PRAISE FOR
WELCOME TO FOREVER

"Tavares reminds us that no matter how far technology advances, human connection will always bind us. This is a sharp and aching portrait of love painted with a deft hand."
Al Hess, author of *World Running Down*

"A hugely impressive feat of layered narratives and big ideas, told with an even bigger heart. I couldn't put it down."
Stark Holborn, author of *Ten Low*

"A thrilling vision of the future and a poignant tale of love and marriage, *Welcome to Forever* is impossible to forget. Tavares keenly engages with contemporary conversations about immortality and identity, and weaves a heartbreakingly beautiful story about the lengths people go for the ones they love."
Victor Manibo, author of *The Sleepless*

"Tavares does what all great writers of science fiction do best. He takes our hopes, fears and anxieties about the way we live today, skewers them to the page and makes the reader watch, helpless and captivated as they wriggle underneath his touch... *Welcome to Forever* is a work of artistic maturity, dazzling imagination and a horrible sense of foresight over what might come to pass—if we let it happen."
Chris McCrudden, author of the Battlestar Suburbia series

WELCOME
TO
FOREVER

Also by Nathan Tavares and available from Titan Books

A Fractured Infinity

WELCOME TO FOREVER

NATHAN TAVARES

TITAN BOOKS

Welcome to Forever
Print edition ISBN: 9781803360409
E-book edition ISBN: 9781803364315

Published by Titan Books
A division of Titan Publishing Group Ltd
144 Southwark Street, London SE1 0UP
www.titanbooks.com

First edition: March 2024
10 9 8 7 6 5 4 3 2 1

This is a work of fiction. All of the characters, organizations, and events portrayed in this novel are either products of the author's imagination or are used fictitiously. Any resemblance to actual persons, living or dead (except for satirical purposes), is entirely coincidental.

A CIP catalogue record for this title is available from the British Library.

Printed and bound in Great Britain by CPI Group Ltd, Croydon, CR0 4YY

For Eamonn

VERSE ONE
THE BOOK OF THE DEAD

"We are sparks. Our experiences, our memories, are electro-chemical impulses dancing from neuron to neuron, across the synaptic divide. These impulses may be mapped and influenced, written and sung out in epics. We are stories."

—Aset, *Philosophies of Memory and Laws of Applied Sahusynics*, First Edition

~

Our story's not so much an epic—I had him and I lost him.

Was he ever really there? Or was he a ghost?

And how well can you really know someone, anyway?

The Memory Options Specialist doesn't give a crap about my questions, and stories, and blubbering about how *I just saw him, and now. And now.* I get it, the waiting room's full of griefbags like me.

She hands me a tablet. The bright screen stabs my rusty eyes.

"Look over the levels," she says. "We're here to help with any editing-related questions you might have."

Happiness is a Choice™.

ONE
FIELD OF REEDS

The staff gave me a picture of me and someone I'm supposed to remember. Every morning, I'm supposed to look at the picture as soon as I wake up, then close my eyes and feel for the memories. I'm supposed to imagine that my shredded brain is like a tree. If you hack a tree down to the stump, new shoots will grow, the Head Therapist told me on my first day here. He called it "coppicing" and blabbed about nature's ability to heal.

Mostly I just need to pee.

I don't remember the guy in the picture frame on the worn wooden desk in my room with its creaky floors in this weird old house. I don't even remember how I got here. Curving lines shaved into one side of his buzzed head, another slashed line in one eyebrow. Bright, gold-ringed brown eyes crinkle at the corners from his smile. A tropical-print shirt unbuttoned to show his brown chest and gold chain. One hand holding a glass of white wine, the other arm draped across the shoulders of a guy with windblown hair, dark eyes, and a sharp nose. White linen shirt against brown skin, the sloppy smile of someone a few glasses of wine in. This guy in white is supposed to be me, and the other is supposed to be my husband. We're on a rooftop overlooking the golden lights of a city at sunset, though hold a gun to my head and I couldn't tell you where.

This will all come back in time, the therapists tell me. *Close your eyes. Breathe deep. Picture the new shoots of your memories bursting up toward the sun, and when you step back there's a you-shaped topiary in a garden of paradise, and you'll remember everything.*

I've got no idea how I remember words like "topiary" but not my husband. None of the therapists here can give a straight answer why, just stuff like *you've been through trauma and your memories will heal in time.* And *have you tried journaling about this?*

No topiary this morning. Instead, I make my bed in my room like we're supposed to. The clock by my bed tells me it's just past eight in angry, red numbers. We only have clocks in our rooms—the gongs keep us on schedule in the manor and over the grounds. I came here with nothing, apparently. There's only the wardrobe filled with dumpy gray sweat suits, with my name—Fox—embroidered over the heart in blue letters, an empty writing desk, and a chest of drawers filled with socks and underwear. I wriggle into one of the sweat suits, then take a leak in the bathroom down the hall that I share with three other residents, and brush my teeth.

In the mirror over the sink, I look like the me in the picture, just a little pudgier and with more lines around the mouth. I don't feel old, though my face says, *you're here to pick up the kids for the carpool, Dad.*

The therapists get on me about my morning mirror affirmations. *Have you been practicing? Have you been really feeling them?* "How about you tell me?" I tossed at Flo, the Facilities Manager and my favorite staff member here, during yesterday's intro session. You already told me about a husband I don't know, and a life I don't remember, so you must know if I'm the kind of person to pep-talk himself.

"You want to question everything, and that's great," Flo said in her kindergarten-teacher voice with her poufy blonde hair, gentle blue eyes behind glasses, and a pink cardigan over her lavender scrubs. She's the one who rings the gong, keeping us in time, while dipping into her cardigan pockets for strawberry candies. "You're getting to know yourself again. And that self is suspicious and sarcastic at times. A wonderful discovery!" Instead of getting mad, she leaned forward, the keys on the lanyard around her neck bouncing against her chest. "Bend into that. Bend into the questions. *Question* the questions. That's why you're here."

Sure, Flo. I'll go with the flow.

Talking to myself in the mirror is about as batshit as the other stuff the therapists have us do—the meditations, and the singing crystal bowl sessions, and the trust-falls—so, what the hell. Deep breath.

"Your name is Fox," I say, still surprised every time the stranger's lips move in the mirror. "You will remember. You are special, and you are loved. And you deserve to remember."

Down the short hallway and the wooden staircase, I join the line of people in gray sweat suits waiting on the faded floral carpet outside the sunroom. The woman with blue-streaked hair at the back of the line turns and nods a *hi* to me. Her name's Minou—it's embroidered over her heart just like mine—and I know from yesterday's group session that she remembers when she was growing up she had a cat named Sprinkles. When she was done sharing her new memory, Seth, the Head Therapist, thanked her and nodded to us. Which was our cue to tell Minou in one voice, *we are memories, and memories are we.*

People dump their memories all over each other here.

Fredericka, who pops up behind me in line, doesn't let me even fire off a *good morning* before she says she won first place in shot put at a track meet when she was fourteen. Up ahead, Pierluigi's talking about how bright the sky was over his childhood home on the Ligurian Sea. We all came here in varying degrees of head-fuck, so Seth says it's important to share happy memories when they come back to us. He calls it Radical Remembrance.

"I honor your memory," I say to Fredericka, still feeling dumb about the line that Seth says we're supposed to say back. She nods a thank-you.

Seth and the therapists in their different-colored scrubs are big on scripted lines. And hippy-dippy therapy concepts like Radical Remembrance, and Memory Mapping, and Moving Meditation. And, I guess, alliteration.

The glass door to the sunroom opens and the line moves. My eyes fall to the carpet, willing memories to bloom in my head like the worn pink roses. We're supposed to spend our morning focusing on the things we remember, as prep for our Memory Mapping sessions. Or, in my case, the things the therapists tell me I'll remember.

My name is Fox.

I'm a memory editor. One of the best, so they say.

There was an attack on New Thebes. A bomb exploded in the city center and a weird signal torched the memories of everyone in the blast radius.

I survived the attack—barely, if you can count having basically zero memory as surviving—but my husband, Gabe, didn't. Too close to the bomb and his memories turned to dust.

So I checked myself into the Field of Reeds Center for Memory Recovery, apparently. For the staff to try to recover my damaged memory code. And to find a way to bring Gabe back.

I wrack my brain for any trace of those memories and come up empty. There's stuff I remember, of course. I'm not one of the residents with the yellow bracelets who the therapists have to hover around. Who remember so little that, according to Flo, they're a danger to themselves. My first solo session with Seth, he talked about core memory. How Alzheimer's patients, before the cures, usually lost their recent memories first, leaving the older, deeper memories intact. He said it's how I know how to walk and talk, and how things in the Center—in some woodsy part in the Western Massachusetts district of Kemet—are familiar. I remember being a kid and living for a while in New Thebes, my parents installing the little silver nub of the memory transmission node behind my left ear. I even remember starting work at NIL/E Technologies, the giant company behind memory and resurrection—rez for short—tech who runs this place, if I squint hard enough. You say NIL/E like the end of the word "denial," I remember. And then a big anchor wraps around my neck with how I can remember the name of the place I worked but not my own husband.

I'm a dotted-line drawing of myself, hoping to remember enough to fill everything in.

I bury my hands in my pockets and dig into my thigh with my fingernails, just to yank me back to my body. I breathe past the anger, like Flo tells me. I'm supposed to be a reed swaying in the breeze when the anger hits, giving in and letting it blow past me.

I hold my breath until my lungs burn. Telling myself to give it time.

Gabe. The name tastes bright green, like the herbs from the garden where we pluck off dead leaves, and snip chives, and plant things as part of our therapy. We poke holes into the warm earth with our fingers, drop seeds inside, and cover the holes with dirt. Whispering *grow, grow* as much to the seeds as to our memories. His name feels like the grass on the big lawn, too. I asked Flo how in the hell I can feel a name and she shrugged and told me, *hon, your brain is so shredded we're just happy you're not pissing yourself.*

Then she went pale and asked me not to tell Seth she said that. I stuck that one in my back pocket, just in case.

The line moves again and soon I'm the one waiting at the door with its glass panes covered with white fabric. When the door opens, J calls for me to come on in and my slippered feet sink into another floral carpet. In the sunroom, three stiff-backed chairs circle a low coffee table that's dotted with crystal knickknacks and fancy china for morning tea. Misty painted landscapes on the walls are windows to somewhere else. Another set of glass double doors leads outside to a small brick courtyard, painted gold by the morning sun. The only thing that feels out of place is the steel reclining chair, mantis-like with how it's leaned back, waiting to strike.

Another *whoops-your-memory-is-mangled* plothole: I asked Seth two days ago when I first got here and saw that chair how I could remember mantises but not my own name until the therapists reminded me, and he hit me with one of his easy smiles. *Memory isn't linear,* he said. *The wave knows it's a part of the ocean.*

Which is just about the politest way to tell me to shut up and stop asking so many questions.

J spins the chair and makes a show of dusting off the seat, giving me a short bow and hand-wave like, *at your service.* Like I'm here for a haircut and not a brain scan.

At least J tries.

"Mornin'," they say, as sunny as their yellow scrubs.

"Looks like someone had their coffee." I try out a smile and sink into the metal chair. I overheard one of the therapists yakking this to another one yesterday and thought I'd give it a go. "Did I say that right?"

J beams. "Bingo! Classic work-appropriate jokey-ness. A-plus."

The sides of the metal chair squeeze a little. I push against the arms that are still warm from the last person in here for their scan. My third morning here, and my third time in this chair, I've learned not to jump when the clear visor from the headrest snaps over my face. Pink and purple lights dance across the visor, in time with the faint, high-pitched beeps blurring in my ears.

"The whole of your memory is your memorystream," J says softly, somewhere behind me. "Watch it flow like a river. Unbroken and eternal, and reaching for the sea."

J's the only staff member besides Flo I've met so far who makes the scripted lines they all bust out—*trust your emotions, healing takes time, the green reed which bends in the wind is stronger than the mighty oak which breaks in a storm*—sound like a prayer. At least starting the day by hanging out with J is starting to feel familiar. Comforting, almost, with their warm eyes, their straight-backed stocky body zipping around the sunroom, their bleached and cropped hair looking like someone dipped them upside down in butter.

And then we wait. More beeps, more lights darting like bees over my eyes. J unscrolls the digital screen of their Reeder by tapping the tube and flicking up their hand, and the display crackles to life. I remember carrying around my own identical device—a gold-capped crystal pipe that's about the length and width of my forearm, with recessed keys and a digital screen—back at work, like all the therapists here. Maybe remember? From the digital display, a projection of thin branches bursts into the air between us. The spindly gray arms look made of ice, and so delicate that they'd snap if I touched them. A memorystream is supposed to look like a river with little creeks that branch off and rejoin the whole, they tell me, but mine looks like someone yanked the plug and sent just about all of the stream down the drain.

I try not to sink. Try. The visor snaps back into the chair's headrest. J sidles up to me and tips their head at the projection.

"Anything?" I ask.

"Looks like we've got some slight budding here." They raise their hands in the air and swipe, zooming in to one corner of the projection where a little nub looks the same to me as it did my first morning. "Maybe."

I don't know if the lie is okay if it's meant to give me hope.

"Have you been doing your affirmations?" J asks.

"Ugh, yes."

J playfully conks me on the shoulder with their Reeder.

"I don't sense boundless gratitude at the wonders of creation in that 'ugh,' mister," they say.

"Guilty. I'll do better."

Here is where I'm supposed to bounce out of this chair and *give in to the process* with a big smile slapped on my face, thankful—like Flo said—that I'm not pissing myself. But then the mystery of the picture of me and Gabe in my bedroom drags me down. I can hear Flo telling me to be like a reed bending in the wind.

I must've been bendier ten years ago. There's white in my hair, now, and I can't touch my toes. Doubt locks up the backs of my legs.

"How will I ever get my memories back?"

When I catch J's eyes, their lips press together. "Memories are like scars," they say, hugging their Reeder close. "Way down, in your neurons. In the deepest part of you. Nothing is ever really gone. It just takes time to get back."

I really want to believe them. Seth says things like *happiness is a choice*, so at least for today I'll choose to trust that I'm not going to be a dotted-line drawing of myself forever.

"I'll wait, I guess." I fumble out of the chair and head to the courtyard door.

"Let's add another affirmation for you," J calls. "'I will be kind to myself. And let the process…'" They stare at me with searching eyes. "'Process.'"

Out in the courtyard, I wince against the sunlight.

TWO
FLASHES

I don't remember loving Gabe, but I remember losing him. Snippets of memories come at me in flashes like someone sliding shards of glass into my head. I wake up in the middle of the night in sweaty, twisted sheets. Flo says it's because trauma really digs into the memorystream and hangs on tight.

I remember standing by a window in an apartment that must've been mine, looking out at a city. The closest buildings crowded like a row of teeth, connected by metal catwalks, with twinkling lights on fire escapes. Narrow streets that gave way to a wide-open city square of pink granite ringed by squat glass buildings and stone towers. A long rectangular pool in the middle of the square reflected the night sky, ending at a wide stairway that led to a white pyramid with a base as big as a city block. The pyramid rose a few hundred feet higher than the surrounding buildings, like a diamond against the night, capped by a digital screen. Blue lights trickled down the pyramid edges.

Some joking pros-and-cons list we made before moving into this place floated to me. Pro: Three blocks from all the action of the city square. Con: When you walk to the kitchen in your underwear at midnight for a glass of water, your office is staring at you.

Flash. Everything white.

The pyramid exploded. *Weird*, I had time to think, before the rolling white cloud, the roundhouse from a pissed-off god, launched me off my feet. I woke up on the floor, covered in broken glass, a high whine blasting through my head.

Red and blue flashes in the streets. Sirens and screams.

Skittering over broken glass. My phone flashing in my hands. Calling him, again and again, no answer. Just the *eeeeeeee* in my ears, drowning everything out. Blood in my eyes. Blood in my mouth.

Running through the streets and the crush of bodies, none of us knowing where we're running. To the smoking crater that was once the city square, or away from it?

Grabbing the shoulders of the people I slam into. All of us caked with dirt and blood, wild-eyed. *Have you seen him? Have you seen him?*

Flash.

A news crawl on the screen in a gray waiting room. Not sure how I got there. Where *there* is. *Memory virus. Neuro-terrorists.* One anchor talks while the other beside her cries quietly. The weapon exploited the memory backup transmissions, using the company's own technology against them. Customers' memory backups were destroyed, even within the secure NIL/E servers, files replaced with some kind of scrambled code. And *more as this story develops.* The anchors don't say *final-death*—because even in the decades since rez tech, those words are a night terror—but what else is it if your memory backup is scorched? Instead, they sniffle. *Hug your loved ones tight, and...*

Flash.

I'm in a training room and someone at the front is telling us something we all already know, that our parents told us when they had our nodes installed when we were kids.

The wireless memory transmissions are painless. Your memories are relayed to our servers every twelve hours, where they will be kept safe in case of critical damage to your vessel and/or node.

I'm running in the street again, dodging rubble. Cars on fire. Blurs that I can't look at, because I know if I stop and look, I'll see an arm. A leg. I hear voices in my head that aren't mine. Or maybe it's the leaked security comms recording that the news plays over and over again. Who knows. Time and memories blur all into each other.

—halt all transmissions until we can stabilize. Are you seeing this? Isolate the memorystreams of everyone at the square. Put them in quarantine. Priority one is keeping our servers safe. Those fuckers. Those fuckers think they can get us. We invented this tech. This is our codedamned house—

My hearing is cranked up way too high in this sad, gray room. The overhead lights buzz like a jet engine. Someone is screaming. Edit to add: I'm that someone, screaming. A folding chair is in my hands and I throw it at one of the walls. Because they promised. They fucking *promised* that none of us would ever die. That none of us would have to say goodbye. And I didn't even get to say goodbye to Gabe, and our separation was temporary—*temporary* until we could cool off—and now they're telling me he's gone.

I know the woman with the tired face and the steady eyes doesn't deserve this, but neither do I. So she gets the screams and the tears and the begging. And the *don't you know who the fuck I am?* I don't know if I'm asking this or telling her.

Someone behind me jabs something sharp into my neck.

Flash.

In one of the folding chairs again in the sad, gray room. Night, this time. The tired woman is speaking but her words don't match the movement of her lips. She's being nicer than I deserve, than she has time for, with all the others in the waiting room outside.

We can offer you an envesseled approximation of your loved one while you wait for memory cleansing. Approximation. A husband skimmed from your memories—traits, habits, behavior—cobbled together. More you than him. Temporary. Hopefully. *Though this virus is craftier than we first thought.*

Or we can delete him. Your choice.

We are doing all we can. Terrible, yes, those monsters. No, they didn't suffer. The blast was—take your time. Look over our new memory-editing levels for your Upgrade. Staff discount. We recommend the Euphoria Special.

THREE
THERAPIES

S eth looks like he's on a beach vacation, in linen pants and a long-sleeved white shirt bright against his skin, not leading group therapy. Me and the three others in my group—Cohort, I'm told, because this place is jazzed over vocabulary—sit on folding chairs in a circle on the lawn in front of the brick patio, the bright morning sunlight blanketing down on us. Minou, Stash with the purple-dyed mustache, Chengmei with her laughing eyes and frizzy gray hair. There are fifty residents here, about half as many staff, and we all usually stick with our Cohort as we move through different therapies. *To really foster trust*, according to Seth. The sun glances off his shaved head at the opposite side of the circle from me. Behind him, birds glide over the marsh. The warm breeze smells like water and dirt.

The first morning I met him, after my tour of the manor, Seth told me he wasn't just the Center's Head Therapist, but also my Case Manager. Though he hoped I'd think of him as a friend. I'd managed to not immediately roll my eyes at him. The first thing I discovered about myself when I woke up here was *Fox has zero appetite for bullshit*. Maybe I should try that as an affirmation.

We start therapy sessions with a pop quiz. My third pop quiz this morning, since a solo breakfast in the dining room with its round tables, dead fireplace with a mantle dotted with landscape pictures, and big windows that overlook the rolling lawn and the marsh beyond. A therapist floats to each of us and hands us a Reeder, while Seth looks over the notebook he scribbles in during each session. Flo said with all the terminology they toss around here, it's easy to get overwhelmed. And they have to test my recall speed, anyway, to make sure I don't have lasting brain damage.

The therapist's screen asks me a question.

```
Which of the following statements are true?
a.  Aset is the mother of memory.
b.  Memories are discrete units of experience
    and may be edited or created using the sahu
    coding language pioneered by Aset.
c.  The memorystream is the total collection of
    an individual's chronological memories, often
    used interchangeably with "consciousness."
d.  All of the above.
```

I tap "d" and a happy bell dings from the device. Still, the therapist frowns.

"Faster, next time?"

"Sure."

Once we have answered our Reeder quizzes, the therapists drift to other Cohorts on chairs and blankets on the lawn. Seth hits us with his big bro smile. I blank out for most of his opening sermon about how resilient the human mind is, and when I come to, Minou's talking about how she remembers a cat she had a couple of years ago. She tells us about Cupcake while I stare at the blue streak in her hair that's tucked behind one ear, so I don't have to meet her eyes. A memory struggled to her through her half-sleep this morning, of orange air freshener and a little rough tongue across her fingertips. She squeezed her eyes shut until she could see the room with wire pens in the animal shelter where she and her wife had adopted the cat. Seth nods a lot and occasionally takes notes. Out of all the cats, Cupcake was the only one to walk over to the door of the pen to say hi to Minou and her wife. And that was when they knew.

When she's done talking, she looks down at her knees and wipes her nose. It's so quiet that I can hear the water lapping the reed-shrouded shore.

"Another memory of a cat, Minou," Seth says, with his low voice that sounds like a hug. "Why do you think that is?"

"She was the closest I had to a kid. I cared a lot about her. More than myself, especially at the end."

Chengmei offers Minou a sad little smile. All I can do is keep staring at the blue streak in her hair.

"And why do you think this memory returned?" Seth leads gently. "Why this moment specifically, and not, say, one of the times when Cupcake jumped on you in bed in the morning, or greeted you after work?"

Minou frowns. "Because I adopted her with Adela. You're trying to get me to talk about my wife."

"I'm not trying to get you to talk about anything, Minou. I just want you to zoom out. You're on a mountaintop looking down at the whole river of your memorystream. Why does your gaze fall on this particular bend in the river?"

She looks past him to the marsh reeds that ripple in the breeze. Yikes. She's keeping it together better than I would, mid open-brain surgery in front of the group. I'd clam up. Flo has been on me about being closed off, but I haven't remembered anything about my life that I want to share yet.

Stash, the guy with the translucent skin and purple-dyed mustache at her right, yelled at Seth yesterday about how this shrink talk was bullshit, and Seth had to remind him, unblinking, *this is why you're all here.*

"Because it's the last time we were happy," Minou says with a tired sigh. "I don't want to remember this shit with Adela. That's why I deleted it."

Seth has an unmoving smile like on one of the faces in the paintings in the manor. I haven't said a word in group yet, and while Seth introduced me on my first day and said I'd need time to get settled in, he looks at me now like, *anytime, buddy.*

"It sounds like your mind is telling you what you need to remember in order to move on." Seth lets this latest wisdom-bomb sit in the air for a while. A ways down the lawn, by the old fountain, some of the other residents putter around the archery range. *Whiz, thunk.* Arrows sink into the targets. Minou tucks a stray bit of hair behind her ear.

"Maybe," she says.

Seth nods to the group. And that's our cue. *We are memories, and memories are we.*

Moving Meditation is always after morning group therapy. Moving Meditation, aka "go for a walk." I'm out of my seat and away from the others as fast as I can without looking like a complete dick. I pass two other Cohort sessions that just wrapped up, and a woman pops up off her blanket and tells me that when her dad cooked Sunday breakfast, the smell of browning butter filled the whole house. I smile at her and look down at her name, Siobhan, embroidered on her chest. The nametags are so you can put a face to the memories, Flo told me, and respect that other people are on the same journey as you.

Between the colored scrubs, the yellow bracelets, the Center-speak, and the nametags, I'm wondering not for the first time if I've stumbled into a cult. Or if I'm going to wake up tomorrow in a bathtub of ice, missing a kidney.

I've wandered off on my own the past two mornings, exploring the grounds. A few staff cottages sit by the small parking lot off one side of the house, empty except for a white van and a little black electric coupe that Seth drives in and out of here. A long dirt driveway leads to the road that cuts through the long, hedge-dotted yard and must meet up with the main road beyond the treeline. My first morning, he brought donuts from his favorite place in town to welcome me. During a tour that day, Flo said that the manor borders a nature reserve that stretches out for acres on three sides. *Nothing to do here but rest and recover.* The huge back lawn flows to the reed-spotted shore of the marsh, and way off in the distance rolls a clipped green field that looks like a golf course. Facing the water, off to the left, a low stone wall separates the main grounds from an old orchard. Flo said I'm allowed to explore beyond the rock wall—and I absolutely didn't miss the *allow* part—because I don't have a yellow bracelet. But that I should bring a buddy for safety because the therapists aren't supposed to leave the main grounds.

Screw the buddy system. The past two mornings I've needed a breather and wandered past the wall, alone. Today, Minou brushes my arm as she zips by, then half turns her head and jerks her chin. *Come on.*

I follow her along a path parallel to the two canoe racks at the shore, while in range of the manor with its terra-cotta roof and black iron garden gates. Over the lawn and past the dried-up fountain near the archery range, down a hill and into the old orchard with knobby green apples on the ground. Minou leans against one of the trees with its flaking gray bark and watches as Chengmei and Stash arrive behind me.

We stand in a loose circle around Minou, who looks like she's cutting chem to smoke behind the school gym. I toe a bug-chomped apple with one slippered foot, waiting for a fresh round of Radical Remembrance, or whatever this is.

"Pop quiz," Minou asks. "How're you settling in?"

It takes me a second to realize she means me. I clear my throat.

"Alright." I look at their eyes on me, the crossed arms, and the blob of the house on the hill behind us. "Un-unless this is a cult. *Is* this a cult?"

Minou barks a laugh. "Close. Mippers Anonymous." She shoves off the tree with one foot. "That is, unwillingly anonymous, because none of us can remember exactly who the fuck we are."

Mipper. Memory dipper. Something about it on a list of words not to use at work because they're Not On Brand. I almost remember gossiping with the other editors and tossing the word around. Like, *check out the hack job on this idiot mipper.* Maybe the client tooled around with his live memory, or paid some back-alley hack—rolling the dice on an accidental brain-scramble—just to get a few blissed-out scenes dropped into his head. Seth said everyone is here at the Center because of their damaged memorystreams, and we don't judge where that damage came from. And that we're not *mippers.* We're *Memory-Damaged Individuals.*

"Sounds about right," I say.

"What're you in here for? I shredded my brain pretty hard with some off-the-books edits, survey says."

"Flo said I survived the attack on New Thebes." I scrape one hand through my messy hair.

The way Minou's eyes bug out of her head, I know I've stepped in it. I swear Stash and Chengmei shift away a step.

Stash whistles. "No shit? I'm surprised Seth doesn't have you locked away. Like, to keep your cooties off the rest of us."

I squint up into the sky, where two birds circle high overhead. I hoped I could find some company here. I guess I'll just have to go at this alone.

Chengmei must see this all on my face with the way she smiles. Before I know it, she's at my side squeezing my hand.

"The fact that you had enough code left at all to even be here is a miracle," she says. Her hands are soft crinkled paper.

"Hell yeah," Minou chirps. "I honor your memory."

"Yeah," Stash adds when Minou glares at him. "What they said." Cult. Definitely a cult.

I drop Chengmei's hand and shift on my feet. "Thanks?"

"And how much do you remember from your life before here?" Minou continues. "Seth said you're an editor, right? Makes sense, since you lived in New Thebes and all."

"Not much. Everything's pretty choppy. Flo said I was a good editor."

"We were all good editors," Stash quips. "Seth's the Case Manager for all the former editors in the Center, meaning us three. Minou headed the Isfahan branch. Chengmei worked with kids doing—what'd you call it?"

"Early editing intervention at a pediatric hospital in Beijing," she says. "Well, retired."

"And Stash ran a back-alley editing farm in New Orleans," Minou says sweetly.

"I prefer 'small business.'" Stash waggles his mustache. "And, no judgment, remember?"

I might as well be the leaves behind Minou, bobbing on the

wind and half-lost with all the bouncing around. "We were all good editors and we screwed up our memories? Shouldn't we've known better?"

"Don't even get me started on the stim habits of some of the surgeons at my hospital," Chengmei says.

Fair. Do as I say, not as I do, and all.

"And what do you remember about Khadija's history with the company?" Minou asks.

"She founded it ten-ish years back, right?"

Minou's eyes gleam, giddy. She practically rubs her hands together.

"Meen, we shouldn't…" Chengmei trails. "Some stuff he needs to recover on his own. You know what Flo says."

"Oh, come on." She flaps a hand. "I'm just giving him some context."

Stash turns to me. "Here's a Radical Remembrance for you. Minou was a history major—"

"Women's Studies, History, and Sahusynics triple-doctorate, excuse you muchly."

"—and apparently it's her favorite thing in the world to school everyone on the story of the founding mothers," Stash finishes.

"If by 'school' you mean I won't let everyone forget how NIL/E was shaped by two of the greatest minds in human history, then class is absolutely in session." Minou tucks a loose strand of hair behind her ear.

"We should be getting back, though." Chengmei glances back at the manor, up the hill. "Flo will gong for morning rec soon."

The gongs might be the most annoying thing here, as much as Flo—holding the mallet—told me I'd get used to it. Morning gong, breakfast. Ninety minutes of group therapy, half hour of Moving Meditation, gong for morning rec. Lunch, then gongs for individual therapy tracks. Then dinner and more gongs for evening programming, depending on the night. Two full days here and I'm already hearing gongs in my sleep. *Going, going, gong.*

"Sure," Minou says. "I'll just give him the quick tour—the real one—on our way back." She nods, and before I know it, she links her arm in mine, eyeing me like I'm a cat in a shelter she's here to save.

We walk in a loose cluster toward the manor as Minou covers the essay portion of the history pop quiz.

Khadija didn't really found NIL/E, Minou says. Common mistake, even for company folks like me who just cash their paychecks—I shrug at her *oops* eyes to let her know I don't care that she's tossed me into this group—she *re-launched* it. It was Aset who created the whole field of Memory Mapping, known as Sahusynics, and gifted her code open-source to the world. We don't know much about her other than her name, which was probably an online handle. Handles hid people. Handles could be masses or movements, handles could topple governments. But we know that Aset was a woman. *It can't be just a woman*, boardrooms, and intelligence agencies, and news anchors moaned. Like, emphasis on the *woman*. But oh mama, that ship has sailed and we gave it a historically inaccurate Viking funeral, lighting it up with flaming arrows, and watching as the charred timbers sank beneath the waves.

Aset founded NIL/E Technologies about thirty years ago, which lets people download their consciousnesses and plug them into new bodies when their old ones wither away. Well, at first just the rich who didn't shit themselves over the price tag, anyway. Immortality never came cheap. Just ask the ancient Egyptians, with their pyramids and temples full of treasures. Aset had a wide-on for that culture, with endless company brand-babble cribbed from ancient Egyptian beliefs.

Then Aset vanished, with a line in her last philosophies saying she was *continuing her journey to the West.* Cue the crackpot theories that she was actually an emissary of an advanced alien race spreading technology throughout the galaxy, or that she died and the company covered it up, or that she retired to a quiet life in the woods because she had no desire to be a megalomanic piece of shit tech CEO like all the others. Which was maybe the most unbelievable of the theories. Ten years later Khadija Banks became the CEO of NIL/E, taking the company from boutique to behemoth by offering memory editing. New product lines, and price drops and payment plans to bring immortality to the plebs. What Aset had started Khadija finished, like rites passed down from master to initiate.

Some people even whispered that Khadija was Aset incarnated, if you believe in that stuff. Especially with the way Khadija had seen the crumbling empires of the exhausted, dying world and had laughed and said, *You know what? I'm going to burn all this shit to the ground and start all over. I'll remake and re-flower this entire codedamned world and you'll all be my kiddos. And mosaics of my countless faces will adorn walls in every NIL/E building in every corner of this world.*

As bored as Stash looks, it is pretty cool to hear this part of Khadija's story. Like, it's nice to know that even if I wasn't a doctor or whatever, I was working for someone who was trying to improve the world. That's something.

We hit the edge of the manicured lawn, where a resident dashes over to us, the name Hotaru on her sweatshirt. I knock into Minou, startled by the manic joy in Hotaru's eyes.

"I'm a gymnast," Hotaru blurts. She doesn't wait for us to say anything, just bangs out a half-cartwheel that sees her flopping onto the grass. She frowns up at us, huffing. "I mean, I used to be better."

"We honor your memory," Minou and the others say at once.

Once we're closer to the manor, Stash and Chengmei split for rec time. We pass Flo, who's chatting with two therapists, and she waves at us with a smile. "Giving him the residents' side of the tour," Minou sings out. Flo flashes a thumbs-up. Minou glances behind us—there always seems to be a therapist within earshot on the main grounds—and the coast must be clear with how she whispers to me, "Here's the real deal."

"Stay away from Octavio," she says. "Sweet guy who loves his Radical Remembrance, but maybe he should think more about Radical Teeth-Brushing. Inyene likes to talk about all the sex she remembers having, and gets annoyed when it doesn't seem to bother anyone. Flo is literally the best. She's like Mom for both the residents and therapists. Seth is—fine. As much as his touchy-feeling talk can get annoying. He's the only one who leaves after dinner, since the other therapists live in cottages on the grounds. Rumor is half of them are boning each other, and good for them. Nights here are beyond boring when you can only meditate for so long. They relax the 'stay in your room after lights-out' rule a bit when Seth is gone. Last week, they let the residents have a dance party in the music room, even *forgot* two bottles of wine there. They're cool so long as you're not outwardly asshole-y to them, which Stash found out the hard way when one therapist subbed out his rec time for *Manual Mindfulness*. Otherwise known as laundry duty. Still, they're staff and not your friends, meaning don't say anything within earshot of them that you don't want Seth bringing up in your next one-on-one.

"Coffee is always in two decanters in the dining room. They switch over to decaf in the afternoon, so if you're a caffeine fiend, be sure to fill an extra mug of the leaded stuff at lunch and leave it in your room. The food mostly sucks. Seth is big on *we must nourish the body if we are to nourish the mind* and loves to feed everyone wilted vegetables that look like they were yanked up from the marsh. Old resident lore says one of the therapists smuggles in snacks as a side-hustle, but I've been fishing for weeks and I still can't figure out who.

"Honestly, it's as good as you can make it. And based on what some of us got into back home…" Minou shrugs. "Maybe better than we deserve."

She leaves me by the coffee decanters. Fresh coffee scalds my hand, even through the mug. I look down at my face warping on the surface of the dark liquid, wondering if I really knew what the hell I was getting myself into before I came here. If I knew that I'd be pummeled with everyone else's memories and trauma every day.

FOUR
WATERCOLOR

My favorite spot for After-Lunch Free Exploration is the greenhouse attached to the resident kitchen. The quiet, glass-walled room opens to the herb garden and looks out over the lawn and the old fountain. The air smells like warm dirt, in a good way. Plants in cracked clay pots line shelves along the walls, with ivy spilling onto the brick floors and flower buds reaching to the sky. I'm trying not to stare at Nduta, the other resident in here, who's sitting at a planting table with a pad of paper, a cup of water, and a watercolor palette like I am, with a yellow bracelet on her wrist. Instead of painting the vase of roses on the table—my picture's an oozy blob of pink and green, but I'm trying—she's licking one fingertip, dabbing it in the circles of paint on her palette, and smearing it on her lips. Until J, who's watering the plants, rushes over like Nduta is a baby stumbling on chunky thighs toward an open oven.

Not everyone came here in as good a shape as you, Flo told me when I woke up. I flick my eyes away from Exhibit A and keep painting.

"I knew I'd find you here!"

I spin in my seat to see Flo in the greenhouse doorway, hands on her hips, her puffy blonde hair haloing her head. She pushes up her glasses and beams at me like I'm her favorite student. She waggles both hands for me to follow and waits until we're breezing through the hallway, past therapists and residents, to talk just loud enough for me to hear.

"Now, don't get your hopes up," she says, in a bright way that's already ballooning said hopes. "We've been able to debug one memory snapshot. Not a big one. Still, this could be a really good sign for your treatment."

"Good is… good?"

"*Very* good."

I keep quiet as this flip-flops in my head. Past the dining room and sunroom, up one of the two narrow staircases on either end of the first floor. She fiddles with the red and green wrapper of a strawberry candy from her cardigan and pops the sweet into her mouth.

"And debug? What does that mean?" I frown as my brain cells crawl like ants after her fake strawberry-candy fumes.

"I know it's frustrating," she says. "All I can tell you is that while you're working on recovering your memories organically— the therapies, that is—*we're* doing what we can, too. We've got the best editors in here trying to scrub the corruption from a save-file of your code. And we will."

A huge window up ahead beams gold squares onto the honey floors. We stop at the central staircase that separates the second floor into two resident wings. The wooden banister posts are carved into swan heads that look like they're following more of Flo's words than I am.

"Save-file?"

"A copy of your memorystream is uploaded to NIL/E servers every twelve hours," she says. "You remember that, right? A company safety measure to rez clients in case of—god forbid—incapacitation, or accidental death, when their nodes aren't retrievable. Well, no need to worry about that."

My head's still running on spin cycle as I follow her up the stairs to an archway of double doors. I've never been to the manor's third floor before, just the public spaces on the first floor and resident hallway on the second. The third floor must've been a massive attic when this was a private house.

Flo opens the double doors, blasting me in the face with sunlight and the smell of old books.

I follow her through, stepping onto a huge, tasseled carpet, turning open-mouthed to drink in the room. The wall of bookshelves opposite the rock wall inset with a fireplace, with one shelf stocked with Reeders in a row like unlit candles. The wall of windows opposite the door, looking out onto the marshlands. A huge carved wooden desk sits in front of the window, stacked with computer screens that trail wires down to the floor and into a big golden slab that looks too much like a coffin with blippy lights. A little silver bar cart stocked with tumblers, decanters of booze, and glass vials of what must be fancy gold whiskey waits by the desk. I wonder if they all knock back cocktails at the end of the day. I sure as hell could use a pull.

"That him?" a round-faced therapist with a red beard behind the desk asks. Three other therapists at folding metal workstations look up.

"The one and only," Flo says.

"I thought he'd be taller."

"Oh, you're always bad." Flo swats the air. "He'll be coding you under the table in no time." Then looking back at me, wearing her auntie smile. "Don't mind Sig. He thinks he's Seth's favorite editor and doesn't want to share the spotlight."

I spin in a tight circle on the carpet and almost trip over my own feet. "What the hell is this place?"

"The Ankh Room." Sig gets up from the desk and flicks open his Reeder screen. He bobs his chin at the gold coffin. "And that's the Ankh. Well, Neb-Ankh if you wanna get all technical like Seth. But not everyone's up on their ancient Egyptian."

"This is our editing room," Flo translates. "Downstairs you work on your minds and bodies. Up here we work on your code."

"And we've got this lovely bit ready for you to gander at." Sig taps at his Reeder until a picture crackles into the air, suspended on three thin beams of light from the Ankh. "Ta-da." He waggles his fingers.

The semi-transparent image looks like stacks of kids' blocks, all warped like I'm looking at it through water. Only when I squint do I realize it's a city street, with a smudge of green on the sidewalk that's maybe a person? Or a blob from my watercolor?

"That's it?" I ask.

Sig frowns, with Flo rocking a little on her toes like I'm opening a birthday gift she just gave me.

"Yeah, not much to look at," he agrees. He tugs at one end of his thick red beard. "It's about what you feel."

His eyes bounce from me to the Ankh. Oh, wait. They want me to get in that thing? I'll take some singing crystal bowls, please. Or talking about cats with Seth and Minou. Or, or…

"Hon, you don't have to be afraid," Flo says. "This is a piece of you, pulled right from your memory. It's like going home."

Flo calls the picture a Memory Excerpt, and with her kindergarten-teacher emphasis on the words, I can see the capital letters. It looks like a snapshot, but that's just the visual trigger, the tip of the iceberg. I have to go into the Ankh, where they'll drop the salvaged code into my memorystream, and I'll live it again for myself.

The therapists draw the curtains, plunging the room into darkness except for the glow of screens and the sharp blue lines on the Ankh. The darkness cranks my heartbeat way up, and my eyes flick to the door. Sig looks heavy and slow, and Flo like the fastest she moves is a power walk with her neighbors. I could probably book it outta here and scramble to the road before they even hit the stairs.

Flo hands me one of the glass vials of gold liquid from the bar cart. "Sedative. It'll help with the transition."

Her smiling eyes hit me while I stare at the glass vial. *Easy, Fox, you came here for a reason. For your memories. For Gabe. And if this is the only way, then bottoms up.* The stuff tastes like liquid sunshine.

"Oh, I'm not supposed to do this, but…" Flo gushes at my side before squeezing me in a hug that's over before I know what it is.

Her words—even the quick hug—help. And, hell yeah, the sedative, too. I'm warm all over, drizzled with honey. I step into the coffin and she eases me back with warm hands on my shoulders. The sides of the Ankh press in close, but already my head is telling me not to mind so much. Already, my bones blur.

"It'll feel like you're dreaming." She squeezes my shoulder. "Sweet dreams, Fox."

A gold mask snaps down over my face from the wall of the Ankh. A picture sparks to life across the mask, of reeds by a shore swaying in the breeze.

FIVE
THE OLD KINGDOM

As soon as Fox rounded the street corner to find Gabe waiting in front of the double doors to the marriage therapist's office, the whole world crunched down to the collared shirt under his leather jacket. Who was he trying to fool? Mint-green cotton screamed against the white faux-marble-fronted building that was glazed with cold winter rain. Wrinkle-free and with a stiff collar that must've been chafing his neck when all he ever wore was stretchy gym gear. From frowning down at his phone because Fox was ten minutes early instead of fifteen—translation: *He's late*—Gabe glanced up. His eyes brightened, and his teeth poked out from between his full lips with his smile. Then, an exaggerated eye-roll-meets-head-loll of *finally*.

But all Fox could see was the minty shirt, like Gabe was trying to win over the therapist with some Respectable Husband drag. When he'd announced after last week's session, *I just can't win with that guy. He doesn't like me.*

"There he is," Gabe said.

"I decided not to bail after all," Fox said.

Imagine if he actually had bailed, after the therapy sessions were his idea. After Yvonne at work gushed about how Darius saved her marriage, and Fox and Gabe had to give him a whirl. When sitting in a room and talking about feelings was, for Gabe, the kind of concrete-cell hellscape cops uploaded suspects into for a little *enhanced interrogation*.

Fox stopped by Gabe at his post across from the glass double doors. Light from the pink sign of two interlocking rings glinted off the gold loop in Gabe's nose. Fox slipped a finger between the buttons of Gabe's shirt and tugged him closer for a quick kiss that was little more than their lips bouncing off each other. Fox lingered, his nose hovering over Gabe's glowing skin and neat stubble.

"Plum scrub?" Fox asked. Tish, the head bodyfication tech at Gabe's work, always surprised him with some free treat when he re-uploaded into his body after a client training session. Salt scrub. Hand mask. Gabe was her favorite personal trainer. Gabe was everyone's favorite person. Except Darius's, but Gabe would win him over unless Fox rope-swung in to keep things neutral.

"Apricot," Gabe said.

"Tish spoils you."

"She does."

"The shirt's nice," Fox said, lips still tingly with that kiss. And the shirt *was* nice with the way it brought out the gold in Gabe's eyes. Fox was being an asshole with his whole *how dare you look nice* thing. Probably. A shirt was a shirt, not a weapon, which he could see when he *considered things from Gabe's point of view*, which the marriage therapist who said not to call him a marriage therapist had said.

"Thanks," Gabe said. "I have a hot date." He bobbed his chin at Fox, smirking. "Long commute?"

And here it was, the one-two jab of shirt, happy hello, and the guilt uppercut finisher, so that Fox knew that Gabe had decided he was late. Even though they both worked a ten-minute walk away from this slab of fake marble, in the flagship building of NIL/E Technologies.

"I stopped to rescue a squad of orphans from a burning building," Fox said. "Lost track of time. What with the smoke." Fox tried to squish his annoyance, which mostly worked.

"Orphans!" Gabe's wide-eyed smile swooped his dark eyebrows toward his freshly trimmed hairline. "Get him the key to the fuckin' city."

"Ready to head inside?"

"You bet."

They always held hands before they stepped inside the fake marble lobby, walking in as a unified front. Gabe's hands were calloused, even with the free salt scrubs Tish swirled over his palms. Rough, but to Fox they always felt soft when they brushed over his skin.

Happiness is a Choice™.

At least, according to the curling letters that glowed from the white wall behind Darius's head. Fox had heard the line before. Hell, he'd yakked it a million times when people bellyached about the price of premium-tier memory editing after he told them he was a NIL/E editor. *Do you wanna bargain shop on your brain? I sure as hell don't. You get what you pay for. Go in for bargain toilet paper, not brain-pokes.*

Fox bounced his knee, he and Gabe on low gray armchairs separated from Darius by a glass coffee table dotted with books and a potted plant. An orchid this time. Darius had to be playing games, with how he changed the plant each week, like he was waiting for them to comment. And the orchid looked plastic, which had to be bad juju, like *welcome to my funeral urn of an office, where only fake stuff grows.*

Fox's eyes darted from the glowing sign to the orchid to the wall of windows that looked out over the city. From here, New Thebes—the neon-lit gold-and-white-marble monument to memory—looked like rows of candle-topped birthday cakes. He sipped on his glass of cucumber water. Shit, how did he and Gabe get here? *Here* in this marriage therapist's office, when they were Fox-and-Gabe—a quick, hyphenated mouthful for all their friends. Like, this life. The other side of forty, shacked up for sixteen years. The last five vanished in a blink. The last ten. Like someone dropped a memory template of two decades into Fox's 'stream.

Gabe reached out and gave Fox's knee a squeeze. Could be he was being sweet. More likely he was telling Fox, *the bouncing is driving me fuckin' crazy, babe-o.*

"Let's get into your assignment from last week," Darius said with his menthol voice. His small leather notebook rested on one crossed knee. "What kind of lives would you like together?"

Yvonne didn't say squat about homework when she'd recommended this marriage therapist after she and her wife had hit a rough patch. And actually, Darius reminded them gently—again—he wasn't a marriage therapist. He was their "Life-Storyboard Consultant." He was supposed to be the best at helping couples squash their issues as they decided if corresponding memory edits were for them. The kind of relative reality couples carved for themselves that sounded, to Gabe—and to Fox if he was being entirely honest with himself, and there was a first time for everything—fucking terrifying. *I'll agree to delete that affair if you agree to lose fifteen pounds. We'll both have this slow lava flow of resentment over the last five years squelched.*

Crap. Fox was thinking about lava flows and not pulling the answer to the assignment out of his ass. Think of something. Quick. The orchids were laughing pink faces. *Don't look at us, asshole. We're just flowers.*

"I'd like to focus on new stuff," Gabe said. "You know—travel. We always say…" Then he stopped, drumming his fingers on his knee. Fox could hear the *we always say we're gonna travel* in that pause, like Gabe remembered he was the one who'd canceled their last weekend trip because of work. "We should learn something together. Like baking."

"That sounds fun," Darius said. "How about you, Fox?"

Wanting to learn to bake was the absolute bullest of shit coming from someone like Gabe, who didn't even look at sugar. Balls, his mint-green-shirt shtick was working with the *that sounds fun* outta Darius. For not being a marriage therapist, Darius was asking a lot of therapist-y questions.

"I'd like the kind of life where I'm enough for him," Fox said.

As soon as the words popped out, Fox wished he could suck them back in. Yikes, the orchids wilted a little. Gabe leaned back into his chair.

"See, you're not even trying." He sighed. "This was your idea."

Who's not trying? They were nearing the end of their session and Fox hadn't even mentioned the Event once! The *Event* being their shorthand for what dragged them to thera—nono, *Life-Storyboard Consulting*—in the first place.

Fox and Gabe had had to spell it out for Darius during their first session. Practically had to draw a diagram with red lines of yarn connecting names and faces, like they were detectives tracking a serial killer.

Gabe was a personal trainer who dropped into the bodies of his clients, often for days at a time, for training sessions. He had a couple of rich clients-turned-friends—for diagram's sake let's call them Client A and Client B—who were getting married and who'd hired Gabe to get them into underwear-model shape. But Client A lost his steam the week of the wedding. He just couldn't do the hill sprints and the juice cleanses anymore. So he'd tipped Gabe a little extra—okay *a lot* extra—on the down-low, to upload into his body and finish out the rest of the pre-wedding dysmorphia binge, all without telling his future husband. And the night before the wedding when Client B pulled Gabe-in-Client-A's body into the hot tub for one last *we're technically bachelors* bonk, well, conundrum. If Gabe refused, Client B would know something weird was up. So Gabe had taken one—literally—for the team.

How's that for math? If Gabe is in Client A's body and he fucks Client B, is that really cheating? If it's just your *consciousness* having sex, how's that different from a fantasy? And what, now Fox is going to police what Gabe thinks?

Wait! This just in. More suspects, with Gabe pulling out another red yarn ball.

Fox had been spending nights in the guest room because Gabe always seemed to be wearing another client's body.

Sure, but how to sleep next to your husband when he's wearing the body of a seventeen-year-old girl?

A seventeen-year-old girl whose body Gabe was in so he could bang out her twice-daily cardio sessions and help her bounce back from her respiratory disease! And then it became how Fox didn't care about kids with respiratory diseases, or anything but himself, or letting Gabe have his own life.

Besides, Gabe wasn't his body, he was the person inside of it. Though—*aha, gimme that yarn!*—if Gabe wasn't his body, what did that really say about the whole Client A and Client B maybe-cheating polynomial fuckery? And how many other situations like this was Gabe not telling him about? How could they move forward if they couldn't seem to decide *what* their marriage meant to each other?

That was session one. Session two, they decided that moving forward was more important than keeping score and figuring out who was at fault. Though it was clearly not Fox, excuse you very much. So, session three: Easier to call all that past junk "the Event" and keep going.

And then came the codedamned shirt.

"I mean…" Fox stalled for time. "New experiences sound good to me."

"He's not doing the work," Gabe said. "He's going to blame his unhappiness on me. When it's because of his boredom, or his big dreams that went nowhere, or whatever."

"And he's not gonna let me in, and he'll say I'm just being needy," Fox added.

"No one can be everything to another person." Gabe's voice carried just a little laugh. He always sounded sweet before he bit the pin off the grenade and hot-potatoed it over.

"I don't want to be your everything."

Fox was sure that Darius was keeping mental score, and—ugh—that lie was going to cost him a point. He *did* want to be Gabe's everything. Ditch the friends, the family, trim their lives down to the four walls of their apartment. Evenings on the couch.

"B-b-but." Fuck. The stutter that Fox wished he'd banished decades ago liked to pop back up when he was frustrated. "I would like a life with you instead of *near* you."

Gabe sputtered something until Darius interrupted him. Very un-therapist-y.

"Can I ask you a question?" Darius smiled with his voice. "Do you want to stay married?"

"Yes," Fox and Gabe said, in perfect unison. Points for not hesitating.

"Then may I offer some advice."

"I thought therapists aren't supposed to do that?" Gabe asked. "Aren't you supposed to, like, guide us as we make our own conclusions 'n' shit?"

"I'm not a therapist."

"Alright," Fox said. "Shoot."

Darius clicked his pen. "Best guess, from all our sessions together, you're both grappling with abandonment issues from your childhoods in Aaru. Gabe, you keep everyone at an arm's distance—including, if not *especially*, your husband—for fear they'll leave you. Fox, you've latched much of your self-worth onto Gabe because you feel he's the one person who hasn't left. The opposing manifestations of your trauma are pushing you away from each other. And unless you're willing to tackle these issues head-on, individually…" With the way Darius trailed, he might as well have been waiting for the fake orchid to sprout.

Fox felt like he'd swallowed the whole pot and the plastic leaves were scraping the inside of his stomach.

"Same time next week?" Darius asked.

Fox looked to Gabe, who winked.

The Coli-See-Um concession area smelled like warm cardboard drizzled with fake butter. The crowd around them bumped too close. Movies weren't Fox's thing—ear-rattling, people kicking his chair, always some asshole nearby blabbing about symbolism to try to sound deep for their date—but tonight was Gabe's turn to pick their post-session hangout. The beers they were powering through helped.

"That hack," Gabe said with his beer-foam-lidded mouth.

"Oh, that *fuuuuuuuucking* hack," Fox added, hamming it up for them both.

"Who the fuck does this marriage therapist—"

"Life-Storyboard Consultant."

"Right, right, Life-Storyboard Consultant. Who does he think he is? Everyone at arm's distance, my ass."

"Yvonne recommended him. She swears he patched her and Shameika up."

"Lesbians are usually way more reliable than this."

"Way."

They'd been sticking to Thursday date nights for months, even before the therapy, as a breadcrumb trail to get them through the week. This Thursday, the stars aligned: A cheat meal for Gabe, Fox had just finished up a monster Happy Vacation with the Family memory template at work, then the release of a so-bad-it's-camp movie. *Spy Flick Part XI: Every City on Earth Explodes.* The big draw was that NIL/E Entertainment was testing out their new immersive storytelling tech in the movie, *audience empathic connection somethingsomething.* They'd piloted it with their InSense social app, which transmitted a signal picked up by memory transmission nodes, letting people experience other memories for a few seconds. Because pictures and videos were unbearably over. Had you ever wanted to feel like you were paragliding off cliffs in Rio, or shaking your ass in Ibiza, or gazing up at a giant sequoia— never mind that those were all mulch by now—without leaving your couch? The NIL/E enclave of New Thebes was like a test kitchen for new products before the company rolled them out to the world. As an editor, Fox had chafed, like, screw you guys! Write a better script, don't just *make* audiences feel a certain way. *That's cool, Shakespeare,* Gabe had told him. *You can stay home.*

"I'm going to get us two more." Gabe waggled his half-full beer. "You get the—"

"Yup," Fox chirped. "Large with extra butter."

"And the—"

"Nachos with barbecue kelp. Got it."

"I was gonna say extra cheese," Gabe huffed.

"No, you weren't."

"Nah, I wasn't." Another wink. "You know me too well."

Gabe spun on his heel and zipped into the crowd. Bummer. Fox should've gone with him. Told him to wait until after they got snacks. Because now he had to stand in line and try to remember what to do with his hands, with strangers breathing against the back of his neck.

The movie opened with a montage of explosions. Enemies skulking around corners. Steely voiceovers. Enter: Moving backstory of the main character arriving as a kid on Aaru with his little brother. Fake-butter-slicked hand of popcorn midway to his mouth, Fox froze as the scene sizzled to life on the enormous screen. Good thing the type crawl across the bottom spelled out *AARU* because the kid's classroom in the movie—construction-paper animals taped to the bright walls, windows overlooking a grassy playground—looked nothing like the refugee nation that Fox remembered. It was supposed to have been the first of many utopian city-states. Gray walls, gray food, recycled water that somehow tasted gray. He remembered a few nice teachers but not much else, thankfully, before he'd been adopted off the island, still a young kid.

He snuck a look at Gabe, his crooked nose, his lips silhouetted by the screen. He picked at the barbecue kelp on the nachos in his lap. He may as well have been scrolling his InSense feed, bored. Fox wanted him to be—he didn't know—bothered? Any emotion at all would be cool. For all the weightlifting personal records Gabe tracked on spreadsheets, his strongest muscle was his noggin. Completely bulletproof to trauma-triggers, and Fox's gentle—then, sure, persistent—prodding to open up more.

They could've met on Aaru, with how Gabe grew up there at the same time, too, though Fox couldn't remember. They were just two of the over thirty thousand people on the floating city-state, anyway. And getting Gabe to talk about his life on Aaru, or in Mexico before that, or even before they met at that bar downtown, was basically impossible. He walled Fox out with warmth, with laughs, and eyebrow waggles. *I was born an obnoxious twenty-eight-year-old, babe.*

With all the bodies he jumped into, maybe the biggest unknown was that when he was himself he was still half a mystery. He'd always be a stranger wearing Gabe's face.

Darius's vapor-y voice cut through the machine-gun fire of the movie. *And is that thought useful?* Alright, Fox was being too harsh. Sessions always made him dramatic, and the movie wasn't helping. Gabe would just say he was looking for a problem. So— *fine!*—Fox switched off his brain and let dumb scenes spiral across the screen as the spy, now a walking pair of bowling-ball biceps, searched the world for his brother. Which mostly involved wiring buildings with C4 and blowing shit up. Fox didn't feel any of the *immersive storytelling* like the InSense tech promised, even at the movie's climax when spy-dude found his brother chained to a chair in an abandoned theater. His voice like gravel in the voiceover: *He's always been there for me, now it's time for me to be there for him.* Gabe looked over at Fox with an *oh, Jesus* eye roll. Maybe they were just too closed off for this projected-feeling bullshit.

In the lobby on their way out, Fox and Gabe almost smacked into an off-duty linebacker, boo-hooing into his phone.

"You've always been there for me, now it's time for me to be there for you." The guy's voice creaked. "I love you, bro."

POP QUIZ

How would you change this night if you were assigned it in your memory-editing queue?

a. Delete the visit to the therapist. Delete the movie and all mention of Aaru. Replace evening with generic After-Work Unwind memory template.

b. Bolster feelings of General Joy after the movie, at the bar.

c. Code a new scene where Fox and Gabe come home after therapy and really hash out their feelings. Insert > emotional breakthrough. Insert > marriage contentedness levels to sustain another two to three years.

d. I wouldn't. Every memory of Fox and Gabe together is perfect.

It was Fox's idea to hit up the bar after the movie—insert > uncharacteristic spontaneity—and they were dopey and jokey, buzzed off each other. Cracking about the table wired with C4, a bartender chained to a radiator in the back and replaced with a double. *You're mine, fuckface! This C4 is wired with even more C4.* Like the old days when they'd run a room with *yes, and* improv shtick, they laughed until the crowd around them in the bar changed. Insert > beautiful people with perfect skin, perfect hairlines, half Fox's age. And holy shit, he'd stayed up past 11:30. He could still hang! But also, get him home immediately.

"Yeah, let's roll." Gabe mugged for an invisible spy behind them in the crowd. "We gotta hurry. The whole goddamn place is wired with C4."

"Synchronize watches. Meet on the roof for airlift evac in five minutes." Fox borrowed spy-dude's razor-blade commercial voice. "The code word is 'platypus.'"

Explosions still happened in the bedroom, though tonight was more like a signal fire in far-off hills. Like they told each other, *I'm still here. We can find our way back.*

Forget the pop quizzes. Fox would take option D, any day.

SIX
CANNED MEMORIES

The bathroom mirror was colluding with enemies Fox made in a past life and could absolutely go fuck itself. It was showing him a picture of this pudgy guy reaching for his toothbrush while simultaneously giving up on himself now that he'd reached middle age. An imprint of wrinkles from the sheet on the side of his face, the lines coming out of his eyes, the dry lips. A guy with close-cropped black hair turned white at the sides—a comic book villain hairstyle without the personality to back it up. Years ago, he'd been handsome in a way that made people say things like he had leadership potential. Now he looked like he needed a coffee enema.

In the bathroom of their two-bedroom apartment, Gabe's face serums and half-used deodorants were heaped into a bucket on a shelf over the toilet. He was always out the door before Fox in the morning, squeezing in a workout of his own before jumping into a client's body for a session. Slicing up life into ninety-minute workouts made him happy, same as helping clients sculpt the bodies of their dreams and scarfing down his pre-portioned meals of oatmeal and cauliflower that smelled like dish rags.

Fox poked at the mound of fat that fell over the waistband of his underwear. Today he would try. Try to try. He'd give up beer and bread and go on hikes with Gabe like they used to. Or at the very least, just settle into this daddy vibe and go with it.

Gabe had never asked him to change. He still grabbed Fox's ass in the kitchen, still liked to drag him to work events to show him off. He knew Gabe meant well, but lately it felt like *show you off in a weird way*. Look at the sideshow freak. At least Gabe still looked human. Gorgeous, yeah, at forty-four in a different—even deeper—way than he was when they'd met sixteen years back. His niche was organic body aesthetics and nutrition, with none of the body mods of his coworkers, their muscle-car quads, and spine-defying water-balloon boobs. He was big with crunchy, earthy types. At Gabe's work things, Fox felt like he haunted the room. The ghost of aging past.

The minty toothpaste burned his tongue. He spat in the sink and flashed his teeth in the mirror like a wolf. He wasn't normally this basket-case-y, but the Event was still messing with his head. Even after date night.

Because the doubt was rolling in.

The doubt talked in this squeaky traitor voice. *How could they build a future if they couldn't agree on what their marriage meant? What they meant to each other?*

And the loneliness from being without Gabe was way worse than the sometimes-loneliness of being with him, right? They'd hit rough patches before, and they were always temporary. Temporary-ish. Gabe wasn't always so breezy and distant—something sharp behind his smiles—and Fox wasn't always so annoyed and needy. His reflection rolled his eyes, like, *sure, babe.*

He showered and got dressed. The first thing he spotted in the kitchen was a stinking pile of cat crap on the floor. Pixie glared at him from her spot on the breakfast nook, with sharp green eyes that glinted against her black fur.

Pixie wasn't real and neither was the crap, technically. The smell in the kitchen sure as shit was, like she'd scarfed a can of tuna that had been sitting in a sun-blasted dumpster. Pixie was a hologram, projected out of the small hand-soap-dispenser-looking thing on the counter, the same device also to blame for the dirty litterbox stink.

When a third disease in as many years had jumped the species divide from animals to humans, NIL/E had outlawed biological pets in New Thebes. Cue the mass lethal injections of cats, dogs, and guinea pigs, trauma that kids would have to get edited from their memories later. But, silver lining: NIL/E's PixelPets line of projected furry friends, complete with their own personalities and occasional around-the-house accidents. And approximated animal behaviors, with how Pixie seemed to know that Fox didn't really like her and decided to shadow him in the mornings, mewling.

Gabe had told him of the stray cats that tiptoed around his fire escape as a kid in Mexico. Fresh off that rare memory-share, they'd picked a PixelPet model that had reminded him of one of those cats. She'd been the source of in-jokes for the first year or so, how she'd hunch over and make circles in her fake litterbox in a dance they'd call the Nutcrapper Ballet.

The only way to get rid of the stink was to use PixelPet's special scooper, to really hammer home the immersion. Fox scooped the poop and it disappeared, along with the smell. If only it was as easy to sort out the rest of his crap.

He couldn't stop staring at the car crash, maybe to distract his brain from the current car crash in the room. Zee's corner office was a post-apocalyptic winterscape of industrial gray carpet, a desk cluttered with abandoned coffee cups and memory-editing manuals, and brushed-steel everything. A wall of windows behind Zee at her computer—in her red suit, she was the only puff of color in the room—looked out over the street ten stories below, where four cars blocked an intersection, fresh off a fender-bender. This high up, the scene was muted. Drivers waving their hands, people in the street yelling, a collective blood-pressure crank-up that echoed in Fox's chest. The crooked bumper of the first car matched the crinkly line of Zee's mouth.

"I mean, of course it's great," Zee said. "It's your work, Shazad."

Oh fuck, by the way she said his name, he'd already cheesed this assignment up. The only people that called him Shazad were Yezenia the Almighty Editorial Director and his parents, who he never spoke to except for the birthday texts they sent him a week late. They adopted him off Aaru—probably just for the NIL/E services discount, though they'd never admitted it—and seemed to think that was where parenting ended. They'd saved him from a bummer refugee-kid life. They'd hired the nanny to shuffle him around and feed him, and had seemed confused whenever this skinny brown boy with the big sad eyes appeared around their house until he'd moved out after high school.

"Thanks," Fox said, gearing up for the inevitable *but*.

"But," Zee said. There it was. "It's… *too* great. As in, too detailed, given how broad Happy Family Vacation was. And you know that one killed upstairs."

"Sure, I get it." He didn't.

Zee spun her monitor, giving Fox a view of the black screen and the white stabs of code.

"Like, here," she said, one red-lacquered nail hovering above a chunk of symbols. "Do we really need seventeen lines of code about how that morning cup of coffee tastes? I'm concerned about resource usage."

With her chirpy voice, Fox knew she was expecting him to say "no." He'd spent hours and hours on that code, like he'd been chipping something out of granite. And when he'd stepped back, there was the perfect example of what coffee should be. Chocolate-y, laced with cherry notes, even though things like "flavor notes" were complete bullshit. And that was just the start of Nailing the Big Presentation canned memory, an odyssey of a slide-show presentation that builds to a slow-clap from the Client's boss. *You, [insert Client name here], absolutely crushed it. Promotion city!*

Zee used to freak out about this level of detail, sending bits of his code around to his coworkers, telling them to take notes. *His memories read like sonnets*, she'd swooned. He was a legend in Editorial—alright, *used* to be—since he'd jumped the ranks unlike anyone in company history.

After he'd spent two years studying Sahusynics in college, the company had hired him and tossed him into the emotional-trauma minefields of the deletion-request queue with the other baby editors. Three years screening memories of car crashes, sexual assaults, and hospital-room panic attacks just to make sure that the clients hadn't been trying to delete evidence of crimes they'd committed. He'd screamed himself awake for weeks in the employee hostel until he'd started popping stimmies and staying awake most nights. Janked-up and slurping instant ramen in the hostel common room that stank of damp socks, he'd snapped open his Reeder and started coding a new memory. A few months later, he'd finished Boring Sunday Evening, a scene where a client is on the couch watching TV with someone they love, and somehow just those hours of comfort help them realize that maybe things aren't totally garbage.

He shared it with his coworkers and supervisor and they'd all flipped out. All it took was a couple of personalizing tweaks and the editors could drop a Boring Sunday Evening into just about every client memorystream in their edit queue. Bam—a surefire way to thread some warm fuzzies into an otherwise crappy stretch of memories. A ten-percent increase in Generalized Contentment Levels, easy-breezy. Think of the hours and the ulcers saved for the editors. With over three billion customers worldwide, and NIL/E editors in facilities on every continent including the cold storage outpost on Antarctica, anything to speed up production was a homer. The editors still used his memory template, twelve years on, so much that everyone shorthanded it. *What're you working on? Just a coupla BSEs.*

Zee, who'd been his boss's boss at the time, had sent the memory up to the top. Way to the top, to Khadija Banks, the CEO of NIL/E. Sure, Aset had invented the whole field of Sahusynics and the symbols—the temple flags, the bird wings, the clumps of wedges that looked like schools of fish, and so much more—that made up memory code. But she'd started too big. Like, gift-to-humanity big, with all her research and philosophies dropped, open-source, to the web.

We are sparks. Our experiences, our memories are electrochemical impulses dancing from neuron to neuron, across the synaptic divide. These impulses may be mapped and influenced. Written in lines of poetry. Epics and songs. We are stories.

Khadija saw the company's real potential twenty years back. *Sure, Aset, I love that journey of epic lines of poetry for you, but I'm a capitalist and we're going to make fucking bank.* Patents on the application of Aset's research in reversing Alzheimer's. Dementia. Memory loss after head trauma. Buying up genetics firms to pioneer body-modding and cloning for perfect vessels. Thousands of editing and vessel facilities to serve the billion-plus customers who wouldn't just fade away when their bodies crapped out. Buying cities and resurrecting failed highway infrastructure to truck vessels around the city-states of North America. Khadija Banks, power-posing from Tomorrow in Tech conference stages. Standing on the banks of a river overflowing with money. Buying governments. Buying the BosWashton megalopolis in North America and renaming it Kemet, building the flagship pyramid in New Thebes—once called New Providence.

And "providence" was perfect, because she was like God stepping down from the clouds in a sheath dress and hip, boxy blazer telling them, *suffering, unhappiness, and even death are diseases that I'll cure. I've got you all.*

When Zee had sent Khadija Fox's BSE, the fucking *founder* of the company promoted him out of the junior pool and into the deep end with the other editors who'd clocked ten, fifteen years. Back when she'd actually shown her face around the office, before she disappeared. He hadn't stopped at BSEs. Next up was Honeymoon and Happy Family Vacation, with a trip destination of NIL/E's YesterWorld theme park in Gulfcoastia. Basically an ad for the park nestled in a canned memory. Zee could've kissed him for the spot-on product placement. And then he'd worked in boutique editing for fancy-pants clients for a while, whipping up memories that crossed off their bullet-pointed obnoxious demands, all without shirking the Big Five editing rules.

You can't raise the dead.

You can't kill the living.

You can't make yourself famous.

You can't make someone love you.

You can't keep someone in your life who left.

Sure, some people bellyached *well then, what the fuck am I paying for,* but the Big Five rules were there to protect the safety of all clients. If your mom died before she bought a backup plan, you're out of luck. You can't just have the editors code someone who thinks they're your mom. And if editors could just delete divorces from people's memories, what's to stop someone from showing up at their ex's new house, all unhinged about why they're not together?

Fox had a tingly sense for storyline pivots and the kind of *aha* moments usually only uncovered after years of therapy. Some schlub might want his ex-wife back, which would be a Big Five no-no. But what if Fox coded him a vacation with an underwear model in the Seychelles and he decided, *you know what? I clearly can do way better than my ex, so peace out.*

When he was tanking it with Zee like this—it was happening too much lately—he wanted to remind her about how Khadija herself put him on the team. Like, *do you know who I am?* Like he meant something, personally, to Khadija. Then again, he did have a problem with exaggerating or completely imagining his importance in people's lives. Look at Gabe.

Instead, he remembered Darius's advice from their sessions. When you want to blow up, breathe. Before you fling an accusation you'll probably regret, stop and think. Frame your thoughts in suggestions. Something that starts with *I feel.*

I feel like you forget who you're fucking talking to, Zee.

I feel like I'm the reason this whole division exists and we're crushing our editing quotas for the fifth straight year.

I feel like if you're not happy with my resource usage, you should absolutely assign Nailing the Big Presentation to one of the hack editors down the hall who'll duct-tape together a bunch of cardboard memories and then go back to stalking their ex's vacation pictures. And you're lucky that I'm even here.

Until he remembered Gabe's hand on his thigh from yesterday, during the session, anchoring himself back in his body.

"Totally get it," Fox said.

He fled Zee's office. The only bit of his life at his desk, against the markerboard walls and project-delivery timetables, was a picture of him and Gabe on a beach, years ago, *cheers*ing with drinks served in hollowed-out pineapples. He could take the picture away and it would be like he'd never been here.

He deleted the memory he'd been working on and started again.

SEVEN
BARRED

A mountain stood between Fox and Gabe. A mountain in the shape of a door with a blacked-out window, set into a wall with more blacked-out windows, under a glowing sign made to look like a white piece of paper scrawled with GAY BAR. Blobs from the sign and the streetlights reflected off frozen puddles on the sidewalk. All Fox had to do to climb to the mountain peak, plant his flag, and do a little victory shimmy was open the codedamned door. One step. Another. Each stealing more of his breath like he was hiking up and up, through the gray flood-season clouds clamped on the sky.

He wanted to be the guy who could hit up the birthday party of Client A or Client B—whichever of the two interchangeable jealousy monsters made of pit sweat and protein shakes this bash was actually for—without making it A Thing. The guy who, even after a day of tanking it at work, could bolt on a smile and gab with strangers. Who didn't forget that the party was tonight until twenty minutes ago, even after The Talks with Gabe about it. *Especially* with The Talks because—praise imaginary sky Jesus—he even wanted to talk. With him promising Fox that he didn't have to go if he'd feel weird, but that Gabe needed to show up himself. These guys were his biggest clients. If they kept him bankrolled, Fox and Gabe might be able to move out of their apartment and into one of the company condos soon. And Fox wanted to be the guy who showed up for his man. If only the door wasn't cemented closed.

When he heaved the door open, the first thing that hit him was the chest-rumble of a deep-house track. Then the huge crowd, every possible age and body-mod cranked out by the Body Gardens and Med Spas, under the disco lights. Seven-foot-tall muscle daddies chomping cigars, with watermelon pecs. Tree-branch models in scraps of dresses flirting with gymnasts with asses you could balance-beam dismount off. Neuropunks with glowing windowpanes fused to their skulls so you could peep at their brains. A few grannies in sequined caftans and bright lipstick, shimmying under the ancient flat-screen playing porn by the bar. The grannies he could get down with. He loved the ones who decided not to plug into younger bodies, or even aged up to fast-forward to that *I've seen too much shit to care about what other people think of me* vibe. Layers of ripped posters advertising drink specials and past drag shows plastered the walls, the floors art-directed to the right level of sticky sleaze. Shot servers floated through the crowd in bralettes and push-up jocks, waggling trays of neon test-tube shooters. Fox snatched a tube. Then—what the hell—one more. Down the hatch. He popped open two buttons of his shirt to try to switch off the *rube came straight from work* sign over his head.

He bopped through the crowd, smiling when he could, on his way over to a corner where he could text Gabe. Turned out he didn't need to. He spotted Gabe with four coworkers by the bar, and when they met eyes, Gabe waved him over. Fox pointed to the bartender first and joined the group once the frigid beer bottle in his hand cooled his nerves.

"Foxy," Gabe said, smooching him on the lips. He'd gotten the cruisey-casual dress code memo, wearing a black tank top and jeans, with his gold chain and favorite diamond studs. He smelled of cologne and minty gum. He'd be sticking to the immune-booster ginger drinks for the night, Fox knew, with how he said he could probably work the room for future clients, flirty car-salesman mode. Especially with how happy Client A and Client B—Rajon and Luka were their names, and Fox could at least think of them as people and not faceless Other Men—were.

He hid the barb with a beer sip. *I bet they were real happy.*

"Hey." Fox squeezed Gabe and nodded to the others.

"How was your work review?"

"Killed it. All hail the return of Fox the Fixer."

"Hail, holy queen." Gabe clinked his ginger fizz with Fox's beer.

"How was your day?"

"Coupla clients, nothing major. Today's highlight is watching pizza guy's special delivery." He bobbed his chin to the porn playing by the bar.

"How do you think that gentleman's able to get his ankles by his ears?" Priya, lifeguard tan in a pink halter and hot pants, asked. "Yoga?"

"He doesn't seem like a gentleman," Reichen with the perfect nose added.

"Boo," Gabe honked. He'd never been ashamed of it, but he didn't talk much about his content-house past. Fox couldn't imagine it was a big subject at work. "We don't get shame-y at Gay Bar or anywhere else."

Petros and Carlos, a couple who Gabe collectively called the Thighnamic Duo, *here-here*'d.

"Besides, the best gentlethems know when to drop the 'gentle,'" Priya said.

"A-fuggin'-men," Fox chimed in, lifting his beer.

Slipping into the Gabe-and-Fox foxtrot was easy. They bopped around the room and got grindy on the dance floor. Gabe introduced Fox to a few new friends and clients, and Fox could rustle up enough *I'm just an editor and you all are sculptors of beauty, aw shucks* charm to score points. Beer helped, and so did the earplugs that Grandpa Fox had smuggled into the club. He almost forgot who the birthday party was for. Until one variable in the Client-A-and-Client-B equation sidled up to him at the bar when Gabe was off taking a leak, leaving Fox to fend for himself. And—oh noooooo—a scream rumbled up from the ground, slicing through his earplugs and melting his brain. Being in the same room as these guys was enough of a Personal Growth Moment for him. They didn't need to actually talk.

Fuck. Dive-bombing over the bar top would be too much. He had to stand there. If only his lips remembered how to smile.

"Fox, yeah?" the guy asked, chest as wide as one of the kegs behind the bar.

Fox remembered the clear green eyes, the sheeny skin, from the week Gabe had walked around in Rajon's body a few months back. Rajon, who Fox had pegged as Client A. Rajon and Luka were chronologically sixty, though they'd gotten plugged into bodies half that age for their wedding. When Fox and Gabe had first started dating, Fox might get a flirty text from Gabe. *Wanna pop by the gym and help me take this body for a spin?* And then in the locker room, Gabe would show off the bells and whistles of the latest model. Sweat that smelled like pine needles, orgasm cheat-button nipples, a dick so *what do you even do with that* huge. They hadn't test-driven Rajon's new body. By then, it had felt skeezy.

"You got it. Rajon, right?" Fox gripped the beer bottle so hard he almost felt glass crack. "Happy birthday."

"Thanks! The big six-oh-fuck. Not that you can tell." Rajon actually lifted his shirt to flash his stomach, rigid as an angry ice-cube tray. Fox died a little. "Gabriel is the best."

No one called Gabe "Gabriel." Maybe Fox could dump his beer on Rajon and he'd run away screaming about net carbs.

"The very."

Fox squashed his Rajon-rage with a smile, chomping the inside of his lip. Just as he tasted blood, Luka joined Rajon in a puff of cedar-smelling pherologne. Crap, Fox couldn't get doubled-teamed by two marble demigods carved by Gabe. Like getting fucked harder than the guy on the screen over the bar.

"Sorry, babe," Luka burbled. "Listen, Buffy's gonna fall off the wagon. I can feel her white-knuckling."

"Crap. I'll get her a tea and hang with her a bit, then shuffle her out."

"Yeah." Luka's glinty brown eyes seemed to register Fox, finally. "Oh hey, Fox! Nice to meet ya. Gabriel told me all about you boys."

Rational Fox knew that Luka was being friendly with the dumbest of party chit-chat. Yeah, but Rational Fox was also screaming against the gasoline-soaked rag in his mouth as Pissed Husband Fox swooped in with the lighter, whispering, *unless this is a challenge*.

He was right. How much of the Event did the two of them really know about? Gabe at least had to have filled in Rajon, once out of his body, in case Luka worked in something like how they'd moved mountains the night before in his wedding toast.

Fox had never been into the Diet Patriarchy version of wanting to own someone, so what the actual fuck was with him lately? Luka's hands and lips everywhere, all over Gabe but also not Gabe. Gabe comparing notes in the bathroom at home, later, like *I sure wish Fox would…* Yeah, Luka knew what was up. *I knew I was really with your man. I made him come so hard his eyelashes singed.*

Words slammed at the backs of Fox's teeth, and he could just open his mouth and they'd rattle the walls. *Maybe you had Gabe for a night, but he's been mine for years. And we've seen just about everything this world can throw at us. Did he tell you, between bicep-curl drop sets, how he held me as I cried when my mother called asking for money for a new body? How the breast cancer came back and she and my dad had blown all their savings on that condo in Hawaii? I hadn't spoken to her in a year, but was I just gonna say no after they saved me from Aaru? And how for years me and Gabe said we'd have kids—we'd adopt or I'd get plugged into a woman's body and carry—until one day he said he wasn't sure there was enough love in him? And I had to hold my breath and let his tears streak my knuckles, and not cry. Because I could grieve the life I wanted later, and I had to hold him together as he broke down. Because he never let me in like that, never.*

More words sledgehammered at the backs of Fox's teeth. *You broke us, and the worst part, maybe, is that you're nothing. I'm an architect of memory and I'll find your memories and black-hole you both to oblivion. I'll erase your names from history, and whatever happens to me later will be worth it.*

Fox watched Pissed Husband Fox lean in closer with the lighter—a canned memory unfolding in Zee's office—and there was nothing he could do to stop it.

"I heard all about you, too," Fox said. The smile in his voice hid a trapdoor, with crocodiles snapping beyond. "Congrats on the wedding, by the way."

Luka and Rajon made bright little *oh* noises.

"I hope you like the gift Gabe got you." Fox was the crocodiles, snapping each word. "Something borrowed for the wedding?" And to Luka, waggling his eyebrows. "That thing he does with his tongue, huh? I hope you've taught it back to Rajon since then."

Fox hid his smile with a sip of beer and watched the color suck from Rajon's face. Luka squinted and then—lightbulb—a tiny space appeared between his lips.

Fox could blame the drinks and tanking it at work and the Event. But he knew, deep down in that moment, hurting Luka and Rajon meant more to him than being good to Gabe.

And when Fox looked back into the crowd, he saw Gabe rooted to the ground by the dim hallway to the bathroom, his eyebrows furrowing into a hard line. He felt Fox's every thought, Fox knew, like they were back at the movie and the InSense actually worked. And that's when they both knew everything was finally exploding all around them.

Fox stumbled home alone, where Pixie surprised him with an encore of the Nutcrapper Ballet. He cleaned up and collapsed on the couch in the small, cluttered living room, just a pile of ash leftover from a detonation sparked by Pissed Husband Fox. Who wore his face, and sounded just like him, and maybe, maybe…?

Pop quiz: If he sounds like you, acts like you, talks like you, is he you?

He must've dozed. He bolted up at the sound of the front door opening, with Gabe captured in a slice of light from the hallway.

Gabe trudged over, his shoulders hunched, and sank to the couch by Fox's knees. Fox could barely see his face, only in the glow from the streetlights trapped behind the curtains, just an outline he could project what he wanted onto.

"Why?"

Gabe's voice was a tired scrape, like he'd been crying. Which, honestly, Fox would've loved. Some emotion—*halle-fucking-lujah!*—instead of beaming it all onto everybody else but him.

"I don't know. I'm sorry."

"You know. At least admit it to me."

Fox's throat caught. "I wanted to hurt you. And me. And them."

"Mission fucking accomplished."

Gabe pushed off the couch, slipped into the shadows of the kitchen, and headed into their bedroom, leaving Fox alone. Pixie padded over and nuzzled Fox's hand that draped off the edge of the couch. She was just a trick of light. He couldn't feel anything.

VERSE TWO
EMBALMING

———◆———

A visit with one of our knowledgeable and warm Memory Options Specialists is the first step to your new life.

Our editing tiers describe the degree of detail with which our editors will work with your memories. At the base level, editors will review only High-Impact Life Events—think wedding days and anniversaries— and polish away any unpleasant sensations from the memory code.

Our most comprehensive, luxury editing level ensures a life free of every worry, every daily heartbreak. A life suffused with warmth, serene sights, and soothing sounds.

Your personalized editing plan may reference specific events (for example, recent divorce or sickness) or contain detailed directives (for example, deleting all memories of recent infidelity).

Your future can't wait. To learn more, schedule an appointment with one of our Memory Options Specialists today!

———◆———

EIGHT
TEMPORARY SIDE-EFFECTS

I scream myself awake. I keep screaming until the puke splashes acid against my throat. Thrashing at the sides of the Ankh, begging them *where am I? Where am I?* until Flo rushes to my side and shushes me.

"It's okay. You're back at the Center. We got you. Just let it out."

I wriggle out of the coffin and onto the floor, the carpet burning the side of my face. *Just let it out.* I hope my puke on the carpet is Fox from the memory—a selfish, controlling asshole—leaking out of my head. Even if we look alike, no way is he me.

"I'll get him a bucket."

A voice above me, somewhere. Luka? Yezenia. *I'm concerned about resource usage.* No, Sig. Right. I'm in the Ankh Room—not on the stiff couch, crying alone in an apartment after I just torched my marriage—and one of the therapists yanks the curtains open. Light floods in. It was early afternoon when they put me under. I must've been out a whole day.

"How long was I…?"

"About an hour here," Flo says. "Always feels longer, with the relative timeframes."

I barf into the wastebasket Sig holds out for me until my eyes burn. Snotty nose wipe.

"Sorry, bud," Sig says, surprisingly gentle. "First time in's usually pretty rough."

"You don't fucking say."

The words hurt the backs of my teeth because for a second I am Past Fox who knows the worst possible thing to say at any given moment. And sometimes thinks, *batter up.*

Sig just laughs and pats me on the back. "Next time'll be easier. Promise."

Fat fucking chance I'm going back in that thing. The strength to grumble that fact drains out of me with my next heave. Flo has to half carry me through the hallways—dodging therapists with sad smiles, the *been there, dude* eyes of other residents—to my room, where I collapse on the bed.

She draws the curtains. I hear the scrape of a chair sliding against the floor. The door opening. Quiet, just my bedframe creaking while I shiver. Then, a cold towel on my head.

"Sleep," she whispers. "The dreams will help you get through it. They'll help bandage up the memories you just felt with the memories buried deep down. I'll be here if you need."

Shivering, body aching, I can see the Gabe in the picture on my desk turning to me to whisper words meant for Fox on the couch. *I'll never forgive you.*

Flashes, again, even in sleep. The memories rush at me in faint sketches and dotted lines.

Time moved differently in the guest room, while Fox and Gabe wintered each other out. The hours dripped by, achingly slow.

Fox called out of work. If he drank enough, he could blank out big chunks of the day.

Their apartment was divided into zones. Main bedroom, main bathroom: Gabe's. Guest room, hallway bath: Fox's. The kitchen was no-man's-land. One morning, Gabe was making coffee when Fox rolled out of the guest room, all bedhead and whiskey fumes.

Gabe left without saying a word, and that was where they were now.

Fox was a ghost at work when he bothered to show.

Flash.

Two days. A note on the counter scrawled on the back of an envelope. *Priya's. Don't call.*

Gabe's things disappeared from the house. His toothbrush. A pile of clothes. His blender. He must've snuck back home during lunch breaks. Each one was like losing him again.

They had to talk eventually, right?

Eventually. *Even.* Evening the odds. Fox had been keeping score for years, of their stupid bickering, of their betrayals that started with *why can't you be...* or *sometimes I wish you were...*

A week rolled by. He showed up for their therapy session with Darius, and of course Gabe didn't. Why would he?

"We call this the fourth-session fallout," Darius said, trying to make a joke. The plant on his table that week: A flowering cactus. Fox didn't feel like joking. Didn't feel like telling Darius what had actually happened, either.

"I had this thought last night," Fox said. "'What if I deleted him? What if I'd never met him?' But I know that wouldn't work."

"He's in you too deep."

"Yeah."

Another week. Fox called to cancel the day before the next appointment, only for Darius to call him back. *I think it's time we start talking about your next steps*, he said.

Darius, again. Alone, again. A tiny fish with a red shredded-ribbon tail swirled around the roots of a water lily in the bowl on Darius's table.

"Have you thought about going up an editing level, now that Gabe's gone? What would you want?"

Fox ignored Darius and chewed his thoughts. He might as well have been that fish, trapped in its little bowl. He wanted to say something about the whole "goldfish have three-second memories" thing being bullshit, but his head hurt from the whiskey, and it seemed too on the nose.

"All I want is Gabe back. For him to want me again. Since he's obviously done with me…" Fox frowned at the empty chair at his side. "That's not on the table."

"Because of the Big Five."

"Ding ding ding."

"What if." Here, Darius leaned in, smiling. The shadows of the grayscale room cast a dark bar over his eyes. "You could forget the Big Five. What if I told you there was a way for you to get Gabe back? A place you could be with him?"

"Where on Earth would—"

"Who said it's on Earth?"

Fox snorted. "I don't know what even to… How to—how is that possible?"

Darius's smile didn't waver. "Technically not illegal. Technically not against our Client Agreements. We've gotten creative with our luxe packages. So, what would you give to have all you ever wanted?"

The stupid fish got tangled up in the flower roots. Like Fox was any better, flash-forwarding to later that night, drunk and alone and tangled in the guest-room sheets.

"Anything. Everything."

"Correct." Darius beamed, pointing to the sign behind him. Because *Happiness is a Choice*™.

Darius led him through brushed-brass back hallways that didn't seem to fit the dimensions of the building from the outside. He talked in more annoying *what-ifs*. What if I told you that you could be a part of something big? What if I told you that Khadija has a new vision for the company—and beyond—that you can be a part of?

"Besides," he said, "Khadija has called you to serve before, right?"

He must've meant how she plucked him out of the junior editing pool. Fox must've said something back. His head was all wonky. The mosaics of people and birds on the brass walls seemed to be staring at him.

Flash. A wide room with five people at computer stations, little more than pencil sketches. One huge screen dominated the wall, with Khadija beaming down at him from a video feed, fountains splashing behind her. The sight of her knocked his clumsy feet into each other. No one at NIL/E had seen her for years, as far as he knew, and here she was shimmering in this gray room, all in gold, with her gold-beaded braids piled up in a crown. Like he had spotted a rare mountain cat and he had to freeze or she'd bolt.

"Well, if it isn't my little intern." Her smile cracked his ribs like an egg, with his heart running like a gooey yolk. "It's good to see you again, Fox."

He met her in passing once at a company party but couldn't imagine she would remember. Hell, she could think whatever she wanted just as long as she kept smiling at him like that. Of course she'd save him. She saved them all.

He must've asked her why she'd disappeared. She met his open-mouthed stare with a laugh and said something about how she was on a personal retreat. *I'm forming a team for my new vision for humanity—where we can all write our own rules*, she continued. *Consider this a vetting process*. Then there was the whole messy thing about payment. What Fox would give. And with the technically *gray area of legality* of what they were doing, he needed to cough up some, well… *collateral* is too messy of a word. Let's say, proof of his dedication before she'd bring him aboard. And he could have Gabe back. A million Gabes. Why stop there? *Think bigger, babycakes!* He could be a fucking king.

Just one minor test to ace first, which he—Fox the Fixer— should absolutely crush.

What'd you tell Darius you'd give? *Anything. Everything*. Let's test that theory.

Kidding! Khadija's laugh again, tinkling like wind chimes. *Don't look so spooked. We just need you to do us a solid and deliver this briefcase to the address Darius gives you, and then wait until I reach out to you again. And I hate to be a stickler for rules and all, but look inside, and my invitation gets lost in the mail.*

Flash. Fox dropped a black briefcase at the front door of a penthouse apartment downtown. The least he could do after she offered to make him a king and all.

Waiting, whiskey. Pressing his face against Gabe's pillow just to smell him.

Darius's office was empty the next week. Huh. Weird.

I love you and I'm sorry. Fox stood at the window, staring down at his phone. Took him probably an hour to type out those words, with how his eyes wouldn't focus, how he swayed on his feet. The whiskey two-step without music. The house stank from Pixie's crap, though it could've been that he hadn't showered in, oh, how long?

He stared out the window at the pyramid of his office building, beyond the silk mirror of the reflecting pool. Priya lived in one of the CondoMansions in the upper floors of the pyramid. Gabe was there, though he might as well have been on Mars.

Fox could just push open the window and *whoopsie daisy* there he went. He'd have to turn off his backup first and put a Do Not Rez in his file. Ugh, the paperwork. Tomorrow?

He typed into his phone. *I will love you forever.* Though that sounded too much like a threat.

Flash. Huh. Not just in Fox's head, either. The pyramid. The windows. Fox. Shatter, shatter, shatter like his empty bottles of whiskey.

And like the windows exploding, I can feel all of these memories blowing away to dust. I can feel myself almost forgetting.

Shivering in my sweaty sheets. I look over at Flo asleep in the chair by my bed, her chin against one shoulder, her big blonde halo of hair glowing in the desk lamp's light.

I'm pulled under, until I bob to the surface again.

"How was I under for an hour when the memories stretched over days?" My throat aches, even with the mint tea she brought me. "And how did I feel Fox's whole life, stretching backwards?"

I still can't say *my* life. I'm not gonna own Past Fox's shit. The words don't make a lot of sense, anyhow. Flo's smile tells me they don't have to.

"We are sparks," she says. Her voice sounds like J's prayer-voice. "Our experiences, our memories are electro-chemical impulses dancing from neuron to neuron, across the synaptic divide. These impulses may be mapped and influenced. Written in lines of poetry. Epics and songs. We are stories."

She kisses me on the forehead. It must be Singing Crystal Bowl Therapy night downstairs with the other residents. Crystalline notes float through the floors, sounding like spaceships taking off.

Past four in the morning, according to the clock next to my bed. The person-shaped topiary, tipped with pink flowers from Darius's office, a gold chain dangling around its neck, shrugs at me.

"Weird how you drop a mysterious package off, 'n' then a coupla days later a bomb knocks New Thebes off the map." Gabe's voice. "The codeword is *platypus*."

The topiary would smile if it had a face. I've got no idea what he means. Sweet, stupid Foxy.

Then morning, somehow. Flo with another cup of tea.

"You did great, hon." She smiles and I want to cry again. "How are you feeling?"

My eyes are crusted with broken cement from Past Fox's apartment explosion. I don't let the cameo of topiary guy in my nightmare from last night—if that's what that vision was—bowl into me.

"Better than yesterday."

"I knew you would. You have a gift. That's why you survived the attack on New Thebes. The others won't tell you that. J, Sig. Even Seth. You have a responsibility to develop that gift. That's why you're here."

Flo's even blue eyes and gentle smile are a warm blanket up to my ears. I don't deserve her. Edit: Past Fox doesn't deserve her, hopefully I do. I'm not him. I won't *be* him. I'll be better.

She pats my damp hand and leaves before I can ask her what that means. I shower. I wipe the fog off the bathroom mirror and tell my tired eyes what J told me to say. *I will be kind to myself. And let the process… process.*

NINE
MONUMOMENTS

Another Memory Mapping session. J in sherbet-orange scrubs in the sunroom, all giggly and slipping me a corn muffin they snuck from staff breakfast like it's my birthday.

"I heard you killed it your first go-round in the Ankh yesterday," J says. "How d'ya feel?"

The visor clicks down over my eyes. "Killed sounds about right. I feel like a corpse."

They jostle my shoulder. "That's a classic Fox joke, I bet! Deadpan, man."

Beeps. Scans. "Oh yeah, *big* budding right here, buddy," J says, zooming in on another branch of my memorystream. Maybe they're right. Maybe there is some budding this time.

POP QUIZ

What's next?

a. Breakfast gong. Eggs and greens in the corner.
b. *I heard he barfed everywhere*, I hear Alexei blab with

     his rich baritone. *Isn't he supposed to be hot shit or something?*

c. Seth looks at me from his usual chair at the start of group therapy, outside by the patio. He doesn't wait for me to volunteer. *Fox had a big breakthrough yesterday. Fox, care to share?*

d. All of the above.

I really wish we'd just let Minou talk more about her cat.

It's another perfect sunny morning in memory-rehab land, all green lawns and cozy breezes. Everyone's eyes knock into me. Minou smiles a little, urging me to go on. Even Stash nods. My head's all fogged up, waiting for the trust-falls or some shit. Hard to believe everything that happened—the years it feels like I've lived since the orchard yesterday morning when Chengmei tried to stop Minou from talking about NIL/E and Khadija. *Some stuff he needs to recover on his own. You know what Flo says.* Then sweet Flo telling me this morning *you have a gift*. Minou's right. Flo literally is the best.

No more time to stall. Chengmei's eyes, Stash's, Minou's—all weighing on me like Luka's and Rajon's did in the bar in that instant before I hefted the sledgehammer.

"I learned I was an asshole," I offer. "I don't know how much of a breakthrough that is."

Across the lawn, a duck touches down in the water with a splash. I'm hoping this is enough for Seth to let me off the hook. Fat chance.

"Are you interested in explaining more?" Seth really masters the *this is a question but not a question* tone. Now it's my turn for his big bro smile.

"No."

"In the interest of fairness to the others in this circle who've been sharing, *could* you share more?"

The duck floats down the marsh in the long silence that stretches over the circle. I wait until it's a white speck on the water, begging it, *take me with you.* I suck in air.

"In my memory, I was with Gabe—he's my husband who died—and we lived in New Thebes and I had almost everything I thought I wanted. I was this big deal editor at NIL/E. Or, used to be. I was coasting, but whatever. I was with Gabe. That should've been enough. Then I fucked things up."

I toe the grass with one of my slippers and want to sink down into the dirt, to wriggle with the worms.

"Is there a word for when you love someone but resent the fuck out of them at the same time?" I ask.

"Marriage," Minou calls. At her side, Stash snorts.

"Minou." Seth frowns. "Interrupting."

"Sorry."

"Fox, please continue."

My nervous laugh shakes my shoulders more than I mean it to. Thankfully, Minou's here. I wouldn't be able to keep going without her mugging at me.

"Alright, marriage," I say. "Sure. We weren't perfect, yeah. But it should've been enough that we loved each other."

I have to stop to catch my breath. I can feel the distance between me and Past Fox wanting to shrink down. I *was* him. I remember feeling everything.

"But it's like… like I had to *own* him. I embarrassed him at this work event he had. Made it all about me. Probably got him fired. I don't remember exactly. Everything's—everything's coming at me in flashes. All I know is that helping people at work was what made him the happiest in the world and I had to break that apart. I wanted to hurt him."

Seth nods. "It sounds like you—"

"Waitwait. I drove him out of our house. Can't forget that. He left because he couldn't even be in the same apartment with me. He was staying with a friend downtown when the bomb went off. His memories turned to dust because of me."

My voice shakes. Keep it in. Keep it in. And wasn't there something else that topiary guy reminded you about? You were in a gray room. Something about someone asking you to bring a briefcase somewhere. What kind of *Spy Flick* corporate espionage shit were you getting into?

Wild flapping against my ribs, bird wings. I trap that thought inside. He wasn't you.

"It wasn't enough that I broke his heart," I barrel on. "I erased him forever. How's that for fucked up?"

"We don't judge here," Seth offers.

"I sure as fuck am j-judging myself."

I'll steal a canoe. I'll swim if I have to. I can't stay here. I'm never doing this again.

"Are you sorry?" he asks.

"What the fuck k-kind of question is that?" My voice quakes with anger, pulled from Gay Bar. Past Fox with the chains on Gabe, each link engraved with a love letter. *That thing he does with his tongue, huh?* He always kept the anger locked and loaded, and now it's bleeding into me. "I'll be sorry forever."

Seth's steady brown eyes won't leave mine. Next to me, Chengmei lowers her head. I hear her sniffling. I can't take that on.

"We call events like this *MonuMoments*," Seth says. "Anchor points in your life that are so strong they defy deletion and even, in Fox's case, critical memory damage. Working through these MonuMoments are essential for your recovery."

I forget how to breathe for a while. All I can think is how the burning in my lungs feels like nothing compared to watching Gabe's stuff disappear from our home. It takes everything I have not to crumple.

"Well?" Seth asks the group.

"We are memories, and memories are we."

Minou's voice is the loudest out of all of them. When I look at her, she mouths, *I'm sorry.*

I saw a golf course green in the distance during Moving Meditation yesterday morning. A green means a country club. A country club means a way out of here. I'd let the golfers pelt me with balls if it means never hearing the word *MonuMoments* ever again.

Everyone knows to give me some space after my memory-bomb. I wait until the others leave their seats before I bolt down the lawn toward the shore—spinning away from Octavio with a *sorry not now* as he barrels toward me for a halitosis-spiked Radical Remembrance—feeling like my feet are sinking into mud with each step.

"You might experience some mild memory tremors as your memorystream adjusts to yesterday's Excerpt," J told me earlier this morning. "A great sign that the Excerpt is knitting into your code and repairing pathways. It'll feel a little wonky, sure! You'll get over the hump in a day or so."

I hear Gabe's annoyed sigh even though I'm alone by the edge of the marsh. The ground seems to shake below me—mild my ass—and I have to stick a hand out against one of the canoe racks to keep from keeling over.

He's sighing because a client invited him to go golfing and said to bring me along. And since I don't really want to go, I'm making this a fight. I'm spinning my annoyance into a never-before-announced hatred of golf while I scrape metal hangers in our closet purposefully loud and yank clothes over my skin. Because *golf*, Gabe, really? Think of the complete fuck-you of water waste, with Lake Victoria drying up and the droughts all over India, just to plant some grass for rich assholes to putt-putt. Not to mention the exploitation horror show of undocumented workers employed there, mostly from Mexico, mind you.

In golfer drag of khaki shorts and an argyle vest he's chopped to just below his bellow button, Gabe's smirking, which only cranks my soapbox up higher. An-and remember the whole *we're gonna cap carbon emissions by 2030* thing? And then 2050 rolled around, and all the politicians were like, *how 'bout 2070?* And that's why NIL/E had to bail out the governments, and maybe the next thing they should do is fucking outlaw the complete gross example of all that's selfish and wrong with humanity, otherwise known as *golf*.

And then we're at a bar and I'm watching Gabe waggle his hips as he adjusts his grip on a golf club, standing on a patch of fake grass in front of a video screen of a golf course. He calls out *foreplay!*, swings, and a tiny white ball whips into the fake sky of the screen.

"You could've told me you meant virtual golf before I went all nuclear," I grumble.

He scrunches his face and the lights of the bar glint off his gold hoop nose ring. "And miss seein' that vein poppin' outta the side of your head when you're pissed? Not a chance."

Deep breath so I don't puke against this memory-golf-ball konking against my forehead. Get to the golf green. Then the country club. A phone. Though, hold up. Who are you gonna call when you don't remember any numbers, anyone else outside? I can borrow the Center's van and hightail it, stopping at a fast-food joint on the way back to New Thebes. Maybe toss a match out the window and burn the Field of Reeds Center down behind me.

"Fox."

Seth smiles when I look up from the marsh reeds, my head still wonky from the memory tremor. His teeth are as blinding as his white linen.

"You must have questions," he says. "I hope I can answer some."

My brilliant getaway plan will have to wait.

"I was going to canoe." I try to sound not manic. "Moving Meditation, all that."

"Good idea. May I suggest a walk instead? I can join you?"

More questions that aren't questions.

"I'd really like to canoe."

Seth looks down at his perfect white threads. "I'm afraid I'm not dressed for…" His voice trails off as he waits for me to budge. I don't. I feel like Minou would be proud, and I'm surprised by how happy that makes me. I need a friend here that isn't Flo.

"Well, spontaneity is useful, yes?" He kicks off his leather sandals and leaves them on the grass.

He lets me struggle by myself to clunk a canoe into the water. I sit on the plank of wood facing the far side of the marsh and grab the oar. He scoots to the front of the canoe and faces me while I paddle.

"Let's just stay close to the shore," he says.

"What, you scared of alligators?" Past Fox's snap again. I have to learn to reel it in.

"You know, alligators I can handle. It's the crocodiles you have to watch out for. Though I'm sure I can therapize them into submission?" His laugh bounces off the water and scatters a flock of birds on the other shore. The only sound for a while after that is the splashing of the oar into the water.

"I understand you experienced a significant Excerpt yesterday. Sig's been hard at work on your memory code. He must be very pleased."

"I'm glad someone is." Water from the oar douses me, cooling me off. I'm probably being a dick. Group therapy wasn't a personal attack against me, especially since I came here on my own. "Sorry. I don't mean to be an ass. This is just a lot."

"There's no judgment here."

"Who attacked New Thebes?"

"An eco-extremist group called the Deathers."

"Why?"

"They created the memory virus to reintroduce final-death and bring balance back to the world's ecosystem. Someday the algae farms won't be enough. Someday we'll suck the oceans dry just for drinking water. That's the official story."

"And the unofficial story?"

He looks behind him to where we're headed, then back to me. "Some people within NIL/E suspect Khadija."

"Why the hell would she attack a city she owns and permanently kill a bunch of her own customers?"

He spreads his hands. "Just a theory. Some note her public split with the company, her disappearance. Then this attack. The company has been trying to contact her with no luck. Some think it's odd that she's offered no help to cure the virus. No public statement."

A tremor in my head hits so hard it almost rocks the boat.

"And what do you think?"

"No opinion. No judgment."

I frown against a trickle of water. "I guess it is weird that she didn't say anything after the attack."

"On the other hand, Aset's code has always been open-source. Perhaps it was only a matter of time before someone used it to craft a weapon. There's the adage, you invent electricity, you also invent the electric chair."

"Bummer."

"No—"

"I know, I know. No judgment."

He laughs. "I say 'no judgment' to stay neutral. I don't want to imprint any beliefs on you. Who knows what you thought about NIL/E—truly—even though you worked there, before you arrived here. It's not my responsibility to philosophize."

I paddle for a bit, hugging the shore and knocking into the reeds with the oar.

"Anything else?" he asks.

"Why are you here?"

"I was a resident a long time ago. Like you."

We slip over the water. In the distance, the maybe-golf-green is still a far-off lush island. Up ahead on a little elbow of shore, a rusty lawn chair with a woven yellow seat faces the water.

"Why?"

He sighs and leans forward, waiting as the muscles work at the sides of his jaw. "My own MonuMoment."

I frown. "In the interest of fairness to the others in this canoe who've been sharing…"

"Entirely fair." He cracks a smile, letting me peek behind the therapist for just a second. "My brother slept with my wife. I did a lot of not nice things to him, and to her, and to others, and to myself because of that. Until I came here to get better."

"Shit."

"Yes."

"No judgment?"

"Some judgment, still. Trying to work through it. It's a process."

"That's what I've been hearing."

"Also, I'd appreciate if you kept that between us." He dips his hand into the water and splashes me with a few drops, laughing. "I'll deny everything, anyway."

So he is human. I stop rowing and let us drift for a bit. I close my eyes as the breeze flows over me, and I try to bend like a reed. Which works a little, even with how I made fun of Moving Meditation and all. Maybe I don't need to roll down the river just yet.

"How is Gabe going to forgive me for all I did to him?" I ask. "If I even deserve it?"

I've been holding the question back so tightly that my jaw aches. I look out over the water, embarrassed to lay myself out like this. His *hmm* is the buzz of a dragonfly that lands on the canoe, hitting me with shimmering green eyes.

"Forgiveness doesn't have to be hard," he says. "You should try to forgive someone you love when they did something that they thought was right."

The oversimplification does squat to make me feel better. I put on a cardboard smile anyway as I keep rowing. After a few minutes, he brightens, straightening to his perfect therapist posture again.

"Can I ask you a question now?"

"Shoot," I say.

"If you could relive your MonuMoment with Gabe again, how would you change it?"

"I'd actually think of him in that moment—how he feels—and not me. Bend like a reed, all that."

"Mm. I'll let you in on a secret."

"I'm all ears."

"You're not here to just remember your past. None of us are. You're here to be better than who you were."

"Therapizing again. I thought we were having a MonuMoment."

I feel Seth's rumbly laugh through the bottom of the canoe. "Come, let's go back to the house. There's something I should show you. I didn't think you'd be ready so soon, but you've already shown tremendous growth. I'll row?"

When I hand him the oar, he leans over the water and heaves. Splash, splash, glide. Seth missed his calling. The manor sails into view in no time.

TEN
INTRODUCTORY EDITING LEVEL

The canoe *thunks* into the shore. Seth hops out while I fumble, stub my toe, and end up tripping, landing in the water up to my knees. The mud sucks one slipper off my foot with a wet *thwack* and I leave it there.

Seth scoops up his sandals and glides up the lawn with me at his side, smiling at everything around him. João breaks off from a Tai Chi lesson on the lawn to chatter at us how he remembers the black-and-white mosaics on the streets of Lisbon. Seth bows to him, hands clasped, and offers such a sincere *I honor your memory* that I almost tear up at the brightness it brings to João. We head through the patio door, through the sunroom, and into the hallways. Seth chirps a *good afternoon* to everyone he sees—the therapists lugging silver trays of food to the dining room, the residents in twos and threes in the halls. He's the mayor of this place while I track clumps of mud onto the floors. He somehow turns on the light switches in the faces of everyone we pass. *Good afternoon! Heard you had a productive Neb-Ankh session, Latterian. So good to hear. J, how's the partner?*

Some of his sunshine is rubbing off on me, with how the manor doesn't look so dusty anymore.

Up the second-floor central staircase to the Ankh Room door, which he opens without knocking. Into the bright, book-packed room with the therapists, and Sig and Flo by the Ankh. My mostly dry feet thud, stopping on the carpet several feet from the gold coffin in the center of the room.

I can't see her face because of the glowing gold mask, but I can tell from the blue-streaked hair that Minou's the one in the Ankh, with its dots of turquoise lights crawling around the gold surface like bugs. Her arms twitch at her sides. I look away, a nauseous echo from yesterday knocking me.

"Good afternoon!" Seth sings out.

Sig frowns. "Really, Seth? We're mid-session. We have the room booked."

"Beg pardon. I'll only be a moment." He nods to Flo. "Florence, how's our Minou?"

"Oh, she's a tiger. Digging into this Excerpt like cake." She looks to me, then down at my one bare foot, and smiles like I'm a kid showing her a crappy finger-painting. Her warmth tugs me into the room. Something about Flo. She makes me feel like mint tea—tingly and warm. I feel better every time she smiles at me. She makes me want to try.

Seth pats around the big wooden desk by the window, then—*aha!*—the bookcases. I step closer to the shelves nearest to me, dust wafting over. Worn book spines in every color. *An Introduction to Sahusynics. High-Definition Memory Dynamics. Unwearying Stars: The Early Philosophies of Aset.* He hop-steps to a corner of his bookshelf and plucks one of the Reeders from the row.

"He ready for that?" Sig calls, not taking his eyes off Minou.

"What'd I tell you?" Flo sing-songs with her strawberry-candy breath. "He doesn't want to share the spotlight. Fox is ready."

Seth flashes his white teeth at me on his way to the Ankh, where he scoots Sig away from a side panel. He taps a few buttons until a glowing gray branch appears in the air, which he grabs, then he presses his fist to the gold tube. He's moving so fast I'm almost dizzy, though it could just be standing so close to the Ankh again. At least they seemed to have cleaned my puke off the floor. Seth flicks his fingers at me. *Come.*

Through a side door and into a small room with brown-papered walls, an overstuffed green armchair at a small desk, and more bookshelves. *Shaping the Void: Memory and You. Entering Forth by Day. The Weighing of the Heart: New Ethics in Editing.*

"The main reason why I'm the Case Manager for the editor Cohort is because you all have an opportunity that the other residents don't," he says.

"And what's that?"

He hands me the Reeder. "Editing. Naturally."

The Reeder is heavy and slick in my hands. And familiar. "I'm not following."

"Your Reeder is loaded up with the most recent save-file of your memorystream. And here—" He points to an icon on the digital display "—you can pull up a copy of your latest Memory Excerpts. You can edit the events. Make a dozen copies, edit them a dozen different ways."

"Which doesn't actually change how they played out."

Seth cheeses at me like I just offered him a beer. "True, in subjective reality. You must've explained this to clients before, surely. But you can have these edited Excerpts uploaded into your memorystream if you wish. Effectively giving yourself—"

"A do-over for past fuck-ups."

"I'd like to think of it more as a chance to put the lessons you're learning here into retroactive action."

"And how does this jive with me taking ownership over past mistakes if I can just, like, erase them?"

He dips his head like I've just dumped a Radical Remembrance on him. "Perhaps it's best to think of this not as editing, but revising. Revision. Re-*vision*. What will you re-vision your life as?"

He sounds so much like Darius for a second that I'm marooned in a white office and staring at a fake orchid.

"There's no wrong or right way down your path, Fox. No judgment. I'm simply giving you the roadmap. You don't need to have the edited Excerpts uploaded to your memorystream. This can simply be a therapeutic exercise."

Tempting, yeah. I blow a slow breath out my nose to calm the stomach-spins.

Before he leaves, Seth says I can stay here for the rest of the day if I want. Skip afternoon sessions and evening activities. Halle-fucking-lujah.

My hands curl around the scroll, my fingers already whispering over the recessed keys.

The study smells like incense has seeped into the carpet and chair.

I pull up the Memory Excerpt. My fingers know their ways over the keys and how to work the virtual scroll wheel by wagging my finger off the right side of the tube. I can switch over to video playback if I'm in the mood for the torture of rewatching Gabe's eyes on me as I wire C4 to our relationship. I stay in the code view, where little symbols wink at me from the screen. Thin wedges clump in shapes that look like sails on a ship. Birds with tail feathers that seem to twitch. Unblinking eyes. Hands up in prayer.

I know I worked at NIL/E for twenty years, even if I can barely remember my early days there in the editing trenches. The muscle memory from probably hundreds of thousands of hours spent coding paints the scene on the backs of my eyelids, without me even having to switch to playback. A door with a blacked-out window that I can open.

Up out of the chair and to the window. My back aches. I've been sitting for hours and thinking. Dozing. A gray cloud floats in the sky, dropping a light drizzle onto the marsh. It's the only rain I've seen in my four days here. White birds up and up into the sky. Already, I'm lighter.

I want to be the type of guy who told Luka and Rajon, *congrats on the wedding, by the way.* And left it at that.

I want to be the type of guy who said, *I hope you're happy. And if you had any part in making Gabe happy, thank you. It's stupid of me to blame the problems between Gabe and me on anyone else.*

I want to be the type of guy who told Gabe, *if you're hiding something from me, I'm sorry if it's because I made you feel like you couldn't trust me.*

I want a lot of things.

I start typing.

~~ELEVEN~~ TEN-AND-A-HALF
BARRED, AGAIN

A mountain stood between Fox and Gabe. A mountain in the shape of a door with a blacked-out window, set into a wall with more blacked-out windows, under a glowing sign made to look like a white piece of paper scrawled with GAY BAR. Blobs from the sign and the streetlights reflected off frozen puddles on the sidewalk. All Fox had to do to climb to the mountain peak, plant his flag, and do a little victory shimmy was open the codedamned door. One step. Another. Each stealing more of his breath like he were hiking up and up, through the gray flood-season clouds clamped on the sky.

His hand on the door wouldn't budge. At least not right then. And that was better. The kindest thing he could do for Gabe—and for himself, when he was like this, when his crocodile smile wanted to chomp on everything until the water was bloody around him—was leave.

Not perfect, but it'll work.

I won't drop this re-vision into my head. I'll keep it as a promise to do better, even if it starts with baby steps of *don't be a complete asshole.*

Until I can rebuild myself from the inside out. And then do the same for Gabe.

ELEVEN
NEGATIVE CONFESSIONS

I grab a few slices of toast for lunch and dinner and hide in my room. I'm absolutely taking the chance of a pass on the rest of the day's therapy to avoid talking about how much of an asshole I am. Was. My tenses are fucked already. *Fox and Gabe were… I will be…* My head's pounding from staring at the Reeder screen for hours.

Someone swapped out my sweaty sheets for a fresh set. I'm still wearing my gray sweats from that morning's river dunk, missing one slipper. I rinse off in the shower and slip on fresh clothes, turning in a tight circle on the carpet. Narrow bed with its metal frame pushed up against the wall. Desk, clock, lamp, and chair. A closet with more shapeless gray threads. If I squint hard enough, it doesn't look much different from the guest room in Past Fox and Gabe's apartment.

I open the window and let the smell of wet grass sweep in. Sweet, over the smell of old wood in the house. But something else, too—*smells are good, they help anchor people to memories*—maybe grease? Salt? Tangy sauce that pinches the back of my throat. And low chatter that sounds like a passing raincloud right in my ears, like when I heard Gabe's sigh at the shore. Swaying to the desk, hands out. Steady, steady.

Where are we meeting again? Cologne. Borrow a shirt from a friend because you don't have anything nice. Right, right, the river downtown and if I don't hurry up—

A memory tremor ripples up the old bones of the manor and into me—I'm hovering in two places at once. No, I'm still in my room, but there's a trace of somewhere else, some other time. An outline superimposed on this moment.

Second or third date in, Gabe said to meet him by the waterfront downtown and that he'd take Fox to his favorite restaurant. And—panic/don't panic?—this is a date, amazing, and not just them hanging out and boning (which, don't get him wrong, was awesome) but he actually wanted to get to know Gabe better. Gabe smiled a lot. He tipped his head back when he laughed. Fox borrowed a collared shirt from someone at work because he didn't own anything nice, and *ugh*, don't even get him started on how he was going to pay for a restaurant dinner when he was still living in the company hostel.

Gabe—T-shirt, frayed jean shorts—kissed Fox and flicked the collar of his shirt.

"Handsome," he said.

"Thanks."

"But not yours."

"No."

"I dig the T-shirts. You don't gotta be someone else."

Which, sweet, that was something you said to people while you were auditioning for each other like this, right? *Just be yourself, I'm such a chill guy, etc*. Until Fox followed Gabe along the crowded waterfront, weaving through street performers spinning fire batons, to Coral Beef, the fast-food joint with the glowing yellow-and-pink sign of a cartoon cow with a fish tail. *Our Moo-rific secret? A blend of seventeen secret spices and stims with real cod- and cow-adjacent proteins.*

Okay, Fox told himself. Relax. Adjust your expectation settings, Fox the Fixer. You're both Aaru brats. "Favorite restaurant" means basically any place where you can eat and no one will clock you in the head to grab the rest of your algaerky bar.

Sticky tables. They split a Cow'N'Cod nuggie combo bucket with BarBMoo dippin' sauce and fries. Gabe scarfed down a beef fishlet sandwich on the side.

"How the fuck do you eat like that and *look* like you do?" Fox asked.

Gabe only laughed, tipping his head back, shoving in more fries.

Back at the waterfront, Fox grabbed a couple of honey cakes from a street vendor and they ate as they wandered, short-handing their lives.

Fox: He'd survived the bird-flu epidemic in Pakistan—couldn't remember it at all because he'd been barely three—and got shipped over to Aaru. Adopted by some distant, Rich Savior-y parents in New Thebes. Put himself through a few years of college, etc., fancy-pants job as an editor at NIL/E.

Gabe: He'd survived the NIL/E trade chokehold against Mexico—remembered it all, thanks—and hey, weird coincidence because he got shipped over to Aaru, too. Rich Savior-y parents would've been cool. No dice in the adoption department. Booted off Aaru with the last wave of refugees after the big storm wrecked the island. Halfway house, then content house to make some bank for a while, etc., and then he'd started as a trainer at one of the bodyfication places downtown.

"Cool." Fox offered Gabe his honey cake, and Gabe swooped closer for a chomp. "Which content house?"

"One of the nice ones."

"Good gig?" Fox wasn't the type of guy to crank it while watching content-house streams and then turn around and get judgy on the performers. Especially with how the houses kept their talent safe. He'd lost track of how many street sex-work shifts gone wrong he'd had to delete from someone's memory in the editing trenches.

"Clients eye ya like you're god waving your dick in their faces." Gabe smirked. "Pretty good. Most of the time."

"And both Aaru brats, huh?" The warm air smelled of popcorn and peanuts. Fox heard a sing-song in Gabe's voice that hinted, *let's talk about something else, yeah?* Still, he'd nudged a little bit more. *Getting to know you, etc.!* "I wonder if we met when we were kids?"

Gabe's big smile, again. "I bet." Then, quiet for a while, chewing on the sweet honey cake.

Fox remembered later: *Most of the time.*

It didn't take much digging to find the content house that Gabe had performed for, once Fox flipped back through a couple years' worth of saved streams. He found one where Gabe had been dressed up like a football player with shoulder pads and a white jockstrap, gliding around the pole as the muscles of his belly moved like liquid. Tossing his head back and laughing for the camera. Thinner, and with fewer tattoos—the cloaked skeleton on his left shoulder and arm wasn't there yet—but definitely him.

———

Flash. Deadlines. Fox was late and needed another landslide like BSE or Zee was going to wonder why the fuck Khadija had promoted him. Zee could always say it wasn't working out and send him back to the trenches. He couldn't. The panic attacks. The nightmares. Why did people watch so many videos of beheadings if they ended up wanting to get those memories scrubbed?

Zee's gaze gobbled up the canned memory that was rolling out in video playback on her screen, one blonde eyebrow arching. The customer template in the memory waggled around on the pole, laughing at the camera. The body type and gender of the dancer could be switched up based on customer specs. Man, woman, non-binary. Every skin tone under the sun. Put them in titty tassels or a cheerleader outfit. He'd nailed the universality, just like BSE. Who didn't want to feel like an orgasm on legs?

"I'm calling it 'Sexpot,'" Fox told her. Awkward to have a boner in your boss's office and to see her chewing the side of her lip, but, well, here they were. "The desire settings are cranked way up. Like, 'the clients are looking at you like you're god waving your dick in their faces.'"

"Whew." Zee hit pause and leaned back, pinching her red-painted lips. "That's some hot shit. I don't know whether to call HR for sexual harassment or get you a bonus."

"I'm lobbying for option B."

She plucked a vape from her desk drawer. "Fox the Fixer strikes again." She puffed out a giant white cloud. The relief puffed in his chest like that cloud, ballooning him up. She even offered him a drag and he watched the white cloud from his lungs spread through the air. Drifting, drifting.

―――

Flash. Years? Another outline projected onto this moment.

Fox didn't remember how Sexpot came up, just that it did. Another ghost that haunted the house.

"You're saying you based one of your shitty canned memories on one of my livestreams."

Fox didn't mistake Gabe's quiet voice as calm. Gabe was gathering, heating the air up around him before he exploded.

"Everyone wants to feel wanted," Fox sputtered. "I was inspired by shame-free sexuality, and—"

"I don't know how to explain to you how gross this is," Gabe continued, cranking up the fire. "That just because something about me is out there, it doesn't mean it's yours to do whatever the fuck you want with. *Muerte*, the editing trenches really fucked with your brain, huh?"

"A part of you gets to live in other people, and isn't that beautiful—"

That lit the fuse.

"How fucking dare you get all philosophies of memory on me."

The lines shaved into the sides of Gabe's head swooped and swerved like storm clouds with how his face twisted.

Editing mental note: Find the code of those last two parts and delete. Delete away.

Before I—no, edit: Before Past Fox even learned to code, he learned the basics of Aset's philosophies. What'd she call the first law?

It butts against the inside of my forehead. The Law of Mnemetic Assimilation. Yeah, bingo.

Edits to memories are dreams to the mind. Edited and created memories fit so well into the memorystream because the mind is trying to heal itself—washing over the new memory, soothing the jagged edges, making it part of the whole.

Dream logic. I dumbed it down during a surprise tutorial for a coworker who just came to my desk to ask me a quick editing question, and then I had to get all philosophies of memory on them, because of course. You'll look down at your hands and see that they're blue. You don't think, *holy shit, I'm blue*. You've been blue the whole time. You just didn't think to notice. The same works for coded scenes. Get them dropped into your memorystream and your brain thinks they've been there the whole time.

J told me that these memory tremors should only last a day or so. And here I'm falling out of my office chair, then through my apartment window before the pyramid explodes, but I land on my bed in the manor instead.

Sure, just how much of my brain will be left in a day or so?

For the first time, the memories scare me.

What if I don't want to be the person I came here to remember? It was his fault that Gabe left, that Gabe was in the blast that shredded his brain. The memories felt like watching a movie, and now they want to wash over me. They want me to drown. They want to dream-logic me into thinking I was always that Past Fox asshole and not this guy I am right this second, who's—alright, probably still an asshole but hopefully less so—trying his best.

I roll up in bed and run to the bathroom to barf. When I slog back to my room and my eyes hit the rat's nest of my sheets, that's when I know.

I can't bend like a reed, and if I don't get out of here—today—I'm going to snap.

TWELVE
POWER OVER WATER

Residents and therapists weave all over the first floor, chatting as they carry blankets and pillows into the dining room, while others push tables against the wall. I dodge elbows as the swarm lugs chairs in from the therapy circles outside. I have to find Seth. He'll let me out of here. He has to. He and Flo told me that I signed up to be here, all on my own. I wish I could knee *that* Past Fox right in the nuts.

No Seth in the redecorating swarm. Fuck.

Chengmei walks over and asks how my individual track went and I barely hear her mention, over the gush of blood in my ears, something about movie night. Then Nicola, chair in hand, stops and says he remembers he always wanted to be an actor. Fredericka adds that a few therapists are in town getting snacks and that Flo is even making popcorn, which cues Hákon to spout that he remembers he was a nutritionist and that corn is poison. And then I'm suffocating as I keep track of all the embroidered names, and everyone is *I honor your memory*-ing each other and ohmygod I can't breathe.

I sprint out the greenhouse door, pass the empty staff parking lot, loop around to the front of the manor, and just catch Seth's black electric coupe scuttling down the dirt road like a beetle as he heads home. Abandoning me. Back inside the dining room, Flo and two therapists are lining up chairs in front of a projector screen, and she gently brushes me off. *Just give me ten minutes to finish setting up, hon.*

So I hide in my room and scream into my pillow until my throat is raw. I scream until all the sounds are sucked out of me, and my room is a frozen bubble of quiet. I can survive another night. I'll skip morning Memory Mapping tomorrow, find Seth first thing, and tell him I'm done. And he'll let me out. Right? Bend like a reed, buckaroo. I can already feel my head cooling to a slow simmer. Yes. Yes, okay—until a tap at my window jolts me out of my skin.

I jerk up in bed to see a bird on the windowsill. This bird is a bird, and also a small dinosaur. This idiot bird with its white body and black head is way too big for my windowsill, when there's a perfectly nice group of trees by the shore. Its black eyes twitch before it taps its long, curved black beak on the window. Its black stilt legs grapple for balance, and then it taps again. More taps, like, *got any fish?* It squishes closer to the window. Tap, tap. *Feed me, Daddy.*

This is officially Weird. J should've warned me that side-effects of memory tremors include suddenly becoming irresistible to birds. *Well, you are a cock, so that makes sense. Har-har. Classic Fox joke.*

My new friend's chirp sounds like a flute half full of water. I slowly sway to my feet and the bird stays put. More taps. Alright, I get the hint.

When I open the window, the bird flaps off, swoops over the lawn, and lands on the canoe rack. And I'm sorry for calling this bird an idiot, because it's an angel here to remind me that I have another way out of the Field of Reeds Center for Coat-Hanger Lobotomies.

I cram a fist against my mouth to muffle my laughter.

The key to not looking suspicious is to crib from the Mayor Seth schtick. I soft-shoe in my slippers down the hallways, bobbing my chin at everyone. I finger-gun to the therapist who's vacuuming the hallway runner. *Crushing that vacuuming, dudebro!* The dining room is empty—they must be waiting for sunset to start movie night. Outside, the late afternoon sky seems brighter for the rain shower that blew over the house, the air just cool enough that I'm happy for my gray hoody. On the grass by the patio, a group of residents bend in downward-facing dog, flowing in one wave. *Namaste, cool ladies!* I hoot at them. And then—alright—maybe I need to dial my mania down a scootch.

My bird bud waits on the shore rack, where the canoes and kayaks are beaded with raindrops, and swoops into the water with another drowned-flute trill when I get too close. I lug a kayak to the water. One last look back at the manor, and then I wobble into the kayak. Clumsy-handed with one of the double-ended paddles, I push off from the shore.

The slow hand of the current nudges the kayak forward, following the black-tipped tail feathers of the bird that's floating across the water. I keep the manor on my left, point the kayak to that maybe-golf-green in the distance, and dig into the water. To my right, a hundred or so feet across from the manor, green reeds clog the other shore. Up the opposite bank, a rolling blanket of tree-shaded land, dark green leaves, and wispy gray tendrils stream off the gray-brown branches.

Dragonflies zip by me in the marsh. One lands on the far

edge of the kayak—a blue-glinted body, four wings that look like cracked glass, two huge sheeny eyes. It twitches its wings before darting off again. The kayak weaves through little archipelagos of squat shrubs that dot the shallow water by both shores. I settle into a rhythm—suck in air when I dig the paddle in at the right side of the kayak, blow out when I dip on the left side—and soon the manor is drifting from view. I bob past the rusty lawn chair with the yellow back that I saw with Seth. The shore warbles into little tree-edged coves. Up ahead, in the distance, the green hills of the golf course are a kid's pillow fort, telling me, *come play.*

The bird gently glides to the right, and I watch the widening V of its wake as it floats to the opposite shore.

I paddle until my lungs burn. I yank off my gray hoody—my white T-shirt underneath is clammy against my belly—and toss it into the kayak. Beams of the low sun filter through the trees. Almost sunset. In the middle of nowhere and I don't know what I'll do when it's dark out here. I'll get lost and end up paddling all night. Something splashes off to my right. A frog?

Suddenly, I don't find all the stupid crocodile cracks from that morning so hilarious.

The golf green doesn't look like it's getting any closer. Two ducks watch me with black eyes in their green heads, quacking to each other like, *look at this idiot,* before floating toward the opposite shore.

Pop quiz, Fox: Did you know that you're a quack at judging distances over water?

For all my bellyaching about the gongs, right now I'd kill for one to tell me how long I've been rowing.

———

I have to stop so I don't hyperventilate, and my palms are numb slabs of the lumpy beetloaf the therapists serve us for dinner. I should've brought water. I remember Gabe carrying around a steel jug of water all the time and trying to get me to drink more. I can see him leaning in to kiss me on the edge of the river in New Thebes, our first date. What's the word, *mirage*? Can you see mirages over the water?

Behind me, the marsh wriggles off into the horizon like a giant snake. I pivot the kayak and row toward the opposite shore, trying to plow through the thick reeds until I give up. Dragonflies with shimmering bodies and black wings. I flail backwards with the oar until I'm pointed at the golf green again. At some point, I've got to turn around and head back where I came. Which was behind me, right? Everything's starting to look the same. The wake from my kayak is one zooming arrow.

I pass the rusted lawn chair again. No, it has to be a different one. I didn't get turned around. I'm sure of it. I laugh so I don't cry, scattering a flock of white birds who lift off, squawking. This is stupid. So stupid. Everyone will be watching a movie and not looking for me. Not that they could find me, this far out in the marsh. Was that a gong? No, another big blue bird splashing in the water. I'm laughing, because why the hell not. The laugh curdles into something sour. I salute the bird with my oar. Captain of the Good Ship Crazypants.

The sun, skimming the horizon, is an orange-gold gong. Sinking, sinking. The pinks and blues are soundwaves, radiating out. The golf green an unmoving, painted backdrop that one of the hack editors at work would drop into a memory thinking no one would notice.

How could that bird stab me in the back and let me die on the marsh?

I just float for a bit. I think I doze.

It's dusk by the time I spot the canoe rack between the reeds and trees at the shore, where Flo is waiting for me. I look behind me at my kayak's wake, which I can barely see in the now-dark water. Except for that pivot when I tried to reach the opposite shore, I kept rowing in one direction, straight toward the green. I'm so fizz-brained with relief I can't even think how that doesn't make sense. *Congratulations, Fox, you're the first person to circle the planet by kayak.*

The bottom of the kayak conks the muck of the shore, and I stumble out. Solid ground. Paradise. Flo's lavender scrubs and her blonde, blow-dried hair in frozen waves around her face. I never thought to be scared of her, or any of them, until I see her frown like I washed ashore covered in blood. *Oh, Fox, what did you do?*

"The bird made me do it," I tell her. I must be delirious, shaking with cold sweat. "How did—"

She flashes me a flat palm. *Stop.* Finger to her lips. Finger pointing behind her to the house. *They'll hear.*

"Straight to your room. Wait until you hear three knocks." Her voice is just a whisper of the breeze through the reeds. "Count thirty breaths. Meet us here."

My head drifts like Zee's white vape cloud, up and up. "Just where the hell *is* here?"

She shakes her head. "Couldn't tell you. You had to see."

Her quick hug is the only thing that keeps me from collapsing on the ground. She pushes a strawberry candy into my hand—and yes, she's smiling, thank god—and then she hurries back to the manor, just a streak of lavender through the fading light.

THIRTEEN
FOR GIVING BREATH

I don't know how the metal bedframe doesn't rattle with how much I'm shaking, waiting in my room, propped up on pillows and sitting on my hands. Laughter from the residents in the dining room billows up to me. They must be watching one helluva comedy.

I measure time by the frog chirps floating in through my window. Noise in the hallway. Just my floor mate in for a shower. I finally hear the knock at my door, count my breaths—adding five more since I'm huffing air so fast—and then I slink through the shadowed manor. By the shore, Flo waves at me to hurry. Others behind her are already carrying canoes and kayaks to the water. I spot Minou's blue hair, then Stash's mustache, and Chengmei's gray frizz.

"Four days?" Stash whistles. "Beat your time, Meen."

"Shut up," she says.

I'm now officially crazy. Tomorrow's Memory Mapping, J will see that my memorystream exploded into confetti. Flo must spot the *what the fuck* on my face.

"Don't worry, we'll explain everything," she says. "Right now, we should get away from the manor. The therapists skipped movie night and are probably two sheets to the wind in one of the cottages' common rooms by now. Still, we should be careful."

The marsh again, hands clawing at my feet. Paralyzed like I'm the one drugged in the Ankh, eyes on the water that somehow led me back here after rowing for hours. I'm suddenly heavy. All I can think is, *please don't make me row.*

"I gotchyou," Minou says. "Hop in."

I'm shaking so hard that Minou has to help me into the canoe, and she leads the boat parade through the water. High overhead, the full moon blasts us with silver light. Minou cuts straight through the marsh until we reach the rusted lawn chair, then she banks a hard right and rows to the opposite shore, sliding the canoe through a narrow break into the reeds. When it hits dirt, we hop out and lug the canoe to dry land. She carries it off to one side, making a clearing for the rest of the group. Then, without another word, she walks toward a gap between two trees and disappears.

Stash. Chengmei. Zip-zip through the trees.

If not for my time-warping solo canoe trip earlier, I'd run screaming.

"It's easier if you hold your breath," Flo tells me before disappearing into the gap herself.

It isn't.

Everything that makes me *me* flies apart in every direction the second I step into the gap between the trees. I would scream, but I don't have a body. Instead, I *am* a scream echoing across a boundless white landscape. Flecks of color down below, hurtling at me faster and faster. No—I'm falling. Dropping from the endless white skies down to what looks like a mound of dirt. *Nonono.* I slam to the ground and somehow fall apart all over again, skidding to a stop in a dark room.

No, I'm back in my body and it's only dark because my eyes are closed. And why does everything *hurt* so much? My joints scream. Even breathing feels like I have to point my whole brain at my lungs to get them to move.

I open my eyes as frosted blue glass slides away above, back into the curving gold wall of the small closet I'm crammed into. I gasp to the water-marked gray industrial ceiling of whatever dim room I'm in, my shoulders bogged down by sandbags. Someone else's pale and slender hands reach up to either side of the curving closet walls to lug me into a sitting position. Wait. *My* hands. I blink down at the thin wrists. Down at the—yeah, those are boobs. *My* boobs, apparently, and my curvy hips and muscled thighs in black athletic tights. Dizzy, I sag against the wall. The outside of the gold, egg-shaped pod next to me reflects a warped and unfamiliar face in the lamplight, all tiny features and a pointed chin, a black braid down one shoulder.

I try to speak, but it only comes out as a wheeze and then a wet cough that doubles me over.

A dark-featured guy with a lumberjack beard sits up in the nearest pod. "Minou."

Someone groans from my right. "Chengmei, here." She winces from the body of a young man with frizzed red hair and a freckle-clouded face.

"Flo," comes a soothing alto like J's voice. I look over to see Flo opening and closing the jaw of the brown-skinned body she's wearing like she's testing a door hinge. She blows fringed bangs from an unlined forehead.

"I hate doing that." Bright, wide eyes blink from the face of a stunning Black Mona Lisa, three pods down. "Jesus Christ."

"We're so happy you dropped down from heaven to visit us," Minou cracks.

"You know it's Stash, you shithead." He plugs one nostril and launches a snot-wad out the other. Minou makes a retching face.

"I can't breathe," I wheeze. "I'm g-gonna…"

"Don't think about breathing." Stash rolls his eyes as he follows Flo's lead and scoots out of his egg. "Just let your body's autonomic whatsits kick in."

"You asshole." Minou swats him. She jumps out of her egg and mirrors Chengmei, dropping into a lunging stretch. "Telling someone *not* to think of something guarantees that's all they'll think about."

"Go easy on him," Chengmei agrees. "You know the first time's rough."

I don't know how they're moving, with the way my bones are suddenly boiled asparagus from breakfast at the Center. I slither out of the egg and flop to the floor, clawing at the impossible weight on my chest. The panic pinholes my vision into a shrinking white tube. Here's how I die. Hands to my neck, *sorry, Gabey, so sorry*—

"You already know how to do this." Flo peers down at me, her soothing kindergarten-teacher voice wrapping me in a warm blanket, no matter what body she's in. "Breathe. Bend like a reed."

I screw my eyes closed, heave air into my cement lungs, and let the panic blow over me. Slow, steady. Bending until I can feel the floor beneath my back. I can see Gabe's gold-ringed eyes hit mine, promising, *you got this*, until I'm strong enough to roll over and stand. The ground quakes, a memory tremor below me.

When I finally feel like I won't barf my insides out, I look around at the five gold eggs clustered in the middle of a small room that's packed with industrial shelves and boxes of paper towels. A single bare bulb hanging on a chain casts sharp light around us. On the shelves, dust-flecked plastic bags of dried pasta and jugs of spices stare back at me. Krill Kreole seasoning.

A vat of creamy Caesar dressing by a tower of toilet paper packs. Bacon Potay-tOH! chips, with added Blisstophan. No windows, only a newspaper-shrouded door leading out of this storeroom into who knows where.

All of us sport stretchy thermals over muscle-corded bods, looking like Olympic triathletes on a ski vacation. New bodies, yeah, though my brain doesn't skip a beat clocking a new understanding of the genders around me. Back in New Thebes, even before me and Gabe first thought about having kids and I planned on living in a female body while I was knocked up, everyone knew that presentation of gender had more to do with dress-up than body parts. And I already knew how to use Gabe's pronouns when he was temporarily in a body of another gender, anyhow.

"He triggered the Ibis Protocol four days in," Stash says, stroking his pouty upper lip like he misses his mustache. "Beat you by two days, Meen."

"This isn't a competition," she says. She doesn't sound entirely convinced.

"The what?" I croak.

"You were visited by a bird, right?" Chengmei asks.

"A big black-and-white one, yeah." I think I've gotten a hang of this breathing thing.

"Right, an ibis, like I said." Stash eye-rolls.

"Sure," I snap. "I'm not a-a bird expert."

"Ornithologist," he corrects.

"C-can you cut the shit, please? Somebody needs to start talking. I can only bend like a reed so far. What the actual *fuck* is going on? Where are we?"

"I'll answer what I can." Flo's eyes crinkle at me. "There's still a lot we don't know."

"Alright." I sigh. "Start with the bird."

"When the Ibis Protocol recognizes a skilled enough editor in the Field of Reeds—we're not sure exactly how the editor proves themselves—it sends a bird messenger," Flo says. "It's supposed to lead editors to a doorway that Khadija created on the edge of the Field of Reeds, a weak spot in the code. I would've noticed the ibis and helped you get here, but I was busy with movie night."

The way she says *code* bird-beak-tap-taps on my forehead. Wait, wait…

"We use that doorway to enter the real world," she continues. "The *real* real world. As in, objective-reality real world, away from the rehab center sim."

Sim. Simulation. How else to explain the magic marsh. Past Fox stared at code blocks on his Reeder screen for years, and each code block is stone, weighing me down.

"How did…?" I manage to sputter before more blocks weigh on me.

She points to the gold eggs. "Those are special Ankhs—"

"Ankh Mark-IIs," Stash chimes in.

"—that Khadija designed for eventual deep-space travel. Upload pods combined with body-stasis chambers. A body's frozen inside until a memorystream is uploaded into it, then it thaws and quick-rezes."

A fresh ripple of *I'm-gonna-hurl* hits me. "Wait, we're in *space*?"

"No," Minou says, a little tight. "Still on Earth, in one of Khadija's old hideouts, we think. We're in an old restaurant storage room, a lil fuzzy on the where. In the Field of Reeds, her power's limited. She can't risk tipping off the sim admin. Seth—he'll snitch. We come here to talk freely, swap stories and all, as we try to find her."

"And the Field of Reeds sim? What the fuck? I thought I came here—*there*—because my memory got blasted."

"You did. It did." Chengmei now, frowning. "It's… it's a lot to take in."

"You gotta try harder than this. *Please.*"

"He should hear it from Khadija herself." Flo snaps her fingers at Stash, who looks like he wants to fight, then thinks better of it.

With a stage magician's *voila*, Stash yanks a sheet off a shape I thought was another pile of boxes to reveal a silver chair plucked right out of the Memory Mapping room.

"Yeah, yeah," Stash says. "Incoming tutorial." He and Flo putter around the chair, tapping buttons in its headrest.

"With open comms to the sim's avatar, please," Flo adds.

I, meanwhile, am floating out of my body again. That's it. I'm not actually here. I died of thirst on the marsh, chasing a magic bird. I let Flo lead me to the chair. *We're gonna tell you a story.* The second my ass hits the chair, I'm somewhere else.

FOURTEEN
TRAINING MODULE

The gray-carpeted training room smells like stale coffee. One of the other new employees behind me in the row of folding chairs coughs. My hand aches from the stack of first-day nondisclosure agreements I just signed, promising not to spill company secrets in this or any alternate universes and divergent timelines. The door by the window, offering a view of the flat gray sky outside, opens and someone from audio-visual wheels in a TV stand. She fiddles around with some buttons, frowns, and gives some wires a tug. Wait, maybe she forgot the batteries for the remote? Someone offers to help. I chew my fingertips, bored, suddenly wondering if this job was the right idea, before—*aha!*—the video pops onto the screen.

Low-rent sax soundtrack. Grainy text against a green background: *WELCOME TO NIL/E TECHNOLOGIES*.

A talk-show stage of a couch, low coffee table, and potted plants. Khadija in her wide-shouldered gray skirt suit, her gold-beaded braids piled in a crown. Powdered lemonade lipstick to match her pumps.

"Hello and *welcome!*" Her smile hits like a lighthouse beam, only for me. "I'm so happy to have you here. You've answered the call and decided to become an editor. And we're *so* much more than just editors. We're surgeons. And friends. And lighthouses in the darkness. Plus, we still know how to get down!"

She snaps her fingers and shimmies her shoulders, like she's taking a dance floor break at a barstool because her heels are killing her, but this song's too good not to groove to.

"Buckle up, we've got a lotta ground to cover."

"First of all, you're in a simulation." Khadija says this to the camera as she walks down the corridor of a cubicle farm, where editors in headsets plunk at their keyboards. "Technically—and we're all about details here!—you jumped from the Field of Reeds sim, to the outside world, to this fancy little tutorial module. Little bit of a mind-fuck." She winces. "Shit, Jillian from HR asked me not to curse in these videos. We'll strike that in post. Anyway, trust me here."

She pops into a kitchenette to pour herself a mug of coffee and sings out a *hey, girl!* to someone off-camera, as bright as the sky on the motivational poster on the corkboard. ENTROPY, the sign says, IT'S JUST A MATTER OF TIME.

I know her. I *know* I know her. The easy song in her voice, the way her eyebrows seem to waggle with every word—it feels like I'm seeing an old friend for the first time in a while. And soon, we're laughing like no time has passed.

"Here's the bullet-point version," Khadija continues, strutting down the hallway with her coffee. "I know the world isn't technically doing so hot right now. Some want to blame the *slightly* inflated human population due to our life-extension tech."

She stops in front of a crowded, glass-walled conference room—long table cluttered with binders, TOMORROWS AND

TOMORROWS projected on the screen at one wall—where two standing guys are hollering at each other. The guy in the suit must be the presenter. The other sports a brown splotch down the front of his white collared shirt. From the looks of it, the presenter must've tossed coffee at him. People around the conference table murmur as others stand and take sides. The glass walls muffle the yells.

"What do I blame?" Khadija continues. "A total lack of empathy."

Suited guy stabs a finger at the chest of the other. And, *snap*. Coffee stain man whips out a handgun and shoots suited guy in the forehead. I almost fall out of my chair at the sound. Blood sprays the glass. Khadija winces for the camera—*awkward, right?*—while people scream and throw themselves at the walls. More gunshots, more gurgling screams.

"That, on a global level." She thumbs at the carnage behind her then rounds the corner, deeper into the cubicle maze. "Just look at the Valholl bombings. And the holy wars, and the genetic wars, and the good old-fashioned *war* wars. Plus, the food shortages while billionaires hop on their space yachts." She ticks off each horror on her fingers. "I started Project Bennu to remind us all of our shared humanity. And that's where you come in."

Khadija's heels clack over to a gray wall with an etched gold sign that says EMPLOYEE OF THE MONTH under a giant oil painting of her. Same gray skirt suit, same Earth Mother smile. "Total babe, right?" She crosses her arms, mirroring the portrait. "See, the problem is the company is absolutely cheesed at me. Been trying to force me out for years. They don't like the direction of Project Bennu, but you know what? Visionaries are always called crazy at first." She winks at the portrait. The portrait winks back.

My ears still echo with gunshots. I'm going to need a training video to explain this training video.

Khadija keeps walking.

"So I bounced, way deep in hiding. And left a few insurance plans scattered around in case they follow through with that whole 'we're going to erase you from existence' thing." She rolls her eyes at the camera after a sip of coffee. "You'd think we could hash this out at a company retreat. But *noooo*. They have to go all nuclear and bomb a whole city on the off chance of flushing me out."

Around a hallway corner, and she's somehow tied to a stake in a medieval square, dressed in a ball gown of gold chainmail and surrounded by torch-waving villagers. Behind her, someone chisels her name off the base of a long stone column. "Eco-terrorist group, my ass. The attack has NIL/E written all over it. Dudes want to burn everything to the ground just to get a woman out of the driver's seat." A joint waggles at the corner of her lips. "Mostly, I'm bored by their lack of creativity." She bobs her chin to the mouth-breathing villager lurching toward her with a torch. "Hey, buddy, got a light?"

The camera pans another corner—I'm dizzy-brained like I took a hit off her joint—and then she's breezing through the front grounds of a squat office building. The manicured hedges along the walkway are shaped into birds in flight. Kids dancing and jumping rope. Couples embracing.

"I mean, technically they don't *love* the idea that I've bounced with a copy of the memorystreams of every NIL/E customer, sure." The groundskeeper in brown overalls snipping at a hedge looks up with a *wait, what?* as Khadija passes. She pats the woman on the shoulder. "Don't worry about that. All part of a bigger vision. You'll love it. A never-ending paradise for everyone, the whole shebang."

I almost fall out of my chair. The audio-visual tech at the front of the room side-eyes me. *Copy of the memorystreams of every*

NIL/E customer. Holy shit. That means she has a copy of Gabe's memories. And I can bring him back and make up for everything I did to him.

"Now, where do you come in?" Khadija asks the camera. "I was almost ready to launch Project Bennu when NIL/E whipped up the virus. Those goons twisted my own tech to shred memories and bring final-death back to the masses, after I democratized that whole 'digital immortality' thing. I mean, girlfriend just can't catch a break here."

She laughs a little—so warm—and maybe her biggest talent besides that whole *forever changing the course of human history* thing is how she can make everyone think she's talking right to them. Even through a video.

"What good is Project Bennu's never-ending paradise if the virus can just black-hole everyone to oblivion? All my hard work? Poof. The next act of humanity gone right before the curtain goes up, bummer of existential bummers. So! We gotta fix the virus. I'm trying to crack it myself, but—well—a good leader isn't afraid to ask for help. So, help!"

She points her search-beam smile at the camera, spreading her hands. "I tasked Flo to round up all the editors in the Field of Reeds therapy sim and give them a copy of the virus. Call it a recruiting test to join my crew. You'll want to stay on the down-low, too. If the sim admin sniffs you out, you're headed to deletion city."

"Hold up." I jerk up in my seat. "Can you hit pause? I have some questions. What does she mean by *delete—*"

"Shh," Khadija snaps from the video. "We're just winding up for the big finish."

Cue the zoom out, cue the marching band stomping through the grass with cymbals crashing, and the color guard tossing their flags in the air, where they flap like butterfly wings. Now, Khadija stands by the office entrance in front of the crowd of her employees, all of them in boxy gray suits and beige sweater sets trying their best to seem excited and mostly failing.

"Our world of tomorrows and tomorrows starts with you!" the crowd chants.

"Seriously, though," she says. "Don't get deleted."

Fade to black.

I jump when the audio-visual aide drops a black plastic binder on my lap. With a cough in the dry office air, she ambles back to the TV stand. The wheels squeak as she rolls it out of the room and leaves us sad-sack newbies in the dark.

I open the binder to the first page.

```
SO YOU'VE BEEN TASKED BY YOUR GODDESS TO:
    1.  CURE THE MEMORY VIRUS WHILE AVOIDING
        DETECTION.
    2.  RETURN TO THE SIM EXTRACTION POINT.
    3.  MEET HER IN THE WORLD BEYOND TO HELP
        CHART A NEW COURSE FOR HUMANITY.
```

Winking eyes, flapping bird wings, and flowing lines of code dance across the rest of the pages of the binder.

I manage not to barf when I find myself gasping in the chair, back in the storeroom with Flo and the others. The way Stash's sculpted arms are crossed over his chest, he looks disappointed when I don't. The marching band from Khadija's video is running laps around my head, distracting me with cymbals and flag flips. *Copy of the memorystreams of every NIL/E customer.* The horn section blasts out of tune. *Don't forget about that whole deletion thing.*

Flo has to explain a lot of what Khadija tried to tell me. The Field of Reeds sim has existed since the early days of Khadija's run with the company, stocked with Caregiver templates to help rehab mippers. Residents pay to get their bodies stashed at a NIL/E facility in the real world while they get plugged into the sim and try to recover their memories. Once they do, they can hop out of the sim, and back to life outside.

"Where is my body, really, then?" I ask her.

"It's in cold storage in a New Thebes facility until your memories are ready for re-upload," Flo says. "According to your intake form."

Flo might've lived out in the real world, once, or she's another one of the templates. Tough to tell. All she really knows is that a few months ago she woke from a daydream and suddenly had the idea to gather all the residents who were former editors and put them in the same therapy Cohort. When each resident is ready— she doesn't know who or what decides that—one of Khadija's old bird-shaped surveillance drones leads the editor to the secret emergency exit to the real world. There, they meet the Scribes— the other residents tasked with finding Khadija—without Seth or the other therapists eavesdropping. Flo introduces them to the others and Sig gives them a copy of the virus to crack on their Reeders. While the therapists help the Scribes heal their mangled memorystreams, the former editors are also remembering how to edit. How to shape code, so they can solve the virus and help Khadija finally launch Project Bennu—whatever that is.

The Scribes meet every few nights in this storeroom after Seth leaves for the evening, to swap code tips and guide each other.

Also to update Flo on any leads they picked up in their Memory Excerpts about where Khadija could be. No way she wouldn't have resurfaced after the attack on New Thebes. The attack on her children. She must be lost somewhere, or buried so deep in nested sims that she doesn't know how to get out.

She saved them from death. Now it's time to return the favor.

Sig's in on the plan. Jury's out on J. Head Therapist Seth is the admin of this whole sim. He's the only one who can log out and return to the real world by driving his car down the dirt road away from the manor after dinner—something called the Commute Home function—leaving the therapists to babysit us for the night. And since he communicates with NIL/E to deliver resident updates to families, it's safe to say that if he finds out what the Scribes are up to, he'll rat us out. And, like Khadija warned, delete us if he needs to. The other Scribes woke up in the sim like I did, fuzzy-brained, remembering scraps of their old lives and traces of their editing skills. Once they triggered the Ibis Protocol, Flo brought them here and filled in the rest.

And then here I came, like popping in a Chosen One module. Magic Fox who somehow survived the attack on New Thebes, the fancy editor who must know how to solve the memory virus and unlock Project Bennu. Once we're back in the Center, Flo says she'll get Sig to upload a copy of the virus code to my Reeder, and if I can crack it, I really am the King of Big Deal she thinks I am.

Sims. Quests. I can remember some of this, somehow, from brass hallways with mosaics staring at me. Khadija offering me something—*a million Gabes. Why stop there? Think bigger, babycakes! You could be a fucking king*—though it could be another brain-blitz memory tremor.

And I must know her, with how her big smile in the video lit me up. I'll remember. And if she can bring Gabe back to me? I'll do whatever she asks.

Darius's voice echoes over the marsh between my ears. *So what would you give, to have all you ever wanted?*

"Why would Khadija want a copy of everyone's memories?" I ask the weird little group in this weird, cluttered room.

"The question really is, what is NIL/E planning with our memories that Khadija must be trying to stop? Why are they scared of her?" Minou says. "You don't torch a city if you aren't scared of what someone'll blab."

"Yeah, but how do we know this is all real?"

Flo smiles. *Canned-memory template.* Even *she's* not real, then? She squeezes my hand.

"Focus on us and what you know in your heart," she says. "That's real."

I don't trust how I feel, and I don't know if she really wants me to answer.

Stash breaks away from the cluster and pulls a box labeled "seeded buns" off the shelf. He opens the box and yanks out a plastic bag of burger buns.

"We don't have all night to splash around the kiddie pool with Fox. Back to business, yeah?" He pulls out a bun and chomps on it, sighing against the shelf. "Shit, I miss preservatives. Anyone have any updates? Leads?"

"Nothing major," Minou says. "Mostly, I've been spinning my wheels on the first block of virus code."

"A staff meeting in my last Excerpt mentioned possible Khadija sightings in Valholl," Chengmei adds.

"That's something." Flo eyes the bag in Stash's hands but seems to think better about asking for one.

Valholl popped up in the news now and then, I remember. It isn't really even a country, more like a truce between the city-states, Canada, and a mob of white nationalist assholes who worship blond Jesus and assault rifles, to see if the idiots will quit bombing shit. They're anti-NIL/E, anti-backups, and anti-happiness, as far as I can tell. Not a bad place for someone hiding from the company to go underground.

"So we go there and look for her." The words come out in one jolt. All I can see is Gabe shrunk down and crammed into the pocket of a trench coat Khadija wears, as she dips in and out of the shadows. If she's the only way to get a copy of his memories and she's out here, why do we even bounce back into the sim?

Chengmei scrunches her mouth. "We don't have a way there, and…"

"She's way too nice to say that your enthusiasm is great and all." Stash chomps a mouthful of bread. "But that's not really how this works."

Minou shakes her head. "For starters, we don't know where *here* is, exactly."

"Y-you haven't been outside?" I ask.

"The first time we arrived through the eggs, one of the restaurant employees told us to stay here," Chengmei says. "This place must be some sort of front for Khadija. We didn't want to put anyone in danger."

"I-I don't get it." I twitch against the bird-beak of confusion trying to peck at my eyes. "Four editors who barely remember their own names are—with the help of Flo—going to crack an editing problem that Khadija, the best editor in history, still hasn't. *That's* the master plan? That'll take forever, if it even works."

Stash just snorts through wet bread. Chengmei wilts a little, while Minou frowns, picking at her fingernails. Ah, crap. The downturned corners of Minou's lips weigh me down. I always push too hard. Still, I'm not waiting for permission. I break away from the group and beeline to the newspaper-covered door of the storeroom. I peel away an edge of the paper—Minou gasping behind me—and peek outside. Just a dark, empty restaurant with chairs upside down on the tables, like someone is sweeping up before they close for the night.

"Looks like the restaurant is closed, anyhow," I say.

"Still—" Minou starts.

"You can go back there and play group therapy with Seth if you want." I thumb at the egg pod Ankhs. "We can look for Khadija in the real world without worrying about getting deleted, and then help her with the virus in person. I'm logging out."

Minou sputters, looking at Flo for backup. Flo just smiles. She pats her pockets like she's looking for her strawberry candies, until she seems to remember what body she's in.

"We're just going to let him shit all over our plans and bust outta here?" Stash rips his roll to pieces. "When we've been meeting here for months, and being careful, and—"

The door handle is cold in my hands. "Yeah, and what progress is that?"

"Maybe Fox's fresh perspective is just what we need," Flo says. "Maybe we've been a bit safe, especially now that no one is outside the storeroom."

"We can poke around some." The slow smile on Minou's face seems fueled by Stash fuming with bread-muffled protests. "Call it reconnaissance."

"No money, no identification." Stash ticks each bullet point on his fingers. "No idea where you're going—"

"Seth is always back before breakfast." Chengmei taps her

fingers on her hips, blowing past him. "And what time did we leave the Center? God, I miss my phone."

"Just after ten," Flo says. "That gives us six, seven hours. Certainly enough time to look around at where we are, then we can return to the Center and start planning our next move."

Let them go back. I'm done being chained in.

"You have fun with that." Stash swallows a mouthful and burps wetly.

"Enjoy your snack," I tell him.

"Really, Stash?" Minou rolls her eyes. "You're not curious about what's outside?"

"Someone should stay here and keep watch," he grumbles.

I flash him a peace sign and open the storeroom door. Evening light struggles through tears in the newspaper-covered windows. Empty restaurant, dust-thick countertops, long-dried beer taps, quiet over the creaky floorboards with Flo, Minou, and Chengmei close behind.

FIFTEEN
INTERMEDIATE PERIOD

The heat is already melting my eyeballs.

We wander past the front door of the shuttered Water Street Café, where a sign taped to the window says CLOSED FOR RENOVATIONS. Four wide streets curve around the middle of a small cobblestone park with benches and a fountain. I smell fresh-cut grass and salt water. We must be near the ocean. Makes sense if we landed in one of the outer burbs ringing New Thebes, somewhere along the Atlantic.

I try not to look at the cars parked along the near-empty street because the reflection of the borrowed body I'm in weirds me out. We pass a drug store. A small diner—two people at the counter, backs to us—casts rusty light into the dark evening, streets lit only by old-timey gas-lamp-looking lights. Squat houses with clipped lawns and flower-packed window boxes border this tiny town square, each building punched from the same assembly line. A woman walks her dog up ahead, someone jogs along the sidewalk across the street, and past the park, two kids throw a ball against a garage door, each rubber thud echoing my racing heart.

I look to Minou and Chengmei, who shrug. Flo is breathing

deep and grinning like she's drunk on air, wiggling her elbows as she power walks.

Everything looks like someone grabbed the remote and turned the saturation down on an off-brand sitcom neighborhood. I can almost hear the laugh track. I remember something about Past Fox working on that Happy Family Vacation canned memory, set in the NIL/E YesterWorld theme park, with facades of malt shops and florists hiding industrial air filters and sprinkler systems. Gingerbread-house-looking cottages camouflaged cooling stations where the park performers could smoke a butt without some kid yanking on their petticoats. The nuts and bolts of the place hidden by hokeyness. We might as well be trapped there.

And the hot air clams up my lungs. I never knew that one of the most annoying parts of living in a woman's body is the sweat that plasters your skin beneath your boobs.

"Anyone else feel like we're slogging uphill?" We have to stop for me to just lean on my knees and suck in air. Minou's nostrils flare with her breaths, like she doesn't want to let on how she's puffing, too. "I'm dying here."

"You're not used to realistic amounts of discomfort," Flo chirps, bouncing on her toes. "Seth has bodyweight and pain settings dialed way down in the sim. It boosts contentedness levels."

"Creepy." Minou squints up at a streetlight.

"Does this place look familiar to anyone?" Chengmei asks, craning her neck around.

"Nope," I say.

The generic street signs for numbered avenues at each corner don't give anything away. Up ahead past the groggy, electronic eye of a traffic signal, a bench waits in a clear bus-station shelter, and beyond that, glass spires of a city. Four shadowed figures jostle each other outside the shelter, their laughter floating over to us.

They'll know where we are. One of us will just have to ask. I'm banking on Flo, since she puts everyone at ease, and I'm wheezing too hard, anyhow.

Turns out we don't have to bother. A sign over the bus stop reads RIVER FALLS in looping script. A post with a digital display, the bright blue letters punctuating the dark, tells us all we need to know. *10:47 p.m. Inland Ocean City free trolley system. Calling at River Falls, Goshute Heights, Pacificus Village, terminating at IOC East. Connect at IOC East to IOC Radius Line.*

A happy chime behind us. I turn to see a squat vintage trolley car pulled from a kid's playset chugging over to us, all shiny tangerine paint and curving windows. All aboard.

The trolley driver in a tweed vest and straw hat nods as we hop on. There's only a handful of people aboard, a few folks probably heading in for their night jobs, and one couple jazzed up in bar-hopping outfits. The kids rustle past us—gems and lights flashing from their memory nodes—and spread out in the back seats, gabbing about a slasher flick they're heading to see. We find an island of empty seats toward the middle and plop down. Just in time. I sag against a pole and will the stars from my eyes.

Minou is our tour guide, dishing out as much as she can remember about Inland Ocean City, the second urban rebuild on the continent after New Thebes. A marvel of engineering that she remembers NIL/E announcing maybe six years back, before her memories get fuzzy because of her back-alley edits. No more arsenic sandstorms scorching the dead earth around the dried-up Great Salt Lake, now that the company had laid some seven hundred miles of plumbing to glug in seawater from the Pacific. The once-evacuated Salt Lake City reborn as a green dreamland fueled by electricity generated by seawater surging through pipes down the mountains. No fossil fuels anywhere, which were supposed to have been as dead as the dinos years ago, anyway—until the ice sheets in Greenland melted to reveal fresh oilfields underneath. An oasis just in time for folks forced out of most of RedLandia by the inner-circle-of-hell heatwaves to find a new home.

Chengmei doesn't remember anything about the city, and Flo's expertise seems to dead-end at the workings of the Center, so she's no help. We fill in the rest from the city map on the walls of the trolley, studded with blurbs aimed at tourists. *Neo-burbs in concentric rings around the Inland Ocean offer all the comforts of modern living within an easy ride to the central city. Did you know? Inland Ocean is approximately seven times the size of the former Great Salt Lake. Fun fact! Brine shrimp provide food for resurrected species of American avocets, marbled godwits, and more. Even you!*

And that's great, yeah. I love that the company I must've broken my back for is making good on all its promises to rehab the world. But unless Inland Ocean City boasts a bullet train right to Valholl, where Khadija will be waiting with a shiny copy of Gabe's memorystream, I don't feel much like celebrating.

The trolley chugs along on one of a dozen thin bridges over the canals, passing through more sitcom neighborhoods, as the central city within a huge stretch of water creeps closer. A few minutes after we stop at Pacificus Village, a wooden-covered bridge putters into view. *This dual-mode trolley switches to magnetic levitation for the remainder of the trip*, a cheerful voice calls over the speakers. *We hope you've enjoyed your ride.* The trolley stops for a few breaths on the bridge, where it clanks and whirs beneath us. I jump at the sound and look around, but none of the other Scribes—I guess I'm one of them, now— seems to notice.

We blast out from the covered bridge so fast that my ribs rattle. Sweating, swaying, stomach on spin cycle like Seth accidentally sat on the remote control and jacked up my bodyweight. The others wince, except Flo, who bounces like a kid in a bassinet strolling through a field of balloon animals. The trolley blurs over the wide lake until buildings on platforms over the water pop into view, glowing against the night. *Entering IOC nodecast zone*, the same voice calls again.

Warm spider fingers tickle out of the node on this body I'm wearing, spreading down my spine. Something ripples like water over my eyes. I blink the water away, and just like a session in the Ankh, I'm somewhere else.

A multi-tiered green-and-silver mosaic of buildings rises out of the water on either side of the bridge, lighting the way to the glass vase of flowers that is the central city. Waterfalls and hanging gardens trickle down the sides of the buildings—glowing terrace windows and bloom-draped patios offering glimpses into plush living rooms and bathrooms with soaking tubs giant enough to swan-dive into. Bashes on rooftops overlook the luxury yachts skimming over the water like fringe-finned dragons. Lights wink from the wingtips of passenger-jet pods and delivery drones. Jeweled chalices of fountains shoot braids of water into the night air as sea birds fly by the trolley, eye to eye with me. The sight of them and this whole cubist psychedelic trip of a city blurs as the tears well in my eyes.

I remember in New Thebes, the apartments in my and Gabe's neighborhood were crammed together like bristles of a hairbrush. We could hear every sneeze, every argument of our neighbors, even over the near-constant rattling of the metal catwalks as the trains rolled by. Here, though, in this garden of light that makes even the golden downtown of New Thebes look like a pile of rubble? Here we could live with each other forever in the spray of salt air while waterfalls shush us to sleep.

Minou's mouth drops into an O. Even Flo leans forward and fans her fingers over her chest.

"How?" I ask. *Nodecast*, the overhead voice said. For an instant, I flash back to the movie theater that date night with Gabe, with that supposed immersive storytelling InSense tech. What was to stop the company from beaming out happy signals and painting a paradise around you? I rip my eyes from the city and look behind us, in the direction we came from. Only endless, open ocean, now.

Chengmei's fingers float from her trembling lips to the trolley window, tears gushing down her face.

"I feel like I'm back home in Beijing," she says. The sound from her lips dances between a laugh and a sob. "I never thought I'd see it again."

The trolley whirs and slows, flowing in a liquid line to a giant silver platform where the pattern of streets and glass-and-chrome buildings is sacred geometry dreamed up by particle collisions. Lantern-topped obelisks, wrapped with ivy, wash the incoming train station in a silver glow. More canals and footbridges thread the platform, with clear water sloshing below. *Alighting at Inland Ocean City East*, the voice coos from above. *Change here for the Radius Line.*

I had a plan, almost, when I tore at the paper plastered on the door of the storeroom and shoved off Stash and his caution. *I'll hitchhike to Valholl if I need to. I'll sell a couple of organs to hop a flight if it's the only way to find Khadija.* As the trolley glides into the station and the other passengers trickle out around us, another voice massages out the knots in my neck. *Stay here a while. Take it easy. Welcome home.*

We weave through the thin crowd in the station. Moving digital mosaics that look like they're made of cut-glass tiles flow over every curving, silver wall of the tube-shaped main hallway. I don't know how suspicious I look, but I can't keep my mouth closed as my head wobbles around to stare at the glowing scenes with their titles describing the legend of Inland Ocean City. *Khadija Tames the Seas.* A woman in a gold sheath dress with a crown of braids—flat and stern compared to Khadija's brightness in the training video—descends from the clouds, waves her Reeder, and ribbons of water race from an ocean, through the desert. *Resurrecting the Birds.* Khadija opens her arms and a rush of bright-feathered birds soar into the starry sky. *Flowering the Earth.* Khadija walks through the desert and flowers bloom from her footprints.

"I dig a woman who's not afraid to toot her own horn." Minou whistles at my side.

One of the women in the mosaics seems to wink at me. I snort a laugh at Minou. This place is more beautiful than any museum, and it's just a train station. A whole garden of glass and chrome waits outside. Still, we can't stay here forever. I have a plan—theoretically. And now that I'm back in the real world, no chance in hell am I going back to the creaky-floored purgatory of the Center.

The station funnels us in one of two directions: Either a curving tunnel with signs pointing to the Radius Line, or out the automatic glass doors marked INLAND OCEAN CITY EAST, to a neighborhood with a green-and-silver-wave mosaic on the pavement and ivy filigreeing the sides of buildings. I point to a row of ticket machines. "I think our free ride is over if we wanna get to the city center."

Flo frowns at my side. "No. We should head back. This is a fine first step. We can regroup, and—*oh!* Chengmei!"

I spin in the direction of Flo's horrified voice. Chengmei already made the decision for us.

She floats, palms out like she's soaking up sunshine at the beach, through the glass doors and into the night. We scramble out to her side. Not fast enough to keep her from traipsing through one of the three metal-detector-looking gates that low glass walls corral everyone through. Me, Flo, and Minou stop at an overhead digital sign that reads PARCEL CHECKPOINT. Makes sense to sniff for bombs after the attack on New Thebes. One of the three goggled guards in safety-yellow shirts emblazoned with CITY SEC—each of them with radios and snub-nosed silver pistols on their belts—waves for us to walk through.

Before my heel even hits the ground on my next step, low fireworks explode over the gates.

Flash, white-hot, across my eyes. I'm in New Thebes that night of the bombing again—stumbling through screams, instantly blind. I reach for Minou. Someone slams into me from behind and growls a gruff, "Go, you dumb shits," that I can barely hear over the screeching in my ears. I bash into Flo, Minou is pinched to my side, and we're shoved through the gates. The flash fades enough for me to see the security guards clawing at their goggles. Sparks shower down from three of the busted lanterns atop the obelisks that line the platform.

The world oozes to a stop and the painted paradise of Inland Ocean City falls away.

The train-station exit and the surrounding block are sucked free of the green and silver of the rest of the city—a stage spotlight in reverse. Jagged edges of the spotlight fizzle like a janky light switch. The level of the crystal water in the nearby canals has suddenly dropped twenty feet, exposing thick silver pipes that belch steam. My feet trip over gray pavement instead of the wave mosaic that was just there. The apartment buildings at the edges of the spotlight are scarred with pipes, cranks, metal grates like the teeth of giants, painted letters—TO EAST PLUMBING STATION ONE, TO ALPHA RADIUS SANITATION—over black catwalks and ladders, like scaffolding holding up the sky.

And the people. So many of them, like someone tipped over an ant farm—people in black overalls and yellow hardhats unleashing glowing sparks as they weld pipe joints on just-revealed metal platforms, and scrabbling up ladders to glowing panels that scream *cast error*. Others suspended from cables squeegee windows of apartments, water patio gardens, and roll gray paint over a graffiti mural of a gold-skinned, winged Khadija beneath a single word. *Rise.*

Beyond the spotlight, the rest of the city is still the same perfect glass garden. Only here, you can see the machinery below the dirt.

Time catches up to the wild sprint of my heart. Flo claws at my arm and the pain knocks me back into myself. Alarms over the gates whoop with bright, bloody lights. *Nodecast failure.* Chengmei is suddenly at our side and then someone in black overalls and a hardhat shoves us out of the spotlight—*move your arses or you're dead*—kicks open a maintenance side door in the closest building, and crams us through.

The hallways are a shock of white after the whooping alarms and red lights of the train station. I'm dizzy and tripping over my feet in the sudden, stuffed-ear silence. The only sounds are our stomping footsteps and the occasional cough from black-overalled people who work at glowing maintenance panels and ignore us. Plus, the stream of abuse from our maybe-savior in a yellow hardhat.

"Ripping, bloody bell-ends will see us all killed." They yank off their hardhat and goggles to reveal a sunburned woman with a taut yellow ponytail. "Faster, fuckface!" she barks when I turn back to her.

Chengmei seems to have snapped out of whatever trance lured her away from us in the train station, murmuring *sorry* and *all my fault*. Flo huffs over Minou's steady stream of *shitshitshit*. My brain is drowning in adrenaline at whatever fresh hell of an espionage canned-memory template we just got dropped into. Which was my bright idea. I bite my tongue until I taste blood.

Ponytail shoves past me to the lead, jerking quick turns and leading us down more pristine hallways.

"We didn't have a drop scheduled tonight," she grumbles, half turning back to us. "Who's your handler? Jasmine?"

I sputter. "We got here from—"

"And why the piss did you leave River Falls? I got the ping that the loaner bods left the storeroom, and I've been using the nodes' kiddie-settings GPS signals to trail you since you stupid cows stomped past the usual drop point and walked on the tram." She hurls her hardhat and it skitters down the white hallway. "I had to shoot out a coupla the nodecast lanterns, blowing *months* of cover, before whichever of you is the parcel carrier mooed right through the checkpoint and got us all killed. Great fucking-fuck. Half of City Sec'll be crawling up our arses, now."

"What just—"

"You're from the SoCalia ring?" She stops at an intersection just long enough for the four of us to knock into her back. She shoves me off with a growl, then we're racing down a hallway marked FILTRATION E-1. "Mandrake, that munter, wouldn't know protocol if it bit him on the bollocks." Right turn, a quick left into a room with screaming vents and pipes that glug trash-flecked water into a giant tank. "Always at me, all, 'Poppy, protocols go to shit when things get fleshy, and—'"

"We don't know anyone named Mandrake," Minou huffs over the noise. "We're not from SoCalia. We got here from the Field of Reeds."

Poppy stops in her tracks, her eyes suddenly taking up half her face. "*Wot?*"

"The Field of—" I start, until she cuts me off with a hand up. When we're out a steel door and into another coffin-quiet white hallway she turns to me with a *well?* look on her face. "The Field of Reeds."

"Piss off." She flashes a wicked smile. I think I liked her better swearing. "Which Field of Reeds? You're not part of the memory-runner ring. You're editors, yeah?"

"Right," Flo says. "We're trying to cure the virus. Especially Fox here—"

Poppy's burst of laughter drowns out the rest of Flo's words. Usually a Flo vote of confidence would help calm me down, but even she can't throw me a life raft now.

"Fucking Shazad fucking Fox!" Poppy claps. More white teeth jut out from her smile. "King editor in a loaner bod in IOC East. Of course. Just when I was having a quiet night."

The wobbling floor threatens to crank into a full-blown memory tremor. "Did I know you?"

"No, but we all certainly heard legends about *you*." She mumbles something about getting turned around, then snaps down a hallway. "Well. *Warnings*, more like."

It's like she dropped another Memory Excerpt on my shoulders. *Here you'll learn how you're not just a screw-up for Gabe, but for everyone else.*

"Can you get us somewhere safe, from whatever the hell that was back there?" Minou asks.

Poppy stabs her fingers at a keypad and heaves open a door that leads into an alley. A fleet of black IOC East Maintenance vans wait in the glow of the floodlights off another perfect, vine-wrapped building.

"Cams have your loaner faces now. We wouldn't be able to hide you, even underground. Not with the sweeps. We'd pop you into new loaners, but the Ankhs are all under lockdown in Central Editing. And the eggs, well, *blast*, we have to consider them compromised. I'll have to crack them, or roll them into the canal after you're out, or..."

I don't hear the rest. *After you're out.*

"The only way out for you is back in." Poppy thumbs a code on one van's door and the doors whiz open.

The passenger seatbelt of the maintenance van cuts across my ribs. The only sounds are Chengmei's quiet sniffles and Flo's gentle *there-there*s as the van's AI nav hauls us off the ground—up and up—leaving my heart in the alleyway.

Poppy pulls a Reeder from her overalls and jams it onto the console. The central display fritzes, fills with code, then glows with a new menu that says *Cast Presets*. She taps *pizza delivery* and the outside of the van changes, from what I can tell by the hood switching to bright red with CHEE-Z XPRESS written in pizza slices. She tugs the steering wheel out of the dash and switches to manual, banking a hard left into a nearly empty lane of aerial traffic. Way off to the right, an army of police vans scream through the sky, their blue and red lights reflecting jewels over the water.

I'm suffocating—trying to breathe and bend at the same time so I don't pass out at the thought of getting shoved in the Ankh again, and more memory tremors, and more Excerpt evidence that I was human garbage. For an instant, I hear Gabe sigh. *Might as well barrel-out, babe-o. Hope you can swim.*

We zip over street grids and canals. Over the open water. Once we pass the nodecast barrier, the rings of the outer burbs blink into view. *Next stop, River Falls, connect to the Field of Reeds Torture Chamber.* I'm barred behind my ribs. Like I'm back in Zee's office when I thought I was hot shit and she reminded me with painted red lips, *think again.*

I get half of what Flo and Poppy blabber about, all logistics. Something about how the Ankh Mark-IIs auto-dial to the last upload point. How Poppy won't be able to find out just where that is, by design, in case City Sec sniffs out the storeroom. Something about City Sec scanning all civilians for memory parcel whatevers, in case Khadija is trying to sneak into IOC.

We touch down behind the Water Street Café. Canned memories, canned movements as I tell my legs to step out of the van, through the restaurant, back into the storeroom where Stash wakes up from a nap on two folding chairs when we stumble in. The others climb into the pods and blue glass screens roll over their bodies.

"You can't make me go back there," I beg.

Poppy softens just a bit. Maybe it's the war she must see in my eyes. "We'll find you. Give us some time. And when you see boss lady, you tell her Poppy is holding the line with the IOC runners, yeah?"

The sides of the egg crush me when I wriggle inside.

SIXTEEN
BUDDING

'm barely through the rift back into the Field of Reeds when Stash's hands claw at the neck of my sweatshirt. For all of this being a sim, his hands sure as hell feel real. His spit flecks my face, and the red veins in his eyes are angry lava flows. I slam my hands into the center of his chest and his animal grip falters. Minou is the one to shove him away.

"We had *one* anchor to reality, *one* maybe lead on Khadija's location, and this stupid prick fucked it up," he snarls.

"It's my fault," Chengmei says, wincing. "The nodecast signal did something to me. Like it pulled me someplace, and—"

"No," Stash barks. "You left the storeroom because of him. Ever since king editor douche got here, the rules don't matter—the rules that kept us hidden—and now we're absolutely fucked. Even if we *do* cure the virus, this asshat bricked over the extraction point. And it's not like Seth is going to let us walk out of here with the cure code."

"You mean now Poppy and her memory runner whoevers know about us?" I snap. "She said they'll find us. An-and maybe I just sent word to Khadija that we're still working on things. That's more than you've done."

I huff and yank at the neck of my crumpled sweatshirt. Gabe would clench his jaw, narrow-eyed. *And now you're the victim. Not even an apology in there. Bravo, Foxy.*

Stash barrels past us and throws a kayak into the water with a messy splash.

"Well, let's look on the bright side." Flo plucks a strawberry candy from her cardigan pocket and the lanyard of keys around her neck jangles. "We still have the virus to cure. That hasn't changed."

"Yes," Chengmei offers weakly.

"Now that we can't visit the storeroom, maybe that's one less distraction," Flo continues. "We'll stay focused on the work. We'll do what we've always done, and only talk shop when we're not around Seth and the other therapists. We'll be more careful."

Minou just sighs and crosses her arms, her gaze lost over the marsh. "We should get back. I know I could use some sleep."

"Yes, we all need to rest," Flo says. "And tomorrow, you all carry on with your treatment plans as usual, so we don't tip off Seth, and—"

"I can't." The breath I'd been holding while in Poppy's van blasts out of me. "I don't know how long I can keep up with the treatments. I…"

Flo squeezes my hands. Her urgent eyes hit mine. "Fox, I *know* you can do this. And it's not just me. Khadija sent the ibis—that means she's watching out for you. You're not alone anymore. You're part of something now. You have us. And I promise, I'll keep you safe."

I want to believe her. Stash is already wildly paddling away.

I trail my hand out of the boat while Minou rows me to shore. Watching the ripples. Feeling the cool water even though my brain is trying to tell me the truth. You're not actually touching the water.

You're a bunch of code floating in a bunch of other code, with other code telling you your fingers are wet and cool.

Every floorboard seems to creak on my way back to my room. Like this whole sim is full of alarms I'm triggering at invisible checkpoints. Until Seth—all *no judgment*—hits me with the searchlight. And would he really delete us? *I'm your Case Manager, though I hope you'll think of me as a friend*, he said that first day we met. I'll just have to be a model resident until I get out of here. I remember something when I'm curled up in bed, locked up again in my cell of a room. Too small to be a memory tremor. Too bright to be a dream. Just me and Gabe in Darius's office, in the real world, our first session with him. We're holding hands. I can feel Gabe's grip weakening as Darius talks, something about *we can storyboard a life together we think you'll both be happy with*. I hold on tight because being here must be what Gabe wants, right? Better than being alone? *You're part of something now*, I could've told him.

"But it won't be real," Gabe says slowly. "Right?"

"Would you like me to explain our company policy on relative reality?" Darius asks.

"No," Gabe says. "I really wouldn't."

I'm screwing up somehow, flash-backed to that therapy room. Even then I should've known he was already gone.

Morning drenches my room in amber, and I'm a mosquito stuck inside, forever. Gold light through the window, shining on the specks of dust in the air. Someone had to code those specks of dust, the physics of their slow loops. Points for the immersion of this place, I guess. Now that I know it's a simulation, I want the sunlight to feel less real. Still, it lights up my skin, warming me.

Affirmations in the bathroom mirror, because why the hell not. *You are special, and you are loved. And you deserve to remember.* Except this morning, feeling like someone took a wrench to the inside of my skull, that *deserve* is a threat. *Your punishment is that you deserve to remember. You don't get to forget what you did. How you treated him.*

Flo told me that Sig would drop a copy of the memory virus code onto my Reeder. I grab the thing off my desk and zip up the screen. A broken wavy line icon waits for me, which I tap, popping open a new window with a giant block of code. No line breaks, no separation into stanzas. Just one unending block of symbols. And down, and down, as the bottom of the window just reads: *Calculating...*

Scribes, Flo called us. She said the others had been working on the virus for a few months, and nothing. What am I going to do that they can't? *Fucking Shazad fucking Fox*, Poppy sing-songed. *King editor in a loaner bod in IOC East.* Another vote of confidence from someone I don't know. And then there was her whole *warnings, more like* barb. And then Khadija's laughing, dark-honey eyes when she said cracking the virus is a recruitment test for her crew. To join her in the real world, she must mean, wherever she is, with her copy of Gabe's memorystream. Ready to launch the never-ending paradise she called Project Bennu— whatever the hell that is.

All the code words and secrets. All the train station moving mosaics fighting for attention.

The Reeder still says *calculating...* while I scroll, the lines blurring across my eyes. A million lines of code, probably. Might as well be a trillion. Fuckofftillion. I giggle with the exhausted sillies while I keep scrolling, and it's like I'm wearing Flo's lanyard of keys, except more keys keep clipping onto the ring until I tip over, then more pile on me.

The key to beating the memory virus and getting to Khadija, who'll bring Gabe back to me, is stashed somewhere in this never-ending pile of keys. *And you'll find it!* Flo's sunny voice hits me. *After all, you have forever. I'll just put a pot of coffee on.*

Coworkers grumbled at Past Fox while he walked by them in the hallways. Asstool. Golden boy. Convinced Zee that his shit doesn't stink all because he could code better than us.

Yeah, where's that savant shtick now, buddy? I try to massage my code-headache away with taps at my temples. Is this thing on? Fox? Hellooooooo?

He's not interested in helping. I snap the Reeder shut, head out of my room, and bounce down the stairs to start the day.

Flo hovers by the door to the sunroom, at the start of the Memory Mapping line, and I know she's there for me. She nods to remind me. *You're part of something now... And I promise, I'll keep you safe.* Minou keeps her lips tight like she's trying not to smile when I pass her on my way to the end of the line. She taps her nose. *Our secret.*

"I mean, I could get laid like concrete, twice a day, easy," Inyene gabs to Fredericka in line. "I remember my neighbor left me a can of joint grease on my doorstep, once, with a note saying my bedsprings were keeping the whole floor up."

Fredericka looks like she doesn't know whether to laugh or run. Instead, she offers up, "I honor your memory, I guess?"

"Damn straight," Inyene says.

I'm a part of something that all of the others, with their embroidered names and Radical Remembrances, aren't. I can keep going. I feel lighter, somehow, now that I have an actual purpose instead of a hazy *get better*. And I can be someone to the Scribes, right? Past Fox had no one else but Gabe, really. When Past Fox was *he* and not *I*. I can feel us blurring together. I'm already doing better than him. And here, as the line moves up, I wish Gabe was around so I could tell him, *see, I'm already more. I'm not just someone who broke your heart anymore.*

Even J's bright smile lights me up, and I let myself laugh. The same choppy bleached hair, the same cheerful blue-gray eyes and tuneless hum while they work. Template or no, J manages to always put a smile on my face. The chair's visor snaps down over my eyes.

"The whole of your memory is your memorystream," J says behind me in their prayer-voice. "Watch it flow like a—holy *moly* have we got a boatload of budding, buddy!"

J zips to my side and flicks their hand at the projection, zooming into one of the branches. I squint through the purple lights of the visor but don't notice anything, whatever it is I'm supposed to be looking for.

"The Memory Excerpt Sig debugged the other day is *really* taking root," J burbles, bouncing excitement into me. "You've been having memory tremors?"

"Earthquakes, more like."

J zooms in closer to the branch of my memorystream. A picture appears—another watercolor blur that's little more than a streak of blue on blue. They grab the picture and toss it to their tablet, then yank the visor back from my face.

"We gotta get you to Sig, *yesterday.*" They haul me out of the chair, chattering, then out into the hallway where we meet up with Flo, J's arm linked with mine and glowing like we just got hitched. Hooting and cheering at every resident and therapist we blow past, *significant organic memory recovery!*

A blur of stairs, of sunlight squares from the hallway windows until I'm in the Ankh Room again. J drops me off before disappearing with another celebratory *significant organic memory recovery!* that has the other therapists in the room murmuring.

"I'm not gonna lie to you," Sig says, frowning through his beard at the floating blur of my Excerpt. "This one looks like a doozy."

I wouldn't be able to get in the Ankh again if Flo didn't rest a warm hand on my shoulder.

"It's alright," she tells me, her strawberry-candy breath wafting. Then soft, so the other therapists don't hear, "She's watching you, now. She'll guide you. I just know it."

Soon, I'm sitting in the cramped Ankh with the sedative's sweetness dying on my tongue.

I know she wants me to call out to Khadija. I can see Gabe's lips instead, and his dark eyelashes against his cheeks one morning our AC busted and we trailed ice cubes over each other's skin. So I pray to him instead. *Wait for me?* Soon, I'm heavy-lidded. Bones bending like a reed in the breeze. Leaning back in the Ankh and breathing out honey fumes.

I'm not going to sleep. It feels more like waking up.

SEVENTEEN
STANDARD MEMORY TEMPLATE 36

G reg spotted more white in his beard than he remembered. Under the salt-white light in the bathroom at work, the strands poked from his chin like toothbrush bristles. White hair and a gray face and popping joints when he stood up too fast. The yellow tile floor in the bathroom that he'd just mopped was ice-slick beneath the grass-green stall doors and the three urinals like snowmen in formation. Back when it still snowed and you could make snowmen, before the melting, and the flooding, and the droughts. He remembered snow sticking to the ends of Zeke's eyelashes when they'd walked their dog.

He remembered too much. That was the problem. These memories didn't help anymore.

He finished cleaning the bathroom and wheeled his squeaky supply cart into the hallway. By this time of night, most of the staff were long gone. Wide glass windows offered views of the green-walled editing lab with its six long tables and computer workstations. One woman was parked at a terminal, pecking away at her keyboard. She didn't look up when he wheeled in, which was just fine with him. Sometimes the editors said *thank you*, once in a while *how are you?* No one ever asked his name.

He swapped the bag in the trash can for a clean one while the woman's fingers rippled over the keyboard. He wasn't jealous of the job. The paycheck, sure, not that he needed a lot to live on out here, in a nowhere town in LakeLandia—three hours outside Minneapolis—working at a giant editing center that the fancy editors from Greater Chicago or New Thebes who rolled in once in a while to hold training sessions called a "mass-market MemoReetailer." The editors here snipped away downer days and dropped canned memories into the heads of coupon-clippers. Greg had cleaned a coffee spill in the back of the lab, once—no one noticed him—while the visiting execs had blabbed about projected happiness curves and *we call this editing level the euphoria special*.

He'd peeked over enough screens to see what the editors watched before they deleted memories. Coffins lowering into graves. Screaming matches over the kids' toaster waffles at breakfast. Dirty bathroom mirrors where someone tried to smear makeup over bruises.

No, thanks. Give him the trash any night.

Greg's tiny house was quiet. The air used to clang with bird caws, and dog barks, and cats chasing balls with bells in them across the floors. He and Zeke hadn't needed much space, just this two-bedroom ranch with its living room off the kitchen and a yard with the hammock out back. Zeke had been a vet and thought it was funny—cute, even—how mad Greg would get at the sight of another animal. *Rescued!* Zeke would say, shoving a wiggling ferret in Greg's face for a cuddle. *Meet your new son. He has your nose. Kidding! Kidding!* And Greg would have to step outside, clamming up another yell, about how *Jesus fucking Christ, Zekie, I didn't sign up to live in a zoo.*

The ferret had been pretty cute, though. Greg had learned to kill the guilt trips, and Zeke learned not to bring any more abandoned pets home, not with the dog that slept between them already, and the one-eyed cat named Pixie that napped on Zeke's belly when she wasn't barfing up hairballs.

Greg flicked on the holo-display, and the projected scenes burst into the living room. A lumberjack of a guy lathering in the shower at least helped Greg pretend he had company.

Dinner was a soy Fauxlognese frozen Mentrée that looked like something he'd mop up and a bleachy-smelling whiskey. When his first whiskey slid down easy, he glugged another into the tumbler and wobbled to the red blob of the couch across from the TV. He tried not to knock back round three too often, but he was on a mission tonight. Otherwise known as *getting after it* when he and Zeke had met in their twenties. Otherwise known as *Tuesday* now that Greg was marooned on the wrong side of sixty, with a husband dead for two years.

Zeke would say something like *this is how it starts!*, hiding the worry with a little song in his voice, like when he'd found Greg in a cloud of booze fumes on the couch the day the foundry had closed. Greg had been a welder until things hadn't needed welding, then he'd driven trucks. Once caravans started whizzing across the highways, shoving the guys like him off the road, he'd started sweeping floors. At least messes were recession-proof. *Nobody wants a drinking problem. This is how it starts!*

Tonight's round three tasted sweet. The *should've*s bowled into him every night, between the commercials and frozen dinners, the handfuls of grease-bomb chips. He should've begged Zeke to sign up for NIL/E's services so they could've plugged him into a new body. Guerrilla holo-ads followed people on the sidewalks, their ageless faces promising *tomorrows and tomorrows in the sunlight*.

"Yeah, but it's not you," Zeke had said, after one of the ads first crashed a weekend morning coffee run, six years back. On the sidewalk in front of the coffee shop, he'd winced and batted at the projection of an ageless couple walking on the beach. The image had blinked away.

"What do you mean?"

"When they dump your memories into a new body, it's some... *thing* that thinks it's you, maybe. What makes you *you*—the real you—is gone."

Greg had swallowed the laugh before it popped out of his mouth, but he knew Zeke had spotted it in his eyes. Greg hadn't meant to be an asshole—but his boom-mic ears had picked up what his husband was really saying. *What about your soul?* The closest they had ever gotten to church was Sunday brunch at the gay bar two towns over, but he'd known that Zeke's parents had been Nuestra Señora de la Santa Muerte missionaries, and those kinds of claws stay in you forever.

"Besides, we can't afford it," Zeke had said, hiding the downward sweep of his eyes with a sip of coffee.

What Greg regretted more than the almost-laugh was not pushing Zeke harder. *Do this for me.*

He regretted plenty, like how his last words to Zeke had been *hey, can you take the trash with you?* before his husband had had a heart attack on the way to work, crashing into a tree, and *Jesus*, he hadn't even been sixty-five. He regretted how three days after that he'd been so blind drunk that he forgot to put Zeke's chickens back into their coop for the night, and a fox had torn them to shreds.

Feathers and blood everywhere the next morning, while Greg blubbered into the dirt, smearing his hands and clothes.

He couldn't do this. He'd waited all of that day and night on the back porch with his shotgun, hoping to nail the fox. It never came back.

Some days he stared at the shotgun a little too hard.

The whiskey burned Greg's tongue. He wondered, before the tide yanked him down to something close to sleep, how it'd taste in the new body he was saving for. He'd signed up as a NIL/E client and had gotten his node installed six months back. The employee discount had helped. He had the rest of the insurance money, and his paycheck, and no real bills except for his food and Pixie's. He'd go for a body in its early thirties, maybe, for his next go-round in a life that was supposed to stretch out forever. Models in their twenties cost too much. Plus, it would be weird to be so young without Zeke.

The night they met shivered through him, sharp as Pixie's claws on his chest as she kneaded his flesh, purring. He'd been so high that he'd almost conked his head on the ceiling fan of the bar. On the dance floor, he'd turned to Zeke, whose gold-flecked brown eyes lit up at the sight of him. So why the hell not—he'd grabbed Zeke by the waist and kissed him. When they'd stumbled apart, they'd laughed over the *thunka-thunka* of the bass.

"Couldn't you just fucking die?" Greg had yelled, his hand gripping some live-wire of joy.

"Fries?" Zeke had tipped his head like a hound's. "Yeah!"

Greg had wobbled after Zeke out of the bar to a food truck outside, and they'd scarfed down cheese fries and algaedogs. Zeke had kissed the ketchup away from the corner of Greg's mouth, old loves already.

Hey, can you take the trash with you? Greg hadn't even looked up from his coffee.

The floor had dropped out from under him when the police pulled up to the house. A drop in slow motion and falling still. He'd get his feet back any day now. Any day.

Flo, we seem to be losing him. He's diving to another extraction branch. Holy shit, he's—someone get a dose of sahusynopane. Intravenous, and fucking haul ass.

He's fine, Sig. Let this play out. We're watching him.

EIGHTEEN
EUPHORIA SPECIAL

I told Gabe I loved him the first night we met on the dance floor at a bar downtown. Of course I was rolling—*researching bliss*, so I could accurately recreate it for clients, suresure—and also told the bartenders, the doorman, and a bottle of beer someone left on one of the urinals that I would love them forever, so there's that. He bought me cheese fries and *I love you* seemed like a perfect way to say thanks. We swapped numbers and the next day met for real at a crowded traveling carnival in the city square.

Gabe glowed, lit by the twinkling lights of the Whirl-o-Wind ride behind him. Laugh-screams from the people strapped to the spinning arms washed over me on my way to him, walking almost on tiptoes, like I didn't want to scare him off. He leaned against a park bench and sipped on a soda, open black shirt tossed over a white tank top and shorts. Arm tattoos and gold chain. Chewing on a straw, looking up at the ride and grinning big.

Well, so much for blaming the *I love you* from the night before on the drugs. I might as well have been strapped to the Whirl-o-Wind with how my stomach twisted itself around my spine. Already, sweat stuck my shirt to my armpits.

"You gonna tell me you love me again?" he called.

I laughed, swooping in for a quick kiss. *Old loves already.* "Let's see how tonight goes, yeah?"

He hit me with those gold-rimmed eyes, and it was like I was zipping off in the Whirl-o-Wind, and into the sky. Up and up, never to touch down again.

We tried to win tickets at some of the games, even though we knew they were rigged. Gabe said he wanted to get all hetero and try to win me a stuffed animal in the claw machine, but the metal fingers couldn't catch a drift. We hefted mallets and whacked cobras that popped out of the holes at Smash-the-Snake, swapping first-date bullet points about where we worked and lived. He worked at one of the bodyfication gym-spas downtown, near my office. We could've crossed paths a million times already.

"Memory editor, huh?" Gabe squinted down at the holes, waiting to pounce. "No shit?"

"Barely," I told him. Whack, whack. Konk the cobras. "Junior editor in the trenches. Mostly on funeral duty."

"What does that mean?"

"People want to be there for funerals so they look like good people, but they don't really want to remember how shitty it was. So customers put in requests like, 'edit my memories of this funeral.'"

"And then what do you do?"

I shrugged. I was still clunking through the early versions of Boring Sunday Evening then.

"Funerals are easy. No subtlety there, most of the times. Just these big volcanos of emotions and the code looks like it's screaming at you. We delete the memory altogether, or squash the big emotional peaks." I whacked another snake, beating Gabe because he stopped to look at me. "Like, we lighten up the terror.

Or the sadness that you'll never make things right with your mom because she didn't get noded."

Gabe's eyes lanced me, just a little, like I was one of the snakes. "So, you poke through people's memories?"

"It's not like I get off on it. I feel like I'm helping people."

He softened. "Yeah, alright. I can see that."

Time was up on the game. We dropped our mallets, grabbed the few tickets that popped out from the machine, and drifted through the crowd. He was quiet, working over something while his eyes turned to the twinkling lights of the rides. Probably wondering if meeting me here was a mistake. I bought us a couple of slices of pizza from a food truck to give myself something to do with my hands.

"I mean, you're noded, right?" I bobbed my chin to Gabe's ear. "This can't be anything weird to you."

"No, not weird. Just…" He trailed. He poked the crust of pizza on his paper plate. A stray bit of cricket pepperoni clung to the crust, which he picked off and popped into his mouth. "I mean, I eat pepperoni. I've just never met someone who makes it, you know?"

A spot of red pizza sauce stuck to the corner of his lips. I reached a sneaky hand to brush it away, because what the hell. He let me, one corner of his lips scooping up into a smile.

"What's it like?" he asked.

"Pepperoni?"

"Oh, fuck off." He laughed, tossing his head back and flashing me his throat. "Editing, douche."

I shrugged. "I try to code for others what I would want."

"Like, a never-ending blowjob?"

I almost snorted pepperoni. Gabe's laugh sounded like a cross between a bark and a cough, and he jabbed my side with an elbow.

"I mean, like, real life. But…" My voice trailed off, eyebrows wiggling. A little chalkboard stuck to the side of the food truck offered double-fried pizza-dough balls topped with powdered sugar, called the euphoria special. "Better."

"I dunno. Call me greedy 'n' give me the real top-shelf shit. Constant bliss, ya know?"

"Nah. That seems boring. You need to trip over garbage every once in a while to really appreciate how good things are." I chomped at the pizza. "If they are."

"No garbage for me, thanks. Twenty-four-seven birthday cakes and blowjobs. Can you make that happen?"

"I'll put in a good word."

In the quiet, I ordered us up some euphoria specials. The sugar lit up my tongue. I watched Gabe in the quiet, the way his eyes swept over everyone who walked by, which made his lingering eyes on me even more of a rush.

"Can I ask you something?" His smile melted away.

"Shoot." Meanwhile, my head was a satellite beaming out a message, begging him to ask, *wanna head home with me?*

"If Aset's code is us," he said, shaping the slow words with his sugar-smeared mouth. "What does the code look like?"

"Now you want to know how the pepperoni gets made?"

"You're fuckin' killing me with the pepperoni. I'm actually asking."

"Little symbols. Looks like lines of garbage if you don't know what to look for. Really boring."

"That's it?"

I scooted closer to hear him, our arms brushing. I had to hold my breath, careful. Because in my first intro coding class I'd asked the teacher something similar. Sure, I'd read all about Aset's philosophies. And with all of Khadija's talk about the human spirit and the beauty of destiny and all that, what juju powered the code to make it *us*? Wasn't there something more?

The teacher had coughed a little, soft-shoeing at the front of the class to avoid my eyes. "This is data, not magic," she'd said. "There is nothing else."

Lesson learned. Soul stuff wasn't something you talked about unless you wanted to embarrass yourself.

"That's plenty," I told him.

Then we hit the Whirl-o-Wind, reaching for each other's hands while we laugh-screamed into the night. Whipping around the circle again and again as the lights of the carnival and the city blocked out the stars. Only the near-full moon like an egg, waiting for giant hands to crack it all over us.

I had to bribe the eight other guys in my hostel room to give me and Gabe an hour alone after we trailed from the carnival and back to my place. Worth it. His lips tasted like powdered sugar in the blue dark, us hunched over each other on my bunk bed. I shivered when he tugged the sweat-slick T-shirt off me. When he squeezed me, I felt him say, *it's okay.* I'd done this before, yeah, but all I could think was that I was drowning with him. Into him. Both of us gulping for air between kisses.

"You might have to show me how to do this the right way," I said, trying hard to make my voice not shake. "Because... because a lot of the things I've seen in the editing queue are things I know you don't do to someone you like."

"I got you," he said. "I'm not losing you again."

When did he lose me? I was his, from that first second on the dance floor. *Couldn't you just die?*

Waves rolled in all around us, my lungs on fire. But what a

way to go—Whirl-o-Wind tossed, as I bucked into him. As he told me, flashing his teeth, *harder*. And then I was shivering his name and trying not to slam my head on the upper bunk, while he cranked his cock and begged, *don't stop, don't*. Blinding carnival lights, carried up and up, until everything was just powdered-sugar clouds in my eyes. And Gabe was laughing below me.

I watched his pulse slow at the soft skin of his ankle—still tossed over my shoulder—and I kissed it before settling down on the narrow bed next to him. I traced the wings and the lines of Spanish tattooed down his arms, asking what they meant, while he nipped the fingertips of my other hand. The cloaked skeleton on his upper right arm. *That one? And that one?* His crooked front teeth poked through his smile, his eyebrows were all smudged with sweat.

I pointed to *Julio* over his heart. "And that one?"

"That one." He swooped in for another kiss. "Is for next time."

One of the guys knocked on the door and called out *uh, hello*. Gabe hopped out of bed and shimmied into his underwear with a snap on the waistband. He smirked as he watched me watching him. And then the door to the room cracked open, flooding us with bleached yellow, leaving me with bedsheets still warm from him.

I played the night over and over again in my head, like I was coding it on the black screen of the underside of the upper bunk.

The thing about Aset's code is that we're all the same. We grow up thinking, *I'm a unique and wonderful individual. I'm made of stardust and I'm the universe experiencing itself, etc*. Well, not so much. Once you start coding, stardust starts looking a lot like actual dust collected on a windowsill.

Because the way you code a smell is the same for everyone. The same string of symbols trigger olfactory nerves, launching you back into the past, so that when you remember a smell it's like you're actually smelling it again. Here's the bit of code that makes you smell fresh-baked muffins. Blueberry, from your favorite bakery on the corner, with crunchy sugar bits on top. And here's the code that makes you remember that bakery, even if you live in, say, the middle of a rainforest. That bakery has always been there as far back as you can remember.

Love is the same. Chunks of code dance around your memorystream, lighting up your dopamine sensors, and nesting instincts, and those deep-history parts of your brain that tell you, *yeah, I wanna go out and club a mammoth, drag it back to the cave and share it with this person.*

But I should've given him what he was asking for between bites of sugar-dusted fried dough at the carnival.

There's something that makes us unique.

The first thing memory editors learn is that there's a soul. It's right there. You can see it through the lines of code.

A lie, sure, but lies can be so sweet.

—*he's stabilizing. I've got a lock on him. We're outta the woods. Mostly. Arastoo, keep an eye on his vitals. If his blood pressure drops again, we have to pull him out.*

See? I told you. Fox is our guy. He's got this.

Alright, loading back into the Greg Excerpt branch, we—

NINETEEN
MEETING PARAMETERS

Holidays were a special kind of hell in the gray hallways of Greg's office. Not so much at home—his days didn't change much—but the staff almost doubled come October. NIL/E hired a bunch of temps to scrub away family brawls and Christmas overdoses. Most nights he heard crying in the bathrooms or some newbie who couldn't hack it puking in the sink. At least he racked up overtime as he waited outside the men's room picking at his bleach-dried knuckles while someone blubbered in a stall.

A flash flood, then a flash freeze, in early November. Greg dug his truck tires out of the frozen mud, and his hands still ached when he wheeled his cart into the lab to find a single guy at a terminal, lit by the ghost glow of his computer.

"Hi," he said when Greg stepped inside.

Mid-lean to the trash bin, Greg stopped. "Oh. Hi."

"I knew it would be rough, but…" The guy gushed a breath. "Sheesh."

"First day?"

"Yeah."

"I guess it'll get easier."

"You been here long?" The guy was around Greg's age, from

what he could tell in the dark, with thick eyebrows and a soft voice.

"Couple of years, now."

"Years? That gives me some hope. I'm Hector. It's nice to meet you."

The flutter at the end of Hector's name was Greg's heart skipping a beat. He'd tried to speak Spanish with Zeke, who'd tried to teach him to roll his Rs. He didn't roll them so much as fumble them.

"Greg." A beat of weighted air, and then, "What're you..." He cleared his throat. "Working on?"

"Divorce mediation. Real nasty one. You?"

Greg waggled the trash. "You know. A novel."

Hector's laugh lit Greg up, the feeling staying with him long after an awkward goodbye and into another night of whiskey and holos. He saw Hector the next night. And the next, when Greg worked up the balls to smile and talk some more. Come week two of their run-ins, his pulse jackhammered at his neck thinking that maybe Hector stuck around just to talk. Hector was from Old Newmexico and the company had put him up with the other temps in a trailer park nearby. Greg talked about himself—not much to say but *this is my job, I have a cat at home, blah*—so he listened. He shut his husband's name against his dry, chapped lips because he couldn't go there. Not yet.

Week three, Greg found Hector eating an Italian sub for dinner and he offered Greg the other half. Greg sat next to him, trying not to drip vinegar on his dirty jeans as he cracked a joke he'd practiced that morning in the bathroom mirror. And he hoped. *Ugh*, the cat's-nails of the feeling scraped against him. Zeke had little white scars on his forearms from cats that had clawed him. *Is this... is this a thing?* He wanted to ask Hector, because he hadn't flirted with someone in almost forty years, only it sounded stupid to say out loud.

Their sandwich dinner turned into lunches in the cafeteria, when Hector introduced Greg to his coworkers, who said *nice to meet you* even though he'd seen their faces for years. At night, tears dripped over his lips, between whiskey swigs, as he asked a woman scrubbing dishes in a commercial, "Is this okay?"

He got better about putting on deodorant and clipping his fingernails. He could almost see Zeke behind him in the bathroom mirror, teasing. *Look at Greggy getting gussied up.* One day, around New Year's, a thunderflood blasted rain against the office. Greg never carried an umbrella, and Hector wouldn't let him get drenched on the way to his truck. Shoulders brushing and breath mingling in the bubble of silence carved out by the umbrella, the two of them plodded through the puddled parking lot. *This is how it starts.* Greg's turn to white knight once he spotted Hector's little electric rental, which would probably get washed off the road. He hauled himself into his truck and followed the hard-candy rear lights of Hector's car through the gushing streets to the trailer park. *This is a thing. This is a thing.* The chugga-chugga of a train in his head. *Don't fuck this up.*

Hector kissed him on the rickety front stoop of his trailer. Just a peck, a whisper on the corner of Greg's mouth. Neither of their lips were soft, after too many years around the sun, but the kiss was gentle enough to spin Greg, dopey and reeling, back to his truck. Enough for him to pull over on the side of the road after the rain ricocheted into hail, and he lost his shit in the car—bawling and laughing on some knife-edge of grief and joy and *Jesus, Zeke, I didn't want this but I guess I have to try.*

The next day at work, they stumbled over each other's sentences, their jittery laughs bouncing against the glass door of the lab.

"I'll cook you dinner," Hector said, "to say thanks."

Greg loved that Hector didn't ask. He *told*. The train, again: *This is a thing. This is a thing.* He swept the house and washed his sheets and chucked his comforter into the dryer to suck up the cat hair. He trimmed his hair to hide the white, the pieces of him all falling in the bathroom sink. When they talked, Hector was always flattening his hair onto his forehead because he hated his thinning hairline. Greg hadn't been called handsome in years, not when the most action he'd gotten was Pixie's sandpaper tongue across his knuckles.

The sight of Hector shuffling around his kitchen dissolved Greg into sparks. The árbol chilies in the pozole Hector whipped up—it tasted enough like Zeke's that with the first bite, Greg had to close his eyes and let the ghost just wash over him—kicked his ass in the best possible way. They dabbed their foreheads with paper towels and moved to the couch when they finished eating, sitting close enough that Greg had to cram his hands under his thighs to keep from cradling the sides of Hector's face.

Pixie was nowhere around. Hector was the one to finally lean in for a kiss—gentle again, at first—and Greg held back the thunderflood in his head. *Wait, wait.* Hector's hand moved to Greg's shoulder, pulling something close to a whimper from his throat. And god-fucking-damn-it, the train in Greg's head rolled into the station and he had to pull away and scrub one bleach-blasted hand over his face. Hiding his eyes so he wouldn't crumble.

"I used to be married," Greg said through a clog of phlegm.

Hector's eyebrows scrunched up as he listened, holding Greg's hand and asking all the right questions. He was the first to cry, without a sound, as Greg stared out the window.

"We don't have to rush," Hector whispered when Greg finished his story. Oh, god. Already—*already*—his voice sounded like home.

They held each other on Greg's bed with its sheets that smelled of lavender fabric softener. They didn't have sex, not yet, not until the wet season withered into a scorched February. Hector's fingers flitted over the buttons of Greg's gingham shirt, his lips trailing kisses down the bare skin. Greg's clumsy hands tugged off Hector's polo and swept over the landscape of his body—the silver hair over his chest, his slim hips, the narrow valley where his upper thigh met his body. Two silhouettes in the silver holo light.

Couldn't you just fucking die.

They skipped Valentine's Day. Hector said he had to work—sounded right since editors always slogged through a backlog of misery that time of year—but Greg figured it was really because Hector didn't want to push. And Greg loved him for it. He tried the word *love* out when he was alone, in the fog of a morning shower, or when he had to lean into the bathroom wall at work against the floor-sways after he saw that Hector had snuck a tube of heavy-duty hand cream into his cleaning cart.

February boiled away to March, when tornadoes seared over the cracked plains. Greg cleared a drawer—one of his, not Zeke's—for Hector in the water-ringed dresser by the bed.

"My contract's almost up," Hector said over dessert of an apple pie that Greg made. He used to bake a lot of pies, before. "I can put in a request to renew it and stay. Should I stay?"

Bird wings flapped over Greg's chest. *Yes, yes.* Syrupy apples coated his tongue.

"You should stay."

Hector left for a week in April to visit his mom in Old Newmexico, and Greg missed him so much that cinderblocks were strapped to his feet. But he had Pixie's sandpaper kisses, and he caught up a bit with a half-finished bottle of whiskey—Hector wasn't around to see him wincing through a hangover—and it was a little fun to miss someone he knew was coming back. More fun to fog up the windows of his truck at the airport parking lot with Hector, until a security officer knocked against the glass with her flashlight, interrupting their prom-night necking with a smirk and *let's move it along, boys.*

The rest of April into May, and more pozole and pies, Greg scooted away from the couch one evening when Hector was sorta halfway moved in, and circled back to find Pixie napping in his lap. The train tracks rumbled beneath Greg and he sucked in a breath, palms up to the ceiling. *Okay. Here we are.* He slipped a house key into Hector's khakis the next morning.

Hector wasn't at work one Thursday when Greg wheeled by with his cart to wave good morning. He frowned. Seven months in—though he had to stop and think because time stretched out when they were around each other, which was almost always—he still measured his days around when he'd see Hector. Greg called after work and got Hector's voicemail. He wasn't a big texter, but Greg typed and retyped joke after cringey joke before settling on *hi, handsome. How was your day?*

The waiting was the worst, when he tried to distract his hands with the dishes. When he circled the creaky floors of the house, sucking in air to quiet his chugga-chugga heart. Hector was probably home asleep with a cold. Hadn't he coughed yesterday? Friday after work when Hector still didn't show, Greg swung by his trailer and knocked on the door. No answer. He peeked through a crack in the blinds—no bodies on the floor, no overturned furniture. Hector's rental car was gone. Lava seared over Greg's face. He left before he caved to the screaming in his head and kicked down the trailer door.

He circled the streets, looking for Hector's car. *Don't do this to me again. Not again.* Smarter voices tried to scream over his brain tornado. Hector's mom was getting up there. Maybe he had to see her in a hurry. Maybe he was pulling away because the stink of Greg's landfill of need had finally suffocated him. Greg called work to ask if Hector had taken time off and he could hear the eye-rolling from the woman at reception, all, *sir, I can't give away that information.*

At home he pressed his face into Pixie's belly on the couch. Her purrs rattled through the panic room behind his ribs. Saturday, he called Hector two more times and left laughing, nervous voicemails. *Hey! I'm fixing up dinner. Let me know if you can come over.* He drank until he couldn't see the numbers on his phone, which was good—it saved him from making an ass of himself by calling again. The hours were a liquid, black hallway that he stumbled through.

Sunday morning, his mind spun movies: Hector on the side of the road, keeled over in his car after a heart attack. Hector lying on the bloody shower floor with his head cracked open. Hector mangled in the smoking wreckage of a plane in the desert between here and Old Newmexico.

That afternoon, through the kitchen window, he saw the woman walking up his front steps, a blur of long blue coat against the cloudless sky. Someone there, right? Not just a trick of the light?

And oh god, he was back to that morning again. He couldn't open the door, couldn't face her. His knees turned to mist and he had to lean against the doorframe, because here it came. Here it came all over again.

———

The woman on Greg's doorstep wasn't a cop. She said her name was Fatima—her voice as soft as the gurgle of the sink as he filled the glass of water that she asked for—and that she was from client outreach at NIL/E. She took off her blue coat and sat at his kitchen counter with her too-young, unlined face, and her lips that barely moved with her choppy sentences. She kept looking down at her tablet on the counter, like she was reading from a script on the screen and *Jesus, what, did they send an intern here?*

Heat rolled into him, like bleach running through his veins, as she talked. Bits about *an example of expanded company services* and *new product lines based on client needs to offer deep, emotional connections.* Past the window behind her, the hammock in the back yard swayed in the breeze.

"I don't understand," he burbled. "Is Hector... fine?"

"I don't know how to answer that. Hector is—he's... We understand you recently lost your husband and that he did not have a memory backup plan. Our editors took the liberty of drafting this Zeke-adjacent rendering to... to..."

In the silence, an invisible hand funneled a whole bottle of whiskey down his throat, burning his guts. He hobbled to the sink in case he puked, standing where Zeke did a lifetime ago with his suspicious eyes and his *yeah, but it's not you.* Here it came, here it—he swallowed acid.

"No. *No.* You're telling me Hector's not real?"

"Would you like me to explain our company policy on relative reality to you?"

"Was he faking every—"

"I promise, he felt everything." Fatima's urgent voice floated over the empty kitchen counter. "*Feels* everything. I promise."

More whiskey-sways, fingertips to the counter to steady him.

"And his mom. Was his visit there real?"

She scrolled down her tablet. "There is a woman in Old Newmexico who believes she's his mother, yes. They wanted you to…" Her voice trickled to a whisper. "Miss him."

"I think I'm gonna. I think I'm gonna…"

Plastic containers of Hector's latest batch of pozole still sat in the fridge. All Greg wanted was to hear Hector's key jangling in the front lock. Then, he'd pop into the kitchen, calling out *kidding! Kidding!*

"We can discuss your options," Fatima said. "I think that'll help."

"And if I… if I don't *want* options?" The backs of Greg's hands were cracked even though he'd been so good lately about slathering on that cream from Hector. And how could he forget about the goddamned hand cream when Hector was so sweet to think of it?

"There's no charge for this trial period."

"*Jesus.*"

In the other room, Pixie chased something across the floor, back and forth over the worn boards.

"I took the liberty of asking one of the editors to mock up some storylines for you," she said with searching eyes Greg couldn't look at. "It's a really nice reunion, actually, and you can just pick right up where you left off. With your new memorystream *immediately* uploaded to your current body, absolutely no downtime."

She stopped and asked for more water and when Greg turned back from the sink with a glass in his shaking hand, her makeup was smudged under her right eye. Her kindness made everything worse—so, *so* much worse—when neither of them wanted to be here and Greg had to lower his forehead to the gray iceberg of the countertop to just breathe. Breathe.

"Hector—he had to rush to his mom's side because she got sick and he was so caught up with everything that he forgot to call. But he wants to move in because nearly losing his mom made him feel… And he feels really *awful* about making you worry—you see—because. Because."

He didn't scream—*monsters, all of you are monsters, shredding memories and fucking over the griefbags like us*—as much as he wanted to. He lifted his head from the cool counter, shaking and tired. Zeke would want him to be kind.

"Please. Please just go."

She left her card. Told him to call her after he'd thought about things. *Take all the time you need.*

Hours scraped by, measured by the dirty sunlight across the scratched wood floor. There was no Zeke to tell him what was real and what wasn't. No Hector. Just this graveyard of a house with the holo-display TV ads and the worn stairs and the tumblers of whiskey that dragged him into a static-brained morning. To do it again. And again.

Whiskey burns. Frozen meals. The boulder that he'd swallowed when Fatima had walked in weighed him down as he creaked over the floorboards to his bedroom, where he white-flagged to his bed. He rolled over onto his back. Soon, Pixie bounced up and settled on his chest, her face to him, her single eye closed to a slit as her purrs rolled down to his toes.

He shut his eyes and waited to forget.

TWENTY
GUARDING AGAINST
THE LOSS OF THE HEART

Greg poured all the money he was saving for a new body into the best editing package he could afford. Long-Term Love Life Pack. Editors would sweep through his memorystream and futz with the timeline, make it so Zeke died ten years back—he could hang on to the happy memories that way—and he met Hector a couple of years after. Hector, who helped Greg love again when he'd been basically ready to walk into traffic. The Editorial staff would even replace all the pictures of Zeke in the house with Hector.

"It's alright to move on," Fatima told him at her desk in the cubicle farm at work, where a single picture of her hugging a smiling woman was tacked to the corkboard. A black cat sat in her lap in the picture. She spoke slowly and let him cry when he needed to.

"Sure," Greg said, unconvinced.

He pushed down his anger—she didn't know him, or Zeke, or what was alright or not—because it wasn't really for her. Besides, it helped to think that all this was just waiting. Waiting to be happy again, like standing in front of the microwave while one of his Mentrées spun around. *Ding*.

The price wasn't so bad. Installments, split up over decades. Investment of your life and *blahblah*. Plus, the employee discount. Sign here. *Sure, sure.* When can we get Hector back home?

"Didn't you use to put more árbol in the pozole?"

Maybe he was just looking for an excuse as to why he was feeling off lately. Hector's pozole had been the same for years.

"I cut back," Hector said through a mouthful at the kitchen table. "Last time you had heartburn afterwards."

"How about you let me worry about my heartburn?" Greg frowned into his bowl, immediately regretting the words. "Sorry. Just the holiday stress at work."

"I'll get the hot sauce."

Had Hector always been so quiet? He used to bite back, right? *How about you worry about your heartburn and your dinner, too, asshole.*

They sang in the truck on the way to work, even the stupid Coral Beef commercial. *There's a place under the sea where the cows and fishies play for you and me.* They drove past Hector's old trailer park and talked about *remember that rainstorm?* Hector made him laugh. They headed to the Coli-See-Um in town for movie nights every other Tuesday, where they held hands in the dark, dwarfed by the giant screen. Greg couldn't ask for much more.

Hector smelled different, Greg was sure of it. What, though? Was he showering at work? Sometimes he went for a run on one of the treadmills in the office gym before lunch. Maybe that was it. New shampoo, new lotion?

His voice was all wrong. Too much of a smile. And did he always look at Greg so much? And the pozole. The goddamn pozole wasn't the same. He knew it, now. The whiskey warped his dreams until one night he woke up screaming next to a stranger with wild, scared eyes. And *who the fuck are you? Where's my husband?*

For some reason, the doctor that Hector made Greg an appointment with had an office at work. Greg wheeled into the cubicle farm on his lunch break. A woman named Fatima popped up out of her seat—a blue flower out of the snow—and introduced herself, then showed him a video of him at her desk, six months ago, discussing editing plans and signing waivers. She could answer his questions.

Flash.

"Backsliding is not uncommon," the editor told him, later that day. "We can increase your contentment levels. Delete your memories of this incident."

Hector had cut printouts of his mom's face and stuck them onto pictures of different bodies taped to the walls of her house in Old Newmexico. Olympic gymnasts. Medieval knights. Arch-backed, glistening bikini babes on Brazilian sands. Above the doorway to her kitchen hung a grim reaper piñata with a frayed silver paper sickle. Enough food to last a winter siege—mini sausages with pastry dough burial shrouds, deviled eggs dyed to look like blood cells—scattered across tables, picked at by Hector's family in the black-streamered living room. His mom giggled with her sisters over glass after glass of sangria. She didn't look sick. Hector had organized her Deathday Party and had invited everyone she knew. Greg had helped him cook and clean for days, with Hector scrubbing the sink so hard the countertop shook. *Hey, bub*, Greg told him, fingers on his back, *take it easy*. They were celebrating. His mom wasn't going to waste away to cancer or chemo. She'd reboot into a new healthy body that they'd sprung for, and Hector never had to say goodbye.

"I know…" Hector trailed. "I know this is better for her. I'm just nervous."

Greg kissed the back of Hector's hand. That way he didn't have to look him in the eyes. That way he didn't accidentally blab, when he was already always wobbling on the tightrope between them, *when did things get weird with us?*

"Mijo!" Hector's mom swatted Greg's butt as he passed and stuck out her empty glass of sangria. A kiss on both of his cheeks when he brought her a refill. He was already family.

Hector was supposed to have white cat-scratch scars on his forearms, Greg was sure of it. In the flickering light from the movie at the Coli-See-Um, he started to ask, *hey, Zekie*, when Hector's face fell.

Migraines. Confusion. For some reason, the doctor that Hector made Greg an appointment with had an office at work. A nice woman named Fatima showed Greg videos of him in her cubicle, signing waivers that he didn't remember signing. In a corner office that overlooked the cracked gray parking lot, an editor told Greg that this was his fourth backsliding event. He recommended antipsychotics.

"Repeated memory excisions to address these events aren't great for your brain," the guy said.

"Can't you delete the memories of Zeke if they keep getting in the way?"

Already, the thought of that was a bright stab, deep in his guts. But he couldn't live like this. Like he could hear Zeke's voice at the dinner table while Hector eyed Greg's second glass of whiskey. *Zeke-adjacent rendering? What are these hacks thinking?*

"He's in you too deep," the editor said, which is something that Greg maybe remembered someone else telling him, in an office that was way nicer than this, with cucumber water and potted plants, a long time ago. Or a long time from then? Time got all bleachy-fumed. Probably the antipsychotics.

What to do when the fox mauls the chickens? Greg pulled the shotgun from the hallway closet and waited in the kitchen. Waited for the stranger who looked almost like his husband to come back from a Saturday morning jog. The shotgun was heavy in his hands. Bloody feathers clouded his eyes. *Couldn't you just die*, he'd shouted at Zeke, a million years ago, laughing over the dance floor. *Yes, and take me with you.*

The stranger walked into the kitchen, a cloud of sweat and muggy fall air, and froze when he saw the gun. Greg blasted out one of the kitchen windows. The noise was the chugga-chugga of a train that knocked him back into his head.

Hector's eyes. Oh, Jesus. *This is a thing, this is a thing.* Hector, who Pixie slept on at night. How could Greg forget he wasn't the only one in this house? How could he forget about his Hector?

———

Zeke wasn't who he's supposed to be, Greg tried to explain to the editor, who kept looking back to the nice woman named Fatima—with her too-big eyes when Greg popped up at her desk—then out the window to the parking lot.

"Hector," the editor said. "You're married to Hector."

The name almost sounded right. Rs rolling like his fluttery heartbeat when they met, and something about kissing in a thunderflood? Sheets of rain blasted against the inside of his head.

"What if we get you looking under the hood?" Fatima offered. "What if you could edit Hector yourself? No one knows Zeke better than you. You could make Hector closer to Zeke. Easy."

That didn't sound easy. The editor *hmm*ed, like *great idea!* Greg laughed, anyhow, because the pills were making his head all wonky lately, and the signals in his brain got crossed. He laughed at all the wrong spots at the movies with Hector. At night, the whiskey tasted like powdered lemonade. Pixie didn't come to him much anymore.

Work told Greg one day out of the blue that they'd pay for him to take some editing night classes. Self-enrichment and all that. *Hey, neato*, Hector said. He was visiting his mom a lot more lately, though he and Greg talked on the phone every night he was away, before bed. Greg usually said, *tell your mom mijo says hi*.

He stayed after work three nights a week with other trainees in one of the gray basement editing labs. He was the oldest one there by three decades, even older than the teacher. Jamie cracked jokes while running their hands through their choppy bleached hair and showing the students how to use their Reeders. They kept telling Greg to call them Jamie and not Mx. Jamie, but that was how nice people talked to their teachers, and Greg was a nice person.

He poked at the buttons with his clunky sausage fingers. Before they even learned to code, they had to watch a ton of tutorials. His starfish-looking guide twirled across his Reeder screen, waving her pointy arms. "So you want to be an editor!" she chirped. "You came to the right place!"

Nina the Neuron was the hot pink of scraped knees, with giant-lashed cartoon eyes and a high voice that sounded like she'd been huffing bleach. These training modules were meant for kids, but they worked just fine for the grown-ups.

"Besides, aren't we all kids at heart!" Mx. Jaime said. "Classic teacher gag. A-plus."

At home alone, Greg watched the tutorials again and again.

"First, it's story time!" Nina giggled, twirling around candy-colored slides. "Let's start with the basics! Memories have *narratives*. Start with a setting and a drive."

The next several slides were slashed with blanks for him to fill in with settings and drives from a word bank, each a possible scenario for a memory.

I am in the SUPERMARKET to FEED MY FAMILY.

I am at the LIBRARY to STUDY MATH.

I am at the BEACH to PONDER THE LIMITLESS POTENTIAL OF HUMANKIND.

Nina shimmied around in dopey bliss at each right answer, cheering him on. "Now you're thinking like an editor!"

"Well, soon you'll be up here teaching *us!*" Mx. Jaime chirped when Greg aced another editing pop quiz. "You sure you've never edited before?"

"Never."

Greg knew they were just being nice. Well, maybe there was some truth to his new editing superpower. The software on his Reeder was little more than a black screen with white text, but it was like he could see colors in the code. Somewhere past it, or deeper in it. Purples and blues and shimmering golds flickered on his Reeder screen when he looked at the copy of Hector's memorystream. Pinks for smells. Blues for sounds. Golds for the way the light hit. Greg could knock around in there and change Hector's memories—more than that, too. His brain chemistry. His feelings. Crank up the orange and Hector's voice would get deeper. Sprinkle on some pink and he'd smell different. Muskier, like dirt out in the garden after the rain.

He'd hidden a picture of Zeke deep in one of his dresser drawers in panic the day before the editors had first swept through his house, scrap-heaping Zeke's stuff, and hanging pictures of Hector and Greg. The memory hit his brain like hail. Because how could he forget their last years together? How could he jam that knife in Zeke's back?

Too late to turn back, though, with the knock at the front door.

Flash. He'd remembered the picture was there, and the memories chugga-chugga'd back. Hector wasn't his. Hector wasn't real. He could turn Hector into Zeke little by little—cranking up the silver, washing over spots here and there in turquoise—and then, once the memorystream was perfect, he could get it plugged into Hector's head.

—seizing. Hold him down. Get the paddles ready. I told you. I told you we should've pulled him out. His brain can't take the trau—

———

POP QUIZ

How do you sneak a shotgun into the office?

a. You wait until Hector is gone—and he's gone so much of the time now, and he doesn't even like to look at you—and then you take the shotgun from the hallway closet and put it in an old duffel bag. You put the bag in your truck.

b. You take the bag from your truck into the office, then into a stall in the bathroom.

c. You wheel your cleaning cart into the bathroom, take the shotgun out of the bag, and stuff it into the cart's trash bag.

d. All of the above.

Fatima wasn't listening. Hard to listen when she was crying so much, Greg guessed. If he thought hard enough, it was like he could crank down the blue in his own head and mute her boo-hooing. *All I want is Zeke and I don't get why you won't just give him to me.* Who knows how many times he'd been in that cube, looking at the picture of Fatima and her wife and their cat. A hundred? How many times had the editor yakked about memory excisions—like Greg was supposed to know what the fuck that meant—and tweaked his pills?

He could see Fatima's face stuck to someone else's body on Hector's mom's living-room walls. *Happy Deathday Party.* The truck in his head backfired with a *blam* that rattled the windows.

He smelled smoke and turned down the pink in his head. He heard a few more truck-rounds over the screams—and not like he was really hurting any of them because *Happiness is a Choice*™ and *tomorrows and tomorrows,* and come tomorrow they could get plugged into new bodies, like they didn't want to barf their brains out over chemo. So, *couldn't you just die?* He rounded the corner toward the editor's office when the security team spotted him, their guns raised. And he dropped the shotgun, palms up, and all he could think was, *thank fucking god.* Hold a spot for me on the dance floor, Zekie. This is our song.

VERSE THREE
WEIGHING OF THE HEART

The code, its proponents, and, indeed, its foundress argue, is irrefutable. This is the code for rain falling on your shoulders. This code portraits a sunrise in a hidden glade with dew beading on palms. Here is the line that sings to this cluster of neurons, triggering feelings of safety.

But where is the spark? Where between each island of code, is some hidden quanta of the soul? Nowhere. What the whole arena of Sahusynics peddles is a lie. A lovely lie, yes. All NIL/E Technologies offers is a work of artifice.

—Januscz Duvall, "Lies in the Dark: Sahusynics and the Void of the Self." *New Epochs*, Volume 21.3

~

MODERATOR: Did you catch that "Lies in the Dark" piece?

BANKS: Oh my god. First of all, what the fuck is up with the unnecessarily gendered "foundress" thing? [AUDIENCE LAUGHS] I checked out right there. What a douche.

MODERATOR: Safe to say you're not looking for—what did he call it—"quanta of the soul?"

BANKS: You know, I started looking deep down on the way over, then realized I was hungry, and rolled into Coral Beef.

[AUDIENCE LAUGHS]

MODERATOR: And what about the reports coming out of LakeLandia about a mass shooting that the media is calling a habitual-editing-related—

BANKS: It's a fucking nightmare. Obviously. Of course it is. And tomorrow we're announcing our latest therapeutic initiatives, and course-corrections, and outreach programming to ensure that these tragedies—we have a responsibility. I have a personal responsibility to make sure that this never happens again.

—Roundtable transcript, "Innovations and Inspirations: Banking on the Future with Khadija Banks of NIL/E Technologies"

TWENTY-ONE
TRANSPOSING

Flo keeps watch over me for a while in my bedroom, bringing me mint tea that I sip between sobs and try to keep down. Rolling in the sheets, sweating and delirious as the room darkens. I'm not sure if my scalding tears are for Gabe or Zeke or Hector. Or Fatima. Greg. Myself. The edges of everything blur. I can smell bleach and gunpowder. Feel the weight of a shotgun, the craggy boulder of grief in my guts. Then Flo rubs my back as I'm puking into a bowl again, whimpering *I'm sorry* over and over.

If Khadija had been watching over me, like Flo said, maybe she could've pulled me out of that memory before I pulled the gun from the closet. I would've gotten the fucking drift.

"I saw Gabe, in th-the in-between, somehow." I wipe barf off my chin with the back of my hand, and Flo has the grace not to look grossed out. "Like I fell out of my—*Greg's* life. His world. And into another." Carnival lights and the smell of fried dough fill me up. "How'd that happen?"

"A memory tremor," Flo soothes. "Or more likely a side-effect of the memory virus you're still purging, something futzing with your sense of time." She rubs another slow circle between my shoulder blades. "You did have us dancing for a moment, there. We've never seen that in an Ankh session before."

And I heard their voices shivering over me somehow, when I was out? "But I'm your guy?"

Another kindergarten-teacher smile warms me more than all the tea I could swallow. "You sure are. I knew you could handle whatever tremor your memories could throw at you. Easy-peasy. Just like you'll cure the virus." She rubs another slow circle on my back. "Though, remind me to have Sig bump up your sedative next time."

Next time. Before the Ibis Protocol, when I stranded myself on the marsh, before Khadija's honeyed talk about copies of memorystreams and paradise, I was ready to leave here.

I felt Gabe in that tremor. I loved him. And I felt like myself for the first time since being here. *Really* myself, instead of watching someone wear my face. Reeled in by Gabe's smile beneath the Whirl-o-Wind lights. My hands pulling off his clothes in the hostel. He made me myself again.

Now? I'll take a million more Excerpts like bullets to the chest if that means finding him.

Another voice in the space between dreams and nightmares and tremors. Zee? Flo? Flo comes in with a mug of mint tea. No, not her voice. A woman's, but someone else.

Babycakes, I know you can hear me. I know it's hard. I'm looking for you, but you gotta keep going. You gotta remember.

———

A shadow at the edge of my bed that night. Seth. He presses a cold compress to my forehead and waits.

The rain on the leaves outside my window sounds like distant applause. The light doesn't hurt my eyes so much. I test my feet and—steady, steady—I sway and stand. Over to the window to shove it open, letting fresh morning air into the room, washing away the sweat. Flo left my Reeder on my desk. I don't feel much like touching it, scared I'll see Greg's knobby fingers on the keys instead.

A knock on the door.

"Come in," I say.

Seth pokes his head through the crack in the open doorway, a little embarrassed to be interrupting, and smiling like my roommate in the hostel, a million years ago, after me and Gabe's first real night together.

"You have questions," he says. "When you're ready, meet me in the music room. Don't worry about mapping or morning group. I canceled it for your Cohort. We can use a day of rest."

He snakes an arm through the gap in the doorway, leaves a plate of breakfast on the dresser, and closes the door. My stomach rumbles at the sight of eggs, toast, and bacon. I can almost hear Gabe laughing in my head. *Real bacon, and you can skip group? Might as well ice an entire floor of an office building every day, babe.*

Word has ripped through the sim like a virus.

Residents brush hallway walls at the sight of me. Therapists won't look me in the eyes. They huddle in corners of the hallways and whisper. Minou's in the back of the dining room, looking out over the lawn and doesn't see me. Stash, though, raises his eyebrows when I pass, on the way to dump his breakfast plate into one of the bus bins. From his smug smile, he hasn't forgiven me for that whole screwing up in Inland Ocean City thing.

He sticks his hands up in surrender, stumbling backwards away from me. "Woah. Just dropping off my plate, man. Easy."

The words build in my gut—*hey, fuck off.* Past Fox winding up for a relationship-ending zinger. But I'm New Fox now, foxing this all up, stuttering like the fork rattling against the dirty plate in my hands.

Stash's honking laugh echoes through the dining room. "I'm just jokin'. Everyone will go back to normal. Give it another day." He leans closer, over the bus trays filled with stray egg bits. "You should see some of the shit in my Extracts. What I've done. Supposedly."

Why's he being almost nice? Unless it's a warning. *Don't mess with me.*

"N-n-no, I'll pass."

His purple-mustache-topped smile fades. "I'm serious," he says, softer, leaning in like we're swapping secrets. "Who's to say you really… did whatever you did? What if the Memory Mapping, the organic memory recovery or whatevs, what if it's bullshit? That's the real kicker. How do we know who to believe?"

The bacon's not sitting so great in my stomach. Stash drifts backwards, grinning and pointing finger-guns at me.

I find Chengmei in the first-floor hallway, staring at a painting of a vegetable garden. Her hair is somehow a wilder gray frizz, her lips open as she barely blinks.

"Good morning," I tell her.

She jumps at my words then shakes her head to clear away the fog. "Morning. Sorry. Lost in thought, there."

I haven't talked to her since we ran from Inland Ocean City, two days back. I can see her on the shore, trying to defend me, soft-voiced. *The nodecast signal did something to me. Like it pulled me someplace, and...*

"I remember something," she says. The smile on her face already fades. "I have a daughter. Or had? Or..."

"I honor your—"

"I saw her in the city, somehow, running past the gates with a balloon tied to her hand. I tried to follow her, until she vanished." She picks at her fingers. "She came through in flashes last night. What do you think that means?"

I dig around in my mental backpack of encouraging-yet-empty phrases I've picked up from Seth and the other therapists, trying to make my eyes kind. *Your mind is healing? Open your heart and let the past in?* None of them feel right. Her squinting eyes are just another reminder that we've all lost someone. I'm not the only one seeing ghosts.

I squeeze her hands. "I hope you find her."

She makes a small noise, nods, and turns back to the painting.

The music room is a long, carpeted space on the other side of the house, with three walls of windows looking over the marshlands, and an upright piano facing rows of chairs. A lone therapist is here on cleaning duty, only he keeps slamming his vacuum into the wall, again and again. *Bang, bang*, over the pattering of rain on the skylight. His downcast eyes are somewhere else. Until his head jerks up, he stabs at the vacuum to turn it off, and drifts out the side door. I watch his banana-yellow scrubs get pelted with rain as he walks along the side driveway.

Flo said all the therapists here except Seth are Caregiver templates. I don't know how I didn't notice the seams of the sim before. How instead of lines pulled from the same training handbook—trust your emotions, bend like a reed, blah—maybe they're pulling from the same source code of canned responses.

"Shall we walk?" Seth says from the doorway.

The rain stops like someone turned off the shower tap, and all I can hear is the creaking floor beneath his feet. Seth offers his big-bro smile, only now I know he's actually admin daddy, with probably even the weather in the sim responding to him.

"Fine."

Seth leads the way out to a flagstone path that cuts through the old bowling green to the long dried-up fountain. My slippers are already damp from the grass. I bury my hands deep in my sweatshirt front pocket, squinting up into the wet trees. The questions in my head are another hailstorm battering Greg's truck.

"How could memories from this Greg guy come budding out of my head? Unless I was Greg? An-and Gabe was Zeke? Or Hector? And why were we so *old*?"

Seth offers an easy shrug. "Let's start with the physical before the mental. You were probably in a recycled vessel. When some NIL/E customers upgrade to younger models, their... unaesthetic former vessels are discounted and sold to cost-conscious customers in one of the less affluent megalopolises."

"That's the most company-y way you can say I was a grumpy old man in a bargain body in the boonies. And what's with *probably*? Isn't there a customer file on me, or some shit, that lists all my past editing purchases?"

"Well, yes and no. Client audit trails track editing services purchased from NIL/E, yes. Not edits from unregistered vendors, or self-administered edits, or…"

"And I was an editor. So I could've just booted up my own memorystream after a solo whiskey-chugging contest and started swinging the hammer around. And no one would've known if I popped those edited memories right in my head."

"Precisely. But we do have a record, yes, of you purchasing a Standard Memory Template 36. Model Greg™."

"I bought a shitty canned-memory package to try to get over Gabe after we split?"

"Seems the most likely. I don't have the specifics. Your audit trail is bare-bones or otherwise redacted. Common for editors of your rank."

I frown. The sky is stacked with bowling balls of clouds waiting to drop on my head. "And Standard Template Whatever comes with *what*, exactly?"

"Greg™ is little more than a dropdown menu of life circumstances and backstory. Loner, modest life and home in a middling megalopolis, NIL/E job that covers the bills and much of the cost of the template itself."

"Gabe wasn't a vet. And I wasn't a janitor. An-and Zeke died when he and Greg still loved each other, and…"

"I'm sure you opted for some customization to this specific template, which was the closest homogenized match to your life based on our canned-memory offerings. Which I believe you had a hand in creating."

I turn this over in my aching head, the thoughts clear as the clouds above us. Flo told me that Seth is real—the only therapist who logs in and out of this sim. Honestly, knowing that he's a human helps. He's not grilling me about what I know about Khadija, or opening with a subtle *what were you up to the other night?* No warning alarms whoop from the parcel checkpoint gates of IOC. I'm safe, here, away from all that. Trapped, but safe, as long as I don't give Seth a reason to delete me. It's like we're in the canoe again and he's giving me the space to row over what's below the water.

"Transposing," Seth tells my searching eyes. "The *song* of you and Gabe was there, just with the tones moved around."

"Please, no more therapizing. I need... I need—"

"Perhaps if we flip circumstances, it'll be easier for you to understand." He presses his lips into a line. "Say you're the Life-Storyboard Consultant, now. A distressed client comes in. He's just had his heart broken. His husband left. Living in his house, his city brings up all these torturous memories of happy times. He doesn't have much money for upper-tier edits. What do you suggest?"

My feet thud down the stone steps of the fountain terrace, past three dried-up basins that lead from the fountain to the marsh shore. I feel like one of those basins. Cracked, and moss-spotted, and clogged with old leaves.

"We string together an approximation husband skimmed from the client's memories, nest that approximation in a canned memory template backstory, and sunset the husband narrative with an unexpected death." My insides bob. "The client as a widower is... cleaner. Divorce reaches back and craps over everything. This way he can hang on to the happy memories, at least." The words taste like sawdust. "Then we get him far away—middle of nowhere where he knows no one, as anonymous as possible. New job. New name. No chance that anything will jog his memory."

Seth offers a small nod. "Did I tell you I was an editor, once? Long time ago. In your case, I would've suggested a similar template to Greg™." He dodges my eyes for an instant—and I swear it's like he can see the imaginary gun in my hands. "Perhaps not exactly..."

"How much of it was real?" I stop his inevitable *relative reality* company line with a palm in the air. "How many of the events I just relived happened on planet Earth and impacted other people, please."

"These templates all transition from canned code to lived, live memory via a specific visual trigger."

My eyes hit the damp grass then move up to the lichen-spotted old stone base of the fountain we circle. "And?"

"In the case of Greg™, it was looking in the mirror in a bathroom at his office, counting gray hairs on his chin."

"And everything beyond that was lived experience. For me."

"Correct. All the lessons learned, and—"

"Lessons." I snort. The smell of gun smoke twists up in my head with the taste of smoked árbol chili. "And Hector. He was an approximation of Zeke. Who was an approximation of Gabe. He was a shadow of a shadow. No wonder I freaked out."

Seth winces. "Given your fresh emotional trauma and propensity for self-edits, we absolutely should not have pre-cleared you for client-outreach sample packs. You should not have been given access to an editing terminal and a chance for your nature as an editor to override your template. Not every NIL/E edit center runs a tight ship, it seems. Or maybe the editors in New Thebes did *too* good a job anonymizing you. That was, as they say, our bad. Still, Hector aside—"

"That's one MonuMomental fucking aside, Seth."

"—what did you feel?"

I can't look at him. I squint into the sky as each step over the grass seems to sink me deeper into the dirt. "I could feel that Greg—*me* and Zeke were really happy together. Like, the biggest thing we bickered about was taking out the trash. I loved the reminder that me and Gabe used to be just like that."

"And is that helping you process losing him, do you think?"

"Zeke had a heart attack. Greg didn't fuck things up with him like I did with Gabe. So, not really."

Was he going to ask about Greg's shotgun, or would I have to bring it up? I can feel the weight in my hand. Flash. Fatima's face. The gunfire-like truck noises. I shiver in the damp air.

"Would you say there's anything you learned from your time in the Excerpt?"

He's going to make me say it. Fine. "Only that I seem to have a big fat pattern. Hurting other people in a big way is fair game when I'm hurt."

"You're referring to the—"

"I think you know what I'm referring to, Seth," I snap, bitter-mouthed from the whiskey flashback. We skim the shoreline, with me definitely not bending like a reed.

"Yes." He waits a while. Above us, birds hoot in the trees. "If it's any consolation, the people you encountered were noded individuals, and—"

"But my *intention* was to go in there and fuck shit up. And blow them away. Aren't you the one always going on about intention and energy?"

"Yes. Certainly worrisome."

"You think? What k-kind of a monster was I—in every single life, in every Excerpt? Why should I bother even remembering?"

"I'm glad you're confronting this. This is important."

I can feel my ribs harden into dried reeds that splinter with my heartbeat. The anger spins my guts like a swallow of bleach. The training videos run through my head—Khadija's warnings about deletion, Flo's advice to keep quiet, Stash saying Seth is the sim admin. I blast all that away, punching train tickets to deletion city.

"Want to talk about confronting? Where the *fuck* are we, Seth? Really? I went canoeing for hours the other day and somehow ended up right back on the shore by the manor where I started."

I know I'm screwing up here, after the alarms, and the chase in Inland Ocean City, after Flo said we'd be more careful. But I can't keep the words in. I have to know what he knows.

"We are in a simulation, yes." The mid-session calm line of his lips doesn't waver. Of course he knows I know. He must know everything here. "We freely offer this fact to residents when they ask. Your memorystream has been uploaded to NIL/E servers and into the Field of Reeds therapy programming. You sustained significant injuries during the attack on New Thebes. Your body is in cold storage while you're here, working on your—"

"I'm working on my mind. I've heard the lines." I can almost hear Fatima's voice telling me to *look over the editing options carefully, take all the time you need.* I've never been careful, anyhow. "Does NIL/E have a copy of Gabe's memorystream somewhere?"

"I know why you're asking."

His even tone hides something. He sees everything here. But if he knew about the Scribes and our field trip, we'd all be deleted already.

"You don't want to put in the work," Seth continues, hitting me with pity-edged eyes. "The work on yourself. You want the easy way out. Poof! Gabe returned to you. Everything's fine. But did you earn it?"

"You call this not doing the work?" I stab a finger at the manor, up the rolling hill. A dozen residents by the brick patio are playing dodgeball, cackling like kids at recess. "I just sat in a coffin and watched myself go crazy. Fucking *kill* people, Seth. Forgive me if I want a breather."

"It's not my job to forgive. And no, NIL/E doesn't store secondary copies of customer memorystreams. The only version of him would've been his standard customer save-file, the one that was damaged by the virus in the attack."

Stash and his finger-guns. *Who to believe?* All the anger leaks out of me and collects like raindrops on the grass. More birds in the trees, hooting at me. Who. *Who are you, Fox?*

"How do I get out of here?"

"You can leave whenever you please. I alert the cold storage staff to rez your vessel. An easy trip to the Neb-Ankh, Sigmund executes the extraction commands, and then you're back in your body in the outside. If that's what you want. If you're satisfied with the state of your memorystream now. Are you satisfied?"

What a dumb question. I hold in the laugh. "No."

I'll stay a while longer. Besides, I still have the virus to try to solve, if helping Khadija launch her secret project is the only way to get Gabe back. I owe him that much. Frogs jump from the shore and splash into the marsh when me and Seth pass. We keep walking.

"Past the confusion, past the anger," Seth says again after a while, "what did you learn?"

"I learned that I couldn't forget about Zeke—or Gabe, or whatever I should call him. Even with the chance to live with someone who should've made me happy, like Hector. I couldn't accept that Gabe was gone."

"He kept breaking through your memories."

Break. I can see that heart-smashing-in-a-million-pieces look in Hector's eyes when I accidentally called him Zekie in the movie theater. "Yeah, literally. Memories of him broke through the walls of the Excerpt and yanked me in."

"We've seen this phenomenon before, albeit rarely. We call this *perforation*—how old memories seem to resurface, even after they've been deleted. How the memorystream seems to reject edits, completely opposite to what Aset's Law of Mnemetic Assimilation states."

"Why?"

"There's much we don't know about this effect. What causes it? What was so strong, so special—of course beyond the wonderful bond between partners—about your connection to Gabe that the editing didn't hold fast?"

"Do you want me to answer that?"

Seth laughs. "It would make my job easier, certainly. I suspect the only way we'll understand is if you keep exploring Memory Excerpts as they arise."

Well, not the only way. My Reeder on my desk, back in my room. I can hear Nina the Neuron's chirpy voice, feel little pinpricks from her arms and legs as she spins up my shoulders and neck, to my ear. *Now you're thinking like an editor.*

TWENTY-TWO
EDITOR'S NOTES

All I have to do to get back to my room and hide is sneak past two dozen of my besties in their gray sweat suits sitting cross-legged on yoga mats on the back lawn, joined by a few therapists. Everyone with their eyes closed while Flo sits facing the group, her back to where I stand by the shore. Flo moves like she's stirring a giant pot, filling the air with shimmering tones from her crystal bowls.

They're probably trying to meditate me and my bad vibrations out of here.

I whisper over the grass. Sun blasts the back of my neck, with the rain dried up and another perfect day in our simulated sunshine-land stretching out. There are maybe ten paces to the patio door when Hákon with the ice-blond hair opens his eyes and spots me, then—*psst*—he turns to Siobhan. And I swear I hear, *yeah, that's him. Fucking creepy.* Minou, at the front by Flo, opens her eyes at all the noise and spots me. I could hightail it to the door in three steps now, but the blab-fest has ruined my cover. All eyes on me. Octavio sucks in a breath, like, *yikes.* Model-scruffy Pierluigi with his sad wolf eyes smiles a little, and maybe pity is worse than gossip. Even Flo looks up, unwavering as she spins crystal tones in the air. I can feel the sound in my eyes, cranking up the angry *eeeee* whine in my head, like my ears are ringing after a gunshot.

And how dare they. How can they fucking look at me with those *back away so his megalomaniac cooties don't rub off on you* eyes. The singing crystals crank up in my head until the words fly out of my mouth.

"Why don't you focus on what *you* all did to land here," I snap. I clamp my mouth shut before adding *you fucking mippers*, so at least there's that. Growth, or something. "I'm trying. Sure, I'm quickly learning I was an asshole—alright, maybe that's simplifying things—and that I hurt more people than I'm proud of." My voice shakes. Anger? Sadness? The colors are all muddy. "But that's not me anymore. And… and…" I'm doing this all wrong. Flo smiles, though. I can feel her telling me, *go on.* "And what about you?"

Slam dunk with this MonuMomental announcement, Foxy, I can almost hear Gabe tease. The others look away, murmuring. Except Minou, with her cat-smile.

"We are memories, and memories are we," she sings out.

I blast through the patio door and slam it behind me.

Minou calls my name. I ignore her, down the main hallway, until she slinks up from behind and grabs my arm. She tugs me into the empty dining room.

"They weren't talking about you." She thumbs outside at the residents. "Well, most of them, anyway. We got some news from the outside."

Classic Past Fox with the paranoia, the *everyone's talking about me,* when really, we're all so obsessed with ourselves.

"And?" I snap.

She looks away, then sighs when her heavy eyes hit mine again. "There was an attack on one of the burb rings in Inland Ocean City. Another memory-virus bomb."

The *eeeee* ear-ringing after a bomb blast knifes through my head. My knees shake. "Is it…" The words leak out of my brain like sand. "Bad?"

"Definitely not good."

"Was it us?" My throat can only scratch out one-syllable words now. "Our fault?"

"I mean…" She trails, her shoulders tightening. "We show up unannounced in a city that's under some kind of memory-parcel lockdown—whatever the hell that means—and this happens."

"I didn't mean to—"

"Of course. Jesus. We didn't… we didn't light the fuse. I heard the company's saying it's the Deathers, again."

"How'd you hear?"

"A new resident got here this morning and said something about it. They heard it on the news. Seth mentioned it to Sig, too, and word spread."

"An-and has Flo heard from Poppy, or the memory runner ring, or-or—"

"Flo doesn't have a line to the outside. All we have is occasional gossip from newbies. And Seth."

So, no. We can't give him any reason to suspect us of working for Khadija, if the noose is tightening around her neck on the outside.

My hand on the door of the storeroom again, before I pull it open, shoving us outside, because I can't leave things alone. *King editor in a loaner bod in IOC East*, Poppy smarmed at us. *Of course. Just when I was having a quiet night.*

"At least we're safe in here," Minou says. "And the best thing we can do is crack the virus, and—shit." She glances over my shoulder. "Incoming. Gotta go."

I look behind me to spot Seth coming in from the greenhouse. And what'd he just tell me? *You can leave whenever you please. An easy trip to the Neb-Ankh, Sigmund executes the extraction commands…*

Tempting to just take him up on his offer.

And in a flash, I'm back at the counseling session with Gabe, screwing up. Again.

See, you're not even trying and this was your idea.

If I keep telling myself that I'm different from angry Past Fox, I have to try. It's the least I can do.

The study off the Ankh Room is a cocoon of worn book spines—crushed, dark petals against the brown-papered walls. I suck in the faded-incense-smelling air, trying to kill the fire in my blood. My room felt too suffocating when I went there to grab my Reeder, shaking out of my body after talking to Minou. I trace my hands over the book spines and pull out one called *My Face is Ra*, flipping past an intro to Aset's philosophies to pages with tips on how to code different types of light. Gold morning rays. Sunset across the water from sherbet skies. Silver shafts of moonbeams through the trees. I can see the light on the backs of my eyelids as I read.

This closet of a room blasts me back to the hallway closet in Greg and Zeke's house. Everything I see and touch reminds me of some other life. Like I'm just living through echoes.

Take what is useful, Seth told me in a private session early on. *Release the rest.*

How useful are the Memory Excerpts? They're a distraction,

really, from solving the virus to get to Gabe. Especially now that I've cocked up our chances of getting to Khadija through our emergency exit, until Poppy or whoever can find us.

I settle into the green armchair and pull up the virus. My fingers fly across the recessed keys of the Reeder, clicking like the nails of the ferret Zeke brought home on the hardwood floor. *He has your nose. Kidding! Kidding!* I force myself to ignore the *calculating...* at the bottom of the screen and the endless lines. Even something that's endless has to have a beginning, right? So, start small. Start at the beginning.

My eyes scrape over the symbols. It starts with two arms raised up like a ref calling a touchdown, which means that the next cluster of symbols are emotional levers. Then, the curvy-beaked bird symbol that triggers interior monologue. Different school-of-fish clusters of wedges paint sketches of settings. A pine tree. Maybe a steel storage container? A kitchen with dirty linoleum floors. But it's hard to shove meaning onto the rest when whoever made this knotted up the code in all the wrong ways. Taste-triggers to describe the air, and then it's like I'm breathing in cherry cough syrup. Sounds are hammered into blocks of shifting hallways.

I scroll through it for what feels like hours until I can see flashes when I blink. A pyramid of solidified sunlight explodes. Flash. Glass windows made of moonbeams shatter. Screams that sound like a rainstorm, and the trolley screeching into IOC East, and then I'm grabbing my head with a growl—knocking my Reeder off my desk so more flashes don't stab my eyes.

The virus is static. Like a million voices screaming at once and they all want to be heard. My hot breath burns the back of my throat. I think of J's cheery pep-talks—*I will be kind to myself, and let the process... process*—to bring me back down. Alright, not perfect, King Editor Fox. But it's a start.

———

The therapist who's serving me dinner—trying to serve, anyway—
looks like he's having a worse day than I am. The long silver serving
spoon in his hand keeps missing the muck pile of tofu and wilted
greens on the platter, somehow. His next jerky swoop-down skims
the top of the green and white goop.

"You okay, man?"

"Sorry," he mumbles. Valleys of wrinkles pop over his forehead
when he stares down at his hand. "Not sure what's…" He trails off
with his next failed scoop attempt, then the therapist bubbliness
bounces back to his voice. "Must've pushed myself too hard this
morning at the gym. Arm day!"

Success. He wallops my plate with dinner slop and I sit at my
usual table, alone. The stuff turns to mud in my mouth, and all
I can think is, if this is a simulation, why make us hungry? Who
made that decision when we don't have physical bodies, and why
not feed us whatever the hell we want instead of rabbit food?

I look down at my plate, pushing the soggy chunks around, and
a shadow crosses the table. Minou drops into the seat next to me.
Her dark hair is pulled back into a tight bun, making her look like
an onion with ears.

"Grass clippings. My favorite." She makes a gagging noise down
at her plate.

I try to smile with dry lips. I can't even make a noise.

"It wasn't us," she says. "Remember that. One thing I've learned
from being here—the *only* thing, maybe—is that you have to move
forward. You can't drown in what-ifs and maybes and should'ves.
You know?"

"Yeah. I get it." I drop my fork on my plate. "If we're in a sim,
why even make us—"

"Hungry?" She spears a tofu chunk. "Don't even bother thinking about it. It'll drive you absolutely bananas. Just another reason we gotta get outta here."

"You have any leads with the virus yet?"

She lifts her fork to her lips to shush me, her eyes darting around the dining room. "Let's take a walk after we eat."

"Alright."

"You know, ears around." She bobs her chin at the therapist in pink scrubs hovering two tables down. "Have the therapists been acting weird to you?"

"Weirder than usual?"

"Yeah, that. Since we got back from the you-know-where."

Maybe her paranoia is rubbing off on me, but it does seem like the therapists are hovering closer than when I first got here. Maybe acting stiff and weird, like banana-scrubs guy earlier today, before I walked with Seth. Though it's tough to say if it's just because now I know they're templates.

Then—I'm somewhere else for a second. Mild memory tremor. I can see a gray-and-steel cafeteria that's different from all the worn wood and fading carpets of the manor, but it feels close enough. Forgotten people crammed in and waiting for something. Me and someone else in the corner of the room in our own bubble, us against the world. *You're my intern. Now go get me some coffee, babycakes.*

"Earth to Fox," Minou says gently. "Flashback?"

"Yeah." I shake my head free, remembering seeing Minou in the Ankh the other day, twitching while Flo watched. And then Sig's voice, maybe, in my ears. *Hold him down. Get the paddles ready.* "Things do seem… off lately. But the Excerpts are fucking with my head."

"This place is fucking with my head."

"A-fuggin'-men." I toast her with my glass of water. "I'll keep a closer eye out. Report things to the you-know-what club."

She laughs through a mouthful of mush. We're quiet for a while. Only the scraping of forks across plates. A faraway tilt in her wide, brown eyes, until she looks down at her plate, and her tired sigh tickles my arms.

"You're not the only one who… *regrets* things that happened," she says. "Things that they did."

I can see that she's having a flashback of her own.

"You don't have to…"

"No, I do. I want to. Radical Remembrance and all. I talked about it in group before you got here. And then *I* was the black sheep. Because everyone else here is a hypocrite."

"I'm sorry," I say. And then I bend like a reed, giving her space.

She grits her teeth and pulls the pin on the grenade she's about to lob.

"My mipping got out of control. Obviously. I mean, messing with your live memory is never going to be *under* control, I guess. It's always… desperate. End-of-the-line stuff." She scrunches her paper napkin. "I could've paid for real edits, but the company started cracking down on too many edits within a short timeframe after a few negative customer experiences. Not great for the noggin. Bliss bumps were my thing, even in the bathroom at work. Drop a hit of code into your memorystream of pure euphoria and, for a few seconds, things don't seem like garbage. That last hit sent me on spin cycle. I was behind the wheel and Adela—she's my wife. *Was.* She was in the car with me. I was so blitzed I thought I was flying a rocket to the moon. Ended up wrapping the car around a tree."

What else do you say but I'm sorry? "I'm sorry. Did she—"

"Hit the brakes! There's more." Her laugh is cracked and

sucked free of joy. "I should say I hit another car first. A car with two parents and their tiny, un-noded baby, and *then* a tree."

The chair beneath me bobs like I'm flailing around in the canoe again. I reach out and squeeze her hand, trying to give her my best Flo. *That's not you anymore.*

"That's awful."

"Yes. The most awful. Those memories came back—not the happy ones with Adela because *of course*—and then I decided I was checking outta here. Took a rowboat out, wrapped the anchor around my waist, and jumped overboard. Screaming lungfuls of water, and I woke up in the Ankh. Then Seth broke out the one-on-one intervention therapy." She threw her napkin.

"Couldn't you have just asked to leave?"

"Yeah, and go back to what? My garbage life that I ruined outside? No thanks."

"I'm—" *I'm sorry* just feels too useless and stupid to say. The single word warbles in the air between us for a while. "Sorry."

"Yeah." She brightens. Flash. "Well, bend like a reed, all that. That's not me anymore, but also it is. Take what's useful, right? I'm telling you this because you can decide who you are. I'm alone here, even with the other Scribes, even with the mission. And I figured you were feeling alone, too, soooo…"

I hold back a shiver, even in the warm, tofu-smelling air. Almost like Minou strapped me into a car with her and drove us into a tree. So *this* is what vulnerability is, huh? Moving tofu around your plate again, hitting me with big watery eyes that beg *say something?* Gabe didn't share. Sometimes I traced the *Julio* tattoo over his heart. I asked him twice what it meant—hoping it didn't sound too much like *who had your heart before me?*—and he only shook his head. *I can't.*

"So we can be alone, together," I tell her. Another hand-squeeze.

"Deal."

On the tablecloth by my plate, a red splotch that looks like a wine stain clouds the white. I scrape at it with one finger. So why the stain on the tablecloth, why the awkward therapy sessions, why force us damaged sad-sacks to try to make each other feel better if this is a sim? Points for immersion, I guess. The wine stain. My god. I stare at it as I force the food down into my queasy stomach, dodging Minou's sad eyes. She's right. Thinking about it too much just drives you bananas.

Minou's dim, lamp-lit room is a mirror-image of mine, only a notebook and laundry basket have exploded everywhere. Scraps of paper and whole pages filled with messy, slanted script are taped in a mosaic over the walls. *Cupcake eats special prescription urinary care food. Adela sleeps on the left.* A pencil drawing of a woman's sleeping face. An unfamiliar city. I don't lean in too close to read the full pages. It seems rude, like I'm poking around in her head.

"Flo said I should try journaling." Minou shrugs, her mouth twisting like she's embarrassed at the pages. "I know it looks insane. Whenever I remember something, I write it down, stick it on the wall, and see if it'll help jog something else loose."

"Is it helping?"

"I'm not sure yet. I'm still in barf-everything-onto-pages mode. Maybe once I have a chance to let the process…"

"Process?"

"Something like that. Sorry about the mess."

"It's cool."

She grabs her Reeder from the desk, shoves a pile of towels and gray sweats off the bed, and plops to the edge. She crosses her legs, zips up her Reeder, and nods for me to sit at her desk. I take her cue and pop open the virus code on my own Reeder.

"First up," she says. "Not even diving deep into the code, what do you feel? See?"

"It's not that I see things so much as I hear them. D-different stories, or voices, talking all at once."

Her Reeder casts a ghostly glow over her face. "That's good. It's different for everyone, somehow. I mean, the *code's* the same, but Stash sees it as a maze. Chengmei sees a treasure map. To me, the virus feels like a booby-trapped haunted house."

"How far have you gotten?"

"I'm still trying to decode the first few lines. It's like the doorknob of the house keeps splitting into a million others once I reach for it."

I try not to let the disappointment hit my eyes. Minou and the others have been working on this for months, according to Flo, and they haven't even opened the front door? Shit. I bite back a wise-ass complaint. Coworkers used to come to me for help until I was a total asshole and they stopped. *Yeah, the light's all wrong in that memory, and you should already know that it's messy to leave sense-triggers dangling like that.* Minou doesn't need a surprise tutorial.

"And the others?" I ask.

"Chengmei noticed a bit of text in the first thirty lines that seems to reference one of Aset's early philosophies, so she's researching that. And Stash? Who knows with him."

We work in silence for a while. I try to focus on the stories and the voices I might hear, but now it's just noise. The cursor on my screen seems to zip me somewhere else. Like I'm in Poppy's maintenance van again, nodecasted over with a fake-pizza-delivery-van skin. We're speeding back to sim purgatory after the dazzling lights of the city, and my stomach is sinking deeper and deeper. Until Minou says something to pull me back into her room, something about a pattern—if you squint enough—on line two. Maybe? And yeah, I tell her, trying to smile. Yeah, I think you're onto something.

I'm a ghost the next day, after me and Minou's coding session that went nowhere. Hiding in my room. Skipping therapy. Ditching the affirmations. Afraid to touch things, in case it triggers feelings of Greg pulling triggers. I watch the greasy light through my window slide over the floor. I half expect Seth to dispatch one of the therapists to kick down my door and lug me over a shoulder, fireman-style, to therapy.

And then I see the feet blocking out the light under my door, the second morning of my hermitude, sometime after I snoozed through the breakfast gong. The knock is gentle but not soft, and I can practically hear Seth's voice volleying a question that's not a question. *Wouldn't you think it's best to attend a session today?*

I'm already loading up the *go away* when my hand hits the doorknob. MonuMoments crumble to sand in my head.

I open the door and Seth's even eyes meet mine. But he's not alone. So bright, so perfect that someone must've pulled him out of the picture frame on the bureau by the door. Behind Seth, and a fluttering Flo by the staircase, his hands plunged in the pockets of his gray sweatpants, is Gabe.

TWENTY-THREE
ADMIN MODE

I can feel my heartbeat thudding in my eyes. Gabe. He looks at me like he has a million times over coffee in the kitchen, or catching each other on the sidewalk outside of our place—half-smile, one eyebrow slightly up. My hand on the doorframe is the only thing keeping me from crumpling to the ground. One shaky breath, then another.

"Gabriel, why don't you and Florence get some air on the patio?" Seth asks.

Pop quiz: What in the absolute fuck is going on?

Gabe bounces two fingers off his forehead in a salute and I die a little more inside.

"Is that…?" I manage to gasp until the words leak out of me.

"Let's sit down? You look unwell."

I stumble backwards until the backs of my knees knock my bed and I plop down. Seth pulls my desk chair out and sits. Surprise therapy session. He hits me with his best patient big-bro smile.

"Please," I beg. "Is that Gabe?"

"Well, yes and no. This version of Gabe is pulled from you. Your memories of him. Your impressions."

"You're saying he's a canned memory." Another twist in my stomach.

"He's a gift. A therapeutic tool. You can control him with admin mode and—"

"*Control* him. Shit."

"—get him to open up to you. Think of this as an enhanced version of journaling. For your emotional healing. We've had great success with these types of constructs before. We call them scrapes, if you'll pardon the slightly rough descriptor."

"So I'll be talking to myself?"

"In your case, Sigmund was able to extract a few lines of Gabe's *actual* memorystream from his corrupted save-file. This is an exciting first for us. You can rest assured that you're truly with a small part of Gabe. A new, innovative treatment for your recovery, which I'm proud to say was my idea."

"And how," I start. Already the words are molten glass shoved in a furnace—a misshapen bubble of scorching heat. "How is this *scrape* different than Hector in Greg's Memory Excerpt? You want me to blow everyone away in this place, too?"

"The key here is that you didn't know Hector was a construct once you chose your editing package. Now you do. You can adjust expectations accordingly."

My gaze falls to my lap where my fingers twist into fists, again and again, with my glass words shattering on the floor.

"How long is he around for?"

"As long as you need."

"I don't know if I… If I need. And what'll he even *do* here?"

"He'll join you in your Cohort. We'll integrate him into the community and treat him like any other resident."

"But the others. They know what really happened. They'll know he's a-a scrape."

"There's no judgment from anyone. We're all on our own journeys toward healing. Including Gabe, now. If you want that."

"This is too much. I can't…"

"Talk to him for a while," Seth says gently. "If you find it's too jarring, we can delete him. It's no trouble."

"No," I snap. "No deleting. I-I'll try. Let me try."

He nods. "I think that's best. It will be strange, at first. But in the long run, better for your recovery."

"My recovery." The words taste bitter. "I bet."

Seth leaves me to have a panic attack in the bathroom. How to dress when you meet a scrape of your dead husband? I rinse my face in cold water and slap my cheeks. I brush my teeth so hard that I spit blood in the sink. I watch the foamy spittle slide toward the drain, slow, bubbles popping. Dead-eyed in the mirror, like I'm the one who's a scrape.

I wait in the sunroom, trying to suck in strength from the ground while I watch Gabe through the window. On the patio, his back to me, the morning light eclipsing his edges like he's cut from the sun. Reeds and bending and all that shit. At his side, Flo flaps one hand around like she's giving him the grand tour. The other hand holds a picnic basket.

I shove the door and they both turn to me. And—*oof*—every time his eyes hit me, it's the same carnival lightshow in my guts, blinky-blinky. *You won the grand prize.*

"There he is," Gabe says, smiling like we're meeting for marriage therapy, and nothing happened.

"He is," I say. Not sure if it's a question.

"You two have so much to catch up on," Flo titters. She rocks on her heels and shoves the picnic basket at me. A little hug. "Oh, hon. You deserve it."

Then she's through the sunroom doors, leaving us alone. A ways off, other residents hover over easels and smear watercolors across canvases.

"Let's walk?" I swing the basket, useless. "We should walk."

"Show the way, tour guide."

It's what he'd say, too. And the voice rings with his tilty sarcasm, like it always does. Always did.

A therapist in black scrubs with an electric weed-whacker pops out of a nearby toolshed, past the circle of chairs on the lawn where I usually have morning group. Some of Minou's paranoia must've seeped into me, but I swear the therapist trails us over the open lawn.

I taste blood as I lead him further away from the main grounds of the manor. The therapist stops at the low rock wall that separates the lawn from the orchard and turns on the weed-whacker. I'm going nuts, picturing these people spying on us. Which, after Poppy speeding the van in the opposite direction from police cars, maybe isn't totally out of the question.

We walk until the weed-whacker's electric whine fades, arriving at an alcove by the marsh shore where we'll be alone. I drop the basket on the ground and open one flap. Flo packed us a red checkerboard blanket, because of course she did. My shaky hands fumble with the blanket until Gabe reaches out to help me. An electric zip when our fingers brush.

He drops to the blanket and stretches out, his slippered feet sweeping reeds. I squat down so slowly that my leg muscles feel like they'll tear. I watch him peek into the half-open basket and pull out a bowl of grapes.

"For fuck's sake," he says. "You're looking at me like I'm a snack. Ease up, Foxy."

"This is just weird."

"Weird for you? I'm dead. How do you think I feel?"

"You're not dead. Can you please n-not say that? I'm bringing you back. I'm… I'm."

"Right. Flo filled me in, and told me not to blab to Seth. You're on a quest or something." He flashes me a big eyebrow-bouncing grin. "You're curing the big bad memory virus, snooping for the mysterious Khadija."

"You're making fun of me. Stop."

"I'll stop if you really want. But you know that this is what I'd say. How I'd act."

"What Gabe would say. How Gabe would act."

His smile doesn't waver. "Should I talk like Gabe? Are you going to treat me like him, or like someone else? Either way is cool. I just want to know, so we're clear."

Oh god. I'm doing this all wrong already. "I-I don't know. Fuck. Talk like him. Please."

"Right-o. And before I forget, if you say 'admin mode' I have to follow your commands. Remember that for when we're in the sack." He winks, flicking up a grape with his thumb and catching it in his mouth. "End tutorial."

"I don't want to do that. I'm never going to do that."

"Yessir."

"And you know this is all a sim?"

"Feels pretty real to me."

Scrape is right. Sitting this close to him scrapes all the skin off my body, leaving me bloody and raw. My hands ache to touch him. God, the carnival lights in my guts burn from the inside out. He smells like Gabe, a little salty with a back hit of earth. The same full lips and crooked nose. The same gold-flecked laughing eyes. All of us look dumpy in these gray sweat suits, except him.

The boxy cut frames his wide shoulders and muscled chest. The line of hair down his belly to his groin is spotlit by the lifted hem of his shirt. It takes everything I have not to lean over and kiss it. Can a scrape even say no if he wants?

"So, are we talking or just eating? Not that I mind eating." He peeks into the picnic basket again. "Oh, hell yeah, charcuterie. You in?"

He lays a plate between us on the blanket, the slivers of meat flesh-pink.

"Seth said you're a therapeutic tool." I clear my throat. "What the fuck does that mean?"

"I've got a therapeutic tool for you right here." He grabs his junk and shakes the handful.

I laugh so hard I almost fall over, brain-fried. That really is just what Gabe would say. *He* would say. I could reach for him, cover his hand with mine and tug. Focus, Foxy.

"I'm serious. Help me—help me understand."

"It means we can talk 'n' I can answer how you think I would, based on our history. How you remember it."

I'm quiet for a while, just letting a pepperoni slice turn slimy on my tongue. *How you remember it*, not *how it actually happened*. There's no objective history of us, it's all smeared with watercolor, mangling mint-green shirts into weapons.

A breeze rustles the reeds. I ache as I watch Gabe gaze at the water, smiling like he's happy enough to stay by the shore forever. I don't want to talk and blow open this moment, but there's still so much about us that I need to remember. Carnival lights. Stiff white bedsheets in my hostel, both of us shivering over each other. His whispered words that I can still hear when I close my eyes.

"The night of our first date you told me, 'I'm not losing you again.'" I rip a blade of grass from the ground so I don't have to meet his eyes. "What did you mean by *again*? We just met."

His crooked nose is silhouetted in the sunlight. He shrugs. "Got me. If you don't know what that means, then I don't."

I shred the blade of grass in two, frowning. "And… and the tattoo." I tap my heart, where he has another man's name branded. "You never told me what that means."

He pulls down the front of his gray sweatshirt and, sure enough, *Julio* loops over his perfect skin, through the dark hair. Someone else that had him before I did. He tips his head like he's half surprised the tattoo is even there himself. "I told ya, I can only answer based on our history as you remember—"

"Rightright." I wait as the water laps the shore. "Could you answer like Gabe would?"

"It's not enough that you've got me now. You want my past, too?" His smile cuts me up—a flash of white teeth poking past his full lips—sweet but hiding the bite of a razor. Just like Gabe when he's pushing me away. "Greedy."

Past Fox would've snapped. *We give each other everything. Is that too much to ask?* I sigh. He's right. "I'm sorry."

"Whew! New Fox apologizes!" Cracker crumbs on the edges of his razor-smile that's not a smile. "I know I'm dead and all, but I didn't think I'd go to heaven."

When I don't laugh, the smile slips from his face. He scoots up toward me.

"Oh, shit." He grabs my hands. "That was asshole-y. I appreciate the apology. Sorry. This is fuckin' bonkers for me, too. I don't totally know how to act. Like, I want to hold you. Touch you. I don't know if that's too much, or…"

I squeeze his hands, dropping my eyes to his knuckles. "Thanks."

"You know, I actually missed you, Foxy." His laugh comes out halfway as a sigh. "Even with what happened."

The words drag my gaze up to his. Make me look. I can hear Darius from a therapy session, a million years ago, echoed again by Fatima. Like every one of my moments is just a canned memory based on another. *Would you like me to explain our company policy on relative reality to you?* Cutting me up. This is all too much.

"I missed you, too."

"You've changed. It'll take some figuring to get back to our groove."

The hope hurts too much. The molten-glass words have cooled down into something that can break. It's probably the nicest thing he's said to me in a while. *Our groove.*

"I've seen a lot of awful shit in the Memory Excerpts," I start, slow. "Us fighting. Me being a miserable jerk." I wait for a correction that doesn't come. Fair. "Were we happy?"

"Not all day every day. But every day."

The puff from his nose might be a laugh. It's just what I'd say. I don't know if that's more of Gabe talking, or me through him.

"Can you forget you're a scrape?"

"Is this you officially admin-mode-ing me to forget?"

"No. Just curious."

"I could. If ya wanted."

We both let his words hang in the air. Birds flap from the marsh. We pick at the charcuterie. Flo packed us cookies and a baggie of her strawberry candies, but neither of us are really hungry. After a while, I slide the food to one side and shimmy closer to him, lying out so that we're touching. He turns to rest his head on my shoulder and drapes his arm over my stomach, and I have to hold my breath just to keep it all together, skin glowing where our bodies meet, even through the cotton. Looking up at the sky. Watching the gold light make shapes on the leaves above. A thought weaves around my head like the breeze. *Some version of him is better than nothing.*

We wander from our grassy alcove back to the manor, close but not touching. None of the other residents seem to notice or care that someone new rolled in—or they're still avoiding me. I can't find Minou, not that I have a chance to shake Gabe and look for her. Not that I'd know what to say. *Seth scraped together a version of my dead husband and I'm supposed to be happy?*

An editor promised me, once, *we can make you happy.* I can hear her voice like a puff of mint tea, only I can't remember where I was.

Anyway, I have to show Gabe around. *Here's the dining room. Here's the sunroom. Here's the creaky front hallway where the other residents pretend that I've faded into the wallpaper.* We skip lunch since we snacked through our re-intro session, and I watch him paint with watercolors at an easel out of the corner of my eyes in the greenhouse during Free Exploration. His lips, his eyebrows drawn into lines. I don't feel much like painting, seeing as how I can't hold the brush straight. Past the greenhouse glass walls, a squadron of sparrows swarm and swoop after a hawk, chasing it into the trees. A war of birds.

I must've spaced out. Next thing I know, he's nudging me and bobbing his chin to his canvas, where he's painted a giant blue dick.

"Whaddya think?" he asks.

"Masterpiece." I hope my smile pokes out of my eyes.

We clean up the paints and then he looks at me like, *what now?*

Yeah, what now? I should be happy but my heart echoes like sparrow wingbeats in my empty chest. Flo breezes in just in time and says something to Gabe about getting him set up in his room, and I hate how I can breathe easier once he's gone.

I hide in my room through dinner because I'm a coward, afraid of a stranger who's wearing my husband's face. Who could be him, who could follow me everywhere and tell me endlessly how much he loves me, if I tell him to.

Admin mode. Like I own him. Like he's living just for me. *All I'm asking for is your everything, is that so hard?* There's a razor behind the smile on Gabe's face—the *real* Gabe—in my picture on the bureau. *Ask and you got it, Foxy.*

I shouldn't have skipped dinner. I shouldn't have stuck my head in the sand. But what do I do now that the moon's spotlighting over the marsh? Knock on every bedroom door in the manor, looking for Gabe? Edited scenes swarm around my head with how this night should've gone. Insert > bedframe-breaking reunion, falling asleep in each other's arms, royalty-free soundtrack.

So I try to sleep. Try. What Flo said before when she, Seth, and Gabe popped up at my door is a threat that slips through the shadows in my room. *Oh, hon. You deserve it.*

I find Gabe laughing with a cluster of other residents over a plate of eggs and tomatoes in the dining room after my morning Memory Mapping. I got there early thinking he'd have no one to talk to, but who am I kidding? It's Gabe, he's already running the place. Inyene swats his shoulder like, *you're bad!* Of course they'd get along. Tomorrow, everyone will elect him class president. Pizza for lunch. A therapist slides a Reeder to Gabe for a pop quiz. Gabe stabs at the screen and the guy whistles. New record.

"Well, there he is," Gabe calls out to me.

His wiggling eyebrows as he laughs crack through my ice. Here I am. Being all suspicious, being a dick. The other residents crane their heads to me, João waving me over, and it's like Gabe is my entry to the group of cool kids. They really don't care he's a scrape. I plop down onto a chair next to him and he wraps an arm around my shoulder, squeezing. He chopped the sleeves off his gray sweatshirt—of course he'd want to show off his guns—and where his bare skin touches my neck, more ice thaws. I let myself be pulled to him, warming in his glow.

Another simulated perfect day in the Field of Reeds, where a light breeze welcomes us outside to the circle of chairs by the patio. Ducks glide across the water, past the swaying reeds. The warring birds must've called a truce.

"As you can see, we have a new resident," Seth says to our group, nodding at Gabe, who slouches low in his chair at my side, wide-legged. He salutes. "Anything you'd like to say?"

"We are memories and memories are we?" Gabe tips his head. "I got that right?"

"Exactly." Seth smiles at his new favorite resident. "I hope you'll start sharing when you're ready."

"Oversharing is my thing." Gabe winks at me. "Just wait."

"Now." Seth turns back to the group. "Who would like to start?"

Stash looks down at his fingertips. Minou has perfected her faintly bored smile. My eyes are already lost on the reeds, because what's Gabe going to share when he's ready? Why is he even in group if we're here to recover memories, and what's he going to recover? The only memories in his head are ones pulled from me.

"I had a daughter," Chengmei says with a strained voice.

I tear my gaze from the reeds. She flinches like she hears some loud noise that we don't.

"What do you remember about her?" Seth asks gently.

"I've been seeing her here. And trying to talk to her, ever since…" Her voice trails off, and she blinks against an invisible, bright light. "Ever since the painted city that we found, after the birds started talking to me, and…"

I beg her with my eyes to be quiet.

"Chengmei, what do you mean that birds started talking to you?" I know from Seth's unmoving smile that he's trying not to scare her off, like she's a wild animal.

"They started telling me to follow them, and then…" She looks to me, Minou, and Stash with wounded eyes. "Tell him."

We betray her with our silence. I can hear Khadija's voice from the training video again—*seriously, though, don't get deleted.* Gabe looks down at the grass between his slippered feet.

"Was this after your last Excerpt, the birds?" Seth asks.

"I don't *want* to talk about Excerpts, or birds." I can hear in Chengmei's voice that she's pulling in air and heating it, like Gabe would. I squirm, waiting for the explosion. "I know I have a daughter. And how could you keep that from me? And how—how come you won't let me see her, and—"

I shiver with just how much she reminds me of Greg yelling at Fatima, like we're all transposing the same songs.

"It's alright," Seth says. Just for an instant, his eyes move from Chengmei to behind her. I follow his gaze to the patio, where J pokes their head out of the sunroom door.

"No, it's *not* alright." Her face twists. She stands and kicks the chair over behind her. *Boom.*

"Chengmei, I'm going to ask you to gather yourself, for your safety."

"Bullshit!" she screams. "It's torture, j-just being here and you keeping her from me. I'll… I'll…"

She stops and huffs, her shoulders shaking, tearing at her sleeves, until she seems to notice the chair she just kicked over. *No*, I try to beam out with my eyes. *Don't*. She growls and reaches for the chair.

"Admin mode." Seth's voice is a cool trickle that's somehow louder than it should be. "Resident safety protocol, please."

J moves so quickly that almost all I see is a blur of their yellow scrubs. They grab the chair from Chengmei, and suddenly two more therapists whip to us from their sessions. One pins her arms in a hug from behind—as she thrashes wildly, screaming—and the other grabs her ankles. I'm cemented to my chair. Gabe swallows hard and looks to me for something I can't give him. All of us are too stunned to move.

"Tell him!" Chengmei snarls like her ankle is caught in a trap. "Why aren't you—"

J stops her by plunging a needle into her neck. Chengmei sags against the therapists, her head lolling back. Just for a second, J cradles the side of her face.

"Thank you." Seth nods to the therapists. "If you could please escort Chengmei to her room where she can rest."

J nods and carries Chengmei like a baby, frowning down at her face. They turn and carry her to the manor as the other therapists float away. The sound of the sunroom door closing breaks my heart.

Admin mode, with the therapists snapping into place for him like toy soldiers. I can almost hear the Inland Ocean City alarms over my gushing heartbeat. Even after Khadija's warnings about deletion and Flo telling us that he's the sim admin, I let Seth lull me into thinking I was almost safe here, blabbing about transposing, and my *journey toward healing* and shit. Trapped, yeah, but not in danger if I played the canned template of the good resident.

Chengmei's limp body is proof that he'll do whatever he wants to us if we force him. Even if it's for our *safety*. Even more of a reason to get out of here.

It's so quiet in our therapy circle that Gabe's breath sounds like a breaking wave. He leans deeper in his chair and crosses his arms. Minou eyes the downed chair and her shoulders shake. Only Stash smirks.

"She's right." Stash waves his hand to the group, then over the grounds. "The talk therapy, and Moving Meditation, and Radical Remembrance. It's all crap."

"What's wrong with her?" Minou asks.

Seth's big-bro smile twists at the sides with sadness. Like this hurts him, because he cares about us all so much.

"We'll get her the help that she needs."

He talks lessons for a while, something about bending like a reed, something else about how not everyone takes to their Excerpts as well as we have. I don't hear him. Before I know it the group scatters like birds, leaving me bolted to my chair.

I know the *we're on official Scribe business* clip to Minou's walk. I watch as she and the others trek down the lawn toward the orchard. The therapists won't go that far past the main manor grounds. Or can't? I hold back a shiver against the coolness in Seth's voice when he called out, *admin mode.*

"Are sessions always that full-contact sport-y?" Gabe asks.

"That's a first." I reach out and squeeze his thigh. "Come on."

I lead us over the grass, past groups of residents who must be gossiping about Chengmei. Minou's blue-streaked messy bun bobs on her head as she glances back at me and Gabe. Then Stash, ten feet to her right, shuffles closer to her. I can't hear what they're saying. Gabe, kicking through the grass and his eyes drinking in the blue sky, doesn't seem to notice the gossip that clings to them like a stink. Ten feet away. Five. Until, finally, Minou and Stash clunk to a stop.

"What the hell was that?" I ask.

"I think—*we* think," Minou says with a quick glance at Stash, "that we want to meet with just us."

I stop in my tracks. "Yeah, there's no one else…" I watch their gaze bounce from me to Gabe. *Oh.* Of course.

"We know he's a scrape," Stash barbs, his purple-dyed mustache twitching. "Or whatever. A Deather spy? A plant from NIL/E to find Khadija? Who knows?"

My face feels like it's boiling. Gabe just shrugs, bored.

"Oooo intrigue." He wiggles his fingers like a birthday party magician. "*Am* I a spy? The codeword is platypus."

"He's with me," I snap. I look to Minou, my gaze grasping for her help. "He's—"

"Fox," she starts, softly, and I know she's already booted me out of their little club. "We don't know what's happening with Chengmei and what that means for us. We… we have to close the circle and watch our backs."

"She's your friend, and you're just going to shut down like that?"

"We can't get distracted."

I expected that kind of ice from Stash, but not her.

"*You* shouldn't, either." Stash stabs the air with a finger. "Shouldn't you worry about finding the real Gabe instead of this, like, fucking NIL/E commercial?"

I've never thrown a punch in my life, and now I want to see blood spraying from Stash's nose. *What's your real weapon, though?* Past Fox is cranking open the crocodile trap door, wanting to let the monsters out. And you know what? Chomp away.

"Good luck solving the virus without me, then, you fucking hacks." I borrow the laughing voice from Past Fox in the bar. "We'll be out in the real world with Khadija, while you're rotting in this sim. Forever."

"Also, eat a big bag of dicks," Gabe adds.

There. Not poetry. I smile at the steel in Stash's eyes, turn on my heels, and me and Gabe walk off back to the manor. I search his eyes for the hurt, for some reaction to Stash calling him a commercial. All I see are the same gold-ringed walls holding me back from whatever's beyond them.

TWENTY-FOUR
SUITE LIKE HONEY

A blue heron swoops down from one of the big trees and splashes into the marsh, its head tucked in flight, its blue-gray feathers the color of the storm clouds rolling in my head. More painting in the greenhouse, me and Gabe mixing white, black, and blue paint to try to match the color of the heron wings, though we can't get it right.

"I don't give a fat fuck what the others think about me," he says.

"Good. I don't, either."

I can't find Flo to ask her what's happening until she flocks to us in the dining room at lunch. Her smile warms away the clouds. She has something to show us, she says, barely reining in her sunshine like she's stashing a birthday cake behind her back. Honestly, it feels good just to have someone be nice to me. I try to ask her about Chengmei until she wags a finger at the dining room, like, *too many people*. We drop our plates in the bus buckets and follow her through the hallways, up a creaky back staircase to the third floor on the opposite side of the manor from the Ankh Room. We stop in front of a wooden door.

"We thought we'd offer you this bigger space in case you wanted to room together," she says, hands on the fancy gold doorknob.

She sweeps the door wide open to a broad room that must span half this side of the house, all honeyed wood floors and cushioned furniture. A huge bay window, veined with silver bits between the panels, pours light into the room through long, gauzy curtains that trail past the tufted red window seat. Under a skylight, a king-sized bed mounded with pillows juts from one wall, a plush cream rug separating it from a seating area with a reclining couch, coffee table, and a high-backed tufted chair. A rolling rack for clothes and a small bureau against another wall, next to a white marble sink and a bookshelf. A round two-person bistro table with chairs where we can have romantic dinners as we gaze out over the grounds. A claw-foot free-standing tub—a white island floating in the gold sea by another oversized window—is big enough for two, flanked by a small brass table cluttered with bath oils and fancy soaps. A little room with an open door offers a glimpse of checkered floor tiles in the bathroom. Welcome to the honeymoon suite of the Field of Reeds Center for Memory Recovery, just missing a big heart of rose petals on the bed.

Gabe whistles. "There room service, too?"

Flo smiles at the crack. "In case you want more privacy. If you're ready for that."

Privacy, sure. She might as well be lighting candles and leaving us a tray of strawberries, lube, and poppers. *You boys have fun now, we'll just be blasting music in the next room so don't think you'll disturb anyone.* She's our college RA giving us permission to bone.

And I thought about *privacy* with him, last night alone in my room. Itching to touch him, so I cranked away and thought of his lips at my neck, biting. Crushing his weight onto me. And how I should've leaned over him in our alcove by the water, and rubbed him until his sweatpants tented, wriggled us out of our gray sweats. I'd told Yvonne, back in that hellscape when Gabe left me, how I still jerked off to him. *That's probably the most romantic thing I've ever heard*, she'd sighed. *A million years in and you still wanna have sex with your spouse.* Funny that I sneered at Minou and Stash about forgetting Chengmei, and now it's like the memory of J carrying her away is locked on the other side of the honeymoon suite door.

I shift on my feet, clearing my throat. "Are you ready for that?" I risk a look at him. "Privacy?"

"Hell yeah. Get me outta the fuckin' convent downstairs." His smirk slays me every time.

"Wonderful," Flo says. "I can ask J to help you gather your things."

What do we really have to pack? We came here with nothing. I have a toothbrush in the bathroom downstairs, a few changes of clothes, nothing else I wouldn't mind torching. Only when Gabe is gone does Flo offer me one of her strawberry candies before popping one into her mouth herself.

"Is Chengmei gonna be alright?" The strawberry goo-filled candy is too sweet, like chewing on a candle. "She's been off ever since the city."

"She's sleeping now. I'm leading her through an intensive Ankh session once she wakes. I'll be watching her, keeping her safe. Keeping *us* safe, too. You just do what you need to do, and focus on the virus."

Candy shards stab at my tongue. Flo, with her sweet *oh, honey*s will keep us safe, right?

"And don't listen to Stash," she continues. "Minou told me what happened. You do what you need to do to heal. And maybe Gabe can even help with the mission?"

"How could he help?"

"He's pulled from you. He has your editing skills, if you want him to use them. It's just a matter of asking him."

Admin mode. Right. "Making him."

Her candy clacks against her teeth. "He'll want to help you. Let him."

I frown, not buying it. I brush past her to get my things from my room—my Reeder, and the picture of me and Gabe. When I come back, I see that Gabe has dragged a little table by the big window and set up an easel. He must've lifted it and the watercolor set from the greenhouse. I skim the corners of the room as I drop my Reeder on the desk, still not really knowing what to do when we're alone together. He launches himself onto the bed, the pillows flopping around him, and flashes his lazy smile, arms behind his head.

"This is officially the manor's fuckpad," he says. "Look at that tub. Ya think Seth gets freaky with the residents here?"

"Ugh, I hope not."

I wander over to him with shaky knees, the glass of the picture frame warming under my fingers. I place the frame on the nightstand by the bed.

"Do you remember that night?" I ask. "The party?"

"I don't because you don't. Follow along, Foxy."

"C-could you answer like Gabe—like *you* would?"

That only gets his eyes dancing. One hand idly scratching his belly and lifting his shirt higher, teasing. "Fuckin' blast. You don't remember because you had one too many. I rubbed your back while you puked in the shower at home."

Sounds about right, with him cleaning up after me. Like he makes up for everything I ever did wrong.

———

I remember what to do when we're alone together, after he yanks me to him.

He feels like my Gabe, running so hot the heat blasts off his skin. Smells just like him—musky with a hint of a grassy soap from the gym—so I bury my face in his neck and the hair on his chest and suck in deep, like he makes me drunk. Floor sways, bed sways. He tugs my shirt off so fast that seams pop. My pants. Scalding skin on skin, both of us shivering as he hooks his legs around my waist, with that animal flash in his eyes. Like, *I dare you*. I flip us so that he's over me. Oil from one of the little bath bottles. Already, he's zipping me back together and healing me with slick fingers, opening me up. Driving, hard, into me. Flash. Fireworks outside the window of our shitty first apartment. *I'm close, I'm*—flash. A pyramid in New Thebes smashes apart just from the bomb of us both coming at the same time, eyes locked, the heat arcing back and forth until we collapse onto each other, spent. Panting. Licking away the sweat from his neck and I know, I know. I never want to leave this room. He's back and I'm never letting go again.

Rain against the skylight in the evening, dozing and wrapped up in the sheets, and each other. Gabe's back is turned to me while he sleeps. In the light from the single floor lamp, his shoulder and hip are mountains. In the tap-tapping of the rain, I have to close my fists so I don't run my fingers across his skin. Scared that I'll wake him up and he'll disappear.

Voices, too, in the rain, cutting through my sleep.

A woman's voice. A stranger, no—Khadija. I know the honey-sweet voice from the training video. Yeah. And I heard it before, right? *You've got Gabe? Alright. Alright, good. We're trying to lock onto him, jus—*

Then Gabe's voice, on the sidewalk in his mint-green shirt. *Why kill yourself trying to bring back the real me if you could just roll around with a copy, right, Foxy? Easy-way edits. Just like you. I get it.*

Gabe's voice drags me out of bed before dawn, like he's calling to me from another room in our apartment. His flicking eyes under his eyelids are somehow in time with the rain on the skylight.

I grab my Reeder, and so I don't wake him with my typing, I tiptoe to the study off the Ankh Room. The room is a mess of shadows, the armchair the waiting mouth of a monster. I switch on the table lamp and settle into the chair before opening my Reeder and pulling up the virus code.

None of the colors that I could almost see as Greg shimmer over the endless lines. I don't even hear the static of voices when I look at the code. The only sound is a faint conversation from the other side of the study door, in the Ankh Room. I scrub my hands over my withered eyes and press an ear against the door. I can't make out the words, but I'd know Flo's cheery voice anywhere. I knock once and she calls for me to come in.

The Ankh Room is a different place at night, lit only by a handful of lamps casting hazy amber across the tasseled carpet. I can barely make out the bookshelf-lined walls and the bar cart by the desk, like the space transforms into a huge underground cavern after sunset. Just Flo hovering by the Ankh, the Reeder light against her glasses giving her cat eyes. I never really stopped to think about if she needs to sleep, since she's a template and all. And then that leads me down a dark, winding cave path of whether I even need to sleep since I don't actually have a body. Which only makes the floor pitch beneath me.

Blue lights march across the Ankh. I peek inside and see Chengmei, so perfectly still she could be dead.

"Don't worry, she'll be right as rain in no time," Flo says. She nods to my Reeder. "Any progress?"

I know that I'm supposed to be the golden child that defied final-death to get here and everything. Flo's been the only one to believe in me, really. I hate that I don't have anything to show for her faith.

"I'll get there."

"You will. I can feel it. Just give it time."

Yeah, I mean, what else do we have here? "And it's worth it? The mission. The..."

"Project Bennu."

"Yeah. Just what is it?"

"Well, you know—we know Khadija always starts with ideas. First, immortality for the world. Now, never-ending paradise." She laughs, and for a second she's not the kindergarten teacher, she's the little girl. "Minor hurdles."

"And how's she jumping over those hurdles?"

"She moves in secrecy. We don't know a lot, to be fair. And that's where the trust comes in." Flo sighs and fiddles with her glasses. "All I need to do is look at what she's done already, outside of here. How she brought edits and backups to the whole world. How she rebuilt Kemet out of the rubble of BosWashton and brought water to the deserts. And so much more."

I don't need to see Flo's eyes to hear the mist in her voice. Minou told me that some people thought Khadija was Aset reincarnated. Maybe an online handle, maybe a god. And she'd basically created

Flo and brought her here to guide us Scribes. Like Flo is a disciple following her creator.

Insert > commandments from the sky. Insert > blind faith.

"I know our mission is another one of her gifts," Flo continues. "I trust her. I believe her, in my heart. And I hope you will, too."

I'm glad the room is dark, so I can shove my hands in my sweatpants pockets and dart my gaze from her cat eyes, hoping I don't look too judgy. She has the same quiet, urgent voice Zeke did when he was talking soul stuff. The arguments crawl over my head like the lights of the Ankh. I barely know you, Flo, and now you're asking me to trust someone else I've never met—though, I met her, right? Somewhere, and... I lose the spider-thread of the thought.

Because I came here to change. To learn to trust. How I loved Gabe, yeah, but did I ever trust him with how possessive Past Fox in the Excerpts was? Eyes on Gabe at parties, watching who he talked to. If his hands lingered on someone's shoulder for a second too long. The silence of a fuse, then the blowup days or weeks later. *And just who was that guy you were all over the other day?*

"Me too," I tell her.

Some trust might do me good.

TWENTY-FIVE
COMING FORTH BY DAY

Me and Gabe spot Chengmei in the corner of the dining room at breakfast. I stop when I see her, tug at Gabe to wait a second, and just watch from the entryway. She's not alone, sitting in a stretched rectangle of light from the windows. Flo's with her. I can tell by Flo's beamy smile that she's cooing sweet words to Chengmei, who lifts a hand—a yellow bracelet dangles from one wrist—and tries to spoon food into her mouth. Tries. Her elbow knocks wide like a wing, the spoon bumps her chin, and she smears food along one cheek. Her face twitches into a smile before turning slack again. Lost eyes.

I'll be watching her, keeping her safe, Flo told me yesterday. *Keeping us safe, too.*

A therapist pushes a Reeder at me, on the way to Flo and Chengmei. The pop quiz question doesn't make sense. *Run system diagnostics? Disk optimization. Resource utility. Gateway connectivity. All of the above.* I swear the screen twitches when I look down at it. I tap one of the answers just to get him out of my face.

Flo looks up before I even have a chance to say anything. "I know it might look upsetting, but everything's fine, Fox," she says.

Chengmei smiles at me like a kid beaming at the sunset.

"S-something went wrong in the Ankh last night?"

"Not everyone takes to their Excerpts as well as you have. Some residents need to hit the pause button." Flo pats Chengmei's hand. "We reset their memories to their save-file from their first day here. Let their minds rest a while."

The words are static in my head. *We'll get her the help that she needs*, Seth told us after J carted Chengmei away from therapy. Help, sure. We'll reset her brain and hope for the best. At least she has Flo with her.

The clouds clear in time for morning session. Maybe it's Seth at work, again, pulling the puppet strings. Insert > rain for evening of moody romance, delete before we move therapy into the stuffy music room. Therapists towel off chairs while me and Gabe wander over, through the smell of wet grass. Minou sits next to me. All she offers is a tiny smile. I don't have the energy to ask her if she saw Chengmei with her shiny new yellow bracelet like I did. Stash takes the chair next to Gabe and makes a show of moving it a foot further away. Gabe, slouched low in his chair, only rolls his eyes and spreads his knees wider, like he's happy for the extra room.

"As you can see, Chengmei is not in session this morning," Seth says. "There's a limit to how much even we can help those who are too far gone. Who fight the process. Who become a danger to themselves. But I'm confident that with some course-correcting, Chengmei will be on the road to recovery again before you know it."

Course-correcting. I'm on the marsh again, flailing around in the water. My stomach twinges. I look to Minou, and even after our fight about Gabe—if that's what it was—her eyes soften.

One corner of her mouth sweeps up in a half-smile, like *here we are again.*

"Now, who'd like to start today?" Seth asks.

"I would," Gabe says right away.

I wriggle under the eyes on us. Seth opens his mouth, stops, and reconsiders.

"Please," he says.

Gabe bolts up. "I remember something this morning. About a big concrete island, and being on stage, all lit up in the spotlight."

Seth nods slowly, his eyes turning over something. Minou and Stash are suddenly fascinated by their fingernails. I tune them all out, staring at Gabe's lips and feeling like I'm bobbing down the marsh on a wobbly kayak.

"What's that supposed to mean?" Gabe finally asks.

"A concrete island is interesting," Seth says. "Island being natural. Concrete being humanmade. Perhaps..." He lets the word die on the wind. I can see the doubt rippling over his face like code. *How is this fake thing remembering something when he shouldn't be?*

I try to tell myself to bend. To breathe in and not kayak over to some insane conclusion. *This could be nothing. He was dreaming, or, or...*

"And the stage part?" Gabe asks.

"Perhaps you feel as though there are eyes on you, since you're new here? A bit like you're performing, surely?"

"Surely." Gabe's smirky eyes hit me and we're back in Darius's office, barely putting up with this therapy bullshit. Me staring at the flavor-of-the-week flower on the coffee table and wondering when our hour is up. Something bugs me about Gabe sharing a memory. Buds me. Flower buds, hope budding in my head, so hard they want to poke out my eyes. I know where we have to go.

I tell Gabe the deal with morning Memory Mapping in the hallway, me with my *mayor of the Field of Reeds* smile hiding the nerves. I need someone in my corner who can help me explain where Gabe's new memory came from. I find Flo in the greenhouse, helping Chengmei with watercolors, and tell her what's up. She flags down another therapist to take over, and soon we're in the sunroom with J and the mantis Memory Mapping chair.

"And you're sure this isn't going to hurt?" Gabe asks.

"Easy-peasy!" J chirps behind him. "The light show is pretty something."

Gabe gives his best *I'm game* shrug and sighs. The silver mask snaps over his face.

"The whole of your memory is your memorystream," J starts their prayer softly.

"Oh yeah, one hundred percent a cult," Gabe says, muffled by the mask.

"Watch it flow like a…"

I see the lights reflected across his cheeks, can faintly hear the bee-buzz as the mask scans his memorystream. J's fingers flit across their Reeder and a projection blinks into the room.

Flo stiffens at my side. "J, could you enter admin mode please?"

"You betcha."

"Let's go ahead and pause your short-term memory registration, please, J."

An invisible hand slides a steel rod down J's back, their eyes still downcast to their Reeder. Lips slack like they're frozen in that space between breathing in and out. *Admin mode.* Code words and commands for the templated memories in this big dollhouse. Seeing this up-close makes my stomach twirl.

"Is everything cool?" The crinkle at the end of Gabe's voice makes me almost yank the mask off him. A quick glance from Flo tells me, *easy*.

"Everything's peachy, hon," she says. "Just want to take a closer look at your scan."

J doesn't even blink.

The first swathe of Gabe's scan looks like the vague shape of my broken memorystream with thin icicle branches. Until the branches thicken, all glossed over with glimmers—a shimmer of pink here, dark purple there—like a rainbow on an oil slick. Flo zooms in with a flick of her hands, and the display zooms the river map in to the actual code, which dances with light, too. She zips back out to the map, where one pulsing bead of light juts from the side. More vivid and shimmery than the colors I saw staring at the code as Greg, even. Flo stabs a button on the chair and the visor snaps from Gabe's face, letting the glowing branches glint in his eyes.

"That's me?" His voice is a puff. "My memorystream?"

Flo leans forward and her nose cuts through the projection. "Well, shit biscuits." I almost snort at hearing the kindergarten teacher swear. "Is that budding?"

"It's beautiful," I add.

A ghost of light pulses over the projection of Gabe's memorystream, the gold of the chain he always wears. Flo pinches her fingers to zoom in on the bud. Instead of the watercolor smudge that budded out of my memorystream, the picture is a pointillist masterpiece. A small pink-and-yellow bucket, all spun from tiny flecks of light.

"I'm gonna need you two to stop talking like you're not standing six inches away from me," Gabe says. "What the fuck is going on?"

Flo's eyes dance to mine. Her quick hands pop a strawberry candy into her mouth. "Organic memory recovery from a scrape is just unheard of. Downright impossible. A gift from Khadija? Or, or..."

"A miracle."

The lights reflected in Gabe's eyes warm me up. Like I have a do-over with him, from that night at the carnival, when he needed to hear that we are more than just code.

Once Gabe is out of the chair, Flo un-admin-modes J—with their chipper *howdy!* they seem fine—and the three of us hoof it through the hallways. We have to hide this from Seth, Flo says. In case the company thinks Gabe is glitching out and they decide to toss him in the trash.

Gabe's arm brushes mine. I shiver, even in the humid air. *Or we can delete him for you.*

Over my dried-up memorystream. I'll light up this place before anyone touches him.

"And I can see this budding thing?" Gabe asks. I'm not used to the crinkle-paper sound of his hesitant voice. His sarcasm is gone, like it was the chair mask that snapped away from his face.

"You betcha." I grin at him, stealing some of J's sunshine.

The only way for us to see what the hell is going on is for Gabe to take a spin in the Ankh. The only way through is deeper.

Flo clears everyone out of the Ankh Room but Sig. She fills him in, almost giddy, and he boots up Gabe's newly budded Memory Excerpt on the Ankh. Once the bucket shimmers in the air between us, she sits Gabe in the Ankh. Me kneeling at his side like I'm drawing him a bath. One of his hands twitches on the gold edge of the coffin. I'm the one to pass him the vial of gold liquid, like Flo did for me. *Sedative. It'll help with the transition into the new Memory Excerpt.*

"This makes it easier," I tell him. "It'll help you relax."

"Is this gonna hurt?"

Well, not so much physically. Get ready for some fucking emotional hot-irons, though. I have to bend like a reed against his fear. Against the dry wind of a voice in my ears. Gabe's voice from a long time ago, after a fight, his razor-blade smile nicking me up. *Look at me all needy for you. This must be what you always wanted.*

Seth called the fact that I couldn't seem to fully forget Gabe "perforation." Sounds about right, like he's punched through me a million times.

"No. I promise."

The swirled lines at the side of his head dance with his sudden smile. "If I die in this coffin thing, consider your ass haunted."

I force a laugh, just for him.

He tosses back the vial and shimmies down into the Anhk. The mask *shicks* into place. I look up at the gold light across the picture of the pink-and-yellow bucket. Like the ghost of Gabe sweeping by, leading me to I don't know where. But I'll follow.

Turquoise lights dance over the gold sides of the Ankh and over Gabe's cheeks from the mask, with lights reflecting on his gray sweats like bugs crawling. I stay with him the whole time and don't look away when he stiffens and twitches. When his breath races beneath the mask, and me and Past Fox fight in my head about whether to pull him out or not.

The sunlight glides across the carpet with the hours, slow like honey. Until Gabe gasps awake and coughs, and I'm the one with the bucket at his side, rubbing his back as he pukes. Carrying him back to our bedroom with Flo, where I tuck him in. And Flo looks at me, and I don't even have to tell her what's up.

"I'll watch him," she says. She smooths the edge of the blanket under his chin. "Go."

The sides of the Ankh are still warm from his body when I slip in.

TWENTY-SIX
HUNGER

Dream logic, I told that coworker, how edited memories make sense because they want to flow in with the whole of your memorystream.

I've been Gabe the whole time. I just didn't think to notice.

The tide pulls me into Gabe's memories, and I let them flow all over me.

Why does this stuff look like worms, kids in the canteen whined, poking at their kelpghetti. I could eat that shit for every meal, licking red sauce off my fingers, stabbing stray krillballs off other trays when kids weren't looking. They didn't know what it meant to be hungry.

Gabe, you should forget it all, a caregiver told me 'n' Julio when we got there. *Everything from before you got here. It's better that way. Easier.*

She was right. You learn to push feelings down into your stomach so they don't eat you from the inside out. Most of the time it works. Except the teeth in your gut when you remember the nurses in the plastic suits rolling Julio's body out of the infirmary, when you're screaming and slamming on the glass. You smell smoke in the streets later. You know they're burning Julio. What's left of him. And the others who kicked it since the last wave of boats, who the caregivers say might spread diseases, and burning's the only way to save the whole island.

That shit stays with you forever. Years later, you see it when you blink.

The other kids thought we were getting barbecue kelpbobs again for dinner. Maybe that was the smell.

My favorite story behind my eyes is Coral Beef.

Má brought home food from work most nights. Every time, me 'n' Julio bounced to the door of our apartment, jumping at the striped pink-and-yellow bucket with the cartoon cow with a fish tail. Má dropped the bucket on the counter and plopped to the ground for hugs, first, always. Time with each of us to kiss the tops of our heads and ask what we did that day.

She smelled like fries and spices. The best bucket was the Cow'N'Cod Combo, with nuggies shaped like cow heads and fish tails, plus BarBMoo dippin' sauce. Má usually conked out on the couch, still in her yellow farmer uniform, while me 'n' Julio made forts on the carpet out of pillows and the empty bucket. The TV blasted light on the spots on Má's arms. I'd poked them, once, asking what they were.

"Stars, bebé. They burn just a little at first."

Sometimes she took us to work and we'd run around the ball pit and the slide of the KidzKorral, and I'd see her through the window, working the fryer. Me 'n' Julio played hide and seek, and I always squirmed down to the bottom of the pit. Stayed there until just before his giggles and his *where'd you go*s turned into screams, and I bounced up out of the balls like one of the dolphins we'd see way past the docks off Aaru, a coupla years later. The way his eyes lit up when he saw me made every day worth it.

Until they shut the playground down. Back to TV nights. Julio was still too young for kindergarten, and Má had to work doubles, so I left school to take care of him. Most nights, he couldn't sleep unless he squished my earlobe between his thumb 'n' pointer finger to make sure I was still with him. One night Má made us stay up with her on the couch to watch President Márquez making a speech. The president pointed a lot, and spotlights hit her face, and she talked all about how *we will not be cowed by threats of a company whose very mission cheapens the sanctity of the human spirit. That robs people of their sacred journey with Santa Muerte into the life beyond.*

Cowed had me rolling on the floor and mooing like that Coral Beef commercial where the cartoon cow with the fish tail swims around a pink reef. Until Má yelled to stop.

When me 'n' Julio 'n' the other kids from Mexico rolled into Aaru, the caregivers talked about how happy they were to welcome us to our new home. I didn't learn shit about what actually went down in our real home from them, though. They kicked me outta class basically right after Julio died, just a couple of months from when we first rolled in. I begged them to give me his ashes and let me go back home, and begging turned to screams, and screams turned to fists since they were's listening. And then they moved me to maintenance training because I was *a roadblock to the education of the others.*

I learned from the guys in janitorial—a lotta things—while we scrubbed the algae tanks. How NIL/E got all us refugees noded after we finished whatever training program they assigned us to—Julio never made it that far—not 'cause we were special. But 'cause if we died it was cheaper to rez us in one of the spare Body Garden vessels than to train someone else. How Márquez wouldn't ship oil to the NIL/E Union City-States, wouldn't let them operate in the country unless the company coughed up the goods on its promises. The offshore farms, the water 'n' waste plants, the waste-recycling centers to help support their rich customers all over the world who wouldn't die. When it couldn't be just up to Mexico 'n' other countries, when companies could do more than countries now. And President Márquez was one of the few to stand up and say we should look at the tanking of that economy over there and pass physical-age labor laws, 'cause chronological age keeled over long ago, thanks to NIL/E.

Then came the NIL/E trade sanctions and the economic sanctions from other nations—'cause what else were they gonna do when NIL/E threatened to pull outta infrastructure deals and jobs packages? And then companies 'n' banks bounced outta Mexico all 'cause of the government's *assault on the personal liberties of its people* 'n' shit.

The caregivers, when they introduced me 'n' Julio to the others, tried to make Mexico sound like a shithole they'd rescued us from. I didn't remember it being bad. Until the Coral Beef shut down. The big grocery stores 'n' banks, then food lines stretched around the block. Back then, Má didn't tell me a lot. The other kids watching their little siblings did, about the break-ins, the neighbors kicking down doors to clear out fridges.

Má thawed out the last Cow'N'Cod Combo buckets for my last birthday when we were all together. Even stuck a candle in a nuggie and placed the plate on the kitchen table in front of me, while Julio sat on the counter and swung his feet, all singing. My shoulders were too heavy to feel much like celebrating.

Until Má hit me with her Má eyes. *This isn't for you. This is for him.*

Smile big. Blow out the candle. Make a wish.

I don't think a lot about the naked stuff before Aaru 'cause I know other kids went hungry when we didn't.

One day Má showed up with a folding computer and put it in me 'n' Julio's bedroom. She hung up a bedsheet in the corner and pointed the computer at it. Her face looked like she'd pushed her lips into a smile in the bathroom and was trying hard to keep it there. One of her old Coral Beef friends had told her this was how they'd made a bunch of money, that people all over the world pay to see other people take their clothes off. Which she'd tried already, and would keep trying, but she was too old to make these people happy. And when they were happy, they paid up.

Me or Julio. There was no question. Clothes off like I was taking a bath. No big deal. Facing the screen, where I couldn't see faces. I could hear voices, asking me to turn around or smile. That's when I learned to disappear into the stories behind my eyes. Bounce back into the ball pit, with the Coral Beef music playing. I got us enough money for Má to fill the fridge and buy a better lock for the door. To get a gun that she kept in an old CowN'Cod bucket in the freezer and taught me how to load. Before she grabbed it that one night when the screams and the sounds of breaking glass filled the neighborhood, then the apartment below us.

"Take care of your brother," she said, giving me her hard Má eyes. She pushed me into the closet with Julio—the one with the shrine to Santa Muerte—and shut the door.

Santa Muerte, wrapped up in her black hooded cloak all studded with stars, her bone-hands holding a scythe, just looked at us with empty eyes. A crown of flowers on her head. The flowers Má had brought for her had shriveled already.

I tugged pillows and a blanket into the closet to make it into a game, when I wanted to scream and run after Má. When the big tears started gushing down Julio's face 'cause he wanted Máma— and was that her making all that noise in the kitchen?—I started whispering the Coral Beef song until he finally went to sleep.

Out in the street, someone at least had covered Má with a sheet.

I didn't have time to be sad, not when I had to keep doing the clothes-off thing to keep me and Julio fed, until NIL/E rolled in with what they said was help. And tanks. And the ship that lugged us to Aaru. Where Má was there for us, I lied to Julio, the only way to get him onto the ship.

After that first time in front of the bedsheet, though, she took us back to Coral Beef. She still had an old key from when she managed the place. It was empty except for the ball pit, and she stayed on the edge, arms crossed tight over her chest while she watched me and Julio bounce around.

The thing about Aaru is *welcome home* and all—and for ten years you scrub algae tanks and scrape lichen off the dock ramp and occasionally get lit off homebrew hooch in the canteen—but at some point they gotta kick you out. A storm banged the island to shit and then it was *we need to evacuate immediately*. Immediately turned into two years 'cause *yeah, we meant the important people and not you slobs*.

I made some friends and watched them leave. I kissed some boys and watched them leave. I met Fox. I had to lock Fox on the other side of a closet door behind my eyes and try not to think of him. Except the closet really was a fish tank all lit up in purple and his face pressed against the glass a lot. Begging me to remember.

The ones who didn't leave, like me, stuck around until the final wave. Twenty-one when they shipped me to New Providence. Jobs pipeline or some shit. Goodbye to that fuckin' gray garbage heap where Julio had died, goodbye to the teeth chewing up my guts when I remembered the nurses in the plastic suits. Just kidding—the teeth followed me even as I chomped on my fingertips, watching Aaru disappear. 'Cause with the long life that NIL/E promised all of us who got plugged in, I would never see Julio again. I'd rip that thing out of the side of my head in a second if that meant diving into the ball pit with him one more time.

I made myself forget about Fox like I hoped he'd forget about me. I kicked off the purple lights in his fish tank.

Then at the halfway house dorm place, with the bunks that the others would clean out when you weren't around, so you had to keep everything you had on you, always, down to the algaebars. Not that I had anything besides a coupla changes of clothes.

At least it was around the corner from a Coral Beef. Two weeks into my stay, I'd started hangin' out by the place. They'd changed the recipe—with the beef shortages and all—but the place still smelled like a spicy grease-bomb, the sidewalk glowing from the pink-and-yellow-cartoon cow-fish sign over the door. Hands in the pockets of my black jeans, in my black T-shirt 'cause the black didn't show the stains and the rips as much, head up and catching the eyes of the people going in and out.

The yellow light from the sign almost looked like sunshine.

"You working?" a guy asked.

He was handsome enough, like the guys in janitorial who I'd help out in the showers, back when, only with more salt than pepper in his beard.

I shrugged. I'd practiced in the dorm bathroom mirror how to scowl to make the muscles at the sides of my jaw stick out. You couldn't look like you wanted the attention too much, or the guys would just brush past you. You had to look bored and somehow busy, like you were waiting for someone.

"I could be," I said.

I followed him into Coral Beef, to the sticky pink tabletops, to the hot smell of fries and seventeen secret stims 'n' spices.

You gotta make the guys you're with feel special. You gotta look at them and bring the heat up through your eyes. It's not enough to look good, 'cause everyone can if they try hard enough. And these kinda games between two people are always about how the other person feels, anyway.

I drummed my fingers on the sticky pink tabletop and popped a few seaweed-dusted fries in my mouth. I knew to lean in when Dean, the salt-and-pepper daddy, talked. I knew to ask him questions, and look him in the eyes so that everyone else but him blurred. Brush his fingers every now 'n' then when we reached for nuggets. Half a bucket down, we kicked the stupid chatting and talked in code. He asked if I worked in entertainment. Let's say freelance, I told him.

"And you're not opposed to working in digital content?" he asked. "With some in-person consulting?"

"I'm game." We had a radio in the algaetank room back in Aaru that we switched on sometimes, dancing in our waders. Not much different than me 'n' Dean-o dancing around what we were really talking about. "In person, though? My wheelhouse."

"Mm."

His eyes swept over me again. You can't look away when that happens, 'cause that'll only make them think you're embarrassed.

"I could show you, if that's part of the interview." Then, when the question mark hit his eyes, I smirked again and popped another fry. "Even if it's not, I'm down."

I led Dean to the bathroom that stank of fake strawberry soap and rust. The Coral Beef bathroom stall doors went down to the floor. They knew what was up. No one just came here for the fries.

Inside one stall, he stuck to the door while I gave him a good view. Pants down to my knees, T-shirt up by my collarbone. I'd known enough to get hard before I'd even offered, with my dick swaying in the air between us, squeezing every muscle I could.

He didn't touch me, but he stared hard enough with his *ohmygod* face that I knew he wanted to.

"Two-week probationary period," Dean said, softer. He tore his eyes up to mine. "Fit in and you won't have to hang outside a Coral Beef."

He didn't touch me once. I shimmied up my pants and dropped my shirt, and he buried his hands in his pockets. Back at the table, I finished the bucket of Cow'N'Cod. And—*Muerte*—the nuggies never tasted so fuckin' good.

TWENTY-SEVEN
DE-FRAGGED

*F*ox. *Fox?* Khadija's voice floats through me like steam off a bowl of noodle soup. *Think we've almost got a lock on him. Keep going, and remem—*

I'm in a million places at once—at a sticky tabletop in Coral Beef, in a ball pit with Julio, hiding in a closet with a statue of a cloaked skeleton wearing a flower crown and holding a scythe, shuddering in the Ankh.

—him outta there because Seth's on the way. The Ankh's mask snaps back into the gold walls like it's retreating from Sig's voice. *The fuck is Flo still babysitting that scrape for? Pull the plug on the Excerpt and haul him out the back hallway, stat. Wipe the logs. What a shitshow.*

Fragmented, free-falling through years and years in the seconds it takes the Ankh to spit me out of Gabe's memories and back into my body. Hands under my arms lug me out of the Ankh. More voices spit in my ears for me to stop screaming.

But Julio. Julio. The name tattooed over Gabe's heart might as well be over mine. I feel the stab of a needle, over and over again. Someone drops me on the carpet in the side study room and leaves me in the dark. I flop onto my back and claw my shirt collar down to see if Julio's name is there. Just bare skin, with my heart pounding against my chest like it's Gabe's dead brother trying to get out.

Already, the memories crack open what I knew about him. The things he saw. The things he did for Julio. How do you keep from flying apart after that? I try to hang on to the fragments. A storm on Aaru, me and Gabe meeting there, somehow. Him leaving me behind, as much as I know he wouldn't do that. The story of Gabe is all twisted and transposed, and every time I try to hear it, I'm shoved behind purple-lit glass walls.

And how did some version of Gabe pulled from my memory even know all this about him that I never did?

Unless he's not just a scrape.

All that matters is that I have the real Gabe back—I *was* him— for a while. I saw the soft parts beyond the shoulders-back swagger that he never showed me before. I got to live in his body, feel his muscles and bones. And now I don't know if I want to *be* him or be with him. Insert > jealusty. I need him so much I want to smash the distance between us and turn us into a Gabe-and-Fox Cow'N'Cod Combo meal and lick the spices and stims off our fingertips. Like I'd drown in him if he'd only let me and I wouldn't even scream as the water filled my lungs.

Maybe that's how I always thought of him.

And we met before that night on the dance floor. When I was in Gabe's Excerpt, I could feel him locking those memories on the other side of a closet door behind his eyes. So how did I forget meeting him, even with my torched brain? He's supposed to be in me too deep.

Well, Past Fox at the movie theater on a date with Gabe is here with another edit. Insert > memory of your brightest observation, Fox the Fixer. *Even with all the bodies he jumped into, maybe the biggest unknown was that when he was himself, he was still a mystery. He'd always be a stranger wearing Gabe's face.*

Sheeny sweat on Gabe's sleeping face in our bedroom where Flo is still keeping watch. She sweeps a cold washcloth across his forehead. The room smells like salty sweat after he housed a Cow'N'Cod Combo bucket. The moon through the window drops a spotlight onto the white bedsheets.

"How's he doing?" I whisper, watching his eyes dance under his closed lids.

"Out of the woods. He drank some water." Her eyes are gentle and blue, her hair a blonde poufy halo in the moonlight. "He needs to sleep for a while. Did you find what you needed to in his memories?"

"I will."

She folds the washcloth in her hands. "What—what is he, Fox?"

"Who."

"Of course. Sorry. Who is he?"

"He can't be just a scrape. He's so much more."

"A scrape pulled from your memories, recovering memories of his own. Remembering who he really was." She presses the washcloth to the side of Gabe's face again. "Like some part of him is defying deletion. Do you know what this could mean?"

She doesn't wait for me to answer. I'm always slow, anyway. "His memories could be the key to solving the virus. Our way to Khadija."

"And whatever it is she's really doing."

"Trust *this* process, too, Fox. What did you see in Inland Ocean City? It was beautiful, sure, but when the nodecast blinked off, we saw it was all pretty lights projected over reality. Is that the kind of world you and Gabe want to live in?"

I wince. "I don't know."

"And the company bombed New Thebes *and* IOC just on the off chance of stopping her. Should we wait for another attack?" She twists the washcloth and a few drops of water darken her lavender scrubs. "They don't care about anything but staying on top. Nothing new there, of course. But this time around, the whole world is caught in the crossfire, with no governments, no armies, no bigger companies to stop them."

My sparkly, mental nodecast over the company falters. And what she's saying makes sense, from what I saw in Gabe's memories, about the chokehold on Mexico, about everyone on Aaru getting noded just so the company could instantly resurrect the grunts who kept the island afloat. Things we never learned in school or anywhere else, not when NIL/E controls the story.

"They're final-deathing us," she continues. "And Khadija? From the start, she's only ever wanted to make us divine. Project Bennu is our way to escape the whole cycle of having no control over our own destinies."

Her thumb traces one of his eyebrows. She looks, for just a second, like Má Flo here to take care of him. I almost want to climb into the bed next to him and let her promises lull me to sleep.

"I want to believe that," I say.

"Then bend like a reed and believe it. *They* did this to Gabe. And think of how many other Gabes there are to other people in New Thebes and IOC. People hurting just like you are now."

"I should tell the others about him. They should see for themselves how different—how special his code is."

"Later. Sig just got word that Seth is on his way in. He'll be here any minute. Something about running off-hours diagnostics on the therapists. They've been off lately, since a new empathy patch a few days back."

I rub a hand over my eyes, hungover from the Ankh. From living as Gabe. I tear my eyes from the upended boats of his eyebrows to the ghost of the moon on the marsh, willing myself to breathe. I tell Flo I've got it from here, and she leaves us alone. I slip into bed beside him and stare at the lines that push between his eyebrows even in sleep. But to see him better, I need distance from the constant pull he has on me.

I wriggle out of bed. Soon bats dive-bombing the canoe racks chirp, laughing at me. I drift over the lawn as the moon cuts through the fog. Over the orchard, kicking fallen apples, and back to the main grounds again. I look up to the manor, and there's only the lamp in my room and the glow of the Ankh Room windows.

I could've helped him.

Maybe I wouldn't have been able to take the weight of losing Julio off him, but we could've shared it. And did we really meet on Aaru? If so, how can I even trust my own memories? And why didn't he tell me?

I harped at him for shutting down. *And what're you hiding?* I begged him in Darius's office, eyes bolted to the fake plant on the table so I wouldn't crumble. He locked his pain behind closet doors, he showed me in the Excerpt. *You gotta hold some things back so you don't cave all the way in.*

Just me and him, now. Actually, edit: There was only ever just me and him. Before was just a distraction.

I'm by the marsh and not there at the same time—miles, years away on a sidewalk that smells of spices and fries.

"You working?" Gabe's voice. I turn and he's not there.

"I sure as fuck am now," I tell the empty air.

J is a shadow in the sunroom when I pass the open doorway on my way back to our room. They hover, eyes down at their Reeder by the Memory Mapping chair.

"J?"

"The whole of your memory is your memorystream," they whisper in their prayer-voice, not looking up. "Watch it flow like a river. Unbroken and eternal, and reaching for the sea. It's been six hundred and fifty-one days since last system hard-reboot. Engage protocols?"

Empathy patch, my ass. J's trapped here, just like we all are, and glitching out.

"Sure, J."

"Requesting admin permissions?"

I squirm at J's blank voice and eyes. "C-can I help you get to bed? Or do you even sleep, or…?"

"Big-time budding?" They frown.

"You bet."

I leave J alone, because what else am I going to do? Up the stairs goes Fox hightailing it back to his foxhole. Back in me and Gabe's room, I sink into bed. Next to Gabe—far enough away that I don't wake him. Lonely in my own skin again. I curl up and hug my knees in close.

TWENTY-EIGHT
FOXTROT

The gauzy curtain by our bed is a fabric disco ball lit up by the sun, all shimmering and gold. I shimmy to the side of the bed and dare to slide one leg to the floor. Wince—did I move too fast? I sneak a glance over at Gabe, who pops open an eye.

"I'm awake." He whacks me with my pillow, grunting. "Stop acting like you're a trick sneaking out."

"It's just, I don't normally go home with someone on the first night." I pitch my voice up higher, innocent, and hunch my shoulders, suddenly the newbie gay he seduced in a bar. I don't even have to try hard, and we slip into our routine, building sketches for each other.

"Yeah, I remember evidence to the contrary, babe-o."

"That's fair. How're you feeling?"

He rubs a hand over his squinty eyes. "Like I'm remembering why I swore off gin."

For a second, the bedsheet wrapped around him is Santa Muerte's starry black cloak in his closet shrine. I blink the memory away. I'd hoped he'd want to talk about what he saw in the Ankh when he woke up. But Gabe offering to talk about his feelings is about as likely as me deciding to deep-throat an exhaust pipe, so there's that.

I'll ask him, I just need to be careful about the whole *I technically jumped into your memories without running it by you* thing. He'll love that.

"I'll grab you some coffee and food. It'll help." I avoid his eyes and drop my gaze to the tattoo over his heart instead.

"I should get up, too. Don't you have to go to Memory Mapping before morning session, 'n' shit?"

"Nah. Let's play hooky again."

"Can we do that?"

"What, are they gonna throw us in detention?"

Seeing him scoot up in bed with a laugh makes me almost giddy. Like I can make up for the crankyface mornings when I grumbled at him for accidentally waking me up when he left bed at the ass-crack of dawn. When he suggested both of us call in sick randomly and I shrugged it off with an excuse about being too busy.

Besides. Not like I'm buttering him up, but Flo did remind me of something. *He has your editing skills, if you want him to use them. It's just a matter of asking him.*

"True," he says. "Yeah, grab some food. None of those scrambled eggs. They're gross. All the food here is gross."

"Really? I thought you'd dig Seth's 'nourish the mind, nourish the body' shtick."

"The food here tastes like powder. Fake."

"I'll order up something special from the chef."

"I'd sell my fuckin' soul for some pancakes right now."

"No guarantees. Also, you should take it easy with the food today. Just wait for the memory tremors."

"The fuck is that?"

"I don't wanna ruin the surprise."

I'm Mayor Fox again down the hallways, tossing out good mornings and smiles. No pancakes in the dining room, as much as I offer a therapist my soul for a stack. She brushes me off, not getting the joke. I fill up a couple of bowls of fruit and balance them on a tray with two mugs of coffee and swing back to the bedroom. Not before stopping somewhere else first.

I don't know if it's because he planted the idea in my head, but the pineapples in the breakfast-in-bed fruit salad really do taste like pineapple perfume sprayed on powder. After we clear away the plates I grab the new Reeder Sig gave me for Gabe—with a copy of the virus code on it—off the bed.

"You want to see the big code problem that's got us all stumped?" I waggle the Reeder. "I could use your eyes."

Gabe flips his mouth into an upside-down U, his fingers tinkling invisible piano keys. His problem-solving tell I've seen a million times. Whatever echo of my own editing addiction or passion—or whatever you want to call it—tugs at him, I know. I won't need to admin mode him.

And a little shadow of his voice laughs in my head. *Here I was, thinking you were all "I'm never going to do that."*

"I'm pretty curious about what actually killed me." He smirks. "And I would be into topping you in something you're supposed to be king of."

"We can talk topping later. First up." I tap both of his shoulders with the Reeder, knighting him. "Welcome to the Scribe club."

Our base of operations is the bistro table by the window, where we sit across from each other. Gabe unscrolls his Reeder screen like he's used it every day of his life and pops open the virus code. I chew the inside of my lip, cautious, as I watch his eyes gobble up the code.

"You tried the usual stuff to snoop out ciphers and stashed messages?" he asks, fingers drumming his chin. "Just peeking, some lines at the top are giving me polymorphic base-class willies. You tried the Amphipolis Method, no-brainer?"

"Obviously," I deadpan.

"Yeah, Foxy, I know your editing dick is so big 'n' huge." He eye-rolls so hard that his whole head swings back. Get him an acting award, please. "Just sayin', 'cause not everyone would've seen."

I want to kiss the line between his eyebrows that squinting at the screen is kicking up. Minou mentioned that she hadn't even gotten past the front door of the haunted house of the virus, and Chengmei wasn't far ahead of her. And here Gabe is already seeing things in the code that none of the ham-fisted editors at the office would've. I laugh instead and tell him, *bring it, bitch. Let's dive in.* And he heads-downs at his Reeder screen, game-faced like I just sprung a surprise race on him and sprinted away.

Our fingers scurry over the keys like cat claws on the wood floor as we scry for meaning in the code. Out of the scrying pan and into the fire. Gabe keeps the voices and the flashes away, somehow, with me calmer at his side. We fall into a sentence-finishing shorthand like we've been working together for years. *Hey, line ninety-seven, you see the void pointer there?* I get the idea that chunks of code hint at scenes, and we spend hours dive-bombing through layers, setting-snooping, and cutting and pasting possible scenes into separate coding windows.

"Did you try separating the code by color?" He looks up at me.

The light on our fabric disco ball curtain is the burnt caramel of late afternoon, somehow. I tear my gaze off the curtain and back at my Reeder, which is just a black screen with white text like it's always been. If I squeeze my eyes hard enough and try to remember the gray basement editing lab where Nina the Neuron invited Greg into the *sizzling storytelling world of editing*, I can almost see colors through the code. Just thin threads in a tapestry, until my eyes sharpen again, and the colors fade away.

"You get going on that." No way I'm admitting he's seeing something I'm not. Both because I'm not letting him win this thing that wasn't supposed to be a competition and now suddenly is, and because I don't know what my code color-blindness means. "I'll stick with the setting stuff."

"Bingo."

More keystrokes that *plink* like grains of sand in an hourglass, and sometime later Gabe wanders off to grab us more coffee and some sandwiches. When my scavenger hunt partner is gone, it's like I can still hear his voice in the room, poking me. *Look at him*, he teases. *You finally found your missing half. Someone who gets all hard about sensory injections and flashback mechanics over candlelit dinners, when I'd be bored outta my mind.*

I zip my Reeder screen closed. But his voice, his laughing eyes, stay with me as Gabe circles back with a tray.

The doubt starts as a coldness in my fingertips that wants to seep up and frost over the rest of me. Gabe chomps a sandwich between Reeder keystrokes. And who is he, really? Who are either of us?

"We must've met on Aaru," I tell him. "We were there at the same time."

"Yeah, probs," he says through a mouthful of sliced turkey. His meat-flecked teeth try to shut me behind glass walls.

"Why did I forget? Why did I think we met at that bar?"

"You probably got your memory sliced up. Hey, what're you seein' at line—"

"And why didn't you tell me about Julio?" His eyes hit me, confused, and I know I have to fess up or he'll dodge the truth all day long. "About how you lost him on Aaru. I went into your Memory Excerpt, and—"

"Wait, you *went* into my memory?" I can already see the closet doors in his head slamming shut, with how his eyes narrow. "Without even asking me?"

"Seth said you-you're a therapeutic tool, and—"

"Fuck what Seth said. That's how you wanna treat me?"

You can squash this, Past Fox whispers in my ear. *Admin mode: Don't be pissed at me. And would it kill you to smile?*

"No, I—"

"Jesus, just when I thought you'd actually changed." He slams against the backrest of his chair. "I guess I was stupid. No one actually changes. I didn't ask to be here, Fox. I didn't ask for them to—for them to make me. Seth told you I'm a tool. But it's up to you to decide if you treat me like one. Or like a fuckin' person you're supposed to love."

"I *did* change. I'm not that guy anymore at the bar, trying to let everyone know I owned you. Th-there's something special about your code I've never seen before. An-and that's why I went in."

"Uh-huh."

We're both sucked free of words for a while. Gabe stabs the crust of one of our sandwiches. I just watch his hands, burning like I'm on the marsh and panic-rowing for hours.

"I wish you'd told me about Julio. I wish I could've helped, somehow."

"I didn't want help."

"Husbands help each other."

When his eyes meet mine, they're softer, like the closet door is open just a crack. "I didn't want to talk about it. Think about it. I didn't wanna connect you to that awful shit."

"I get it. But we need to show up for each other for the awful shit." This dose of relationship wisdom would make even Darius cringe. But I still search Gabe's eyes, hoping the words will sink in. "And we met on Aaru, right? What happened?"

"I pushed you away. I don't really remember what else." He sighs and zips his Reeder screen closed, like he realizes just how much he hates being behind a desk.

"I'm sorry. I should've asked before jumping into your Excerpt. Tha-that was some old-me shit. I'm better than that now."

"Say that all you want. Now you gotta show it."

"I know. But I'm serious about your code. It looked a-alive. It got me thinking about that night at the carnival, honestly. When you asked me what code is and I told you it's just symbols and nothing else. I think you're proof that I was wrong."

"Get a loada that." Gabe laughs. The razor slips back into his smile. I preferred him angry. "I'm special when it means I shouldn't be pissed at you. Of course."

"That's not what I meant."

His chair scraping over the wood floor makes my teeth ache. Fuck. I'm doing this all wrong. He presses his palms to the table and rises slowly to his feet, his smile cutting deeper.

"I'm so bored already." He flicks his hands at the Reeders, the sandwich plates and coffee cups of our command center. "This isn't me, anyway. I'm goin' for a walk."

I have to swallow against the acid wave in my gut, with my body trying to remind me how pissed I am. I let the wave burn over me while Gabe slings his shoulders back and breezes out of the room. I almost stop him before he gets to the door so we can keep hashing this out. It'd be so easy. I grit my teeth and bite back the *admin mode* so it doesn't fly out of my mouth.

———

A cheery therapist in peach scrubs shoves a Reeder at me once I'm off the stairs from my bedroom, on my way to escape the manor. The question on the twitching display doesn't make sense.

```
To whom shall I announce you?
a.  To her, whose ceiling is fire
b.  Firewall reset in progress
c.  Whose walls are sacred cobras
d.  Whose house-floor is the flood
```

I jab at the screen just to get her out of my face. I'm two steps toward the door to the lawn before another therapist stops me with a hand to my chest. Another screen.

```
Purge parameters?
a.  You shall not catch me in this net of yours
b.  In which you catch the inert ones
c.  You shall not trap me in this trap
d.  In which you trap the wanderers
```

The static-smeared screen, and the garbage poetry, and the line of more therapists with more Reeders are all going to drive me right into Greg crazy town. Beyond the open sunroom door, Seth and Sig frown at their Reeders by an immobile J. Flo— outside, leading what looks like all of the residents through a yoga session—said something about off-hours diagnostics on the therapists last night. She must be trying to keep the others away from the widening cracks in the sim. And who else knows we're in a sim? What if word got out to everyone?

Khadija's voice fills the room like perfume. *Seriously, though, don't get deleted.*

Another screen: *I sleep and I am reborn. Renewed and rejuvenated each day. Resetting security parameters.* I shove it away and plow through the doors.

My feet fall on the half-worn trails of the grounds, and over the lawn and by the shore, where my hands graze the reeds. Out to the orchard, where I chuck apples against the rock wall and watch them explode in wet chunks.

I wander for hours, stopping to lie in the grass, and then skip stones across the marsh. I stumble back to the manor for dinnertime, where the therapists must be back in their invisible loops with the way they offer smiles instead of screens. I spot Gabe and Stash—I don't need to see his purple mustache to recognize the bald back of his head—talking at a corner table alone over empty plates. Gabe's leaned back, arms crossed and smirking, while Stash stabs the air. Hoooo boy. That can't be good. Each finger-poke jabs my skin.

Gabe must not see me yet since I'm lingering by the bus tables. I'll give him space. I'm about to grab a plate and hide in our room when his voice cuts through the quiet conversations and plate-scraping of the others.

"Hey," he announces to the room, standing. "Me 'n' Stash want ice cream."

Stash spins in his chair to look out over the dining room, his purple mustache twitching with his cartoon-villain smile.

"Ice cream for everyone," he corrects Gabe.

"Hell yeah," Gabe agrees. "Everyone!"

Therapists mumble to each other. Two of them amble to Gabe—as I slink closer to the wall, face burning—and I'm sure they explain how ice cream is a big no-no for Seth. Gabe shrugs them off.

"If this whole place is a sim, we should be able to eat whatever the fuck we want."

Gabe's voice ratchets louder now. I can feel it in my eyes. By me, Octavio—with his paint-wilting breath—mumbles, *wait, what did he say?*

"It's not like you gotta make a grocery run." He cups his hands around his mouth, yelling for Seth now, wherever he's hiding. "Just code us some fuckin' ice cream."

More chatter. Gabe eggs the other residents on, pounding on the table, leading the whole dining room in a chant of *ice cream! Ice cream!* Like we're kids at summer camp rising up against the counselors. Therapists run out of the room while others try to shush residents. Inyene winds up and throws a plate against the wall.

I can almost see Seth running in here to admin mode Gabe, just like he did to J when Chengmei flipped out. Or to delete us all.

Gabe catches my eye from across the room and winks.

Suddenly, Flo zips in with a tub of ice cream, flashing her best *oh you crazy kids* smile. Therapists flow behind her and clear away the dish-bussing station. More therapists with more tubs of ice cream and stacks of plates and candy dishes—a whole procession cheered on by all the residents laughing and whooping—and they set out a kid's birthday-party-sundae spread. Flo laughs and flaps her hands to the floor, trying to get us all to chill. Seth brings up the tail of the ice-cream-delivery line, brandishing two cans of whipped cream like a game-show assistant.

"We certainly appreciate your childlike excitement," he calls out. "We lose much of it as we grow older. Thanks, Gabriel, for the reminder."

His words are airy as whipped cream. But I'm close enough to see the edge in his eyes. Like he's trying to calculate if bringing Gabe here was a mistake, scrape or not. Because even something based on a single memory of him is not going to be penned in like an animal.

"You bet," Gabe sings out.

Seth tells us all to have fun and then turns on his heels and marches away. Residents clatter into a line and scoop ice cream into bowls. Candies rattle against porcelain. Gabe doesn't even get in line. The leader makes sure his underlings are fed first, I guess. I smell hot fudge and can almost taste the sticky sweetness while I'm glued to the wall. Trying to blink past an ice-cream headache, at Seth caving in when he could've just controlled Gabe and wrestled the crowd back with two words.

I wait for the line to fizzle out before I make my own sundae. Smiles on all the residents' faces, globbed together in groups, sugar-buzzed with fudge-coated lips. At a table with three other yellow bracelets, Flo spoons ice cream into Chengmei's mouth, who claps at the sweetness. I'm glad she looks happy, at least. I haven't seen Minou in days. I work up the balls to look at Gabe— still in the corner with Stash—and he waves me over. He's all smiles when I slip into the chair beside him.

I don't know if this is one of those *we're not going to fight in front of someone else* situations. Or if he really has forgiven me already. What Gabe am I getting, the one who's pissed or the happy ice-cream revolutionary?

And these kinda games between two people are always about how the other person feels, anyway, Gabe said in his memory.

"Guy's a riot." Stash thumbs at Gabe. "What the hell does he see in you?"

And what the hell could you possibly have to say to each other, I want to ask, especially after Stash called you a commercial? Except Greg has to chime in, *hey, pal, that sounds a little Past Fox-y, and take it from me and let's squash that anger, yeah?*

Gabe always wins over everyone, anyway. His razor-smile draws a fresh line of blood.

"I had no clue you were so passionate about ice cream," I tell him, sweet like the candied cherry that's bleeding red all over my bowl. I fall back into our Gabe-and-Fox foxtrot. It's easy once I remember that he's always the one to lead.

"It's never about ice cream," Gabe says. He drapes a lazy hand over my upper thigh, his pinkie lightly grazing my balls. I shiver over the sweetness. "It's about sendin' a big message that we're not gonna do whatever they tell us anymore."

Call that a threat to me. I don't know. We'll hash out the whole *I dropped into your memories* thing when he's ready. If he's ready. If he thinks I didn't change from Past Fox, maybe he'll always be Past Gabe who shuts me out. Insert > wall. Insert > disarming dick joke.

He steals a single chocolate candy from my bowl and pops it into his mouth, the sugar coating crunching between his teeth.

TWENTY-NINE
GRAVE ROBBERS

Gabe disappears after dinner. I know better than to ask where he's going.

Flo gathers the rest of the residents in the music room for another movie night, while I hide, since I don't feel much like hearing more stories. And who do I have here, really? Gabe's gone. Stash has always hated me. Chengmei doesn't even know who she is. Flo's busy actually doing her job. I should check on Minou and talk to her about Gabe and the virus. If she'll want to talk. Maybe she could share another story with me about how she's screwed up worse than I have.

Needy Fox, always whining for someone else, I guess.

The floor creaks beneath my feet in the dim hallways on the way to her room. I knock on the door and call her name. A slam against the door jolts me out of my skin. Another one—*bam*—like a body pummeling the wall. I shove open the door, wild-eyed and searching for a bloody body. All I see is Minou in the center of her room, pink-faced like she was crying, fists bunched at her sides. My eyes drop to the floor, where her Reeder knocks against an open leather-backed notebook, covered in her handwriting just like the pages on her walls.

Before I can even ask her if she's alright, she kicks the Reeder. It skims my leg as it skitters into the corner between the open door and the wall.

"It's all garbage," she spits through gritted teeth.

"You alright? Should I get Flo, or—"

"Everything. The virus. The mission. Fucking trash."

A flashlight beam sweeps across the window behind her. She must see it, too, in the mirror over her bureau. She wobbles to her window. When she doesn't say anything—only lifting her fingers to her lips—the Excerpts in my head start whispering. *And did you hear that? Motorboats? Maybe you wanna split?*

"Meen?"

I follow her to the window that faces the back of the manor and the marsh. Flashlight beams over the tree branches and sweeping over the reeds. No, not flashlights. Headlamps from a group of people, crouching low as they slink off a motorboat onto the shore. Another full boat behind them, and another—a boat parade far down the marsh. The ones already ashore sweep red beams from the tips of the black tubes in their hands over the grass.

Not tubes, bud, Greg reminds me. *What to do when the fox mauls the chickens?*

"What the hell's with all the boats?" Minou asks.

As soon as I hear the screams from downstairs, I run.

Fuckfuckfuck. No time. I tear into the hallway with Minou close behind. Gabe's not in our room. I sprint down the hall, pounding doors and yelling after him. Doors fly open. I flash to piles of rubble again, and bloody shapes in broken streets. *Nonono.* The bullet fire of my pulse cuts the signals between my brain and my body. I scramble down the stairs, nearly flailing over my own feet.

Through the dining-room windows, I see invaders in black body armor holding black Reeder-looking gun-tubes, spreading up from the shore like a disease.

Gabe breaks away from the line of residents and therapists staring out the dining-room windows and bolts to my side. "What the fuck is going—"

"We're here for Fox and the editors," erupts a voice from a bullhorn outside. "This doesn't need to be hard."

"Admin mode, all staff," Seth snaps from the cluster by the windows. "Prioritize resident safety. Enhanced force authorized."

Gabe grabs my hand. The closest therapist to the back door rips it open—wood splintering, residents screaming, Seth yelling for everyone to run to the music room. Three more therapists stampede past us, brandishing Reeders, joining a line at the back door. What the hell are those things gonna do to the boats, air-traffic-controller them to shore?

Nothing makes sense. Therapists on the lawn flick their wrists and gold bursts of symbols blast from their Reeders. One of the blasts knocks the nearest soldier off their feet. Green bolts of light spark from the tips of the black gun-tubes in the invaders' hands. I can feel the sparks in the air like a sickness, like cold, wet breath on the back of my neck.

"We gotta make a run for it, out the side door," Gabe barks. I barely hear him over the screams.

"You think we're gonna outrun guns?" Minou snaps.

Flash. A green bolt hits one of the therapists, who drops to her knees and dissolves into static. Drifting like ash on the wind. A green blast hits one of the trees at the water's edge, and the tree shimmers away, leaving a gaping black hole in its place.

That jolts me back into myself. Gabe yanks my hand and the three of us bolt across the ground floor—*you better bloody well stop them*, orders the bullhorn voice—and he kicks open the greenhouse door. We sprint over the grass. Each time my feet strike the ground, the rattle shudders through my bones. I bend through the pain, sucking in white-hot air, and crank up the pace. I'm close enough to Minou to hear her ragged breaths. Don't look back, don't look—

Two soldiers sprint after us down the lawn, maybe a hundred feet back. Two therapists behind them. One of the soldiers blasts with a gun-tube and—*zip! pop!*—a black hole of nothingness at my side. I cover my head and scramble away—stumble, foot-flail, almost careening over. One of the therapists vaults into the air and tackles one of the black-armored goons to the ground. *Zip! Pop!* Another black hole.

A blast tears the ground to the right—so close that it sucks the air from my lungs—inches from Minou.

The blast missed, but it slowed us enough that we're already dead, I know. Gabe's grip tightens on my hand.

Ten feet behind us, the soldier is a black watercolor blur. They plant their feet and fire.

Gabe twirls away and I'm tethered to him—always, always—with him yanking me aside.

In the eternity before the blast hits, I'm Greg again, back in the office building with Fatima in her cubicle. And she's crying. She's crying for herself because this stranger is pointing a gun at her and all she wants to do is be home with her wife and her cat. The green blast of sickness hits Minou.

What kills me the most is the panic that ripples neon-green over her face. How she knows—and I can see it in her eyes, like moon-white code—that she might've tried to off herself here before and only ended up back in the Ankh, but this blast of nothingness is something you don't come back from.

She dissolves like a gust of sand. I scream in that instant, waiting for my own blast.

One of the therapists tackles the remaining soldier to the ground, both of them wriggling and screaming. J crests the hill ahead of us and all I want to do is cry, begging for one of their cheery *you betcha*s. Because that blast should've been for me.

Another soldier tops the hill—and why is Flo with them now?—and squats to the soldier that's pinned to the ground by a therapist. "I meant *stop* as in *immobilize*, you knobber," they yell. "We need the fucking editors in one piece."

A few steps closer and I see J is not my J, of course. Blank eyes. *Admin mode.* Two soldiers at their side. J's fingers dance across their Reeder. They raise their hands—I'm cemented to the ground and at least I'll die with Gabe's name on my lips—and hit me and Gabe with a round of gold code-bullets.

Invisible, icy hands claw over my whole body, freezing me in place.

I'm screaming behind my eyes—for Minou and how I'm next—but my legs don't listen. I can't move. My body is a coffin, and as much as I pound against the lid, it won't open. Gabe's gold-ringed eyes flash to me from his paralyzed face.

"What do we do with this one?" one of the soldiers asks, wagging his gun at Gabe.

"We need him," Flo says. "Bring him along. Careful, please."

"You heard the lady." Even with my frozen brain, I remember Poppy's voice and how she told me back in IOC that she'd find me.

J has to pry open our frozen hands to separate us.

Buried alive in my own body and tossed over J's shoulder as we march back to the manor, I'm starting to remember more, now that I can't fight. Now that all I can do is let the past roll over me.

I've been body-numb and screamy-brained like this before. Too many times. I'd scrounged up one of the node-to-Reeder linkup cables that were all over Aaru and plunked some sedation code right into my live memorystream. And then held my breath and waited for the code to wash over and let me sleep a while.

People will get all high-and-mighty later about back-alley edits in places without apricot salt scrubs and deep-moisture foot masks. They'll call these underground edits *mipping*. We called it just trying to stay alive.

The editors carved a bunch of mazes and dead-end hallways into the bedrock of my brain. *Yeah, you really saw some shit, huh?* Insert > adopted off Aaru. Insert > well-meaning, distant parents. *Hey, look, I added some Adolescent Achiever memory templates in there, free of charge. Just don't mention it to the boss, right? Har. I mean, seeing how we're swapping out your pain and depth and leaving you a dotted line of yourself and all.*

The symbols hacked into the maze walls are spells and stories. *Guarding against the loss of the heart. To escape the slaughter-place.* Animal-headed people, people-headed animals. Thrones and scales weighing hearts, painted in pain-code blacks and burning reds. *O my heart of my mother! O my heart of my different forms! Do not stand up as a witness against me.* The mazes and the dead ends are to keep out the robbers and to stop me from going too deep. I'm wandering around now as I eye the torch in my hand—even as J strides over the lawn with me bouncing on their shoulder—and wasn't I already down this hallway? Another stone wall. Fuck. The flame flickers. I'm running out of air but whatever's in this tomb must be close.

One of the figures on the walls—a crowned woman in white on a throne—clocks me with bored eyes.

Yeah, but it's not exactly the treasure you think it is, babycakes.

Flash.

J lugs me up the back lawn. People swarm everywhere, trickling out of boats and wandering the grass, weaving through stunned residents and therapists. No more bullets and blasts. Flo's at my side. I can feel her warm hand on the middle of my back.

"And this was supposed to be an extraction?" She flicks her hands at the groups of huddled residents, the therapists trying to soothe them. "Look what you've done."

"Tell that to the templates that were shooting at us," Poppy grumbles.

"You couldn't have found a gentler way to—"

"Listen, lady, we couldn't right well ask nicely for NIL/E to let us in. It took us forever to hack into the therapist templates and open a back door. And we needed the jump on them. Besides, I thought this was a mipper rehab. Why was security so hot?"

Flo pauses. "We've had resident... incidents before. In the early days, when treatments weren't as kind."

"Right." Poppy snorts. "Kind."

"Just who are all these people?"

"Refugees from IOC, and most of the SoCalia ring. Things are getting real dodgy on the outside. The IOC attack was the start. It'll be all-out war unless Khadija shows herself. And she won't, she—"

"We don't have the bandwidth to support this many consciousnesses in the sim. It could trigger system-wide lags, draw-time errors..."

"I suggest you find a way, yeah? Now that we handed you the bloody keys."

Flash.

After he graduated the Preparedness Programming and right before he got his permanent work assignment with the other early wave of kids to Aaru, the company installed their nodes. The next day Khadija saw him in the Delta canteen where they'd been meeting up for nearly a year, the skin around the silver nub behind his ear still numb. She said something about needing to pull up his first memory to make sure everything had saved right since none of the caregivers really knew what they were doing when it came to memory stuff.

She pulled up a scene on her Reeder and switched over to first-person playback.

The screen filled with blue. The ocean? No, the blue carpet in the place that used to be his home. When he looked down between his doughy bare feet, the carpet was the blue of the ocean. The ocean being the thing on the TV that the cartoon animals with the big eyes swam in, which looked something like his bathwater when Amma washed him with the blue bubble-y soap.

The carpet looked more like the ocean when he spun and the floor bobbed all around him. When he toppled over and landed on his knees, he stopped—scrunching his eyes and wondering if he should scream. Was it worth it? Amma was busy cooking not far away. In their tiny house, no one was ever far away. Even the screams from the neighbors and slamming doors sounded right behind you. Amma was cooking so that meant if he screamed she'd stop, and it would take longer for whatever was in the pan to get to his belly. He didn't scream, and even still, Amma scooped him up.

"Shazad," she cooed. "Wiggle-bug."

Here, Khadija stabbed at her Reeder, pausing the playback of the memory on the screen years after Fox lived that memory.

I lived it.

See, now you're getting it, Khadija says in my head.

The playback was a blur—following my eyes on my flight up into my mom's arms—of that blue carpet and the tiny electric stove in the background. Little bubbles of text crowded the screen. One bubble sprouting in a straight line from the carpet asked, *search for similar products?* A bubble by the pan asked, *search for recipe "karahi gosht?"* Another, from a small bowl by the stove, *add garam masala to shopping list?*

Khadija frowned and said something about the text bubbles looking too *post-apocalyptic heads-up display* chic. She'd delete them. She just somehow knew everything.

I had to keep my eyes on the bracelets stacked up her wrists. The caregivers had buzzed everyone's hair off after the latest lice outbreak. Khadija was always dying her hair or painting her lips with stuff she'd scrounge up from the kitchen, like powdered drink mix. This week, her hair was beet-juice ruby.

Not a lot of color on Aaru. Even the water looked gray. Not Khadija. She was color, and gooey honey smiles, and bowls of broth. She was everything.

Some part of me misses Amma—my real mom, not the woman with the always glazed-over eyes who let me live with her for a few years after Aaru—but it's a dull ache hitting different parts of my body. My cheek on her bare shoulder. Her fingers in my hair. A warmth that if I cram my eyes closed, I can try to bring back a little bit of.

But how do you really miss someone you don't even know?

"Shazad's your name." Khadija asked, "Did you remember that?"

"N-n-n—" I had to stomp under the table to free the word, clamming up again when I'd been so good about talking lately, especially those last few months. "No. That's not me."

I never saw the ocean in real life until the ship that took me and Ammi to Aaru, stopping for weeks to pick up others. Amma started coughing before we got to the docks. Clammy skin. Her arms around me were so weak that I had to grab ahold of her neck and hang on. Hang on. Until someone with a plastic bubble around their head lifted me away. Said they'd get me medicine, and back to her.

I remember she reached for me. *Freeze the playback there, yeah*. Amma's wobbly arms halfway to me, her dry, cracked lips open. Brown eyes ringed with dark shadows—relief, maybe?—and her arms fell. Too hard to keep them up.

The rest came in pieces at night, years later. Needles in a room with other bubble-heads, one of them asking me what my name was. *Sh-sh-sh*. All I could stutter. Words gone, breath gone. Amma gone. Tired bubble-heads saying something about how *echo's full, he'll have to go to foxtrot*. Then one of them brought me to a fenced place outside with a slide, swing set, and a seesaw that the other kids—so many of them—tried to launch each other off. Beyond the fence, seaweed clumped at the concrete shore.

I stared out at the water. All I could think was that the water wasn't the shining blue of the cartoons. Wasn't the streaky-blue water of the bath.

———

POP QUIZ

Which of these statements are true?

a. Maybe Aset didn't really think things through when she decided to kill death.
b. Aaru was never supposed to be a permanent settlement.
c. Aaru was a gift to humanity from Aset, and may the voyagers on the sacred barges on the rivers of memory sing out her ten thousand names as for long as this earth flowers.
d. All of the above.

Into the Ankh Room. The soldier holding Gabe props him against one of the bookshelves like he's a rolled-up carpet. We lock eyes as two trapped corpses.

J lowers me into the gold coffin.

"You have another one of those, yeah?" Poppy asks. "We got a shiny new deep-memory linked Excerpt, smuggled in through the ring." Poppy tosses a Reeder to Sig. "Debugged by boss lady herself, I reckon."

"Linked Ankh sessions are too unstable." Sig's voice. "Dangerous, even, given the fragility of their—"

"You can't just come in here and tell us what Excerpts to run," Flo huffs. "We have protocols and timelines, and Fox is showing wonderful progress on his own."

"Right, well, Project Bennu'll mean sweet bollocks if most of humanity's final-deathed to hell. Bugger your timelines. Plug them in."

"Does anyone have eyes on Stash and Minou?" Flo asks. "They've made such progress, and we can't have this whole mess getting in the way of…"

I hear whispers. Mumbles. I can't make out whether someone tells Flo about how Minou dissolved into sand and drifted into the air. I can feel the particles of her cutting through me. I can't cry out. A door opens and I hear something heavy being wheeled in. I strain so hard against my paralyzed bones that a gurgle spills from my lips. A therapist carts another Ankh over on a rolling dolly and it *thunk*s to the carpet next to me.

"This is a heroic dose," Sig says. "I'm not sure they're ready."

The soldier drops Gabe into the other Ankh. I gurgle again with how they're tossing him around.

"No choice," Poppy answers for Flo.

A scene spins in the air above the Ankh. A little playground on blue-painted concrete by a dock. Ships that look like giant, rusted-over bath toys, and the open ocean beyond.

Flo just sighs.

Wait. Wait. I'm screaming in my head, even as the mask of the Ankh snaps over my eyes. With no one in here but voices from the Excerpts to hear.

THIRTY
BIRDS

Me and Gabe are at the docks of Aaru, somehow, faces up to the sky, where seabirds swoop and scream. A wave konks into our backs and we stumble, grabbing each other so we don't fall over.

Glass walls spread out like curving, clear wings on either side of the docks. Up ahead, a little playground on the blue-painted concrete, with maybe a dozen kids waiting for turns on the swing set and poking at things on the ground. One small kid—five, maybe—alone, squatting with his back against the glass wall and facing the others.

"I'd recognize those big sad eyes anywhere." Gabe points. "Baby Foxy. I can't believe you were ever that small."

The salt-smell and the quiet of the place locks my knees. I might as well still be stuck in my frozen body. "Are you okay?"

He doesn't have time to answer. Another wave knocks into our backs, and we're launched up the ramp, slamming into each other, surging toward Baby Fox.

A squeeze, a rush—the whole world sneezing—and then the glass walls between him and me shatter. We're the same. One consciousness, one heart, one mind, squatting against the glass wall, eyes out over the group of kids. Waiting and watching.

———

My scream scraped across the broken body of the bird on the painted concrete until one of the caregivers bolted over. I didn't have the words, yet, to ask the caregiver with her big watery eyes what was wrong. The glass walls kept out the waves and let me see out over the dark water that seemed to stretch to forever, but the problem was that birds conked into the walls.

The caregiver knelt down, cooing at me. She scooped up the bird and rubbed its chest and head until the bird blinked and bounced out of her hands.

"That happens sometimes," she said. "You'll get used to it."

The bird bobbled on unsteady legs before flailing off into the air.

I tried the rubbing trick to wake up birds for years. Especially when I was alone, which was most of the time. Alone and waiting. Waiting for my turn in line at the canteen that smelled of instant coffee and kelp stew. Waiting for Preparedness Programming—the training on coding basics and how to work the protein lines—to be over. The caregivers taught short units on art and history, sometimes—*humanities to combat the inhumanities*, one cracked early on, though I didn't get the joke. The caregivers were big on ancient Egypt because of Aset and all, telling us how the Egyptians colonized no lands. And how the world's evils could be traced back to colonization. And here we are in Aaru, named after the Egyptian paradise, to do better.

For a while, me and the other kids from that first refugee wave invited each other to sleepovers in our dorm bunks after games of freeze-tag on the playground. When I figured out that maybe I wanted to kiss and hug some of the boys was when they turned on me. Like they held some secret meeting and decided I was creepy instead of quiet, that my stutter meant I was dumb and not someone who just needed a little more patience, like the caregivers said. So I learned to be invisible, slipping in and out of the shadows, skimming walls. I could take being alone, just me and the birds.

Sometimes the birds didn't wake up, and I tucked them into extra-large krill cans and launched them off the cement beach. Which—yeah, I can see now—carrying dead birds around didn't exactly help the creep-o vibe.

I met Khadija one night after I'd picked up an extra protein-line shift, before I got my node installed. Well, met her for real since we'd been in the same coding-basics class until she'd graduated. She'd smiled at me sometimes. I'd missed dinner in the Foxtrot neighborhood canteen, so I lugged my aching bones to Delta with the rest of the third-shift zombies. Grown-ups, mostly, working the Body Gardens and algae tanks. I was somewhere in between: Not the stutter-y kid with too-big eyes. In the mirror in the dorm bathroom in the mornings, bones stuck out in weird places, and hair sprouted at the middle of my chest.

The walls of the canteen in Delta were the same corrugated steel as everywhere else, though covered in places by tapestries, hanging beaded curtains, and dart boards. A few bedsheets draped across the ceiling, rounding out the hard beams of the overhead lights. The noise of the crowd—fifty, at least, clumped in groups at a dozen metal tables—rolled over me like a rainstorm. The other islanders in their gray sweats laughing over dice games on the floor, or zipping darts across the room, with funky-smelling spliffs at the corners of their lips. Their eyes on me cranked up my heart. Tossed sandbags on my shoulders. I plodded to the line that trailed from three giant pots on a table by the kitchen, ladled noodle soup into a metal bowl, and faced the crowd again.

Craaaaaap. Where to sit? A barking laugh cracked my ears from a circle of people on the floor in one corner, leaning back against the wall or propped on giant bags of rice. They passed around a thing that looked like a silver pen with a wire dangling off one end. One of them plugged the wire into the memory node behind their left ear. Beaming their giant full-moon eyes through me, or up at the ceiling. Memory dipping, Khadija would tell me later. Mippers off mipping. Dropping blissy code right into their live memorystreams, even if that meant maybe scrambling their brains.

My feet stuttered and I bumbled into a folding paper screen off to the side by the doorway to the kitchen. Without even looking up from the chunk of code on her Reeder at the small metal table, Khadija propped up the falling screen with one hand. I was maybe sixteen then, and she looked a few years older than me, though it was tough to tell because the caregivers guessed all our ages based on our teeth. Each of her fingernails was painted the yellow-orange of powdered eggs. Her lips, too. Almost as loud as her bright pink buzzed hair.

"Did you not see the sign?" she asked.

FUCK OFF was written on a paper plate in black marker and taped to the screen. Pretty soon I'd know that the sign counted for everyone else but me.

"S-s-sorry."

Shitshit, I'd said that out loud and had to slash one more word off my daily count. Twenty words a day that I gave myself at first— years ago, when the caregivers taught us about rationing since we all had to cut dinners in half for a while because furycanes had delayed the supply ship—and now I was down to fifteen. Staying quiet meant no one noticed my stutter as much. Stares mostly slipped past me, which I was fine with.

Khadija looked up, her frown softening. "You're cool. I thought you were one of the others." She looked at my bowl, up to my eyes again, then pulled out a chair with her foot.

My pulse *thunka-thunk*ed at the sides of my throat. I plopped down in the chair, broth sloshing into my lap. My eyes gobbled the symbols dancing across her Reeder. Colors seemed to rise out of the code. The smell of onion-y chicken soup and the warm funk of bodies. The rain-sounds of dice clattering against a metal table. An argument over a dart game.

"Y-you're coding what's happening around us?" I asked. A lot of words but I had to know.

Khadija smirked. "You can read code that fast?"

I could code almost faster than I read. One perk of no one talking to me in class was that I actually paid attention. "Y-yeah."

"You got your Reeder?"

"Y-y-y—" I had to bite the inside of my cheek just to get the word out. Stutters never counted against my ration. "Yeah."

"Try to keep up."

I didn't touch my bowl of noodles at all that night. We coded together, barely speaking and I even had a couple of words left, until sunrise torched the rainbow tapestries of the canteen.

Khadija started with coding assignments that felt like jokes the next night, when I crept out of my bunk to meet her. Code a glass of water. Code a blade of grass. Code a sneeze. And I'd spend hours stringing together dozens of lines—sure, I'd never seen a blade of grass outside of the movies the caregivers sometimes played in the canteen—until I could practically feel the pokey-poke of the grass against my finger.

She didn't even live in the Delta neighborhood and wasn't technically supposed to be there. But she could pretty much do whatever she wanted, I soon learned. Caregivers and cooks slipped her extra bowls of soup, and beet juice and drink powder for her hair dye. I figured out why when one of the caregivers lugged a screaming guy into the canteen and practically dropped him at Khadija's feet. Full-moon eyes like the giggling people on the floor of the canteen the night before.

"Hold him down," Khadija snapped.

I stumbled forward until her eyes blasted code at me. *Not you.* The caregiver held the thrashing mipper. Khadija snapped and three more people bounced up from a card game and helped. Her hands were steady while my head screamed at me to bolt, like the guy's brain-melt was contagious. Khadija plucked a long gray cable from one of her pockets, stabbed it to the guy's memory node, and connected it to her Reeder.

Twenty long breaths while her fingers tip-tapped across the Reeder. The mipper slammed his heels on the ground—over and over, bone-rattling—until he sighed, brows slack, mouth dropping open like a dead bird beak.

Khadija called her mipper fix "parachute code."

"The problem with the mippers is that they jack themselves up with code hits that are, like, seeing the face of god and shit," she told me the next night over more noodle soup. "Their brains can't make sense of the sudden drop back down and their memorystream gets wonky."

"And they lose their sh-shit?" I asked. *Lose their shit* felt like a very Khadija thing to say. A big word-waste but I loved it. I loved even more that it got her to crack a yellow-painted smile.

"Bingo," she said. "I whipped up some parachute code to bring them down easy. Tuck them into bed."

"Why?"

Khadija always touched below her collarbone when she was thinking. Creepy, quiet Fox with the X-ray eyes, striking again. She told me once that she'd had long braids as a kid. We shared weed and memories and homebrew hooch—Mei's specialty with orange peels and sugar was pretty gross, as much as it did the trick. Khadija had lived with her dad in a city named New Phoenix in RedLandia, before Aaru. He'd been a genetic patent lawyer with neon suits and orange fakeskin shoes, from a place called Jamaica before he moved to RedLandia and tried to sand away his accent. People there didn't really like when other people talked different.

Her dad used to braid her hair, always knowing not to tug too tight. We all had a *how did you get here* story. Word rationing clammed up my stories, so I'd listened to everyone else's. Until they all agreed to stop asking, because talking about someplace other than here didn't help a whole lot. Khadija told me that a rival firm had broken into their apartment and her dad had yelled at her to run. To not stop running. And she hadn't—out the window, down the fire escape—not even when the gunshots cracked the sky.

She'd wandered the streets for days until NIL/E found her.

"I'm not a caregiver or whatever." Fingers danced at her ghost braids. "But when you see someone who needs help? That's on you to do what you can."

The mipper could've been back, slamming his heels on my chest. Oh. *I* was a charity case, too. Creep-o Fox with the krill-can bird coffins, who she rescued and carved out a place for next to her in the canteen.

I told her, then, about my word rationing, since time with her had me blowing past twenty words, anyway. Her hands fell off her Reeder and she pressed her lips together, her honey eyes squinting a little.

"Oh, babycakes," she said—she called me that when it was time for real talk, and I loved it. I'd babycakes to her bosscakes any day. "Lots of people will wanna shut you up. Don't let them. And most of all, don't do it to yourself."

My own personal parachute code. Goodbye, rationing.

I'd spend years trying to figure out how to thank her, when the caregivers dragged me into the kitchens and pushed extra broth bowls at me, when the others who'd stuttered at my back when we were kids ended up wriggling on one of our tables. When I ran my fingers across their scalps until the parachute code drifted them back to Earth.

Now, though? I sucked in a big breath, thinking of all the words that were knocking around my lungs—me floating up with them—and all I could say was, "Show me."

THIRTY-ONE
LINKS

S ummary is critical to memory, Aset wrote in the philosophies
we read in class. You couldn't remember every bit of every
day. Your brain would buckle under the snoozer details. *For
when sharp-edged hours dull to time, what remains is the lingering
sweetness of honeyed days, reaching out.*

Not that me and Khadija ever tasted honey. The bees had
conked out from colony collapse disorder decades ago, anyway.

Days and years blasted by like the pollinating drones over fields.

I finished up Preparedness Programming, got my node
installed, and worked in the Body Gardens—the purple-lit rooms
with glass tanks where we grew new vessels to ship all over the
world. Sometimes the conveyor belt arms got stuck and I'd have
to sploosh in and haul bodies out myself. When I wasn't gooped
in grow-goo, I was side-kicking for Khadija—clamping down arms
and getting socked in the face, watching for teeth. That pop quiz
left me with a bite-mark scar on my forearm.

More mippers, with the food rations, with the crap-your-
brains-out virus outbreaks. One year honey-drizzled into two, and
more blissy-brained zombies tore through the concrete streets like
furycanes across the ocean. So many that Khadija had the idea to

clear out a kitchen storage room in Delta for our—what to call it, clinic? Easier for mippers to find us there, just two small desks, a couple of chairs, a plastic crate topped by a chickpea flower vase, beneath the FUCK OFF plate on the wall. A joke we were never chucking out.

The mippers tumbled off rocky cliffs, and we helped them float back to Earth. I watched their full-moon eyes clear, and the thoughts rolled over me. Verses of a song I could almost remember. What if we could help them before the full-moon eyes? What about edits slicing away bad shit so the memories wouldn't rot them from inside out? What about new memories dropped in their heads, like gifts?

I started asking the mippers, what would you fix about your life? What would you want to forget? Do over?

If we couldn't fix the world or the island, maybe we could change people's minds. Literally.

The thing about hanging around mippers is that you get ideas. You take their linkup cables and the pen things—for their own good!—and stash one inside your pillowcase. And didn't Khadija ever wonder what mipping was like?

"Maybe if we try it out, we can understand our c-clients better," I offered, spinning the pen. "An-and besides, we know what we're doing."

Clients was a new word we were using, another Khadija idea. She'd been working on a business plan. Her dad used to write a lot of those.

"Market research," she agreed. "Hand it over, intern."

We took turns plugging the pen to our nodes for quick blissy hits. The playground around me shimmered into confetti made of starlight, my body rolling into one big giggle. Khadija's eyes were two moons, her mouth one laughing black ocean. *I wish there were a hundred more of me*, she'd said, once, scrubbing her hands over her face while the mipper line stretched out the clinic door. And now I could see a hundred Khadijas floating toward that black ocean on yellow parachutes. The giggles washed all around even when I unplugged the pen, with both of us falling onto each other. Khadija rested her chin on my forehead and rubbed my back. She smelled like fruity drink powder. She was always warm.

"Sometimes the code looks too familiar," she said, another two hits in. The sky above us was a blanket of instant lemonade mix, winky-starred. She propped herself up on one elbow and we both looked up into the sky.

"Duh, we've been coding for years."

"Duh nothing! It's like I can remember... making the code. Like I can hear it like, like... music." Her giggle was a glob of honey.

"Okay, Aset. You—"

"*Queen* Aset, thanks."

And then we were falling all over each other again.

"All the code, all-all the memories and junk you've seen," I said after we'd zipped up our giggles to breathe. "What's your favorite?"

She twirled the pen. "I bet if I peeked under the hood at this exact moment—bingo. That'd be it."

Her words, her smile exploded my insides into sunshine more than the bliss-hits ever did.

I tried to bury my face in my bowl of noodles in the corner of the canteen months later. Khadija, my security blanket, was off, hanging with a boyfriend in another neighborhood. She'd made me promise to leave the clinic, so I figured eating alone in the canteen counted. I wished I'd lied and stayed in the clinic, as much as the walls seemed to be inching closer. Because then I wouldn't have to pretend I couldn't see the clump of guys at a table across from me, jostling each other and pointing. *Holy shit, it's— Shh!* The ones who used to kick my sneaker-backs when I skimmed the walls near them, still word rationing. And I got sucked back to creeper Fox with the dead birds, words all broken-winged in my mouth.

I wasn't him anymore, I tried to tell myself, head down as their eyes grazed. Even the words in my head stalled—like a noise that started in my ribs, shattering my head until it blasted out my mouth. Until I grabbed them, glowing hot and—

Screams, not from me but from the alarms overhead, and flashing lights. The third storm drill this week, and still every time the sounds lobbed cannonballs between my ears. The *tweeeeeeee* of the giant bird screech rattled my teeth, jolting me at the table and I dumped noodles everywhere. The broth scalded my lap and I scrambled to the ground like the caregivers always told us to. Even under the table, even with my hands crammed over my ears, I could hear them laughing.

Until a guy at the other end of the table stood up, wound back his canteen tray, and cracked one of the guys in the back, sending him sprawling on the table. The caregivers pretended not to notice. The way they doted on Khadija had rubbed off on me a while ago.

The guy walked, almost bored, to the kitchen window and dropped off his tray before plopping on the ground by me.

"Scoot over," he said.

And here, it was like the video playback on all the memories I'd cracked at on my Reeder slowed to a crawl. Just at the sight of him—gold-flecked brown eyes, smirky lips, crooked nose with a bump in the middle like the slide on the old playground.

"Why'd you do that?" I could feel my heartbeat in my tongue.

"'Cause they're assholes."

He smelled like the lemon stuff the janitors used to mop the floors, mixed with a favorite T-shirt, worn for days. A diagonal line shaved into the side of his hair pointed straight up, a diving board I flopped off, dopey and *umm*ing next to him. He said his name was Gabe, and when I told him mine, he said he knew who I was, since me and Khadija had helped one of his buddies a while back. I don't even know what we talked about—a gold spotlight blur, *where you from, how'd you get here?*—just that we stayed under the table even after the caregivers cut the alarms. And met up the next night in the canteen. And the next. My days shrinking down to just scenes with him. Watching how he talked with his hands, flapping them like bird wings in the dinner line and then out to the playground where we swung on the swings at night. How he waggled his eyebrows when he said sometimes he and the other guys went commando under their rubber waders when they scrubbed the algae tanks. Just the idea that he wanted to talk to me kicked up fizz in my stomach and made my head all bubbly. And I had to stop him, a lot, with a waitwait, tell me about commando?

"Lettin' the boys fly.'" He tickled an imaginary sack in the air. "Brotherhood of the Half-Mast Boredom Boners."

I laughed so hard that I must've sucked a noodle down my throat. "You want algae on your junk?"

His laugh tipped his head back. "That's what the group showers are for." Another eyebrow waggle that had me wondering what extra muscles he had in his face.

Mostly, though, I was happy we were on the swings and I could move around and camouflage my own rising mast while picturing him and the guys in the communal shower.

"I work in the Gardens," I told him. I tried to keep my voice all *who-cares*, even with how my mouth filled up with sand whenever he was around. His laughing, gold-flecked eyes, though, seemed to wink. Like, *relax*.

"That place sounds creepy as hell." He shivered, overacting a *brrr* with his lips.

"Nah, it's nice. Quiet." I waited just a second, charging my battery with the energy that crackled between us. It seemed to whisper, *this is a thing, this is a thing*. "I'll take you there sometime. Or something."

"How am I gonna turn down an *or something*?"

Gabe didn't know me as the Fox slipping into the shadows, with the train-stalling stutter. Like with all the coding tricks Khadija had shown me, I could remake myself however I wanted. Who I wanted him to see me as. Starting now.

Behind the conveyor belt in the Body Garden, rows of purple-lit tanks with hazy shapes inside stretched into the darkness. The shapes were bodies that looked like they were sleeping, with thumbs in their mouths, others just skinless webs of muscle. I looked down to my heart, beating hard enough it quaked my loose gray shirt. All at the sight of Gabe's open mouth, dropping *woah* and *gross* while I led him by his fingertips through the tight rows.

Me and Gabe didn't talk much, except with our hands. I'd done stuff with other guys before—tugs in the showers—nothing like this. A blanket of clothes between the tanks. He stretched me back and did a thing with his tongue that exploded stars in my head. And I tried the same for him. It must've worked with how I had to shush him, laughing. The other techs were cool and all—everyone came to the rows for the same reason—but they didn't want to hear the whole show.

Only the bodies in the tanks saw. They could've been dreaming. I was, eyes open, stumbling over him. Dream-walking through the streets until I was alone in my bunk, realizing he'd swapped our shirts. I wadded it against my chest. Because there— ohgodohgod—there was that whole *I can make you happy* thing I'd been trying with mipper memories. Now I could see it like gold dancing over code.

—Yeah, I'm not entirely comfortable with us watching this kid get his dick wet. Beyond invasive, even for us.

Focus. The entry point is coming up soon. I can feel it. Hold on.

Enough mipping, and I could see the colors from the code even when I wasn't looking at my Reeder. Budding everywhere, in everyone. Gabe was gold. The sunlight in his eyes, his crooked smirk like he bent sunbeams around him. Khadija was yellow-orange like her powder mixes. I'm still not sure what I was. Algae-green. The blue-black water past the glass walls. Paradise was purple, no-brainer. Me and Gabe's purple paradise in the Body Garden tanks. I staked out a spot between two broken tanks in the back, and we practically moved in. Old bedsheets and spare T-shirts on the floor, folded empty rice bags for pillows. A crank-radio for some tunes. We left each other notes.

I wrote on my skin for him, too, crescent moons that I dug into my thighs when he'd disappear for days, and I'd see him laughing in the canteen with some of his buddies and his color would look all wrong. Burnt bronze. When he wanted to be a dick because, he said to me, laughing, what was the point of hanging out when we'd never leave here, when we were dead already?

He and the guys in janitorial sang out *what's the point, we're dead already* when shit happened. The algae filter was clogged again and—who cares!—we're dead already. Even if we're noded, because one day the sun will torch the Earth, so might as well do yourself a solid and shrug it off. Everything was bullshit, including you. *Especially* you.

Khadija never yelled at me, even when she must've known my colors looked all wrong. She hit me with her yellow-orange beamy eyes and told me, get a grip, babycakes. You spin life out of symbols, and you're chasing someone who doesn't want to be chased?

Besides, Gabe's burnt bronze always warmed up again to gold, after a while. When he found me again in the Body Garden and crushed me to him, his lips fluttering an *I'm sorry for being a dick* against my neck. And *I won't ghost you again. I promise.*

His arms around me rationed away my words again when I wanted to ask him, *don't you want to try to be happy?*

You can't say those kinds of things, you've gotta show them.

I didn't tell Khadija. I knew she'd big sis me. *What are you, fucking crazy? You could lose yourself.* Maybe I would. Hopefully? I'd already coded a million scenes for him, those days he'd disappeared. Building us a life past this place. We met in a city at a bar with drinks that tasted like starlight confetti. We had a house in Mexico and we watched birds in the lemon trees in the backyard. We could have whatever we wanted, even if we could never leave Aaru. A hundred years together, floating gently back to the ground every once in a while on Khadija's parachute code.

Even in the purple light, the night of his latest rush back to gold, the node linkup wire looked like a gray snake that might snap at us.

"That's the thing?" Gabe popped up from our sheet-bed, biting one corner of his lips to pin down his smile.

"Yeah."

"We just, like, plug in?"

"Just for a sec. That'll be enough."

"Cool."

No better way to show him what he meant. No better way for me to not be so lonely in my own head than to let him in it.

I plugged the gray cable to the node behind my ear. "You ready?"

Gabe scooted closer. "Blast off."

And before I could chicken out, I stuck the other end of the cable to his node.

Everything whooshed. The world dropped away, and we were falling—up and up. No *we*, though. I was Gabe, and Gabe was me, and we both splashed through the cartoon blue ocean of the carpet in the house I didn't remember, with waves that sparked with the first code that Khadija had taught me. And then the ocean smashed again with the first time we kissed—sweet as the plantains Gabe's Má fried up. On the edge of something—starfaces streaking the sky all wippity-wippity—until I yanked the cable out, and we melted into one pile of oozy giggles.

"Holy shit," we both said at the same time.

Holy. Whole-y. I could feel him like an echo in my head. Like he'd smoothed over every crack I'd tried to forget. Like I missed him already when we were still twisted up in each other. His laughing eyes seemed to flicker with gold for just a second.

"Do it again," he whispered.

Plug in, blast off. I saw myself reflected in his eyes, but at the same time I was him seeing himself in mine—bouncing around and echoing, out into forever. And then, and then—

THIRTY-TWO
PARALLEL MEMORY BRANCH

The twinkling lights of the city stretch out beyond the windows of me and Khadija's private office, high over the city. Her eyes are lost on the lights, like she doesn't hear what I'm saying.

"Therapeutic linked Ankh sessions," I continue. "Think what it'll do for intimacy, for understanding, if you can see—if you can *live* as your partner, and experience some of their memories for yourself. And…"

When Khadija looks back at me, the mix of pity and patience in her eyes boots me way back into the past. I'm a little kid again in Aaru, bugging her in the canteen.

"Yeah, but look at what linking up did to you," she says softly.

I know she means this like *look how it screwed you up*. But the mess that spills out of my head and all around me is worth it—beyond worth it—just for the memory of that perfect moment of being connected with Gabe.

—he's jumping forward and nostalgizing the Excerpt events, Gabe must be helping him try to shake us, he's—

Well then bloody drop them into Gabe's Excerpt. We already got to the direct node-link point. The doors are open between their 'streams. That should help with stability.

With this many narrative levels, memory integrity is bound to collapse, and I'm worried that they can't—

Sig, she's right. This is the only memory branch that might possibly lead to Khadija. We've never been this close. Fox can take it. And Gabe, well—this is why he's here.

Me and Gabe are in the middle of the ocean, somehow. We're standing on what looks like a door that's floating flat across the water. An archipelago of doors stretches out ahead of us. I look behind us and more doors float off into the horizon, to vague gray towers in the distance. When I spin back to him, he's rigid, gaze locked on a small ship at the end of the line of doors, his jaw muscles poking out as he grits his teeth. I can just make out a younger Gabe on the deck, his eyes out to sea, his tattoo-less arms crossed over his chest.

"I'm not goin' back there," he sputters.

The door bobs beneath us as an invisible hand winds up to throw another wave. I grab his arm, and the panic ripping up his face suffocates me. He scrambles to the edge of the door and tries to jump in the water as I'm tethered to him, begging, *it's okay, it'll be okay.*

A wave knocks us from behind. His screams—*nonono*—become my screams as the wave launches us at the boat and we tangle up together again, into one mind. The way we've always supposed to have been. Like our time living separate lives was the illusion.

———

I told the boys at the Stable that the only way to get by is to lock things from your past behind doors that you don't open. You don't talk about them. You don't even think about them. When the rescue boat took me from Aaru to New Providence, it was like I could look back at the water and see all these floating doors I was leaving behind.

Yeah, what do you mean, they asked. Since we shared everything, and since I was teaching them, they got the short-story version.

Mexico, Má, Julio. One double-locked door.

I met a boy on Aaru named Fox. The problem was I loved him, so that's why the door came in.

A storm hit Aaru and the company had to evacuate us. So me 'n' my boyfriend's best friend met in secret to get him off the island. See, that door gets three locks, one for each big bad thing I did: Trick, Lie, Betray.

(Here I can see the questions in the boys' eyes. Like, *how can you forget something that awful that you did?* So I have to stop and tell them, the thing about doors is that the worse the thing that you did is, the bigger the door, the bigger the number of locks that it gets. So many that you can't even open it if you wanted. And they nod like, *we gotcha*.)

Two years on a half-drowned island, knowing I'd fucked up big-time. Door.

Evac to New Providence, quick stay in a halfway house. One last door.

And then I opened the door to the Stable and locked all those doors behind an even bigger one. That's how I can be happy here. And you should, too. It's just easier this way.

———

I leave my body when I dance. When the lights burn up my skin and I close my eyes, tipping my head back. On stage or in the private rooms, grinding my hips around in the lap of a client who's shooting me his *ohmygod* eyes.

Every time their eyes hit, I'm someone else. Might as well be fucking god sucking them off, with how I patched them up. And anyone who tells you what we did at the Stable—just 'cause we were dressed up like professors 'n' army sergeants—isn't medicine is just being an asshole. And you don't know what it's like to look down at someone's closed eyes after you've made them come so hard they might as well be dead, and know it was you who walked them through some real shit. That you looked through the stories behind their eyes and gave them what they needed. Took their pain for an hour. Even loved them for a few minutes, while you were doing that tongue-thing and they were whispering, *holy, holy*.

And who doesn't want to feel wanted? And maybe you're not supposed to say this 'cause it freaks people out, just like how you're not supposed to say that your Má got you to pose for pedos to keep food in the fridge, but I fuckin' loved the Stable.

The leaving my body stuff didn't happen the first night that silver daddy Dean drove me from Coral Beef and brought me to the big brick-walled old warehouse that was crammed with gym equipment. Spotlights reflected off the mirrored walls, and a football player was shaking his ass on stage. *Friday night revue*, Dean told me, before he handed me off to a guy named Coach, whistle bobbing from a silver chain between his tank-topped pecs. He probably had ten years on me, though it was tough to tell with his smooth, deep-brown skin and muscled legs that poked out from his black shorts. He'd show me around later—the locker room, the pool deck, my private room where there were no cameras in the ceiling like everywhere else—and talk about the rules of the place. *Rule number one—everyone dances the Friday-night livestream.*

He brought me to a group of guys standing in the dark in front of the stage, waiting for their turns. The place smelled like bar soap 'n' glass cleaner. A bead of sweat splooshed from my armpit and hit my hip under my boxy halfway-house shirt. I slapped on a smirk 'cause Dean must've wanted the cocky walking cock from Cow'N'Cod, and nodded at the boys. They didn't notice much.

Coach blew a whistle and football dude left. A guy in a cow-print thong, cowboy hat, and chaps jangled his spurs on stage. Ranch-hand thick, spinning to shake the golden globes of his ass. Looking over his shoulder with a wink, firing finger-guns and *Muerte*, I knew. I was a fuckin' goner. Cue the slide guitars, hoss.

Cowboy—Colt was his name—swooped to my side after his dance with a twangy *howdy* and stuck so close that I smelled his sweet sweat. I screamed for the next dude on stage. I screamed for them all. Sarge. Biker bear. Frat bro. Whooping so loud that the boys eyeballed me and started cheering, too. The boys that would be my brothers, later, spotting each other at racks, flashing pits and pecs at the cameras, keeping each other company when the bank-rolling clients booked us for off-site weekends. Asked to call us baby. I whooped until we were all banging on the weight racks, cheering for each ball-smashing split, each pole-spin. Until Coach took to the stage, pointed into the crowd, and the spotlight swung over to me.

Rule number one—everyone dances the Friday night livestream.

"Gentlethems, please help me welcome to the stage," Coach started with his announcer voice. His eyes swept past me to one of the walls, where I spotted a vintage poster for Surge Studios.

All us studs cribbed our names from the old skin studios. Colt. Falcon. Titan. "Surge!"

Cue the lights 'n' the music, the boys cheering 'n' jostling my shoulders. What the hell. I jogged to the stage. I didn't know what to do, so I shook my can, laughing. Peeled off my shirt, crammed my hand in my shorts.

And the boys, thank god for them, their screams hit the fuckin' walls.

"You could feel what we were trying to do," Titan told me, over grain bowls after he showed me how to knee-hook the pole. And *Muerte*, the food—actual chicken, and greens, and pea protein shakes. Natural fuckin' grade-A proteins for us on the meat farm. And we were natural meat, too—natural-ish, if you don't count a few hormone jabs here and there—free-range with the big backyard past the pool to roam and tan. "Other new guys come in too hungry, pissin' all over the place, tryin' to steal clients. Not you."

Applause, applause. Coach had to shuffle over, pat me on the chest and say, "Alright, time to take a bow."

I coulda swam in that spotlight all night.

Colt 'n' Surge stayed on the other side of the closed door of my room, Dean-o's two-week probationary period long past. My brick-walled room only had space for Gabe 'n' Levi. Levi—head plonked on my lap, me running a hand through his reddish-blond hair—held up the joint. I sucked in a lungful. The paper was still wet from his lips.

I only called him Levi when we were alone in our rooms. We tried not to do that too much, all googly-eyes and excluding the other guys with handholding in the cafeteria 'n' shit. Coach only had to remind us once to have fun 'n' all, but we were on the clock.

If we busted all our happy-feeling wads on just each other, upstairs would hafta reassign one of us to an affiliate house. We made sure to bone enough of the other guys for the ceiling cams on the main floor to keep everyone happy.

The purple smoke from Levi's joint curled around his face, lit up in the noon sun. The weed dipped me in the cuddly water of the pool downstairs. Mostly, the warmth was from catching the view of Levi's head on my bare thighs, his stubbled cheeks, his squinty blue eyes looking at me all heart-shaped. Like he's not supposed to.

"Don't." I huffed out another lungful of smoke.

"I was just gonna say…" He puffed a laugh. The weed slowed his voice, some of the twang gone when he wasn't laying it on for the cameras. "That you should show Falcon how to do those upside-down pole spins."

"Sure y'were."

He didn't need to open his mouth to say what was in his head. Love gushed all outta him at everyone. When he poked the boys to drink more water, when he snuck the fresh meat candy bars and showed them how to find their light before their dances. When he pushed them to take web classes in the library lounge— the actual classroom, not the set for horny teacher livestreams. Coach took care of us like it was his job. Levi took care of us like we were his family.

I only let him say it once, 'cause when you tell someone you love them you're talking future shit. And I'd already told him about the algae tanks, and the fishing nets, and the *babe, what's the point*.

We couldn't stay at the Stable forever, he started saying. We could put away some cash. We could find a place on the cheap in New Providence. *Could, could.* In my head, it sounded like fists against a door.

Hold it in. Close it, even halfway.

"Where's this one from?" I traced his wrist, along the scar with its spiky edges like the spurs in his cowboy getup.

We did the history lessons a coupla months back. Swapping stories and scars. I told him some about Mexico 'n' Aaru. He brushed his thumb over my node—he didn't have one—and told me about growing up in Valholl. Freaked every day that someone would clock him, then off to the reeducation camps 'cause of adultery of the flesh. Meaning, being a faggot.

"Dug out my tracker," he said.

I don't know how his eyes didn't dim. How he kept the smile on his face, blasting warm fuzzies out—then, or ever—after running from his family who wouldn't take him out of Valholl to save him. Hitching by himself to the city-states and across the continent when he was sixteen. Still a kid.

"It does look pretty fuckin' punk." I stayed light, just for him. Even laughed. "If you'd stayed, would they'da let you outta the camp, after the reeducation or whatever?"

"My body, yeah. Dead or alive. But the thing inside it?" He sucked the joint again and whistled out smoke. "Gone-zo. And that woulda been worse, almost. Because I'm not my body."

Sounded a lot like the *we are all special and sacred* stuff, from Má, and the president, and how Santa Muerte watched us and carried our ghosts off to God when it was time.

"Really?" I traced his collarbone. "Bummer. I gotta thing for your body."

He laughed and kissed my knuckles. "This body's gotta get ready for livestream. Yours, too."

Yeah, I never told him with words. I told him with my eyes, especially after that night's livestream when we snuck back here and I told him about Julio. Voice shaking, his hands rubbing mine, 'cause of how his eyes hit me. *I got you.*

He rolled off the bed. He tried to hop back into shorts and ended up bouncing against a wall—both of us cracking up 'cause nothing had ever been this fuckin' hilarious, or stupid. Dopey from the weed 'n' each other. He slipped on his shirt, smacked my lips with his, and left the door open behind him.

—still a ways out from the entry point and their code-forms can't take much more. Someone—Parwan, get a towel for Fox's nose. Fuckin' shitshow this is, it—

Let's bump playback speed, then. Poppy's right—this is the only way. Sometimes we have to bend like a reed, too, Sig. Stay here. Stay strong. If we get stream collapse, we'll look to a hard-reboot. You know the protocols.

Protocols. Flo, it's… they're people.

The green shakes started tasting like powder. Some of the gym equipment busted and took forever to get fixed. More studs rolled in and we fought for livestream times. Coach blamed the new content house, the extreme kink stuff that sucked our traffic. We leaned more into the in-person content, the private sessions 'n' the group shows. The hyper-gonorrhea outbreak—Coach figured another house whipped it up, couldn't be sure—had us trying to be more careful. Unfolding condom things up our asses and in our mouths. The sprays before each client that made fluids roll off.

No wonder the clients complained. Like fucking a non-stick pan.

Rajon liked to book me 'n' Levi for weekends in his fancy apartment. Nice dude. He kept our numbers way up by rigging his social bot farm to buy passes to our livestreams each week, even when we didn't ask. So how do you pay back that kindness? We fudged the rules a little with Rajon. Let him finish on us or in us and then we'd hop on an extra round of antibiotics when we got back home. His clipped silver hair, his lined forehead, the way he moved over his sheets—he coulda been one of the studs there, anyhow.

We helped him feel loved 'cause he looked out for us even when he didn't need to.

He'd usually head to bed early, tell us to relax, and ring up some food. Those weekends didn't even feel like work. Like me 'n' Levi living together with a roommate snoring in the next room. Friends, with him telling us on the drive over from the Stable how, by his third life-exploding divorce, all he could handle were weekend dates now 'n' then.

"You remind me of—" Rajon started to say to me in the car, once, until he looked away.

Before the nodes rolled out to the whole world, guys always came to the Stable looking for someone gone who we reminded them of.

He made us breakfasts of fried eggs that looked like jiggly yellow boobs, while Levi talked about getting outta the Stable. He had a friend in LakeLandia with an actual farm who needed help. After three years of pretending to coach guys in the gym, it stopped being just pretending. I dug it. I started taking online physio classes, memorizing muscle names while I poked Levi's body. Trapezius. Latissimus dorsi. *Could, could.*

"He's right," Rajon said. "You boys'd need a place to stay and some money to get started. And livestreams can't get you there. Just let me know."

The corners of his gray eyes always crinkled up when he

smiled. I poked at one of the eggs with my fork and watched the bright yellow yolk run on the plate.

Levi left one Friday afternoon to take a group of boys on an off-site just like a hundred other off-sites. Almost like. He didn't come back Sunday. Monday, Coach said the limo got hijacked on the way home. They were probably halfway to one of the houses in SoCalia by now. Coach had some hookups there. He'd see what he could do about finding Levi, but. *But.*

I need to keep him, but can you help with the memory. It... It...
    Of course. Let's take a peek at the editing levels in your price range. We can make something work.
    Insert > emotional dampening.
    Insert > abstraction.
    Insert > time compression.

Blurs, flashes. Mostly back to the closet with Julio, where I wrapped him in a blanket. Singing the Coral Beef song to keep him from crying.
    Numb by the pool. The boys tried to help.
    Stoned, catching Santa Muerte as she slipped through the trees, just a flicker of her black robe. One bony finger brushed a tear from my cheek and I rolled back, barfing acid. Begging her to bring me with her. Or at least go to Levi and set him free from wherever they had him.
    Nets caught up in the algae tanks.
    What's the point. We're already dead. My fault for forgetting. Never again.

———

Flashes as the streetlights streaked against the windows of Rajon's car. He squeezed my hand, crinkly-eyed. *I got you.* I tried to follow his lips. Something about how the real cash was in memory storage and movement. Something about how the people he worked with shelled out buckets to get copies of their memorystreams plugged into walled-off sections of someone else's brain—a runner, the clients called them.

"Parceling," Rajon said. "You won't even know the memories are there. You won't be able to access them."

Hot blood in my mouth.

"Yeah, whose memories we talking?"

"You won't know. That's the point. Usually some paranoid, loaded asshole who thinks their partner is gonna off them. Or someone trying to throw off the banks."

"And how does it work?"

"Runners get the parcel uploaded. If the customer needs it, they call the runner back, toss them a fat bonus."

The inside of my head was already carved out. Why the fuck not.

"Even if they don't call you in, the cash's more than enough to get you set up somewhere," he said.

He parked in the back alley of a bar. Broken glass like stars, crushed under my sneakers. The inside of the bar looked and smelled so much like the Delta canteen that the floor did a knee-hook spin. Crowded, beer-spill smell, death metal on the speaker. I knocked through the crowd like a ball in the pinball machine with the spinning lights around the name. *Aset's Spellbook.*

Rajon talked to a few people and then handed me to a bartender, who handed me to someone else.

"I'll be here waiting," he said.

I hoped whoever was gone—whoever he loved that I reminded him of—made him happy.

A maze of back hallways, a door at the end. A hand pushed me through and into a garage lab that stank of church incense, ringed with screens and gold coffins that sparked with blue lights. Khadija, in a boxy neon suit, floated around with a Reeder. Another Khadija with buzzed pink hair sat at a computer. Another Khadija in bright yellow yoga clothes tapped at the screen of one of the gold coffins.

"Holy shit," Suited Khadija said. "Gabe the Babe."

The other Khadijas looked up. "Been a while," they all said at once.

I almost barfed yellow acid again. How did, how did, how did…

Variations, Suited Khadija called them. Insurance policies. Three Khadijas headed the runner ring outside of New Providence. A dozen Khadijas were implanted in various teams across the company. Thirty more around the world, at least, in non-cloned bodies, in hiding. Then more parcels stashed all over.

Fox had told me once about how she'd heard her dad get gunned down by other lawyers when she was a kid. That'd make anyone grow up suspicious as hell.

"Are any of you the real Khadija I knew?"

"Khadija created all us variations after Aaru, in New Providence," Suited Khadija said. "So, technically we're all the Khadija you knew."

"And 'variations' is bullshit," Yoga Khadija said. "We're equally valid co-Khadijas."

They weren't so chatty like this with just any runners, Pink Hair gabbed. *Besides, talking to yourself gets fuckin' boring. And it's you, Gabe. Call it old time's sake.*

I slammed the door shut against *old time's sake*, against the last time I met with Khadija in secret.

They got me coffee. Helped me into a chair. The story behind each of their eyes: Pity. They could help me. Money, a job, a place, whatever I needed. I could stay with them. *After all that we...* Suited Khadija didn't finish the sentence.

Guilt offers. No thanks. Being with her like this again made the closet door that locked away Fox fly open, gushing purple light everywhere. It burned my skin.

"The parcel," I said. "Then I'm out."

The Khadijas looked at each other. "Fair enough," they said together.

The Sisterhood of the Three Khadijas brought me to a reclining chair thing. Could've been the same chair the caregivers on Aaru plonked us in to get us noded in the first place. "How the hell does my head have enough space for another whole memorystream?" I asked.

"We pick one memory for the parceling," Suited Khadija said. "That's all we need. Even one memory contains the code of the whole 'stream, folded in on itself. Like how individual cells of your body contain your entire genome."

Sure. Whatever. Things stopped making sense once Levi didn't come back, anyway. Santa Muerte's cloak fluttered in one of the curtains by an open window.

"We'll give you a good one," Pink Hair said, squeezing my shoulder. "Not that you'll be able to see it. But it's the thought that counts, all that."

"You have to be awake for us to map available neural pathways since live code is more flexible," one of them said. Or all of them. Voices like overlapping echoes. "Then we drop in the parcel and goodbye, Gabe the Babe. We can even scrub memories of the installation if ya want."

"Will it hurt?"

"No."

A gold mask snapped over my face. Heartbeat, pounding. *Could. Could.* Blue lights.

They lied.

VERSE FOUR
TO ESCAPE THE SLAUGHTER PLACE

"Memories are not islands. Memories are interconnected, shuffling. Out of order. Every past memory colored by every memory experienced since. Try to hold a moment—exactly as it was—still in your mind. Impossible. See how the code dances! Such joy. Give in to the dance."

—Aset, *Philosophies of Memory and Laws of Applied Sahusynics*, First Edition

~

"Your girl's going to get uncharacteristically mushy here. It just means the world to me to welcome you all to the ribbon-cutting for the Field of Reeds Center for Memory Recovery. The first of what will be a lot of these places around the world, I know. This is just the beginning. Out of everything we've done so far... this is just. It's just. Memory treatment is so completely at the heart of why I reimagined the company. And wherever we go next, I'm so thankful we're here now."

—Khadija Banks, the Field of Reeds Center for Memory Recovery dedication ceremony, Nueva Yorkersey City

THIRTY-THREE
RECALL, RECOGNITION, RELEARNING

Soft sheets beneath me, in my body—alone, as myself—again. Gauzy dawn light filters through the drapes of our bedroom. Gabe is out cold next to me, head back, snoring softly through his Ankh hangover after the therapists carried us here, hours ago. I feel stronger than ever, like after a twirl on the pole, fired up by muscles that can go for hours. I stare at him so hard that a mean voice from the last Excerpts remind me, *hey, creep-o Fox with the dead birds, cool it.*

Pieces of the mosaic are finally snapping into place, now that I remember me and Gabe plugging into each other's nodes when we were kids. Names and faces. A group of Khadijas in a hidden lab. Khadija, who told me she'd wished there were a hundred more of her. Once she left Aaru, who better to help carry out whatever master plan for humanity that she's working on than copies of herself? Rajon, in a younger body when I met him at his birthday party at Gay Bar, but still the man who helped Gabe. Levi. I can feel my hands threading through his hair, his head on my lap. I'm glad he got to love Gabe. That Gabe got to love him, as much as Past Fox would've made it about him. *How could you love someone else?*

Because Gabe loved me again, after Levi, even when he promised himself *never again*. And how could I ever be so lucky?

Well, maybe put a pin in "lucky," Foxy. You know a storm hit Aaru. You know Gabe and Khadija tricked you somehow and got you off the island. Maybe I should take a cue from Gabe's master compartmentalization, throw all that behind a closet door for now, and deal with one world-ending problem at a time.

Because I may have arrived here as a dotted-line version of myself, but I'm filling things in now, beyond the canned identity the therapists handed me. Let's break out the can opener and let the metal lids cut me up. Like Darius might encourage me in therapy to *think about things from a different, broader perspective* while I frown at the fake plant on the table.

My name is Fox.

Amma, my mom, named me Shazad. I was one of the thousands of refugee kids who lost their names on Aaru. The caregivers put me in the Foxtrot neighborhood and didn't know what else to call me, so Fox it was.

I'm a memory editor. One of the best, so they say.

I was the first memory editor. The best, even better than Khadija—who was the first memory therapist—and I carved trauma out of the minds of refugees even though it sliced mine to shreds. Khadija Life-Storyboarded a new direction for the company, and together we brought editing to the world. Well, she did, mostly. I stayed at the sidelines as a silent sidekick, always her intern, because it wouldn't look so good if a mipper was helping call the shots.

And here—here's where a therapist shoves a Reeder at me. NIL/E was a little boutique company catering to the richest few on the planet until me and Khadija brought it to the billions who refuse to die, even as the planet buckles beneath us all. And sure,

NIL/E is building new cities for all the souls, and watering the deserts, and pinky-swearing about renewable energy, but someday we'll even suck the seas dry. And until then, we can just paint over the pain.

Khadija saw that the company is too big to answer to anyone. She left and she's trying to stop them. *Project Bennu is our way to escape the whole cycle of having no control over our own destinies,* Flo told me.

So, pop quiz: You accidentally helped break the world. Now what do you do?

I have to make things right. I have to help Khadija fix it.

There's one stop I should make to see if it'll fill in any more blanks. I slip out of bed and look out the window to the grounds, where residents stretch in yoga poses to the sky, and smear watercolors on canvases, and wobble on uneven legs as caregivers guide them along the shore. Yellow bracelets on all their wrists.

Piano music floats up from the first floor of the manor as I wander the empty hallways from my room to Minou's. I open the door without knocking to find Stash in her bed, surrounded by pages he must've pulled from the walls, with an open leather-bound book in front of him. The book's pages are covered in Minou's handwriting. I remember the sound of her throwing the book against her door and it's like she's launching it at my ribs. The horror in her eyes while she shivered into sand in front of me washes over me in a cold wind.

"Finally awake?" Stash asks.

"Not sure yet."

He shrugs, tries to smile. I walk in and sit at the edge of the bed because we've both been through enough that whatever beef between us doesn't seem to matter anymore.

"I knew I wouldn't find her here, but part of me was hoping," I tell him, my eyes lost on her handwriting.

"I know it. Meen is—or *was*—or, or… She made me feel better than I deserved. You all had your shit together, back in the real world." He frowns down at a page. "She was a big-time editor, Chengmei was helping kids or whatever. Me? I dropped bliss-hits into people's memorystreams in bar corners for beer money. I never went in for that Radical Remembrance shit because I didn't have any good memories to share." His gaze sweeps over the room. "She told me I wasn't that guy anymore. I believed her."

"Yeah." My throat aches. "She told me to take what was useful from my past and decide who I am. It helped."

"You were with her, when…?"

"We tried to run for it, during the attack. She got—it was quick. She didn't seem like she was in pain."

"Yeah." The word is a puff of air. He turns another page in her journal. "Yeah, that's good."

"How many others?"

"Four therapists. And Hotaru and Nicola, before Flo was able to cool things down. I hid in a closet downstairs as soon as I heard the screams. Always hiding."

"And after that? I got hit with some freeze-ray and trapped in the Ankh for what felt like years. What happened to Poppy and the others? I heard something about IOC refugees, and…"

"System hard-reboot to wipe every resident's memory of the attack, and the truth about how we're in a sim." I jump at the hard snap as he turns another page. "Flo blabbed how it was going to reset the sim to its original specs and patch up the damage."

I shiver, even through my sweatshirt. "Yellow-braceleting all the residents."

"Right back to square one. And boot out any—what'd she say?—unauthorized users. She brought me to the Ankh Room for *protection*, she said—you and Gabe were still in the Ankhs—so I could keep my memories for Scribe stuff. I looked out the window, things got blurry for a second, then poof! Another sunny, perfect day."

The edges of the pages slice me up. I start to say *they couldn't* and shut my mouth. NIL/E made the virus code and bombed cities ahead of an all-out war that's in the making, according to Poppy, just to stop Khadija. Of course they'd delete a few stray refugees and SoCalia memory runners.

"Scribe work." He puffs air. "Minou's gone. Chengmei's a vegetable like everyone else. You're... whatever the hell is going on with you. You don't need me. I'm clocking out."

"Sh-she told me the mission was bullshit right before the attack. L-like she found something."

He tosses the book closer to me on the sheets. "She's been out of it for days, ever since she said that she found a journal hidden in this room from the person who stayed here before her."

"And who was that?"

"Her, apparently. Before her last hard-reboot."

I look down at the pages that are filled with name lists from her Excerpts, possible timelines, theories. Whole paragraphs scratched out. *Born in Isfahan. Where'd I meet Adela? Adela, canned memory? New Angeles, infiltrate Khadija's SoCalia cell. Timeline doesn't match. New Thebes, Egypt?*

Pages torn out and ripped in half.

Bullshit. They coded you. Minou isn't even your name. You don't even have one.

"Take it if you want," he says. "I don't need it. I'm done. Seth always said we're here by choice. I'm going straight to the Ankh from here and leaving. Whatever life for me is outside has got to be better than this. I just came to say goodbye to her."

The piles of pages are snowdrifts between us, muffling sounds.

"I hope you find what you're looking for out there," I tell him.

He nods to the door. "You, too, bud."

Who knows what raw hell Minou saw in her Excerpts. Stash, too. I don't need anyone else to tell me who I am, now. I leave the journal on the bed.

This new sparkling update to Fox comes with early-bird tendencies and thirty percent less existential terror. I swing by the dining room for a couple of mugs of coffee. Therapists in the hallways sweep clean white paint over the dusty yellow of the walls. Vases of flowers sit on tables. A yellow-braceleted Inyene stuffs a carnation in her mouth before a therapist swoops in and guides her out the back door, to the lawn with the others. Gabe's still asleep in our bed when I slip into the room and leave a mug by his nightstand. I'm careful to not make too much noise. Kid Fox from Aaru taught me how to move in and out of the shadows.

He taught me a lot of things.

I boot up Gabe's Reeder and open the save-file of his memorystream, watching the river branch and flow. I only need to flex my eyes like I'm trying to focus to see the gold wash over his code, the same color that I saw in his eyes in Aaru. Float up on enough bliss-hits and you can see everything below you with clear eyes. Seth told me when Gabe first came here that he was a scrape pulled from me, with a bit of salvaged code from Gabe's actual memorystream. *Even one memory contains the code of the whole 'stream, folded in on itself,* Khadija told Gabe in a garage lab. Which explains how he was able to remember things beyond his scrape parameters. Since we'd connected to each other on Aaru, and mingled our memorystreams, it was like I carried all of him with me, always. An almost-impossibility that only happened because of how close I was with Khadija.

And Project Bennu is her gift to the world, I know. Like the parachute code she made on Aaru, for us all to drift down back to ourselves. The years spent helping at her side remind me of who I am.

I only need to focus a little more to punch through the folds—perforation, like Seth said how I could never really forget Gabe because he was in me too deep.

All of Gabe's memories are spread out in one ocean of gold on my screen, except for a walled-off island that must be Khadija's memory parcel. He started out as a tool just for me to use until he bloomed into so much more. The real Gabe, unbroken into forever—the proof of that is right in front of me. The same gold I feel in my gut every time our eyes meet. The same gold in his eyes. Beautiful, beautiful. But how to pull it out of the folds?

I switch over to the virus, my eyes still focused. Sometimes Gabe would mumble at me when I grabbed my Reeder from the bedside table at night, its screen cracking the darkness. What was I doing working so late? Except he didn't know that sometimes it was like I got a message from someone else—somewhere else—and I had to sit back and take notes for them, for some new *we can make you happy* fix.

I'm taking notes, now in code. Bird wings, hands up in prayer, triple-wedge, temple flag. A search string threaded through whatever energy the code actually runs on. A fix for the virus, and how didn't I see it before? I see now that the other code in the virus isn't just junk noise, it's other colors. A billion other lives all crammed up in one never-ending stanza. I can't see any of Khadija's yellow-orange, or any of the algae-green or blue-black or whatever color feels like me. I copy over a bit of Gabe's code and drop it at the end of the search string. Telling my code, *find the rest*. Holding my breath as invisible fingers reach out and out, feeling the threads of him. Feeling how the bit of gold recognizes all the other gold in the one stanza—soul recognizes soul.

One keystroke after all the years I lived in the Excerpts to get here, and the other colors fall away, leaving Gabe's. The long gold river of him only punctured by a blue island of a single code symbol. A blue crown surrounded by shimmering walls—that must be Khadija's parcel. I try to peek behind the walls but they don't budge. The gold flows around it, seemingly forever.

Gabe sneaks up and hugs me from behind, resting his chin on the top of my head.

"Pretty," he says. "What is it?"

"It's you."

I don't know where else we can go from here, with the light brushing through the gauzy curtain. And that's alright. It's enough to just have him beside me.

Water drips from the oar in my hands as I paddle us down the marsh in a canoe. Gabe faces me with his hands wrapped around his coffee cup. The ducks glide away from us across the sun-glinted water. We drift from the manor grounds and the morning sessions. On the way to the shore after refilling our coffee cups, we passed flocks of yellow bracelets drifting over the lawn. Therapists try to wrangle them to circles of chairs and blankets for a session, while Seth keeps his back to the manor, his face out to the water. Good luck with that.

I have to close the door on everything else right now—Khadija, and world wars, and the company can wait—while I'm willing Gabe to look at me. We've been quiet for so long that it feels like I'm back to word rationing. I stretch the silence out, hoping it'll give him the space to figure out what he lived in the Ankh. And how I was there with him. The manor floats from view, hidden behind the reeds and trees.

"I'm sorry," I tell him gently. "I know you didn't want me to see those memories."

He shrugs. "I know you didn't have a choice."

He stares down at the coffee cup until he bursts up and chucks it into the air with a growl. A long, ragged scream of *FUUUUUUUCCCKKKKK*. The canoe flails under us. I hold my breath against the panic that we're going to tip, and let his anger torch out. The cup splashes the reeds by the far shore. A duck flaps into the air, quacking like, *I didn't do shit, I'm just a fucking duck*.

"*I* didn't want to see those memories," he says when he's sitting down again, the growl burned away.

I wait until the canoe stops rocking before I paddle again, hoping each dip of the oar will stitch my insides back together.

"I'm glad you and Levi had each other." I mean it, with no Past Fox to tell me otherwise. I can finally slam the closet door on him.

"Me too."

"Did you look for him?"

He squints into his hands, the shaved swoops on the side of his head wavering. "I must've. For years, poking through livestreams. There's a lot after meeting the Khadija crew I still don't remember."

We float by a small island in the marsh, its shore ringed with tree roots, offering no place for the canoe to land. Just like Khadija's parcel of memories in Gabe's code, the walls I couldn't burrow through before Gabe came up behind me.

I want to ask him how and why he and Khadija tricked me to get me off Aaru. To beg him for answers, until Darius's voice floats over the water, reminding me to *let go of the past*. We'll figure that out later. Here's hoping. Right now, I need to be the one here for Gabe.

"You could have all those memories back now," I say. "I pulled the full copy of your memorystream from the virus code, and you could hop into the Ankh and we could give them back to you."

"We've been thinking about this all wrong." He shakes his head, one corner of his lips cresting in a half-smile. "That Gabe died in the blast. I'm not him."

He leans back, legs wide, his eyes on his steepled fingertips. I don't think I've ever seen him look this small and lost. Someone must've drilled a hole in the canoe with how I feel it sinking beneath me. I swallow hard.

"But you," he says after a couple silent oar-dips from me. "You must be happy you can pull a copy of yours outta the junk code."

"Mine's not there."

"What does that mean?"

"I don't really know."

I don't know for sure. Just one stop to make before I do—one that I'll have to make alone. He sighs, like I'm draped over his shoulders and weighing him down. He can't carry me through everything.

"I can't take any more Excerpts," he says. "I'm done."

"I know," I say. "I'll get us outta here."

One thing at a time. We can't get to Khadija and help her stop NIL/E if we're stuck in here. I crane my head at the shore behind us. We either have to turn around or just keep paddling for hours until we circle back. I stab the oar into the water and cut hard, banking us and bringing us closer to the reed-shrouded shore one wobbling stroke at a time.

At least the other residents look happy. Pierluigi giggles and half flops a cartwheel down the lawn while an orange-scrubbed therapist scrambles to make sure he's safe. Chengmei stretches out on a blanket like a cat napping in the sun. A group sits cross-legged on the grass in front of J, who's reading them a story like this is a kids' daycare center. They poke at the dirt and burble while J reads something about how memories are interconnected, shuffling, and out of order. Double the amount of therapists—Seth must've just duplicated their templates—hover close by, making sure the residents don't trip into the marsh or eat dirt.

After I rowed us ashore, Gabe walked off alone and said I'd know where to find him. I get it. It hurts my head to see all the bracelets—yellow like old bruises—and wonder just how much of this is all my fault.

Only Seth stands apart from the playtime, by our group-therapy circle of chairs where me and Gabe should've been pouring our hearts out. He's surrounded by therapists chattering at him and waving at the residents who are yanking at their own hair and earlobes, scratching invisible bugs over their forearms. Full-moon eyes. *Not everyone came here in as good a shape as you*, Flo told me a million years ago. Seth's shoulders rise with even breaths. I can see him trying to bend like a reed. Looks like his system hard-reboot will have him working overtime. Serves him right. He pushes away from the group when he sees me, his pace quick as he clips over the grass.

"You're one of the Scribes, then?" He points to my bracelet-less wrist.

"I'm not sure that means much anymore." I shrug. "Me and Gabe would really like to leave now. I think we learned enough about who we are. Were."

"I'd love to hear what the Center's administrator has to say about that."

I start to say *I thought that was you* until I stop myself. I must be caught canoeing round a loop again, flailing over the water. Ah, Fox the Fixer. Coding golden boy, last place in critical thinking and everything else. Poppy's voice from when I was paralyzed as J lugged me up the lawn floats back on razor-tipped bird wings. *We handed you the bloody keys.*

"Flo," I say, dumb.

"Then you didn't know?" He squints into the sun. "Changing of the guard, it seems, with how that rebel group hacked their way in and switched the Center's administrator access from me to her."

She must've wanted this all along, with the way she's been banging the gong to keep us all in time. "And this system hard-reboot…"

"She ran it. Hard-reboots were only ever meant for resident safety events if they became a danger to themselves. And system-wide reboots were only to receive code updates when the Center is empty of residents between Cohort admissions. Not for whatever she's trying to do. Not for deleting unauthorized users outright."

Holy shit. Flo's call to delete Poppy, and the SoCalia runners, and the IOC refugees with a couple of keystrokes. A trolley rolls into my head, and when the door slides open, Flo's smiling in the driver's seat wearing a tweed vest and straw hat. *All aboard for deletion city.*

"She'll—she'll let us leave?" I sputter.

"Please." Lines ache across his forehead with his furrowing brows. "Whatever you and Flo have planned, please let the other residents go." He waves behind me, where one of the yellow bracelets sprints, laughing, toward the marsh, and two therapists bolt after. "Flo cut off my access to log out of the sim. Not that I would just abandon everyone here. Let me contact their families. Let me arrange for their transfers to another facility where they can continue their treatment, and you can do whatever it is you need to with this Center. Whatever conflict Khadija and NIL/E— or you and NIL/E—have, it doesn't concern them. They need help."

I ache for one of his "no judgments." But I can see in his eyes: *Judgment, judgment.*

"I-I'll try."

He stabs a finger up to the wide windows of the Ankh Room before he turns back to the mess behind him. Residents hoot around me on my way over the lawn and through the hallways that smell of fresh paint.

My code fix for the virus shimmers in the air of the Ankh Room, projected from the gold coffin. Made up of tiny flecks of light and spinning slowly, glowing on the faces of Flo, Sig, and the other therapists. They cluster around it, murmuring at the sight of this holy marvel. The bird wings in the code flap, the waves ripple.

"It's elegant, really," Flo says, still eyeing the code, as I stiff-leg over the carpet. "Almost simple. But even with a code sample, how is your search string able to find and reconstruct the discrete memories of an entire 'stream? Is there some marker assigned to each client memory that we didn't know about?"

I don't know how to tell her that I was wrong when I told Gabe that there was nothing behind the code. Just that I didn't have the eyes to see it at the time.

Instead I ask her, "What am I?"

Minou's torn journal pages flutter by the window behind Flo, sounding almost like bird wings. I blink them away. It's just a trick of my eyes.

THIRTY-FOUR
EDITOR TEMPLATE 17

Flo looks at me with her melty blue *oh, honey* eyes. I don't know why I didn't see the edge in them before. The kindergarten-teacher-cardigan and voice, yeah, but she has to be patient because the kids she's dealing with are dirty-handed shits who can't help how dumb they are. They need her to guide them.

"Oh, hon—"

"Don't."

She nods, then turns to Sig. "Sig, can you and everyone clear the room, please? Fox and I should catch up."

I can feel the *yikes* simmering off Sig's shoulders. He and the others scoot out of the room in a blink. When the heavy wooden door behind me shuts, Flo floats around to the big carved desk in front of the windows and sits down. Of course. That's always where she wanted to be. *She had you focused on Seth as the boogeyman,* Gabe reminds me. *She knew that obsessing about the wrong people really is your wheelhouse.*

Not now. I shake my head to brush away his voice.

"Why don't you have a seat?" She motions to the chair across from the desk.

"I'll stand."

"Whatever makes you happy."

She pulls a strawberry candy from her pocket. I eye-stab her as she unwraps it, the foil crinkling in the dead-quiet air. She pops it in her mouth and the sound of it rattling against her teeth clanks my brain. Finally, I sit down.

"Why the system hard-reboot?"

"We needed a good spring cleaning."

"Even if that meant deleting a group of refugees who c-came here for help."

"Poppy barged in here with over two hundred people and zero warning. The sim architecture was hours away from crumbling under the strain of that new code injection. I'm talking total cognitive collapse of everyone here in the Center. I did what I did to prioritize the safety of the residents and continue our mission."

"Mission." I snort. "What even am I? A canned memory you booted up to help you with it?"

"Not quite. You came here as a…" She falters and offers a Flo smile. "Are you sure you want to know?"

"Please," I beg.

"It's easier if you think of Fox here in this room—you, that is—and Shazad Fox who once lived out there as two different entities. Shazad grew up on Aaru, met Khadija and Gabe, helped launch NIL/E Editorial. All that you've seen in the Excerpts. Until the blast in New Thebes that killed Gabe. Shazad's memories were damaged, yes, that much we know. The rest is a bit unclear. He vanished. It's likely he—he obliterated his own memories in his grief. Accidental or not. Which is unsurprising, given what we know of him."

She stops and I see the shimmer of tears in her eyes. And how dare she—how fucking dare she cry about *me* in front of me like this.

"I didn't know that Shazad, but I would've liked to," she continues. "I know that his gentle heart was his biggest strength and his biggest weakness."

My heart doesn't feel gentle. I swallow hard to keep the lava flow behind my ribs so I don't burn the whole sim down around me.

"And the Fox that's sitting in this room?"

"NIL/E recovered what they could of Shazad's memorystream and uploaded it into the Field of Reeds to monitor him on the off chance that he'd recover any memories that might lead them to Khadija. They created the story that he admitted himself here and put it in his client file in case your Case Manager ever needed to review it as part of your care plan."

"S-so I *am* Fox. Or Shazad, or, or..."

She shakes her head. "As much as you could call a pint of blood a human, I suppose. A—a severed arm—"

"I get it. Fuck."

"The Fox in this room was completely unrecognizable as a person—never mind Shazad—in any way when he first arrived. The residents outside that we rebooted to their day-one protocols? They're rocket scientists compared to the ghost you were. It broke my heart. Until slowly, over the years, you were able to walk and talk. And start treatment. Which is nothing short of a miracle."

I should've brought Gabe here with me for strength. *We've been thinking about this all wrong,* he said. *That Gabe died in the blast. I'm not him.* He can always see things more clearly than me.

"How many years?" I have to squeeze tight to not sag onto the floor.

"Since New Thebes? Seven."

Time crunches down to instants. Gabe on the edge of the couch after I broke his heart at Gay Bar. The flash over New Thebes. *Oh, that's weird.* The exploding windows of our apartment cut me up all over again. I squint, trying to get the guys from the Excerpts to chime in here. They don't say a word.

"Y-you told me the other Scribes got here a few months ago. That's how long they've been working on the virus."

"A few months in this iteration, yes. We found that if the malgs—amalgamated intellects, which is how we classify you Scribes—don't notch significant breakthroughs on the virus after eight, nine months, they start to backslide. Or, like we saw with Chengmei, what they experience in their Excerpts is too upsetting. Then we hard-reboot them and start over. Try different Excerpts and memory parameters to see if the editing mastery that we need surfaces."

Flash. Back in the Ankh. My first day here, affirmations in the mirror. Flash. Again and again.

Gabe forgiving me. Gabe loving me. Me seeing all of his memorystream as a gold river, with new eyes. I know she's wrong.

"B-b-b-but what does amalgamated intellect even mean? The budding. And the organic memory recovery, and how to explain me being with Gabe, an-an-an—" I can't get the rest of the words out. I'm back to the little boy on Aaru again with no voice.

"Is this helping?"

"I-I don't know. Keep going."

"We started with that tiny piece of Shazad. We folded in some editing training intensives, a handful of canned memories from other editors, summaries of Aset's philosophies. Some actual Memory Excerpts, yes, that you organically recovered during previous script-run iterations."

Script-run. *Some version of him is better than nothing.* Me and Gabe stretched out by the shore during our picnic, when everything seemed like it might've been fine.

"Yeah, but *why*?"

"Khadija created the Field of Reeds Centers—virtual and physical—to help heal memory trauma. When she left, NIL/E kept things running here as usual. You arrived and were basically a prisoner for years in your room. In whatever your shattered mind showed you. Until she reached out to me using a back door she left in the sim and tasked me to create the different editor templates, and the Scribe program, in secret. Using the company's resources against them. She hoped you could access Shazad's latent editing skills from his memories—his past—to help cure the virus."

"She spoke to me. In the training video, and sometimes I hear her voice. And…"

Flo waits for a while as I drown in all of this before she throws me a line.

"Editor Template 17—that's you—does have some quirks. Chosen One module inlay. Some self-mythologizing parameters, some entitlement boxes ticked." She hits me with her strawberry-candy smile.

"Minou. She found out."

"She is—was—special, Editor Template 11. The last several iterations, she emerged as a guide to the others, an emotional tether to keep them on track. Though sometimes her editing skills didn't rise as quickly to the surface. She discovered the truth of the Scribes many times before. Probably too observant for the sim parameters." Her eyes fall to the swirled wood of the desk. "We shouldn't have lost her. We've already sacrificed so much. But that's what happens when you move in shadows, away from your allies, even. We had to. You saw how the company is hunting Khadija. Still, Poppy was reckless."

"And the other residents?" Embroidered names carve over my heart. Radical Remembrances. All of them remembering their pasts, a memory at a time, until Flo blew that all away.

"Actually here for memory treatment, with their bodies in cold storage. We hid our work from them, and the therapist templates, save for the Ankh Room staff. Even Seth. He took over from the last Head Therapist about six months back. I'm not even sure how much of NIL/E's plan about you he was in on. Maybe he just thought you were another resident."

"He sure as fuck knows what's up now. What are you going to do with him? Trap him here with the other residents?"

She folds her hands. "He's a go-between for us and the company. We're working with him on the possibility of escorting the rest of the residents elsewhere—"

"A hostage exchange."

"—while we keep this sim to continue our work. He's good at what he does. He's the one who suggested the Gabe scrape as a recuperative tool for you, which just unlocked everything. Brilliant, given how intertwined Fox and Gabe were after their node-link. I don't know that you can really say they were even two separate people after that. Or, *you* were. You know what I mean."

"He's not a scrape."

"Yes, we've seen some beautiful surprises in his code. Still, at the end of the day, he's a scrape pulled from a template based on someone who once lived. Three layers removed from objective reality."

"His colors—"

"I had no idea—none of us could know—that he carried a Khadija parcel with him," she barrels on, ignoring me, "until Poppy came in with the installation Excerpt. Which was too unstable to access on its own, which is why we had to use the strength of your Memory Excerpt and your connection to Gabe to access it."

I look down at my hands where a blob of blood streaks from a jagged strip of skin on my thumb that I don't even remember ripping. The bright pain shoves me back into my body. My sim body. Whatever that means.

"And what now? Poppy s-said NIL/E'll bomb the whole Earth looking for Khadija. We need to help stop them, and—"

"You've done it, already. Let them keep crowding the Earth and dropping their memory bombs. You've cured the virus and removed the last roadblock to Project Bennu. Of course it makes sense, given your past role in supporting Khadija's efforts. You've set her—all of us—free from our chains."

"And now she can bring—what did she say?—never-ending paradise to Earth, or whatever," I smarm. "While we're stuck here."

"Not paradise on Earth, exactly. There's much Khadija's keeping to herself until it's time. But I know the next phase of humanity is that we'll live out in the stars, where we belong."

From the start, she's only ever wanted to make us divine, Flo told me, once, in a prayer-voice. And I looked out at the stars here, over the marsh. Just pixels in a sim.

"I'll send your code fix to her." Flo spreads her candy wrapper on the desk and flattens out the wrinkles, her head bobbing with a song I can't hear. "She'll be so happy."

"You sure do. S-seem happy."

"Well, I fulfilled my directive here, so I suppose that makes me a little tickled."

"Congratu-fucking-lations. What about me? How—how do I get out of here? We go to Khadija and help her—or the runners, or whoever—with the launch?"

"We don't even know where she is. All I have is an encrypted email address for messages. She's never responded. Poppy convinced me, when you were connected in the linked Ankh session, that once you and Gabe experienced the point in his memories when he received Khadija's parcel, we could somehow use it to find her. Tell her our progress. Ask for her help." Her smile fades as she fiddles with a candy. "Tell her how dedicated we've been."

She wants a pat on the head from her god. Problem is that gods never listen.

"We're trying to break open the parcel," she continues. "No luck as of yet. You?"

"No. I'll k-keep trying. If-if you send her messages, can you just *send* my code and Gabe's code to wherever she is? Or let me leave here in the Ankh, like Seth said residents could? Like Stash did? Get uploaded into a new body and try to find her, and…"

Wait. *Wait.* For a second, I can see Gabe on the edge of Flo's desk, swinging his feet, popping grapes into his mouth. His teeth poke out from his smile. *Come on, Foxy, you almost got it.*

"That's not how this works," I finish. More rattles against Flo's teeth as she moves her candy to the other side of her mouth.

"Stash—Editor Template 9—has degraded the last several iterations. You've seen how bitter he gets. It clouds his judgment, distracts him from the work. And his ice-cream tantrum with Gabe could've blown our cover. He wanted out, so I let him go."

"You deleted him?"

At the carnival, our first date, me and Gabe played that Smash-the-Snake game. The mallet in his hand slams on my chest with each word. High score. *Let's get the boy a prize!*

"It's for the best. Sometimes the templates react… poorly with the Excerpts. I know it sounds scary, but honestly, there's no pain."

More snakes. *Wham. Wham.*

"And you could let me and Gabe go—*really* let us leave, not delete us—with the other residents. If you wanted to, as the admin. There is a way out."

"You templates belong here, not in the outside world."

She must have a set of secret admin-mode settings at her desk that she stabs, making all my bones vanish, making me sag, heavy, into the chair.

"B-but if Khadija *knew* Fox, wouldn't she want to see me? Or-or him. This is too much." I hate how weak I sound. The fight leaks out of me. "I-I thought I was special."

"You are!" She leans just a bit over the desk, closer to me, still so gentle. "Just think. You discovered the virus fix. You fulfilled your purpose. How many people can say that about themselves? That they truly achieved what they were meant to? That's special. So special."

"And now that I fulfilled the mission?"

"Maybe there will be more research and we'll be called again? Or she'll call to us to join her, as a reward for all we've done? To be honest, I don't know. If you prefer, you can always…" Her voice trails off, her eyes flicking behind me at the Ankh. *You can always delete yourself.* She knows not to finish that sentence.

She reaches over the desk and pats the edge by me. I know she's trying to look comforting, and the fact that even after all this—all her lies—I want her to make it all better slides a shard of glass between my ribs.

Editor Template 17 has some "Mommy, please save me," issues, Gabe offers.

"In the meantime, Gabe's here with you. You have him back," she says. "That's all you've ever wanted."

She gets up and walks around the desk. I'm glued to the chair while she wraps one arm around my shoulders and the other around my head. And presses me to her in a hug, while my gaze is gone out the window—too tired to fight her—looking out over the marsh. One long ribbon of silver that stretches out to the horizon.

———

The worn floors of the manor creak under my feet as I wander from the Ankh Room, cement-footed. The walls are freshly painted and two therapists roll out a new floral runner down the main hallway. Still, it's the same place. I can't look at the grinning faces of residents bobbing around me in the halls. Hopefully Seth will get them out, leaving me, Gabe, Flo, and the therapists in sim purgatory until the slow death of the universe.

Template or not, I miss Minou. Her cracks during therapy. Her sarcastic eyes as she gave me her tour. How she tried to off herself and only ended up back in the Ankh. I miss her even if she was an emotional tether, according to Flo, to keep us Scribes on track. *Would you like me to explain our company policy on forced friendships while imprisoned in a simulation?*

The Excerpts in my head are screaming now that I'm away from Flo's strawberry-candy breath. Past Fox who wants to drown under a wave of whiskey. Even Gabe, whipping out his razor-smile. *What's the point? We're already dead.*

I find him on the back patio sitting alone by an easel. His hand with the brush moves, slow and steady, adding fringed blue-gray feathers to his painting of a heron. He missed his calling. He really should've been an artist.

I wait, just watching him and trying not to drown. Stalling before I swoop in and ruin his life. Because he doesn't deserve this.

"Staring," he calls without turning around.

Of course he felt me.

"You got me."

He drops his paintbrush in the cup of water by his easel and swings to face me, his face falling once it hits mine.

We walk in silence—him letting me turn over everything in my head while we follow the grass to our alcove by the shore.

"You're killing me," he says, frowning. "What happened?"

I sit down and he follows, legs folded up and facing me. I take his hands and stare at his knuckles, then—no, he deserves for me to look at him. His gold-flecked eyes, his eyebrows that crinkle with worry. I don't cry. At least that I can be proud of, as I tell him everything Flo told me. Stuttering at first, then pushing through. I'm a malg. None of this is real. The mission from Khadija was just to get us to carry out some stupid research project. *He's a scrape pulled from a template based on someone who once lived. Three layers removed from objective reality.* That's what hurt the most, the strawberry-scented words falling from Flo's lips. I don't tell him that part in those words.

He drops my hands and faces the water. Quiet, chewing on his fingertips until a tear glides down his cheek. His hands fall to his lap and then he bowls over, his shoulders shaking, his sobs slamming over the water. It's shitty to watch, feeling like the wound on my thumb from where I ripped my skin widens until I'm raw all over. Hurting more for him than for myself. He collapses into my lap—head slamming into my shins—and we both shake under the weight of all this. And I've never seen him half-ass anything as long as I've known him, so why would now—when he finally blocks out the stories behind his eyes and gives in to what he's feeling—be any different? Like everything he's ever held back explodes out at once and the whole Field of Reeds shakes with the blast wave.

I can't crumple. I let him wheeze and cry until his face is red, his chin quivering, until he almost can't breathe. Shaking with him. Until he's quiet again, and I trace the curved lines shaved into the sides of his head. Until I can drown out the Excerpts and listen to my own voice, even if it stutters, reminding me of what I know, deep down.

"Flo's full of shit," I say. "She has to be. I don't believe her."

Gabe clears a wet clog from his throat. "Why?"

"Because of everything we've seen. The-the *proof* of it. How-how you remember things you couldn't if you were just an Excerpt. The proof I've seen in the code that we're something more. And—how Khadija said one memory contains the whole. You're not just a scrape of Gabe, you're all of him."

Only his tired breath, slowing like storm winds.

"You made me see all that," I tell him softly. "What do you think? Feel?"

"I'm real. I *know* I'm real. Because if I'm not, what does that mean about Julio, and…" The way he squints shoves the dried reeds through my heart again. "But why would she lie?"

"She just doesn't know what we do. This whole place is fucking crazy. Our only hope is to get outta here. Find Khadija's location and maybe Flo will let us out. An-and we can join her, wherever she's going. So we don't stay in this sim forever, rotting in a server on some bombed-out Earth."

The sadness in his eyes kills me. He told me, a million years back, in Darius's office, *no one can be everything to another person.* And now he's stuck here forever, because of me, with nothing else to do but be by my side.

"And how do we do that?" he asks.

"I'll find out."

I cram my mouth shut before I can finish the thought. *I'll find out. We have forever.*

———

Gabe glides out of bed in the light of the moon. The drapes rustling in the breeze of the open window make more noise than he does. He needs time to work all this out, and so do I. I pretend I'm asleep and let him go.

You templates belong here, not in the outside world, Flo said. *Or she'll call to us to join her, as a reward for all we've done?* I could feel the need shimmering off her like colors over code. My only bargaining chip is to find where Khadija is so Flo can go off and meet her god.

How's that for polynomial fuckery?

I try to hack into the parcel for hours, every way I know how. No luck. If we're going to find her, we have to dive deeper into Gabe's mind. Forget about linked Ankh sessions. We have to take a cue from Kid Fox and Gabe from Aaru and plug into each other again.

But I can't be the one to ask. Not after all I've done to him already.

All we've done to each other, Past Fox reminds me and tries to stick his head out from behind one of Gabe's closet doors. *Remember the whole him and Khadija lying to you, and tricking you, and…*

I lock him away again. I wish Khadija was here. Or the Khadija I knew in the canteen, the one who dragged me around the neighborhoods, and taught me how to code. Who showed me how to breathe through the stutters and find my words. Who gave me a future without asking for anything. So she could tell me the truth. And save me from myself again.

I can see the scene I coded for her, like the ones I coded for others after I asked them what they wanted to change about their lives. What they wanted to do over. She's a kid again in her living room, sitting on the cushy carpet with her back against the couch. Cartoons in the background, her belly full of her favorite

Cow'N'Cod nuggies, her dad's warm fingers tickling over her head as he braided her hair. He always knew not to pull too hard. Her dad was with her, and everything was perfect.

Khadija's eyes swam when I showed her the scene on my Reeder in the canteen, the noise of the dinner rush falling away.

"I've been working on a basic conversation simulator, too. So you can talk to him." I had to keep my voice low so it wouldn't shake. "And say whatever you need to say."

I would've said *so you can really say goodbye*, but with the way her chin bounced and she didn't reach for a zinger, she didn't need me to nudge her off the edge. I'd loaded the memory sim on one of the pen things we'd lifted so she could plug into it whenever she wanted.

"Why?"

"You gave me my voice."

She cleared her throat, squashing her tears with a smirk and an elbow to my gut. "And now I can't get you to shut up."

I wish me and Gabe had some of her parachute code handy, now, to save us. Floating, floating, with the world coming into view down below.

The way the morning light makes the colors of the dining room look too dim lances at my eyes. Something's different. Wrong. Insert > doubt, dry and sharp like reeds. I know the hunger is fake, that I'm code without a body, but tell that to my stomach. Sunny Gabe is back at my side, grinning at me through a mouthful of kale and eggs like he hadn't smashed apart in my lap yesterday. The wall's back up. Therapists spoon food into the mouths of residents around us. Siobhan asks for some coffee, and the therapist at her side makes a big show of pouring a mug, practically throwing her a parade for stringing a whole sentence together. I ask Gabe if he wants to take a walk and I'm honestly relieved when he shrugs me off, saying he wants to paint for a while.

Outside, half of the patio bricks are suddenly cracked. One of the window shutters snaps off its hinge and swings against the manor. The sound is like a creaky knee. I pass by Seth on the lawn, sitting with another resident, looking like they're having a one-on-one session. I stay away from them and the others. They don't need me infecting them.

The breeze off the marsh fogs my head. At the archery range, two residents poke at a leaf that's suspended in the air. A therapist with hedge clippers presses her forehead against a tree, her legs moving beneath her on an invisible treadmill. Ducks swim backwards over the marsh. Everything, all of us, lost off our tracks for some reason. My head throbs while I wander over the shriveling grass to the orchard, where rotten apples stud the ground. The low moss-flecked rock wall that separates the orchard from the rest of the grounds looks like it's carved from polystyrene. I toe one of the rocks and it dissolves into sand.

Just the first barrier I need to break to get us out of here.

I roam the grounds for hours, piecing cut-glass mosaics in my head. On the way back to the manor, I spot Flo sitting in a lawn chair facing the shore. I stay far enough away that she doesn't look up. She just unwraps a strawberry candy and pops it into her mouth. Balls up the wrapper and adds it to the pile overflowing from the coffee cup on the armrest. The glinting red and green plastic spills all around her, onto the grass.

THIRTY-FIVE
FIELD OF MEMORIES

I've never been big on art, but Gabe's heron painting is so
beautiful I almost cry. I'm in the tub in our room when he walks
in and rests the canvas against the wall by the big bay window. The
heron's wings are the blue-gray of stormy skies, fanned in mid-
flight, its yellow beak spearing the air. It looks like it could flap
off the canvas and out the window.

Right now, I wouldn't be surprised.

Gabe lugs a footstool from the lounge and *thunks* it on the floor
by the tub.

"What the fuck is going on around here?" he asks. He's my
Gabe again, shoulders back, in the spotlight. I knew he just needed
some time.

"Did you see Flo?"

"In her candy coma by the shore? Yeah. I also saw J in the
sunroom talking to a houseplant about big-time budding, and
snow coming down the dining-room fireplace like a goddamned
Christmas miracle."

"I think Flo is wrangling with an existential bummer after
fulfilling her purpose as the Scribe ringleader, and it's cocking up
the sim now that she's the admin."

"Can't she just bend like a reed like the rest of us?" He leans forward and presses his fingertips into in a pair of bird wings. "We gotta get outta here."

"Yeah."

"And we know the only bargaining chip we have with Flo is in here." He taps his head.

We bleed into each other. We share thoughts. Call it perforation. Call it being together for sixteen years. Of course he'd have the same idea.

"I know."

"We save off a copy of my memorystream, boot it up on a Reeder, and editor tag-team again? Try to crack the walls of the Khadija parcel and find out where she is."

"The code is too static."

"So we plug into each other? Just like old times."

The water of the tub is so hot that steam scalds my nose. "We'll both be too delirious to really be useful."

Past Fox would come at this with a chisel and a hammer. *Just admin mode him and be done with it. Why are you dragging this out? Tell him what to do and then tell him to forget it.* I doubt that admin mode would even work on Gabe now—he's so far beyond a scrape or an Excerpt—not that I ever would try.

I have to look down at the murky bathwater in case my thoughts beam out of my eyes and nudge him. I can't be the one to bring this up. I won't. If he wants to take this road, it has to be him to suggest it. It's his memorystream. Like we're both him again, stumbling through the doors of Khadija's garage lab. *Live code is more flexible. You have to be awake for us to map available neural pathways.*

"Then we need you clear-headed, and me out of it. So…" I watch the valley between his eyebrows as he thinks. "So we take a hint from Auntie Flo on your first day in the Ankh. Sedative."

"'It'll help with your transition into the new Memory Excerpt,'" I quote her.

"She's not wrong. My memorystream'll be more receptive to you poking around 'n' shit. I can let you in deeper that way."

"If that's what you want."

He leans back with a smirk. "I usually don't gotta be sedated to take you deeper, babe."

I love him so much for making a joke right now. I laugh and end up splashing water out of the tub.

I slosh out of the bath, towel off, and get dressed. Me and Gabe head to the Ankh Room, where books litter the floor, half of them open with stray pages flapping in the air like birds. Sig's alone in the room, his back to us as he sits on the windowsill and watches the yellow bracelets down below. He doesn't say anything—barely moves—as we brush through the floating pages and swipe a vial of gold sedative from the bar. One of the pages slices my hand, drawing a thin line of blood. In my head I can hear the rollercoaster from the carnival as a car clanks up the first drop. If the sim is breaking apart, what does that mean for us?

Back in our room, we sit on the couch and Gabe stares at the vial. Rolls it in his hands.

"So you'll just be rooting around all of my memories?" he asks. "You'll see everything?"

I can see the question behind his eyes—flecked with the same gold as the liquid in the vial—that he doesn't ask.

"Nothing I see in there will make me love you any less," I tell him.

"How do we know this'll even work?"

"We don't."

"Are we fucking up here? Is this stupid 'n' dangerous?"

"Not any more than all the linkups we've already done. And we have a copy of your memorystream saved, in case…"

I'm back in the editing clinic on Aaru again, asking *what would you change about your life?*

He sighs and rubs his hands over his face. I almost stop there, with the skin-over-skin whisper lacerating the backs of my arms, the doubt turning down the corners of his lips.

"I want you to know that I'm doing this for me, not for you," he says. "We still got shit to work on, and I can't be in this place forever. I'll go crazy."

"I know. I'm sorry that you have to go through this. I'm sorry about a lot of things."

"Yeah." He presses his lips into a hard line. "If this is the only way, maybe it's…" He looks up and his squinting gaze glides past me. "Maybe."

"Yeah."

The wall of my ribcage might as well explode at his words. With the way he reaches for my hand and flips it to trace the lines of my palm, closing the space between us. Like we slugged up a road together and can maybe turn around and see that we were alone in the same relationship for so long. For our own reasons.

"Alright." He sucks in a breath, suddenly bright. His Gabe costume confidence, scaffolded by a story behind his eyes. "Bottoms up."

He knocks back the vial and then lies back on the couch and closes his eyes. I wait, locking my breath tight, until his chest slows with long and steady exhalations. Until I call his name and he doesn't answer. And then I grab the linkup cable from the dresser, sit on the floor next to him with my back propped against the couch, and plug in.

———

The rollercoaster car creeps up and up—until the instant of weightlessness at the top of the ramp where I have just enough time to think *oh holy fuck I made a huge mistake*—before the car rockets down, through thunderflood clouds that smell like apricot scrub from Tish at Gabe's work, and past floating mint-green shirts, and cyclones of balls from the playground of Coral Beef. A hilly field along a never-ending river peeks into view from behind the clouds, the landscape a twilight of blues and reds against blackness. And shouldn't the car be slowing down? Wait, wait—a giant invisible thumb squashes me deeper into the seat as I blast beyond giant buckets of Cow'N'Cod nuggies and flying cat PixelPets. The sides of the car glow and spark before catching fire as my screams come out in watercolor herons that squawk, look at me with glassy eyes, and fly away like, *good fucking luck, man.*

The car crashes into a hill and the invisible hand of god fast-balls me through the air—*I don't have a body here*, I scream in my head, *this won't hurt, this won't hurt*—until I slam onto the grass. I bounce once, twice, and crumple into a heap of smoking friction burns.

So much for the *not having a body* thing.

Breathe deep. Bend like a reed. I cough and try to piece myself together. A faint, slow and steady drumbeat of distant thunder rolls through the air. Gabe's heartbeat, I know. Everything here is part of him. He let me in and he wants me here, I say to the landscape more than to myself. Insert > guy who keeps fucking up his and his husband's life and is just trying to make it right.

Please don't let me drown here. Please don't let me lose myself.

I ache up to my shaky feet and look around. The rolling grass along the river looks not that different from the Field of Reeds, if I ignore the half-translucent scenes that float down the water like ghost barges. A laptop on a footstool pointed at a bedsheet in a small bedroom, the only flickering light from the screen. The bow of a ship where Gabe holds tight to Julio's hand. Gabe in his rubber waders in the algae tanks, laughing as he sprays someone with a hose. Him on stage at the Stable. Both of us lying in the Body Garden, folded into each other. That one aches. I have to hold my breath against the view of myself through his eyes. I can feel his love for me—throbbing like the thunder heartbeat overhead—that I never trusted was there, that I always begged him to spell out.

I could stay here forever and just relive every part of him. But Gabe's waiting for me to make this right.

Affirmations in the bathroom mirror. You will remember. You are special, and you are loved. And you deserve to remember.

Yeah, I remember, suddenly. I'm not really here. I don't have a body, as much as the burns on my arms and face scream otherwise. I'm a bunch of code in a bunch of Gabe's code, in a simulation that's built of code. It's all the same, flowing into each other. *Now you're thinking like an editor*, a mash-up of voices reminds me. Nina the Neuron. Greg. Seth. J. Gabe. Even Flo. Khadija has been calling out to me since I saw her face in the training video, and I know I can find her.

Everything I am shrinks down to a search string—and how many narrative levels deep are we?—with glowing gold bits of code circling me like fireflies. *Show me where Khadija is.*

The symbols blast away in a gold wave that shudders through this field of memories. Off in the distance down a hill, a huge spotlight flicks on—illuminating what looks like a giant block of glass—at the end of a gauntlet of smaller spotlights. In each spotlight waits an Excerpt his subconscious dreamed up for me. Stories behind his eyes that he needs me to see.

"Gentlethems, please help me welcome to the stage for his debut performance," Coach's voice booms overhead. I look up, and a galaxy of livestream cameras blankets the sky. "Fox the Fixer!"

The applause is a rain shower of code. The clouds overhead crack open, raining wrenches and bolts down on me. For a second I'm in just a tool belt and skivvies, ready for Friday-night livestream. Coach doesn't have to tell me twice. I haul ass down the hill.

Flash.

I'm running through the empty streets of Aaru as my wild breath rasps against the shipping container buildings. I'm Gabe but also Fox. A Cow'N'Cod nuggie combo bucket, now with nuclear-winter-ranch dip. Running and watching as Excerpts of Gabe and Fox play out in each spotlight.

A roar behind me. I really, really wish I hadn't turned around. The wave surges around a street corner, blasting away neighborhoods and train cars.

How do you outrun an ocean?

One night, the storm drill alarms whoop through the air. Well, hold the phone on the *drill* part. A furycane pointed right at Aaru. The mother of all storms. *I asked you nicely these past several hundred years to cool it with the greenhouse gasses, and now I have to yell because how the fuck else am I going to get you kids to listen?*

The storm knocks three spokes of Aaru into the ocean. Eight thousand dead, easy. It takes months and months, but NIL/E drops a lot of them into new vessels, because the algae farms and the Body Gardens aren't going to run themselves.

The line into Fox and Khadija's editing clinic wraps around the island. Each memorystream that Fox edits—slicing away memories of drowning in shipping container dorms, or kicking past bodies to get on top of a train car above the water, or seeing your kid pummeled by a flying Body Garden tank and then get dragged out to sea—stays with him. He drowns, he dies each time. Gabe brings him bowls of noodles and begs him to sleep. Fox blinks too much and squints, like he's caught in one long wince. The line out of the editing clinic never seems to get shorter.

"You can't keep doing this," Gabe says. "You gotta stop and eat something. Sleep. *Muerte.*"

"Now you don't care about the others?"

And he knows it's because Fox is scared and tired and confused, but still, that shit hurts.

I forgot how small the editing clinic really was. I wore away the gloss on the concrete floor around my desk from all my fidgeting, over the million hours I was there. Deleting thousands of deaths by drowning. I can feel everything—the hours, the deaths, the shitty memories I carved away—slamming into me like Body Garden tanks tossed on a tidal wave, now that I run past that Excerpt. Suffocating me. But I can't break, since Gabe is waiting for me. I have to be strong for the both of us.

For once.

More storms.

The storm cracks the foundations of Aaru. Literally—the seawater seeping up through the canteen drains, chunks of other spokes floating away—but figuratively, NIL/E thinks they did a pretty bang-up job! All their utopia-lite humanitarian lessons and editing curriculums and industrial algae farming and Body Garden advances would help humankind reach toward their Tomorrows and Tomorrows™.

They built an island and raised a generation of entrepreneurs and go-getters and Big Thinkers. Just look at Khadija Banks, who dropped a novel-length proposal on the next evolution of NIL/E Technologies onto the desk of the Aaru bigwigs a week after Furycane Set round-housed the island.

The digital immortality was an adorable start, babycakes, she told the Head Caregiver. *What me and Fox built here is the pilot program. Now it's time to scale up. You gotta roll out boutique editing to the rich memory-backup customers first, then use the cash flow to go mass-market. We can bring backups and bespoke bodies and editing levels to the whole world. And look, I'm not saying let's make NIL/E a charity. Let me help you make more money than god. And then we use the money and the tech to fix the planet, switch to solar power and suck up the carbon from the air, and drain the flooded cities. And then we all live on this dirt mound until just before the sun swallows it up, and then we sail off to new worlds and start all over again.* And then, and then, and then…

Twenty-three, and Khadija Banks is going to save the world. NIL/E Corporate staff agree the Aaru experiment got the thumbs-up. Handshakes, company-wide bonuses.

The company plans to evacuate Aaru in stages—because this was the old days, before the centralized NIL/E client servers, when they could just send someone's saved memorystreams to one of the million Body Gardens around the world for a quick rez.

They wrangle a nearby yacht to rescue critical staff first, two days out, with more to come soon. Fingers crossed. The first yacht has room for sixty. Khadija's not staff, but they're making an exception for her as a Key Citizen.

She's not leaving without Fox. This is his idea, too.

He's not leaving without Gabe, Fox says to the Head Caregiver in her office. Khadija, beet-red hair at his side, links her arm in his. *What he said.*

Head Caregiver smarms something about *we don't exactly need a janitor on this boat, which is staff-only and it's a miracle they're even letting you two on, blah.* They'll put Gabe on another one, soon. Unless Fox wants to convince one of the Aaru staff to leave one of their kids behind, or stay themselves, and free up a space?

She is, of course, being a total asshole, but that doesn't stop Fox from begging down the list for someone to do just that.

All of this that Gabe didn't want.

"Stop bein' an idiot," he tells Fox. "You can't help people if you're dead. I'll go on the next boat. I'll find you."

Fox looks more and more like the banged-up birds he used to save as a kid. He cries and begs until he can't breathe, and the stutters clam him up. Gabe yells at him. He doesn't want to, but he knows he has to be mean. He can't have Fox's death on him, not after Julio. He says Fox is embarrassing himself. That Gabe never really loved him. That he has the Brotherhood of the Half-Mast Boredom Boners to keep him company.

When Fox doesn't believe all of that, Gabe corners Khadija the night before the yacht reaches the docks.

"We lie," Gabe tells her.

Khadija's smart. She knows what's up. "We get your ass on the next boat. Start packing."

Even with the lie to Fox about how Khadija scored Gabe a ticket, they need backup. Fox patched enough memorystreams that plenty of people are all too happy to help repay the favor and get him out. Mei scores some top-notch downers and whips up Fox's favorite noodle soup, loading it with extra kelp kimchi to hide any new bitterness.

Fox is dopey and sweet after he slurps down his noodles, already drooling a bit. Burbling how he loves Gabe. How they're both leaving, when that's all Gabe ever wanted, *and then we'll, and then we'll…* He doesn't finish the sentence before he sags down in his seat.

Gabe almost crumples. Almost. He stuffs a slip of paper in Fox's pocket. It might as well be a ransom note for a stolen life. *I'm sorry. I had to.* One of the other Body Garden techs scoops up Fox's sleeping body, hauls him out to the docks. Gabe had planned on carrying Fox but suddenly he can't lift his own arms.

I watch Gabe at the docks of Aaru as the yacht with Fox sails off. The glowing scene of Gabe turning back to the yacht for one last glimpse before shoving off into the shadows floats down the river of memories, away from me. I'm frozen to the shore. Water trickles into my shoes.

Let me drown. Just let me drown, knocked by the tidal wave of code, and the past, and what me and Gabe did to each other, over and over again.

Thunder rolls over the sky. I look behind me as lightning stabs the sky again. I should learn from the tidal wave on Aaru to not look back. To keep going. If I stop and let myself feel any of this, I won't be able to move again.

It's raining torn-up scraps of paper from the livestream-camera sky, now. *I'm sorry. I had to.*

———

Citizen priority lists. Evac boats. So much for Khadija's whole *we get your ass on the next boat* thing. Gabe drowns two years in the algae tanks. When he thinks he made a mistake by booting Fox out, he wanders, aimless, to the edge of the Echo neighborhood, where the splintered road and toppled buildings sink a little more each day.

Enough boats come that one morning there's actually room for Non-Key Citizens like him.

New Providence. The halfway house. He rings up the main NIL/E customer hotline once—in the two years since Khadija and Fox left Aaru, NIL/E offices popped up all over the world—feeling like an asshole as he asks to leave a message for the CEO. The operator asks, *and who are you, exactly?* Khadija doesn't call back. Too busy saving the world and all, he guesses. Whatever. He never went for handouts, anyway.

The stability at the Stable, finally. Hours, days, three years with Levi all compressed down into an instant, a single scene with Gabe and Levi in Gabe's bedroom that I run into, shivering as all the ghosts pass through me. Like *wait, wait, stay here and feel this all.*

Almost to the last spotlight in the field of memories where the block of glass waits for me. *Come on, tubby, you can wheeze for a few more minutes,* I told myself a hundred times on the treadmill in the gym at work, trying to make myself better. For him, which is why it never worked. I never wanted to be better just for myself.

Each time I blow through an Excerpt and back into the field, another crackle of lightning stabs the sky. Overhead, huge blossoms of light collapse into tiny fireflies, like fireworks in reverse. Only the distant glass block waits for me.

Another boom of thunder from Gabe's heartbeat that I feel deep in my chest more than I hear. No, actual thunder. I splash through an inch of water, and when I look around I see that the river is overflowing. Way off in the distance of the endless fields, a growing tidal wave of glimmering blue code builds, sucking up strength as it warps the landscape around it. Furycane Set to settle the score. *Look who's back, bitch*.

Shit, I'm gonna drown. I'm gonna—

"I understand you're having some problems with perforation," more than one editor told me and Gabe when we went in for edits together. "Let's see what we can do."

All the edits are knocking together and damming up his memorystream. I'm the invasion, the virus in his mind, and now it's fighting back. Another gut-punching thunderclap. I don't belong here. I don't have long.

Another memory. Hold on. Keep running.

Lights streak against the windows of Rajon's car as he drives Gabe away from the Stable and New Providence. Later, he'll let Gabe crash in his guest room for a while, and they'll stay in touch even when Gabe leaves. And he doesn't ask, but the least Gabe is happy to do for the man who saved his life is toss him a fuck once in a while until Rajon meets Luka. Gabe can hold Rajon some nights. Love him for a few hours.

For now, Rajon just rolls up to the bar—where broken glass confettis the pavement outside—drops off Gabe for his parcel installation, and waits. He lights a cigarette while Gabe, foggy-headed, reads over the storage agreement and extraction plan.

When the Patron requires extraction, extraction coordinates and instructions will be transmitted to Insurance Policy via Constructed Memory Dream Sequence. Monetary bonuses are awarded for Insurance Policy rendezvous at Extraction Point within twenty-four hours of transmission. Failure of Insurance Policy arrival at Extraction Point within seventy-two hours of Dream Sequence delivery will result in remote-wipe of Insurance Policy wetware.

Begin installation.

The water flooding the field of memories is so cold it blurs the edges of my vision. Trudging the last leg through knee-high water, finally—*finally*—I reach the glass block at the end of the spotlights. It's fifty feet high, easy. Warped reflections of myself run at me as I sprint to the block and bash my whole body against it in a blast radius of code. Nothing happens. I run my hands over the block, looking for cracks, brushing away the ransom note rain. Nothing. Nothing.

The water gushes up around me. The thundering of the tidal wave at my back twists into a scream—an animal sound that feels like fangs on my neck. I think it's my own scream until Gabe swoops through the air from behind me on watercolor heron wings, his black Santa Muerte cloak hovering around him like he's underwater, and heaves a canteen tray at the glass block.

The block shatters. Shards ripple out into a loose bubble but then freeze in midair, spinning and slowly shrinking back together. Beyond the shards I can just peek someplace that looks familiar.

Of course Gabe would be here. Of course he'd save me. I look at him—his sly smile like he just made a dick joke—and could shatter into a million pieces like the block.

"Go!" he shouts. The voice echoes through the blue-red twilight. "I'll buy you time."

I don't have time to answer. He zips up into the air like one of the gods in the stories back on Aaru and beats back the tidal wave of code with his canteen tray.

The shards cut me up as I squeeze through until the glass un-shatters closed behind me.

THIRTY-SIX
SCALPEL

The second my feet hit the blue-painted concrete, the memories of the playground on Aaru knock into me like a wave. The rusty slide, the swing set, and there Khadija and kid me are on our backs and giggling all over each other by the creaky seesaw, stargazing mid-mipper trip. I'm in a piece of her mind, re-seeing, reliving. I know what happens next.

"All the code, all-all the memories and junk you've seen," me and Kid Fox say at the same time. "What's your favorite?"

He looks happy—even here in this tiny concrete playground on this gray island, because he's with Khadija, and tomorrow he'll see Gabe, and his whole life is ahead of him—and it breaks my heart. Because now I know the Khadija I loved so much is going to drug me and shove me on a boat one day. Even if she thinks she's saving me.

I miss her and hate her and love her so much still, with the signals all jamming up in my head.

I can't think about that now, not while Gabe is fighting a tidal wave outside. I've got to move.

Khadija twirls the mipper pen. "I bet if I peeked under the hood at this exact moment—bingo. That'd be it."

She chose her favorite memory of us as the parcel to drop into Gabe's head. I wonder if he feels honored?

The playback of the memory stops, pausing Kid Fox and Khadija mid-giggle. Moths frozen in flight around one of the floodlights, a stray krill chip bag stalled midair over the concrete. Only the ocean lapping at the dock ramp by the playground moves. When I walk to the water's edge, the black ocean looks like it stretches out into forever. Bits of code flash off the waves instead of starlight, with scenes glowing and fading from the deep. Khadija on stage waving to a crowd. Khadija as a little girl running down a fire escape and trying not to look behind her. Khadija in our editing clinic in Aaru, wrapping a blanket around my slumped shoulders, where I'm asleep at my desk.

Even one memory contains the code of the whole 'stream, folded in on itself. Like how individual cells of your body contain your entire genome, her voice reminds me from above. Though it could be just the thunder.

"Show me what I came for," I tell the frozen stars in the sky.

I step into the water. Flash. Another wave knocks me into somewhere else.

The huge windows of the airy bungalow I instantly find myself in look out over sand and craggy outcroppings of rock. I've been here before, surrounded by the glossy wood furniture with clean lines and the mural of birds. A jungle of plants on one wall, across from the framed FUCK OFF paper plate and mounted flat-screen where the memory of her dad braiding her hair that I coded plays on loop. Khadija's private pad in RedLandia, far from her penthouse in Kemet and the board meetings and product launches that grated her so much, years after the scaffolding around New Providence came down and she'd renamed her new-jeweled city New Thebes. I used to hop on her AI-piloted private jet-pod out here with her for intensive coding weekends. Or more often, to break out the old mipper pen. Flashback to old times, when things were simpler and we didn't have a company to run. We'd turn to each other, like, *reshaping the world sure chaps my ass sometimes, huh?*

I wander through the living room and into the glass cube of the dining room to find Khadija sitting at a semi-circle of six Reeders at the table, surrounded by abandoned coffee cups, and Coral Beef buckets, and piles of wires. She's pushed away the chairs to make room for an Ankh, where lights from the gold mask flash over someone's face. Pause, revision: *My* face. I could be looking at my younger self from the picture in my room back in the Field of Reeds, except this version of me is stiff and clawing at the sides of the Ankh. Screaming.

Ageless Khadija—pulled from the training video, in white linen and gold, with her crown of beaded braids and so, *so* much patience—sucks in a breath, and keeps going. I can feel her thoughts seeping into me like the freezing water from the flooded field of memories, making me all ice-brained. I can feel the riptide of her memories yanking me down.

I'm pretty sure I'm already losing my mind. At that, I hear J's sunny laugh. *Can't lose what ya didn't have, Fox! Har. A-plus colleague-appropriate humor.*

Khadija jetted to LakeLandia the second she heard about the whole *NIL/E employee and client icing his coworkers* thing, filling the tiny security office where cuffed and drugged Greg was slumped over in a chair with her patchouli perfume and Earth Mother rage. Some shit you don't send minions for. There would be incident reviews, and process reviews, and review reviews, soon. She'd get

Media to hammer out a name for whatever happened—chronic excision-based cognitive buzzwords. First, mission abso-fucking-lutely critical for her to peep at this poor bastard's code to figure out what had happened. And before word spread and clients got freaked about their next round of edits accidentally insta-sociopathing them.

She cleared the rent-a-cops out with a flap from her gold-caped suit and a *go*. She plugged her Reeder into his node, and—*great fuck, my incisors are Aset the goddess*—she could see past the finger-painted templates and hacksaw edits.

Fox.

She hadn't seen him for over a year. You can only support someone while they tear themselves apart from the inside out with whole-scale edits and backstory overhauls that never seemed to stick before you realize you need to stop being a crutch. You need to step back. For both of you.

She owed him, he screamed at her all the time. A week off the yacht from Aaru, she'd fessed up to what she and Gabe had done and held Fox while his cries shook both of them. They'd get Gabe off Aaru on the next evac wave, but NIL/E said they had to wait until the seas calmed down. They were still two kids with ideas then. They had to prove to the company and the world that they were fucking worth something, then they would call the shots. Soon. Hell, she'd hire a submarine to chug on over to Aaru once their checks cleared. Once their proposals poured into concrete foundations for editing offices all over the world.

Fox had to trust her. He had to give her some time.

And of course she'd helped him, mostly with hope and promises at first, the two years after Aaru while they co-piloted the Editorial rollout and remade the world from the NIL/E flagship in New Providence. Looking for Gabe, suturing emotional dampeners and light edits just for Fox to get through the days without crumbling. But at some point, he had to move past the past and focus on all the beautiful work they were doing, with editing centers popping up everywhere. All the trauma he was axing out of their clients, the squads of editors they were training. They were breathing his dream into the world, continuing his work from their Aaru clinic, now with basically unlimited resources. It's what Gabe wanted him to do, too.

She didn't judge the edits Fox hacked into his own head as he tried to forget about Gabe. Raw-dogging reality bit big time, though she stuck to weed and wine like her pop. Fox would vanish for weeks, then stumble into the office stinking of panic and crying about bodies in tanks dragging him into pink water. Something about an emergency meeting of a brotherhood of the half-mast boredom boners.

Jesus. He needed a breather—sabbatical, she said. They had hundreds of editing teams now. Let others pick up the slack while he traveled, and took up yoga, and maybe got laid. *Work through your shit*, she'd told him. *I need you.*

Then he had to take the easy way out and get a bargain-basement Greg™ template.

Shove all that out, boss. Think of the mipper lines out the clinic door and ignore the migraines trying to drill out your eyes. You got this.

She handed Greg's body over to Uploads—no use in wasting it, they could just slash twenty percent off asking for the next client, anyhow—and sent for one of Fox's vessels. That was easy. Fox had extra bodies. Both of them had extra everything, those golden years after the first editing clinics opened in New Providence and Beijing to customer lines down city blocks. When the world collectively lost their shit over Khadija Banks, the architect of memory who'd save them all, who would've shared the spotlight with her little intern Fox, if he'd wanted it. She bought beach houses and heels and tailored bamboo-silk suits to show off her (killer) pins. He bought bodies—a fleet of them, like the board members whose pockets they lined bought vintage sports cars— and stored them in his cryowardrobe at home. He jumped in and out of them—*this one's sense of smell is too strong, that one lags to the left.* He was trying to be someone else, of course. Until she and everyone else in the company barely remembered his face.

She sent for a vessel with his original genome—normcore-chic and all—and had her assistant overnight it to her RedLandia pad. She scrubbed the Greg template from Fox's memorystream on the jet on the way there. Even after that, his fragile memorystream was like filling a paper bag with water and knowing it'll leak out. Tick tock. She stopped for enough Coral Beef to feed a small army, stocked the fridge, and the next day she was hugging her little bro on the couch, fresh from his memory upload in her private Ankh. She rubbed his back like they were mipping on the playground again.

"Precision edits," she told him. "The only way I can think of outta here."

"Yeah," was all he could say, like he hit his word ration for the day.

This time she couldn't drug him and lie. She couldn't save him from the pain, not when she needed him awake and alert to hunt down the corruption and the painful memories wherever they popped up in his live memorystream.

Sometimes, she knew, the cure burns worse than the poison.

She laid him down in the Ankh and plugged his node right to her Reeder. The cursor was her scalpel.

Who knows how long I've got here, splashing around in Khadija's memories, before Gabe's mind spits me out. Or mangles me. The thought of him thwacks me with a canteen tray and knocks me back into my head.

Young Fox under the mask is screaming. I'm screaming. Our double-helix of screams rattles the glass-cube walls of the room, and still Khadija won't stop.

"Aaru," she says.

The word wakes memories in the code on her Reeder screens, sparking the symbols like spells. Her steady fingers flick over the Reeders, and me and Young Fox scream as she deletes the glowing code. Hacks the memories from our mind. Each keystroke slides hot glass into my eyes. Her gold bracelets jangle like sleigh bells.

I'm awake for my own open-brain surgery.

My screams shred my throat and I claw at my ears. Reeds from the shore of the Field of Reeds stab under my fingernails. Young Fox screams ten thousand names at her, begging her to stop, begging her to keep going.

Gabe. Slice. *Delta canteen.* Slice. *Body Garden.* Slice. Her voice only shakes once.

A memory earthquake snaps me in half, hands on my knees, barfing onto the floor. I cough up code—wedges, and symbols of seated little guys in skirts, and wavy blue lines, and crescent moons. Horned snakes. Birds with fringed wings. And even the word *baaaarrrrrfffff* that flows in a black river out of my mouth.

When Khadija seems to run out of words, Young Fox screams

more from under his mask. *Purple lights in the Body Garden. Julio. Don't you fucking stop.*

"Bosscakes," me and Young Fox blubber together. "You gotta save me."

"You know I always will," she says.

The pain burns out the sun. Off in the dark sky, lightning cracks over the sand, blinding me.

Khadija never understood quite why Fox's edits about Gabe never stuck. She knew Fox tried to turn Gabe from the only man he'd ever love into Some Guy From Aaru by digging out the emotional scaffolding of his memories as a kid. Deleting him outright didn't seem to work. He'd show up again, first in dreams, then in hallucinations, haunting him.

In their private penthouse office, the music from the rager downstairs thudded through the floors. Their whole staff was celebrating the ground-breaking on the New Angeles facility, the Beijing extension, and the billionth customer sign-up, knocking back spiked punch from ice fountains carved into statues of Aset. Khadija eyed Fox sitting on the loveseat in their brainstorming lounge area, turning over a glass of whiskey. She looked down at the lotus in the chickpea can on the coffee table between them because his big dopey eyes hurt too much, like he was holding a dead bird in a krill can out to her.

She held in her *what the absolute fuck were you thinking*, when he fessed up how he and Gabe had connected their nodes together as kids. And since then it had been like their memories all bled into each other, even when they were apart.

"The only times I have ever not been miserable was when I was connected to him," Fox blubbered, whiskey-slurred. "When

I was mipping with you." He jammed his fingers to the side of his face until his fingertips turned white. "We were never meant to be alone, Deej."

"Babycakes," was all she'd been able to muster. She'd swallowed the rest. *You'll never be able to dig him out.*

Connected to Gabe, feeling everything he felt, swimming in all of his memories, so tangled up still, years later. Parts of them forever anchored in each other. Were they even a single mind anymore? Absolute batshit.

Unless.

Unless he was onto something?

A back door to what the caregivers were trying to teach them on Aaru about fellowship with humankind, and kindness, and responsibility for the Earth. Which we'd never get to on our own.

Thoughts of that back door cracked open for years, stayed with her long after the precision edits on Fox. After she had to scalpel out even his memories of their time together on Aaru—she couldn't separate his memories of her from Aaru, couldn't separate Aaru from Gabe, so they all had to go—and replace them with a combo Generic Childhood to Early Adoption template. She had to get creative with the timeline, ret-conn his memories so he wouldn't remember launching Editorial with her and would think he'd only been at the company as an underling for a few years. She sent him back to New Thebes and set him up with an easy job so they could babysit him in case he came down with the Greg™s. She would always, always save him, but she had to put up the FUCK OFF plate between them for a while and bounce out of New Thebes. When the company pivoted from paradise on Earth to immersive flicks and canned memories. Hawking pop-up armies—vessels with reinforced titanium skeletons and built-in Krav Maga mastery. Paradise could wait while the board slobbered over bonuses.

In the mipper clinic, she'd told Fox she'd wished there were a hundred more of her. So she plugged in a hundred dupes of her memorystream into a hundred cloned bodies, and, *bam*. The bad-ass-est brain-trust to strut through history. An underground Khadija Technologies. Avatars, daughters of Aset, fucking queens walking the Earth, and bringing her brightest idea to life.

How many memorystreams could they link without complete collapse, whipping up buttresses and giant limestone blocks of foundational code for stability? Connection would remind us that we're all part of a bigger whole. Get us all to stop being such assholes. To each other. And the environment, and...

Until the company got wind that something was up and sent their goons to hunt down the queen of queens. So she had to go into hiding and parcel out insurance plans, just in case.

She could save them all. Just like drugging sweet lil bro Fox and saving him, because he couldn't see the big picture.

One big over-soul-y puddle of humanity. Sounds, what, spiritual? Perfect.

Forget bringing mippers back down with parachute code. She'd keep going up and up and up—bringing everyone along for the ride.

Gabe's voice rattles from an air-conditioning vent above the dining room memorystream surgery—*ox, I can't keep the wave back much longer. It's too strong, it's co*—and slams me back into the right moment.

Young Fox in the Ankh is screaming for Khadija to stop. I'm screaming for her to stop—I have to stop her because she can't. She can't mean to turn every NIL/E customer into a mipper, billions and billions of them, everywhere. I hear Coach's voice calling her up to the stage. *Twenty-three, and Khadija Banks is going to save the world.*

Something growls behind me. I've got to get out, I've g-got to—*bosscakes, you gotta save me*—flailing over my feet through the open kitchen door, out into the sand.

Flash. Darius frowns from his chair in his office. *Don't turn around. You never learn, do you?*

I turn. The tidal wave surging over the sand is the fist of every angry god in every myth the caregivers poured into us in Aaru, reaching up beyond forever.

I don't have time to scream.

Gabe on his watercolor wings slams into me just before the wave hits. The code-water knocks us through shipping-container neighborhoods, and Body Garden tanks, and exploding gold pyramids, and Memory Excerpts—screaming through mouthfuls of water, drowning a thousand times over, and holding on holding on, until the wave washes us out to sea.

THIRTY-SEVEN
THE NEW KINGDOM

I slam my forehead against the carpeted floor of our room back in the Center as I scream with lungs that still burn from drowning. My heaves flip-flop me onto my back, where another wave-launched shipping container knocks me in the head. *Gabe.* I bolt up. He's lying on the couch still, twitching and baring his teeth. I kiss his forehead and run my thumb over his lips, whispering *hey, hey, we're here. We did it.*

His twitches fade and he sags into the pillows, his breathing deep and heavy. He must be asleep. I'm not sure how long we were out and how long the sedative will keep him under.

And he'll wake up, right? The wave was just his memorystream knocking me out of his mind?

Then I remember the floating scenes in his head, and the rain of ransom notes, and the riptide grabs my ankles.

I'm sorry. I had to.

Did you?

I can't look at him right now. I can't be around him. I shove off the ground, over the creaking floorboards and into the hallway, leaving him islanded on the couch, alone.

———

The air of the hallway fangs my skin with cold. Blue light leads me down the stairs to the first floor, where someone has spread rock candy everywhere. No, ice? J streaks over the slick floor of the hallway, slipping on sneakers, laughing and pelting one of the other therapists with a snowball. In the dining room, a dozen residents cozy around the fireplace with blankets and mugs of hot chocolate. Chengmei roasts a marshmallow on a stick, bouncing as she hums a sweet tune to herself. Nduta and Octavio stuff marshmallows into each other's mouths. João adds a broken chair leg to the fire and the air smells like roasting varnish. The only ones who aren't in on the winter wonderland are Seth and Sig, arguing about something I can't hear in the sunroom. The bay window in the wall that faces the grounds is gone, like it was a rotten tooth yanked out with pliers. The edges of the wall even look spotted with blood. In the evening light, I see snow over the grounds and the frozen marsh. Pierluigi waves me over and hefts a mug, calling out, *vieni!*

I ignore him.

Through the back door and out onto the lawn, my slippered feet crunching through an inch of snow. The chill of the air burns my face. Flo still sits in her lawn chair by the water, her back to me, only now she's draped in snow beside a three-foot-high mound of red-and-green candy wrappers that looks like a bush dusted in powdered sugar. Our only way out of here is to tell her that I think Khadija's somewhere in RedLandia and that we should hop outta here and find her, but I walk past her for now. I think she's the only person who's having a worse day than I am.

Besides. What kind of a world would I be uploaded back into?

One big over-soul-y puddle of humanity, Khadija said with her full-moon eyes. Has she done it, yet?

I'm sorry. I had to.

In the middle of the marsh, water tumbles into a black sinkhole and vanishes. Moving Meditation over the snow.

I don't know what's worse, honestly, and which I should care about more. That fact that my husband and my best friend basically drugged and kidnapped me, even if they thought it was to save me. Or that it was me and Gabe—indirectly, sure, though that'll mean jack shit when humanity is one big manor of giggling yellow bracelets—who gave her the idea for Project Bennu.

Call me selfish. Whatever. That's hard-coded in every version of Fox.

The sun and moon rise and set two times before I plod to the edge of the main lawn where the snow singes into gold sand. A sun-torched desert stretches out, flecked by withered trees of the once-orchard. My slippers hit the sand, and the snow melts and trickles around my damp socks.

The manor is a thumb smudge on a watercolor painting behind me. In the desert, I finally let out a throat-ripping scream from deep in my guts. The noise knocks a withered brown apple from the big tree where me and the Scribes first met up. I scream until my throat is raw. It doesn't calm the furycane ripping through my guts.

Nothing I see in there will make me love you any less, I'd said before plugging into his mind.

An invisible editor controlling this whole sim rolled up their sleeves like, *yeah? Game fucking on.*

I would've stayed on Aaru with Gabe. Would've followed him to the halfway house, where we could've shared a shitty twin bed and wandered the streets. We'd've been together.

Way high over the dunes up ahead, something long and thin pokes up from the sand and into the air next to a few low shapes that might be houses. I don't have anywhere else to go. Might as well keep walking.

I still don't remember my whole life, but more memories hit me like the debris I smacked into when the tidal wave knocked me and Gabe around.

Flash.

The motion-sensor lights in me and Khadija's glass-walled office flick off, with how still I've been, long after even the cleaning crew left. The pen is cool and slick in my hand. My new Life-Storyboard Consultant said I should try journaling with real pen and paper—something about the physical sensation of actually writing is therapy in itself, blahblah—and it's like someone chucked dynamite at a dam, with how the words keep coming.

Perforation. A lingering after-effect of live node-to-node link, where link-mates break through each other's consciousnesses even long after the connection is severed.

Gabe's here again. Fuck. He's supposed to be gone after my last round of edits. His drawers are empty at my place, next door to Khadija's. I can't remember if his stuff was even there to begin with or if I just imagined it.

I hear his voice. I see him, through the glass walls of the office, running down the hallway in his gray Aaru overalls, laughing. Spraying his hose everywhere, shouting, *look at Foxy pulling an Aset and writing out his philosophies.*

"Leave me alone!" I chuck my coffee mug at the wall and it explodes in white chunks.

I scratch out the word "link" on the page, digging so deep with the pen that the pages rip. Edit: *Node-to-node chains.* Links you can break. Chains? Chains can feel good—biting the skin at your ankles and wrists—when you don't want to be free.

Up ahead, a stone obelisk atop a hill points to the cloudless sky. Colors flap beneath it. A mirage? No, sheets on the wind, strung up by a few squat houses. I need the shade.

The voices, the Excerpts, the memories—everything I've learned about myself since waking up here, my first day—are telling me to bend like a reed and remember how much me and Gabe love each other. And how we both hurt each other, and it's not so easy to point fingers one way or another. Even Minou's sighing for me to take what's useful and forget the rest. I swat those lessons away like the biting flies at my sweaty forehead because maybe Past Fox in New Thebes had a right to be pissed. Even if he didn't really understand why he was so angry all the time. Why with each year it felt harder and harder to be kind.

I huff up the hill, and when I get to the top I see a handful of mud-brick houses around a single well with a red sheet tied from one roof to a couple of posts. Two lawn chairs in the small oasis of shade. On the other side of the hill between more dunes, a Whirl-o-Wind rises out of the sand, its lights still blinking. Gabe makes his way from an empty food truck by the obelisk—bare-chested and with a T-shirt tied around his head—and waves two cans of soda.

"Hey," he says, trying to smile through his squint. "Thirsty?"

Flash, us meeting and re-meeting a million times over. Each time is a bolt through my heart. Like I miss him already every time I see his face.

"Dying."

He tosses me a sweaty can. I crack it open and slurp it down. The cold soda douses the sandstorm in my throat. We meet up in the shade of the red sheet, and our shadows are black shards on the sand, all at wrong angles based on the white sun above.

"How'd you get here?" I ask.

"I woke up and you were gone. I figured you needed alone time. Same." He sips. "I walked past the therapists making a snowman in the sunroom. Down the front driveway for what felt like hours. Then sand. Then, here."

The red sheet snaps in the breeze. I swear I see cobras slithering over one of the dunes, and my hands itch to Smack-the-Snake them just to distract from the ache behind my ribs.

"What'd you see?" he asks. "In my head? It's a blur."

Easier to talk about the *Khadija mipping the world* stuff, instead of us. I buy time with a long sip and wait as the bubbles zip across my tongue.

"I dropped into Khadija's parcel in your head and it pulled me into a few memories. Mostly me and her in her home in RedLandia."

"So we head there? That's a start. Here I was thinking we'd stay 'n' move in here." He thumbs at the mud-brick house behind him.

Always jokes and dodges with him. When I don't answer and just toe the sand, he adds, "So our plan worked?"

"Yeah, except I found out what Project Bennu is."

"Don't leave me hanging."

"She's going to—if she hasn't already—connect the memorystreams of every noded person on Earth. Seeing what node-linking did to you and me gave her the bright idea."

"Hmm." No more cracks, just his eyes sweeping over the sand. "Yeah, not great."

"So we're gonna stop her. We're gonna get her to see what she's planning is absolutely nuts."

"And how do we do that?"

"I'm still working on that part. But if the company is trying to find her, maybe we let them?"

"What does that mean about getting copies of our memorystreams from her? About getting ourselves back?"

"What happened to what you said before, about how we're doing all this wrong? How Gabe died, and you're not him?"

"You made me want to remember him." He squints off into the dunes. "Us."

I whack a thought-snake down with a mallet. *Yeah, but do we deserve ourselves back?*

Past Fox would ignore her plan and trust she knows what she's doing. Or not care. I can't, not after learning about what my life was like on Aaru, and remembering how I really met and loved Gabe. And what I did as Greg.

"This is bigger than just us," I say. "Living the Excerpts—or remembering them, or whatever you wanna call it—it made me different. Made me the kind of guy who's not gonna ignore all of this."

"You could get everything you want back, and now you wanna boot Khadija in the ass? That's, what, ungrateful?"

"That's not what I'm doing. I need to stop her—"

"I need. Not *we* need." His bitter smile nicks me. "Fuckin' nice, Foxy."

"I'm doing this for the... the..."

He snorts. "No, finish that. I want to hear you say 'I'm doing this for the world.' I want to hear if you really believe it."

I swallow hard. "Why are you getting so pissed?"

"Because you're blowing up shit for the both of us, and—"

"I'm sorry. I had to."

He freezes. I see the rainstorm of ransom notes behind his eyes. I see him remember.

"If we're on the subject of blowing shit up for the both of us..." I trail, with even Past Fox from Gay Bar telling me, *hey, easy...* "How about we talk about how you and Khadija drugged me and shoved me onto a boat, and. And."

"He did it—*I* did it to save you. Because I saw you shredding your brain for everyone else, and I knew you wouldn't stop. And I knew you had to get off Aaru, even if that meant me being alone and..." The anger leaks out of him and into the sand. "And what about you? Pushing me away back home, and then coming here, and fuckin' around with my memories. Going into them without even asking me. You think I wanted that?"

I wish the ocean of sand would pull me under. I wish I could delete this fight. Delete this moment. This moment thinking about that moment. This moment thinking about that moment thinking about that moment, spiraling down into forever. But I know this has been building between us for days, for years, and if we're going to move on—whatever the hell that even looks like— we have to kick this all out into the sun.

I sink into one of the lawn chairs that face the sand-drowned carnival. It's easier this way, so I don't have to look him in the eyes. I toss the empty soda can into the sand.

"No," I say softly, the chair Whirl-o-Winding beneath me.

"We've both been shitty to each other. And selfish."

"But we keep coming back. Why? And how?"

He sits in the chair next to me, his fingers just barely brushing mine on our armrests.

"'Cause we're a part of each other," he says. Mostly to himself.

"The connecting stuff. Perforation. We need a better reason than that. Don't we?"

We're so close to understanding that I have to hold my breath, in case the sand slides out from under us and Smash-the-Snakes us into the valley below. I look at Gabe and try to smile, telling him with my eyes *I can't be the only one trying*. His mouth tightens and wobbles, and the lines on the side of his head are storm winds as he clenches his jaw again and again.

"I love you," he says, and threads his hand into mine. "I'm sorry I hurt you—the Luka 'n' Rajon shit, how I pushed you away on Aaru and in New Thebes. 'Cause I couldn't handle someone else disappearing, unless I did it to myself." Eyes up at the sun. "I'm glad you saw all that shit in my head now. Yeah. I'm done hiding things from you. Myself. I don't wanna be alone anymore."

The words are a bliss-hit from one of the pens on Aaru. Even better, because I can feel him next to me, and the empty space he leaves behind, at the same time. The poisons and paradises from our past wash over each other. The whiskey burns of those nights alone in our apartment, and the night in the hostel after our first date the second time around, where he tugged my clothes off and held me as I shook. *I got you. I'm not losing you again.* All of it—the whole ocean of us stretching out backwards and forwards.

Happiness is a choice, right? I can see the sign behind Darius's chair. I used to laugh at how stupid it was. I used to laugh. In general.

"I love you, dumbass." I elbow him, and see the light switch in his eyes, shock to relief. "You know that. But I used to think that gave me the right to try t-to hold you hostage with it. Seeing how you loved Levi, seeing how even after losing him you still chose to be with me—that was a fucking miracle. Showed me how I was such a possessive, jealous asshole who drove you away. And got you killed."

His eyes swim. "That wasn't your fault."

"I mean, who the fuck *were* we at the end?" My words are a laugh-shout that roll over the dunes.

Gabe laughs, and then I'm laughing, and we both double over, swatting our thighs.

"I don't know!" he says, wiping tears. "*Muerte.* That wasn't us. We were, we were…"

"Fox and Gabe."

"Fuckin' Fox and Gabe, like, against the world. We got tired and annoyed and forgot that."

"And it only took both of us trying to piece our broken brains back together to remember."

"God, we're dumb."

"A little."

Every laugh from him unstraps more stone blocks from me that I didn't even realize I'd been lugging around for so long.

"Darius would be so annoyed with us." Gabe rolls his eyes. "Whaddya think he'd say?"

I clear my throat and snatch back in my lawn chair, straight-backed. "What kind of lives would you like to lead together?" I rumble.

"And don't make me remind you again that I'm not actually a marriage therapist, you pieces of shit," he pipes in with a slapped-on soothing voice.

I crack up again and lean over the lawn chair arms into him, kissing his knuckles. "Alright. For real. What kind of lives would you like to lead together? Serious this time."

"I guess we can start with saving the world." He sighs. "Goddamnit."

"Woo!" I hoot into the air. Fist-pump. "Let's fuck shit uuuuup!"

"Chill!" He laughs. "Compromise, yeah? Aren't relationships supposed to be all compromise 'n' shit?"

"Allegedly. Shoot."

"We get our whole memorystreams back first—proving what we both know, that we're not just scrapes—and we stop Big Auntie Khadija from mipping the world."

"Seems fair. And if we can't get the rest of our memories back, and it's just us, like we are now?"

He shrugs. "We've got the bullet-point version. Enough of our big mistakes to know not to repeat them."

"I mean, what's the worst that can happen? We've already done every fucking awful thing to each other that we possibly could."

Gabe's elbow in my side jolts an *ooof* from me. He levels me with one of his head-back, fangy laughs that makes me feel so lucky that I brought it out. "Think again. You should see what I've got cookin,' Foxy."

We stay there for a while, just watching the wind whip little sandstorms over the dunes as the sun sinks lower. Whirl-o-Wind lights on the sand light me up. The perfect, highest editing level I could ever dream up would be this moment. You and the love of your million lives about to do something big and wonderful and maybe stupid, but at least you know you're together.

And who is this goofball Fox, easy to laugh, and hopeful, while he and Gabe trek over the desert and back to the manor? And this Gabe, who's the one to grab Fox's hand, with his eyes beaming out, *I promise we got this*. The group therapies and the affirmations and the rest of the Field of Reeds garbage must've worked, because I want to spend the rest of forever finding out just what these new levels of us are.

THIRTY-EIGHT
BARGAINING

Gold pollen clings to the air around the manor. The breeze is thick with the sweet stink of flowers and honey. Me and Gabe walk across the lawn, and I can see sunflowers and roses pushing out of tree trunks along the marsh's edge. A lattice of vines covers the blown-out bay window with creeping green fingers reaching out for the rest of the house, cracking bricks as they crawl. The black hole in the marsh is plugged up by a dam of lotuses. Birds and blooms frozen in the air. Residents and therapists—all of them giggling, now that Flo isn't ringing the gong—roll down the lawn, and weave flower crowns, and make out in grassy patches out of some springtime-horniness animal instinct. A therapist with garden shears trims invisible hedges, glitches, then keeps trimming. Another naps in the grass by the archery range, covered in vines. At least I think she's napping.

New reeds shoot up from the ground, and I watch one spear through a small boulder at the shore. Only a matter of time until the reeds reach the house. And then what?

I liked the snow better.

As we walked across the desert back here, we pieced together a plan.

Still, Flo unwraps strawberry candies by the water, only now she's covered in cherry blossom petals. We'll have our sit-down therapy session with her soon.

"Place is falling apart," Gabe says, frowning in the flower-clogged air. "I think I miss the gongs."

"Me, too."

The ice has melted in the empty manor where vines and flowers tumble out of vases and devour the furniture. Butterflies flit around a chandelier of birds of paradise. The hallway is now a carpet of real grass and roses, and we step over thorn-studded stems on the way to Seth and Sig in the sunroom. Seth's tight voice floats over the sound of bird chirps, saying something about Inyene, and how Pascal needs out, too.

"I don't understand why we can't just evacuate the whole Center." Seth sighs at the vines creeping up the Memory Mapping chair. "I can't effectively care for fifty day-one protocol residents at once, even with more therapist templates. Never mind that the sim stability is declining rapidly. It's clearly unsafe."

Sig glances at me and Gabe like *oh, great* when we walk in, then squeezes the bridge of his nose. "She's worried that if all the residents are gone, the company will find a way to delete the whole sim. Herself included."

"We're talking about people, not bargaining chips," Seth says.

"I'll get her there, I promise," Sig adds. "For now, it's ten."

Seth winces. "Yes. Pascal, then. He's the tenth. No—Inyene. She's in worse shape. And Florence is allowing me access to the Commute Home function again?"

"Temporarily. You have to escort the residents out, then come back." Sig shifts on his feet, his eyes worrying over the room. "We have to move now. Before she changes her mind. She's... degrading."

"No shit," Gabe chimes in.

"Of course I'll come back," Seth says. "I wouldn't abandon the others here."

Honestly, how I pegged him for a NIL/E goon niggles my conscience. I'll have to tell Flo to update her specs for Editor Template 17. Edit: He's a shit judge of character.

"And you two." Sig frowns at us. "I suppose you guys are here to beg your way onto a lifeboat."

"Not quite," I say. "We found out what Project Bennu is. And it's—we have to talk some sense into Khadija. Get her to call her plan off, if we're not already too late."

"And her plan is what, exactly?" Seth asks.

"That." Gabe thumbs out the patio door, to the yellow bracelets rollicking in the riot of flowers. "Everywhere."

"She's going to link every noded person," I add. "Some kind of forced spiritual awakening for humanity."

Seth scrubs a hand over his forehead and glares at Sig. "Did you know about this, and Florence?"

"Jesus! No. Bare-bones shit, that's all. Next step for humanity, making us all divine, rah," Sig blurts. "We're templates trapped here, same as these other schmucks, not exactly top brass."

"And you know where Khadija is?" Seth turns to me and Gabe. "I can tell the company when I'm out of here, and they can find her."

"Not exactly." I suck in a steadying breath. "Somewhere in RedLandia, we think."

"Wonderful." Sig rolls his eyes. "From 'somewhere on Earth' to 'somewhere in a nation state hundreds of thousands of square miles big.' Huge help in narrowing things—"

"Hey, asshole," Gabe snaps. "You've been helping her this whole time, so how 'bout you step the fuck off."

Sig's mouth opens to say something, until his shoulders drop. "You're right. Sorry."

"What're you thinking?" Seth asks.

"We need a-an insurance plan, if we can get to Khadija and she won't see reason," I say. "We need to call in the big guns. Flag the company to our location."

"How?" Sig sputters.

"Fox logs in to the kiddie settings on his node and switches on the GPS." I love that Gabe's voice carries his *you dumbass* tone. "Then the company rent-a-cops follow the big treasure map to us. X marks the spot 'n' shit."

Switching my GPS settings on is an easy box-tick with a Reeder or an editing terminal, which Khadija's base must have. Seth waits a long breath as a pink flower bursts from the vine that's creeping up the Memory Mapping chair.

Sig tugs the end of his beard. "There's nowhere on the planet NIL/E can't reach within twelve hours. That's smart. It might even work."

"I'll bring it to the company," Seth says. "I'll see what they say and bring you the news when I come back for the next resident evacuation group."

"While we're on the whole *evacuation* topic," I say. "If we signal NIL/E to stop Khadija, we gotta be sure that they'll evac us to safety."

"Fair." Seth nods.

"Seth." Sig actually tugs at his arm. "I'm serious. You need to leave, now. Round up the residents. I'll get the van."

"Yes, right," Seth bumbles. He's halfway out the sunroom door when he stops and turns back to us. "And why? Why stop Khadija when she can probably give you both of your memories back, and you have everything you've ever wanted right in front of you?"

I grab Gabe's hand to try to slow my heartbeat. He gives it a squeeze.

"You told me… you told me 'you're here to be better than who you were.' And now we *are*. The therapies, the Excerpts—I don't care if Flo or the company or whoever were just using all of us for different reasons. Because you know what? It worked. Me and Gabe *are* better. The Fox and Gabe out there, before all of this? Those assholes didn't deserve each other."

The words come out in a gush. I might be trying to convince Seth of something, but I'm right, anyhow. Me and Gabe were wrong for each other, before all this. I can see that now.

"So we stop her," I continue, "because now that we've fucking got it *right*, we actually need a world to go back to. Even if we're in some NIL/E nodecasted city. I'm not going to let Khadija fuck us all over."

Seth tips his head, considering. "How selfishly selfless."

"Still counts," Gabe says.

"You know, Fox, for all your initial resistance to our methods here, you and Gabriel might be our biggest therapeutic success yet."

"Put us in a commercial when we're outta here and safe," I tell him.

He hits us with one last big-bro smile before he walks out the door with Sig.

Mosaic pieces are slotting into place, but there's still someone else we have to convince. Hand in hand over the lawn, dodging spiny cactuses and wild strawberry bushes. Flo's pile of candy wrappers is a mound of cherry blossoms that drift away on the breeze. When we round her lawn chair, her blank face brightens at the sight of us.

"Hi, boys," she says in her old Flo voice. "Sorry, I've just been. Been..." Her voice trails off, her watery blue eyes blinking away a fog. "Been a little out of it." She cranes her neck to the riot of flowers behind her, then back to us with a wince. "Oh. Oh, dear."

A little vine of pity creeps over me with the way she's falling apart, remembering her sneaking me candies and hugs when I was so lost.

"You think?" Gabe cracks.

Flo unwraps a candy, stops with a frown, and then shoves it back into her cardigan. "It's just—just, how do you keep going? What you both remember from your Excerpts, out there in the world, how did you keep going when you knew that there was..."

"No point?" I offer. "No mission?"

She winces over the marsh. "Yes."

"Welcome to the fucking club," Gabe smarms.

"We need you to send a message to Khadija for us," I say. "I want to remind her of something, and I think it'll get us out of here."

"That's not how this works. We wait for word from her, and—"

"Look, Flo," Gabe cuts her off with a hand in the air. "I get you're having a rough go and all. How 'bout this. You send our message, we get her to pull you outta here, too. Real world, at the boss lady's side."

His voice is hard. Bees buzz in flower-drunk figures of eight around us. Gabe always knew when to be mean, even if it was behind a laugh. I thought of it as a weapon before, but now I know it's a tool. Sometimes you have to sting. What'd Khadija think when she was slicing up my memory? *Sometimes the cure burns worse than the poison.*

"You did complete your mission," I tell her. I give my best good-cop glance to Gabe with a shrug. "I mean, you think she should reward you, right?"

"Don't *you* wanna get out?" He niggles the knife again. "Or are you gonna let her just forget you, and leave you here forever?" He looks to me, suddenly bored. "Or there's always peacing-out in the Ankh."

The way the fear shadows across her face like the sun moving behind the leaves, I know we've snared her.

"I know it sounds scary," I toss her words back at her, honey-sweet even after her lies, too. "But honestly, there's no pain."

Gabe *hmm*s and nods at me, arms crossed. We're ourselves again, soft-shoeing through an improv in front of friends at a party. Like two caregivers that want what's best for her, as much as it seems like it'll hurt.

"You think she'll really answer you?" Already, the light creeps back into her voice.

"She'll be interested in what I have to say, yeah."

"Which is?"

"Tell her, 'bosscakes, you gotta save me.'"

I can feel the ghost of Khadija's Reeder scalpel dragging across my brain in answer, echoing what she told me that day of precision-editing hell.

You know I always will.

Flo says she's in. She needs to clean up first, though, in case we have company. And imagine Khadija, here! She hops off her lawn chair, pushes past us. The frozen birds and falling blossoms in the sky glide through the air like they're supposed to, as Flo finds herself again.

The springtime on steroids didn't seep up to our room. We hide there for a while, and I collapse into the window seat and eye the black hole in the middle of the marsh as it slowly knits back together. Gabe cleans his paintbrushes over and over in silence. Until Seth knocks on the door, breathless between evac runs, and lays out NIL/E's terms.

We go to Khadija. We turn on our GPS settings. They come in and get us out, away to New Thebes. Where we can have our whole memories of all of this—the Field of Reeds, Khadija's quest, our work with NIL/E to stop her—scrubbed. We can start fresh.

I blink and see my own torn-up note shoved into Khadija's pocket. *I'm sorry. I had to.* I'm not ratting on her unless she gives me a reason. Unless I can't save her from herself.

I look at Gabe and his big toothy smile, and it takes everything in me not to burst into tired giggles. We're almost there. Hold on.

Lying on the couch, I watch the sun glide across the picture frame in our room. The picture of us from a million years ago, smiling on a roof deck during some party I can't remember. Gabe's at the window overlooking the grounds as the therapists weed-whack reeds and tap-tap at Reeders by the shore, forcing flowers to shrink back into the tree trunks until they vanish. This whole place is knitting itself back together again.

The picture, though, gives me something to hang on to through the nerves and the doubt. Now that my *let's fuck shit uuuuup* fire has cooled. Maybe it was the effort of the whole psychological manipulation of Flo. Not doubt about our plan—I mean, can you even call it that? Doubt about us.

Seth gave me that line about coming here to be better. And I am better. I hope. Different, definitely, now that I know things about Past Fox that I never let myself see. How I turned Gabe into a canned-memory version of himself—all withholding, with a razor-blade smile—because I didn't want to deal with our problems. How I needed him to fix the cracks in me that started when my mom stumbled onto the docks of New Thebes and handed me to one of the caregivers, her exhausted face and her searching eyes telling them, *you have to take him, because I can't*. When she was supposed to be the one who cared for me, and stayed with me forever, as much as I know now that her letting me go then was the best thing she could do.

The cracks widened over the years, and more appeared, until I fell through them and became some ghost of who I was. Some template who wore my face and had my job, had my husband. We were lucky for a while, when love might really mean finding someone else with as many cracks as you. And you try to line up all those cracks so that you fill each other in. Even if maybe you can't patch each other up.

So who knows if the Gabe and Fox from New Thebes need another shot. But the Gabe and Fox who crashed through each other's lives to get here, who faced the worst possible parts of themselves and still held on to each other, and laughed it all off— they do. We're the ones I'll fight for. I can feel the doubt sliding off my shoulders like sand trickling out of the Whirl-o-Wind seats as it rises out of the dunes. Leaving me lighter, all lit up.

Gabe must feel all of this while he's quiet at the window, with how we wash into each other. He looks at me lazing on the couch, and the sun behind him sets. The moon rises. Like the whole universe beyond this house revolves around him.

A voice that I remember well cuts through the air with a crackle from a non-existent public address system. Khadija, tapping the microphone, then calling out, *boss to babycakes*.

"Now boarding first-class passengers Fox and Gabe," she sings out with her honeyed voice. "Please make your way to the river rift, which we've rerouted for your one-way trip home. We hope you have a pleasant flight."

Gabe bounces from the window, laughing. "I dig the voice from the sky. Every CEO has a god complex, huh? At least she's more honest with hers."

Is it weird that I'll miss this place, where we learned to love each other again? Where all we had for a while *was* each other? Through the creaky, shadowed hallways. Past the other residents who Seth is hostage-negotiating out of Flo. Over the lawn. Slipping across the mirror of the marsh on a canoe, and then I cut a right at the rusty lawn chair like Minou did that night we all landed in Inland Ocean City. I lead him to the gap in the trees that will toss us out into wherever Khadija wants us to go.

Both of us look at the empty air between the trees. I don't let myself wonder just what happens if we're making a big mistake here with who to trust. With thinking we can pull a fast one on Khadija, if that's what we're really doing.

I start to say *I love you*, but Gabe's eyes stop me. A half-smile, just a little sad. He's right. Any *I love you* now would seem too much like goodbye.

THIRTY-NINE
BARGE OF THE SUN

I feel gentle rocking beneath me and fuzzy warmth all around. I open my eyes to a skylight with vanilla ice cream clouds scooped over the blue sky beyond. My eyes sting in the dimness of what looks like a small lab with workstations pushed against the curved walls and blinking blue server lights. I'm on some sort of gurney and wrapped in a pink knit blanket. Gabe at my side on another gurney, with a gold mask ripped right out of an Ankh over his face. The wires that pipe into the mask and into his arm snake woozy panic into me. A second ago I turned to Gabe and brushed through the gap in the trees, and here we are—wherever this is. Together, at least.

I hiss at a pinch in one arm and see a guy in fancy private-doctor athleisurewear looking sheepishly at me, raising a thin, blood-tipped IV tube he just pulled from my arm.

"Sorry," he says. "Some stims to guide you awake."

"Break out the espresso, he's been dead for seven fucking years."

I crane my head behind me. Khadija leans against one of the walls, a cream blanket draped over her shoulders, her neon yellow-painted smile like she just called me babycakes in the canteen.

A circular gold-framed window by her head offers a glimpse of the water. We're on a ship. Her crown of braids is threaded with gray now, though her face is barely lined. Words leak out of me like the drop of blood from my arm. I expected to want to rail at her. *How could you and Gabe do that to me.* Mostly I just want her to tell me that everything will be alright.

"If this is heaven, I'm disappointed," I tell her.

"Well, not yet. But getting there." She pushes off from the wall. "Come on. We should catch up. Rezzing Gabe will take a little bit, still. I'll have you back here before he wakes up."

I'm woozy on my feet for just an instant. Then, strong and straight-backed. I catch myself in the window's reflection and see my face from fifteen years ago staring back at me. A slimmer body without the creaks and aches of middle age, all in black.

"We have one Bennu Egg aboard," she says. "Those are the quick-rez grow-chambers my team built, that grow a whole body in a few hours. We're thinking they'll be key for off-world colonization. I took the liberty of borrowing your genome from your company file—Gabe's, too—and whipping up younger bodies for you." She winks. "I need spry brains. You're welcome."

What to say to her? I had friends in New Thebes, but no one like her—a friend, a big sister, a mother combo bucket. I can hear Seth's voice rumbling at me, *forgiveness doesn't have to be hard.* A mother I can barely remember. Parents who adopted me that weren't real. Even when so much of my past is gone, maybe forever, it's hard to hate some reminder of it. Even when a part of me says I should.

She lets me flounder through this water behind my eyes. Lets me be quiet. She hands me a cream blanket from a coat hook by the door to this inner cabin. I follow her through a dim hall and a narrow stairway, up into the light.

―――

Sea spray and white-capped wavelets, with no land in sight. I follow Khadija over wood decks so lacquered they could be made of gold. The *Barque of Ra* is her ship, she says, her mobile base. *Ship* isn't what I'd call this massive superyacht of curving lines, its observation deck topped with satellite dishes, a helipad, a single gold mast pounded with symbols that stabs the sky. Her deck hands—or whoever they are—float by all in white, sweeping decks and tying ropes, nodding to their queen. With the brightness that hits their eyes, each smile from her might as well be a blessing. Off in the distance, a group of dolphins spurts to the surface.

"Where are we?" I pull the blanket tighter around my shoulders against the sea spray.

"Somewhere in the North Pacific. The supply drones keep us self-sufficient, with a few nodecast-equipped AI-nav sea pods stashed in the lower decks in case we ever need to split in a second. Never in one area long. Never near land, not with the company lurking behind me like they wanna stab me in the gut and grab my purse."

She sneaks glances at me with black-lined eyes as we walk. The calm rises from her shoulders like code. If she feels any of the jangly awkward nerves that I do, she's hiding them behind her tour-guide voice.

"Ah."

Years together, when she taught me to push away my stutter, and the best I can do is *ah*.

"We're actually not far from Aaru," she continues. "What's left of it."

She points one ring-stacked finger out to sea, where I can maybe make out a few gray shapes against the horizon. Though it could just be my eyes.

I suck in a breath, trying to borrow some strength from the sea mist. Like each drop contains part of the ocean. *Every piece contains the whole.* Here we go.

"Where do we even start?" I ask.

"It's good to see you. The *real* you. Let's start there."

"It's good to see you? B-but it's…" My voice trails off. I want to say *hard*, which is such a blank Reeder screen that I can hear Gabe laughing, *aren't you supposed to be a fancy editor?*

"I know. Hard. Crazy hard. Beyond batshit."

I manage a clunky laugh. We make it to the bow of the ship and Khadija leans her elbows onto the gold railing, face out to the water.

"How much do you remember?" she asks. "I can never be sure which Fox I'm meeting, with all the edits. With all that's happened."

"I don't remember everything. I remember meeting you and Gabe on Aaru. I saw, in his memories, you and him tricking me outta there. I know you and me launched NIL/E Editorial, and I went off the rails. The Greg stuff. You t-trying to edit me. Me and Gabe meeting again in New Thebes." I frown down at the mist-splattered railing. "A lot is still patchy."

For the first time since I opened my eyes here, her neon brightness fades.

"We spent a lot of years together after we left Aaru. You were angry for a while. I understood. How could you not be? We had a mission to bring editing to the whole world, not just the royals, and you'd cut the memories of Gabe out of your head to keep going. Then they'd come back, and you'd spin out, and square-one us… and it was hard." She laughs. "There's that word again. I'd say *fucking* hard."

My gut spins, dizzy, not just from the waves.

"I would've left you with Gabe on Aaru if I knew all of this would've happened."

"Then why didn't you, when you knew I didn't want to be without him?" I'm the kid with a croaky voice again, stumbling into her screen in the canteen. More dolphins splash out in the water.

"Ever since that night when you knocked into me in the canteen with your baby-bird legs and big eyes, it was like I saw myself as a kid wandering around New Phoenix. And then all the time we spent together in the editing clinic. I had a family again. I knew I had to save you even if it hurt. Even if you wouldn't do it for yourself."

"We were all we had, for a while." I swallow past the gravel in my throat.

"I've said goodbye to you a million times. And then I get word that Fox is magically resurrected in a therapy sim that I built, and recovered from the memory virus. Of course I'm gonna drop everything and bring him here."

"Bosscakes, you gotta save me," I remind her.

"You know it." She's laughing again. I didn't realize how much I missed the honey-sweet sound until it bowls me over with warmth.

"What was the virus?"

"You know what it is. You have to."

"It's a copy of everyone's memorystreams, all jumbled together."

"An earlier iteration of my work on Project Bennu. Weaponized, unfortunately."

"I thought the company promised not to stash copies of clients' memorystreams."

"*Individualized* 'streams. Not that we wouldn't lump all the memories together—mixed and mingled, one big ocean of everyone,

one collective history of humanity. Or, say—*hypothetically*—an anonymized, searchable database for product projections. Like, 'show me what the average gay guy chronologically aged forty to eighty with an armpit kink would want in a canned-memory projection and new vessel with bells 'n' whistles.'"

Ocean of everyone. I can see Gabe flailing in black water, an undertow of code trying to yank him deep.

"Why?"

"How else could we get the money to suck carbon from the air, and send reparations to the global south, and a million other miracles because governments have done fuck-all for centuries, without targeted memory-editing offerings based on aggregated data from billions of 'streams, and..." She hits the brakes on the runaway train of her words, stops, and breathes.

I can see in her eyes, *bend like a reed.* The regal tilt to her chin, the straight shoulders sliding back into place.

"Besides, a little fudging here and there never hurt anyone." She taps her nose, her warm smile back. "Also, *you're welcome.* Because of said fudging, that bangin' search string you created to cure the virus means you can toss Gabe's memories a life raft and pull them out whenever you want. Instead of sitting through decades of group therapy and waiting for organic memory budding, which was working. Slowly, according to Flo. I get that patience isn't your bag."

"She wants you to rez her here as a thank-you for all her help."

"Why the hell not? Many hands make quick work, or something."

So easy. *So no one ever has to say goodbye.*

"Why weren't my memories in the virus code? And yours?"

"Security. Neither of us wanted our full memorystreams in there in case someone figured out how to unravel them. I went the parcel route for my memory insurance plan. You've got a copy of yours still stashed in our private dev server, which you can access from a terminal in the lab. I'll even give you your old log-in back." She's quiet again, eyes on the water. "There's more I can tell you—more of this that you were even directly involved in—but it's not my place to. You got those memories sliced out. That's the rule we've always lived by. Relative reality."

Years with her, edited. And years with Gabe, too. *That's the rule we've always lived by.* We're never actual happy, even when we get what we want.

"Th-then I'm not just a template. Or malg, or—whatever, like Flo said. I'm real. Gabe is."

"Maybe the *you* that's flapping his gums with me started as a piece of my little bro's memories that the company squirreled away in the Field of Reeds, and I shuffled a few resources around to get him to help me. But now you see that even one piece contains the whole puzzle…" An easy, Earth Mother shrug. "What do you wanna be?"

Sunlight dazzles on the water. Gabe. I need him here. He'd help me make sense of all this with one of his smirks. *You got this, Foxy.*

"It sounds a lot like you're saying happiness is a choice."

"With all I've seen, you start to realize that the boundaries don't matter. You're Fox. Hell, I'm Fox. Any separation is just glass walls that we put up and can knock down. With all the work you and Gabe did, we finally get to remind people of that."

She sounds so much like Aset with her philosophies that the kids in Preparedness Programming would've been like, *can she give us a rip of whatever she's smoking?*

And glass walls. The glass walls in Gabe's memorystream that I slammed into. My fists ache from pounding on those walls.

No, wait—I snap my eyes from the water and look down and see I've been clenching them. Thunk-thunk of trapped blood in my fists.

"You're talking Project Bennu. Khadija—you can't," I sputter. "Whatever you're planning, we both saw how broken the mippers were on Aaru. You can't do that to everyone, as much as you think you're saving them. It's not what they'd want. Look at what it did to me and Gabe."

Khadija shakes me off with an easy smile. I know she might as well be pointing at the FUCK OFF plate in the canteen and booting me out.

"We were never meant to be alone," she says. "You told me that—you *knew* that—over and over again, didn't you? When you live-linked with Gabe? When you met him and re-met him and your eyes locked all those times, and you felt connected to him and everything all at once? I've live-linked to so many—you gave me the idea. All the other Khadijas out there, and more. It's like I've lived a thousand lives at once. Why would you keep everyone else from that?"

She leans back against the railing, her full-moon eyes on me. She makes all this sound beautiful. And honestly, I almost want to believe her. Until Gabe's voice cuts me. *I want to hear you say 'I'm doing this for the world.' I want to hear if you really believe it.*

"Because what good is a whole world of mippers going to be?"

"Oh, reel it in, drama queen. I'm not scrambling everyone's brain permanently. I'll flip the switch for a little while. Just long enough to remind everyone that we're all variations on the same song. Can you imagine what good it will do for us all to be connected for a shimmering moment? All of us experiencing the same needs, and aches, and hungers? A big wallop of global empathy? It's like—like what Aaru was supposed to be. But better."

"I assume you'll keep the switch in your back pocket, in case we need reminding again?"

Another honeyed laugh. "Kids need to be told things a few times before they stick, huh? Come on. Lighten up. The human brain is a tough cookie. Proof enough that both of us are still standing here. It'll be a brief, shared vision. And after that taste? Everyone'll be begging for the whole meal. I'll happily bring that paradise to them again, forever and ever. I promise you, Fox. It'll be beautiful. Spiritual, even."

Mama Khadija swooping in to save us all, again. Saving us from ourselves. *I'm deciding this for you all because you're my kids. My beautiful, dumb, weak kiddos. And—shh—this will only hurt for a moment.* The spot where the doc yanked the stim-pumping IV out of my arm twinges.

"And when should we expect this beautiful, spiritual moment?"

"Once Flo sent us the fix, I sent word out to all the Scribe cells and runner rings to get to safety. Things'll be dicey for a bit after the signal. A transition period, you know. I'll give them another two days. And now that you're here, even better." She looks up to the sky. "Dawn on the third day? I know, I know. A little on-the-nose biblical. But it feels right. Like we're greeting a new day for all of humanity."

I promised Gabe I'd try to get our memories back. One fucking potential apocalypse at a time.

"And then when it's done, I can get all of my memories back. And Gabe's."

"Hell yeah!" Her neon-lipped laugh again. "You can get your paws on those copies tonight, if you want. We already incorporated your search string into a fancy new searchable memorystream database. De-frag away. I've been dragging my whole archive around with me." She points behind me at the gold ship mast that's studded with symbols. "My life's work. Seems a shame to hide it, so why not let it shimmer in the sun?"

Shimmer is right. What I thought was sunlight on the gold mast are flashing lights. Symbols, and birds in flight, and hands up in prayer. Sahu code. And each of the flashes is probably a new backup transmission from someone on Earth, adding more memories to the ocean. Young immortals, all of us.

FORTY
CLOSING RITES

'm late to Gabe's side, of course. It wouldn't be me if I was ever on time. I find him laughing with athleisure doc, sitting on the gurney and swinging his feet. Flirty Gabe style, charming anyone around him, lit up by spotlights of computer screens around the lab. The lights flick against a table scattered with Reeders.

Khadija's words followed me while I circled the decks, alone. *When you met him and re-met him and your eyes locked all those times, and you felt connected to him and everything all at once?* And yeah, she's right. The sight of his laughing eyes and his head-back smile shivers through me with warmth. We're young again, and together again, with everything we ever could want ahead of us. In the doorway to the lab, I'm almost afraid that if I step foot inside he'll vanish like a mirage on the dunes where we made up.

And maybe. Maybe? *Beautiful. Spiritual, even.*

Doc spots me before Gabe does and smiles. "It's not every day we get newcomers, never mind two editors."

"Fox's your editing guy," Gabe answers for me. "I'm more of a jack-off-of-all-trades."

He hops off the gurney and in the next second he's in my arms. Wait, wait. Breathe through it. The real him, not just lines of code fooling me into thinking I was really holding him, brighter and more solid than anything the hacks who finger-painted the Field of Reeds could ever dream up. We've survived the hell of reliving the worst parts of ourselves, and each other, and I'd do it all again just to be skimming the clouds like this, high off the smell of him, the weight of him. Hugging so hard it's like we're trying to cram ourselves into one body. Swaying, face in his neck even in front of a stranger.

I can't think it too hard, because what if he feels the doubt? The hesitation. The *maybe Khadija is right and we just trust her.* Look at what all the work on curing the virus did for us.

No work talk for tonight, Khadija decrees over the ship's PA system. Tonight we're feasting and glugging wine and toasting me and Gabe joining the crew. Coming *home* to her and the family. Her dozen or so disciples in white—editors, Scribes, whatever they are—listen. All hail the queen on her floating throne. Doc, whose name is actually Kareem, politely shoves me and Gabe out of the lab, where I'd been snooping on what kind of tech they have stashed, and shows us to a cabin on the lower deck. The cabin's honey-cake walls curve with the ship. A huge bed swathed in white. A marble bathroom. A desk with a single flower in a chickpea can is a gift from Khadija, I know. A sliding door fringed with sheer curtains beckons to a balcony, where a loveseat faces the ocean. Gabe's hands brush the walls, his smile for Kareem wiped off his face.

I tell him Khadija's plan, bullet-pointed. *Beautiful, spiritual.* Most of all, temporary.

"We get our memorystreams and then bounce the fuck outta here," he says. "Stat."

"I'll get them tonight. And then we figure it out."

He won't let me hold him for long. He just shrugs out of my arms after a few seconds. I get it. Weird place, weird people. He drifts out of our cabin and to the private deck, shoulders back, his eyes over the waves.

We pass bowls heaped with figs and nuts, fresh from a drone drop-off yesterday. Pastas flecked with fresh mint and whole grilled fish that are so beautiful their fins ripple in the gold lamplight. I lick the smoke off my fingertips. Khadija is neon, casting light onto everyone, glinting with her collar necklace and stacks of bracelets and rings. The smile that never leaves her face like a painted mural. I watch her like I'm rationing words—falling in love with her as she codes the world.

And I see everyone else has the same shiny-eyed half-smile look on their faces, too. We're in the same room as someone who's vibrating. Who knows things we can't ever know, and we're just happy to breathe the same air.

Except Gabe, who's not himself. He's quiet. Probably not jazzed that we're not Gabe-and-Fox foxtrotting around and running the room. He and Khadija must have a lot of shit to hash out themselves, too.

They'll have time.

All of us disciples share stories about how we got here. And ask Khadija about where we'll go.

"I've lived a whole lotta lifetimes," Khadija says, leaning back when we're all full and giggly with wine. "And thank you for all your hard work. Everyone here." She looks around the table to each of us, even Gabe, and I see glints in eyes. I feel them in mine. "I've been working on the greatest gift I can give back to you. To all of humanity."

She has us. Everything else fades away, even the gentle rocking of the ship.

"Before this planet buckles beneath us, we need to find a way out. The tower here—this moveable vault—is a beacon, sending our memories out into space. To local clusters. To distant galaxies. To worlds that have instruments pointed out into the darkness, waiting for signals from other civilizations. We'll load memories onto barges that'll launch off in a thousand different directions. Different worlds that we'll colonize with people who still remember Earth. So that it will—*we* will—stay alive. When Earth is a smoldering bit of ash, we'll still live forever. Out there, among the stars. The Bennu signal will unite us all. And it's just the first step."

Tears streak the faces of the others. Some of them raise their wineglasses. I look at Gabe and squeeze his leg under the table. It's just so codedamned beautiful, I tell him with wet eyes, because we wanted to live together on one world, and now we get to on a thousand? Gabe smirks, stabbing a stray fig with one finger.

"And how *does* this Bennu signal or whatever work, Deej?" he asks. Oh no. I almost shush him. The edge of his razor-blade smile glints in the lamplight. "I know, I know—we said we weren't talking work tonight. But don't be a tease."

"Ah!" Kareem pipes up. "Well, it's all thanks to the company temporarily reversing the upload flow for the mass-rollout of a security patch to deliver your search string as like a pre-exposure inoculation to the virus, and—"

"My man, enough work for the night!" She shushes Kareem with a gentle hand on his arm. Then to all of us with her laughing, honey eyes: "You'd better've saved room for dessert. You're all having honey cakes."

She passes a dish of slivers of cake topped with honey and almonds. Still warm, and so sweet.

———

Security patch. Circuits zip together in my head, alone in the lab where we woke up, with Gabe off to lie down after dinner. Because, he said, he was tired. So tired of all this shit. And don't you see, Fox?

POP QUIZ

Now that you've got all the answers, what are you gonna believe?

a. A big bomb drops on New Thebes and spreads a nasty memory virus that me and Gabe help Khadija cure, and then she parachute-codes us all to safety again.

b. And don't you remember a flash of something? Darius bringing you to some brass-walled place, Khadija offering you Gabe back. A million Gabes. Why stop there? Think bigger, babycakes! You could be a fucking king. You just gotta deliver this package for me first.

c. Weird that NIL/E would send out a big security patch of your search string—the cure to a virus they created, right? A virus that *is an earlier iteration of my work on Project Bennu,* Khadija said. *Weaponized, unfortunately.*

d. Yeah, Deej. But by who?

———

Fox the Fixer, answering these quizzes always takes you longer than it should.

The doubt starts as a bird tap-tapping against the window of my forehead, at one of the workstations, logged in to Khadija's archive database with the password she gave me. And how did the birds get here, so far from land? I key Gabe's name into a search field, and a result blinks to the screen with a numerical code. The system asks, *begin defragmentation?* I hit *yes.* A tiny green progress bar blooms at the bottom of the screen. It only takes a minute for the system to thread the scattered pieces of Gabe together again, until the cheery *ding!* from one of Greg's sad-man microwave dinners. I copy Gabe's memorystream onto a blank Reeder from the shelf.

I switch over to her—*our*—private dev server. My name in the search field next, my memories rolling in like the tide. *Ding!* I copy my memorystream onto a blank Reeder. Then, what the hell, I dump the copy into Khadija's archive, where my memories will swim with Gabe's and everyone else's.

Just one more thing to do.

The doubt-bird tapping against my head calls his friends until a whole flock of them blots out the light in the lab.

I plug the Reeder with my memorystream to my node and then I'm in the parental settings tab, about to switch on the GPS locator. Bird wings, cold, against the back of my neck. Hold up, edit: Not yet. The whole flock of their beaks and talons scrape my skin. I have to know, first. I have to know.

I follow the birds out to the front bow, under a moon so red it looks like it stole some of noon's heat. The yacht slices through the water. It's too dark to know what's beneath the waves. Khadija's alone—waiting for me?—on a balcony off what must be her room. Her shrine. She waves me up. My feet seem to move on their own, up a narrow staircase to her balcony.

"Beautiful night," she says, so easily. She's wrapped in a gauzy robe, her jewelry gone, but her braids are still the only crown she needs. And what happened to the girl I knew who painted her lips with powdered drink mix, who split her bowls of noodles with me?

Me. I ruin everyone.

"Sure is," I say. I can bring the breeze to my voice, too.

"We got some big days around the corner. I came out here to think."

More birds—feathers of white, of code-blue—on quiet wings that blot out the moon for just a second, before scattering.

"I need to know," I say.

I can't really see her eyes by just the moonlight. "Shoot. Just remember, only ask what you really wanna know, babycakes."

I have to pull from the Excerpts to keep myself from shaking. Greg loading up his shotgun. Gabe about to hit the stage. In control, in their bodies.

"Was the attack on New Thebes you? And did you get me to do it?"

"Alright, you asked. Now it's my turn."

"I deserve an answer, Khadija. After all this."

"You'll get it. Just—humor me. Like you said, after all this."

Gabe's sleeping in the deck below. Or probably not sleeping. I'll get us out of here after this. I'll steal a lifeboat. We'll swim if we need to. Kayaking over the folded ribbon of the Field of Reeds marsh again.

"Fine. I'll bite. What's your question?"

"First! The wind-up. Story time. They're both true, of course." She elbows the air, laying on the shtick. "The first story is that those pieces of shit Deathers bombed New Thebes. Fighting for the planet, but no problem blowing up a city, huh? The second story is that the attack was a necessary bummer to get us here, on the verge of perfection. Gabe sleeping in your fancy cabin, and—hey!—is that a Reeder with patched up copies of your memorystreams, ready for you to dive in?"

"Is that your question?"

"My question is, if everything is true—relative reality, all that jazz—which story do you like best? You can pick. And isn't it better to be kind to yourself?"

Gabe's right. I'm sick of this shit. I let her question die on the breeze.

"You wanna hear the real kicker?" Khadija asks.

"Why should I even answer when I know you're just going to tell me anyway?"

Bingo. Nina the Neuron squeaks, *now you're thinking like an editor!*

"I built the Field of Reeds and a ton of other sims. You should see them. Paradises. And Aset's code isn't just for our memories." She taps at her collarbone. "Look at any scrap of matter in this world down deep enough, and you see that it's code, too. Unbreakable and perfect and fucking beautiful. Because we made new memories and worlds and didn't think, or maybe didn't care, that we were a world that someone made, too. And that someone had made the world that *that* someone was clickety-clacking us into life in. Way, way up until forever."

I head back down the stairs, ignoring her.

"Somewhere it all had to start, right?" she calls to my back.

Through the gold hallways of the ship. Not that I'm even really here. I'm in me and Gabe's apartment in New Thebes, and a million different stories and narrative levels. I meet a guy named Gabe on Aaru and we like each other for a while but it doesn't work out. Gabe dies in a blast and then I bring him back, and we love each other harder than before—more than anyone has, ever—because we flipped off death when it's not supposed to exist in the first place. I'm in a storyboard meeting with Darius, who brought in his manager for help because I'm never happy. Today's suggested editing level: *We'll start you off as an entitled, selfish asshole, and through loss and struggle you'll blossom into a better person really worthy of Gabe's love.* Except I'm like, *sure, but what about adventure, and mystery.*

Insert > warring gods. Insert > quest to save the whole fucking world.

Levels, leveling me down.

Gabe has slipped out of bed. I see him wrapped in a blanket on the loveseat on the balcony, silhouetted by the red moon. I drop the two Reeders on the white sheets.

I part the gauzy curtains and join him in the night air. He looks up, just a hint of a smile on his face, and kisses my shoulder when I sit. Wraps me in the blanket with him, and just like that—all of Khadija's promises or lies fall away. Just the two of us. There's only ever really been the two of us, right? Come morning, maybe we should drop the Reeders over the balcony. We don't need those ghosts of who we were. We have each other, wrapped up in the cool breeze, so close that our breath is a shared ribbon that flows between us. And in the morning, me and Gabe can hop on one of the AI-nav sea pods and sail off to start our lives together.

Start them again, for the hundredth time.

Only the sloshing of the boat over the waves. Only the flapping of wings and a distant mark in the sky. One of the doubt-birds swung back around? The chugga-chugga is the sound of heron wings lifting off from the marsh. No, a helicopter streaking right for us. Closing in, closing in. I shut my eyes. I lean against Gabe and he kisses the top of my forehead. His arm slides around me and he tugs me close. *It's okay. I'm here.*

Flash.

Our eyes meet across the dance floor of a bar, then in the purple twilight of the Body Garden. Rounding the corner of the sidewalk, early for our appointment. All those times, we met. We met. I open my eyes. Flash, then another, as two rockets flare from the bottom of the helicopter. Two metal birds with tails of fire carve through the darkness toward us.

I open my eyes and Gabe hits me with his fangy smile, his laughing eyes. I know what he's thinking. *I'm sorry. I had to.* He knows I would've choked and let Khadija roll with her plan if that meant leaving here with him. He must've switched on his GPS the second he woke up and got Kareem to help. He knows me better than I know myself.

He is myself. And I'm him.

And we're already miles away, anyway. *We met. We met.* That's all that matters, so hang on. Hang on.

CODA
EXCISIONS

Darius took such good notes. In his planner for this week's session, he'd written: *New assignment check-in. Progress?/ Breakthrough?*

What plant to pick for tonight? He knew it was going to be a whopper of a session with the way he'd felt the pressure behind his eyes, like a trapped sneeze. With the way he knew them and their stories. He rooted around in the botanics room by the suite of offices— ha! Rooted, he didn't mean to be so punny—and picked a vase of red roses. Call it too on the nose for the lovey-dovey breakthrough (fingers crossed) session he hoped was in store for Fox and Gabe that week, but whatever. Classics were classics for a reason. Simple glass vase, half a dozen roses, which the Life-Storyboard Consultant Handbook said should *foster an environment of intimacy.*

He dusted the coffee table between his chair and where Fox and Gabe would be sitting soon and set the vase in the middle. Then moved it an inch to his right. Couldn't look too planned. Especially with how he noticed Fox's eyes on the flowers the first few minutes of each week, like Fox was onto him. Fox, who'd been testy again lately, which could only mean he and Gabe were gearing up for another round of deletions.

He almost hoped Fox would open with something like, "What the shit is going on with the plants?" Better when he's feeling something, better when Gabe is laughing and winking even when it's hiding a lie (stop there and cross that out in his mental notes. He should be more neutral. Suggest: *Not total truth*). He'd take the big emotions over the dotted-line versions of them, when they come in for their first sessions. Well, their first sessions *again*.

"My coworker Yvonne said you saved her marriage," Fox had said practically every first-session go-round, which had Darius thinking, *is he fucking with me?*

Second thought: Roses were too hokey. Sometimes you needed to chuck the handbook and go by your gut. Darius swapped them out for his favorite orchids—the live ones, not the silks—that he kept on his desk, just for himself. Even though he wasn't supposed to have favorite clients, Fox and Gabe stood out. Even if Khadija hadn't told him herself when she brought them to his office the first time—the *first* first time—that they were special and he had to take care of them.

It was how they came here, year after year. First-session fibs. Fourth-session fallouts. That one memorable thirty-seventh-session *how could you do that to me and I will never forgive you* (note: Tiger lily on the table that session. He'd like to think that set the mood for sudden passion). Honestly, that go-round seemed like they were breaking down some walls. Actually dealing with their trauma instead of bailing with edits, which technically Darius was there to hawk, but *noooo*. Enter the excisions, the editors with their shiny scalpels, with their *we can make you happy*. Or the rollouts of new premium, ultra-premium, diamond-premium editing levels.

You'd think Fox and Gabe would piece together, eventually, why they neared the tops of their fields yet could only afford their tiny apartment, but top-tier edits included forensic financial scrubs. And some willful blindness.

At least Fox and Gabe were consistent. Plus, even with the employee discount, they were paying the mortgage on his condo in Gulfcoastia, so hey, there was that.

CLIENT HISTORY SUMMARY

Shazad Fox: Grew up on Aaru. Befriended Khadija Banks, great aptitude for editing. Established historic first editing clinic on Aaru. Began relationship with Gabriel Encarnación; memory perforation via node-to-node link. Moved to New Providence with Khadija Banks. Anger. Discussion halts session progress. Extensive edits to excise trauma of Aaru, separation from Gabriel Encarnación, et al. Co-founder of NIL/E Technologies, Editorial Division. Propensity for self-medicating. Propensity for megalomania? Interim CEO of NIL/E while Khadija Banks began and completed the New Thebes project. Continual extensive edits, self-administered. Sabbatical from NIL/E; anonymity, financial ruin. Relocation to LakeLandia, Standard Memory Template 36, subset Greg™ editing path. Chronic excision-based cognitive fracturing. Recuperative precision editing by Banks, temporary stability. Return to NIL/E in junior role, suggested by Banks. Re-met Gabriel Encarnación in New Thebes. Recurring night terrors re: Furycane Set, other reemerging self-excised traumas, amplified by proximity to Gabriel Encarnación.

Gabriel Encarnación: History of childhood sexual exploitation; deceased mother, deceased brother. Discussion halts session progress. Late childhood removal to Aaru. Late teens, began relationship with Shazad Fox; memory perforation via node-to-node link. Conspired with Khadija Banks to remove Shazad Fox from Aaru. Remorse, sadness. Discussion halts session progress. Final-wave evacuation from Aaru to halfway house outside of New Providence. Three years' work in content creation, temporary stability. Gap of many years; discussion halts session progress. Enrollment at Kemet College, study in kinesthetics, nutrition, body aesthetics. Position at NIL/E bodyfication boutique. Re-met Shazad Fox in New Thebes. Propensity for distrust, emotional self-harm, amplified by proximity to Shazad Fox. Occasional infidelity as weapon, self-aimed?

Treatment history: See related list of sanctioned company editing. Extent of non-sanctioned memory editing unknown. See related history of successive vessels, genetic save-files.

Treatment plan: Couples therapy. Individual therapy declined. Experimental therapies?

Swing big on this one, Darius. I've got a plan. These are my boys. I need them back.

—*K.*

Gabe never really wanted to be there in Darius's office. His eyes skimmed the windows of the room, most sessions. His leaned-back smirk shirked responsibility, and it was only a matter of time before Fox fell into step with him, marching on over to *this is bullshit* land.

This time felt different. The slow reveals week after week had helped out (poppy, blue lotus, chrysanthemum…), the constant reminders for Gabe and Fox to talk, and trust, and think about things from each other's point of view, even when perforation swung back around and the old memories started to resurface. Gabe and Fox remembered most of their real histories now, and here they still were.

Fox's eyes were down at the orchid with a slight crease in his forehead. Gabe, his knees bouncing, looked out the window at the watercolor-blue sky. Darius had heard NIL/E finally got those weather-architecture machines right. He liked to end sessions with questions. Last week he'd asked them, do you want to stay together? Why should you? Then, he'd given them the assignment: Forget the past on Aaru, think about your current lives in Kemet, pick a memory where you knew you loved your partner, and Darius's support staff would load it up on a Reeder to play at this session. The InSense tech that NIL/E finally got right would allow the other to feel the memories, beamed right to their nodes. Darius would have the dampener settings switched on his node. He didn't need to eavesdrop. What better way to move forward than for them to see through each other's eyes?

"Shall we begin?" Darius asked.

He placed the Reeder on the table between them. A tap on one of the keys and the holo-display knit a scene to life out of beams of light.

GABE

Dancing in the crush of bodies on the dance floor wasn't the same as leaving my body on the stage of the Stable. But sometimes, it was enough. Hip-sway, shake shake, bounce on over under the disco ball, and eyes up to the sparkling lights while a woman's voice promised me, *I feel love*. The smell of warm bodies 'n' sweat over too much pherologne, catching eyes as I shimmied by, occasionally brushing a crotch, *hey my bad, bud! Unless you're into it?* I'd been alone too much the last few years, and the bass in my chest and the laser lights flashed me back to the early days at the Stable. Like, even if for a night, we're all in this together.

Until I saw Fox, his head tipped up to the lights, in the middle of the floor. His eyes closed, but definitely still him, and the sight blasted me up through the disco ball, surrounded by a million reflected versions of ourselves from way back.

His eyes slammed into me. Flash. I was in the Body Garden with him, a million years ago. I saw him from across the street in Aaru—on the way to meet me in the canteen—and before he saw me, and I just got to watch him. Head down, probably thinking about how he could edit the world around him to make it better, and warm goo was trying to pump outta my heart, over all the cracks. I had to get outta there before he made a scene, I had to—

Fox hooked me by the waist. Yank. Big sloppy smooch like no time had passed, so close that our eyelashes brushed. We stumbled apart before the fireworks could even reach my brain, and both of us laughed through the nerves.

He said something I couldn't really hear over the music. Maybe it was, *wanna get some fries?*

Fries were not a *let's hash out the way you destroyed my life* kinda thing. He'd forgotten about us. Edited me outta his life, of course. Could you blame him, after what I did?

The disco ball rained shards of light down on my shoulders. A story tried to pull me behind my eyes—*tell him you're on a date with the Brotherhood of the Half-Mast Boredom Boners, tell him he's not your type*—but wait. Stay here.

I still thought about Levi every day. Losing him had bulldozed all my years with him, leaving just a big empty space. Spaces. Holes of someone I used to be, whose voice I couldn't remember until he'd pop up in the mirror and remind me, *never again*. The memories of Julio 'n' Fox, too, never far behind even when I ran through New Providence for years. Even when I left and only came back after everyone called the city New Thebes. New name, same hurts.

Fox's big melty eyes blasted holes through my chest.

Stars, bebé, Má had said, when I'd poked at her fry grease scars on the backs of her arms. *They burn just a little at first.*

But then I knew, you get to love him again. You get to forget all your mistakes, even when they burn. Ghosting him on Aaru just 'cause you were an asshole and scared you were getting too googly. Forcing him away with Khadija. You get to love him all over again. And isn't that a gift? And more than you could ever ask for? *Could, could.* And maybe. Maybe?

Why the hell not. Fries sounded pretty fuckin' awesome.

FOX

From the roof deck, the whole city spread out like a candle-dotted sheet cake, topped by the sunset. Even the wine past my tongue tasted gold. If a client rolled into my office for me to edit them a perfect summer rooftop bash, I'd whip up something like this. Coworkers and friends but not too many. Music, but not too loud. The sounds of traffic below muffled, like even the city had decided, *hey, Gabe's been having a rough go lately, let's give him a breather.*

I'd had to book a facial with Priya at the bodyfication place where she worked with Gabe so I could get her alone without tipping him off and we could plan. *Love the idea of a surprise party,* she'd told me, *now let's talk about those pores*. Somewhere along the way, all the hushy texting with Priya became, honestly, fun. She was the one dragging Gabe over from work. *Just bash him over the head in the street, and get him in the elevator*, I'd suggested. *As long as there's wine waiting for me*, she'd shot back.

Gabe would be like, who's this comedian pretending to be my boyfriend?

A text buzzed in my pocket. Priya: *Five mins*.

I drank in more wine, and the city lights, and spun to the crowd. "He's almost here. Who needs more drinks?"

The crowd whooped. The star of tonight's editing level: Party Host Fox, camouflaging jitters by refilling glasses. All the late nights with Gabe, quizzing him with flash cards and helping cram for his Trainer II certification test would be worth it, just to see his face.

I still didn't believe I was here, sometimes, three years after me and Gabe met. Him drawing me out of my head. Me arm-twisting him to move in four months ago, and now he was the one saying we're staying in this weekend to repaint the bedroom because the apricot baby-shit-colored walls were driving him bonkers.

Not that things were perfect. Some nights he'd clam up, or start a sentence with *hey remember when*, and then stop, his lips in a line. And I knew not to ask who he was thinking about, who he was remembering, because that didn't matter when he was here with me. And then on the nights when the drowning nightmares clawed at me—moaning and confused—he was the one to massage my forehead until I found sleep again.

Besides, perfect happiness didn't really exist, I'd had to tell more than one disappointed editing client. Sometimes perfect was a boring Saturday night at home with the man you love, a couple of cans of paint, and some takeout algae kabobs. And you stopped for a second, looked around, and remembered, *yeah, this is all I need.*

The elevator door dinged open. The whole crowd screamed, "Surprise!"

Gabe, at Priya's side, jumped and one hand flew to his heart. Whooping louder than everyone, I watched the smile paint over the panic on his face.

"Gabe told me you're an editor," one of his coworkers said at my side, after the cheers, as Gabe made his rounds. Which one? Carlos, Petros? "So you make people happy?"

I started to say something about how you couldn't really *make* people happy, how editors could only really reinforce fuzzy feelings with scaffolding scenes, until I hid a smile with another glug of wine. Carlos/Petros didn't actually care. He was just trying to be nice.

And you know what? From across the roof deck, Gabe's gaze hit me and I could hear his voice in my head, laughing, *you bastard.*

"Yeah," I answered. "I do."

Even if it was only one person for one night, it wasn't a lie.

Gabe swooped to me by the deck railing, smirking. "Workin' late tonight, huh?"

I pulled from the Gabe playbook and winked. "Surprise!"

He kissed me hard and fast, then draped his arm around my shoulders. He waved his glass of wine over at the guy who I'd been talking with. "Hey, Carlos! Snap a pic." Then in my ear, not much more than a warm breath, "Thanks."

That was as close to an *I love you* as I was going to get today. And that was okay. Better than that. Perfect.

A-fuggin'-men.

"Smile!" Carlos called out.

Gabe tugged me closer. Flash—so bright, so white that for a second it blotted out everything around us.

———

Years, sessions later. How long, really, was tough to say with all the edits. Fox stumbled out of the lobby of Darius's office, fresh from a session previewing the latest premium memory editing level. Never enough, because Fox still left the sessions alone. On his way out last week, he thought he'd spotted a glimpse of a mint shirt heading into the lobby elevator. Maybe it had been Gabe. Who knew what he'd been up to in his own sessions, if he was still going. Fox couldn't even be sure it was him.

He walked out of the elevator late today, his head filled with sand from fading memories. And Gabe was always early for his sessions. Chances were they'd bump into each other in the street, eventually.

Especially if an old friend decided they needed a nudge and *accidentally* scooted into the scheduling server and shuffled things around, babycakes.

In the lobby by the glass front door, Fox froze. He could've been seeing Gabe as a memory, backlit against the gold streetlights. A little more gray in the hair, a few more lines at the eyes. No, real. Hands in his pockets, like the ghost of him that Fox felt still floated around their place. Well, *his* place. Gabe hadn't been there in a year. For an instant, headlights from a passing car seemed to cast a silver river of light that flowed between them. Fox pushed through the front door.

"Oh," he bumbled. "Hi."

"Oh, hey," Gabe said, through a single nervous laugh.

I used to love you—I still do and now we bump into each other and say oh, hey, was just about the coldest level Fox could think of. Mile-deep under glacial ice.

"Darius?" Fox asked, jerking his head to the lobby.

"You know it."

"Any progress?"

Gabe shrugged. "Happiness is a choice."

"So I've been hearing."

Gabe rocked on his heels. Fox had to bite the inside of his smile just so he didn't blurt out, *what are we doing? Come home.*

"I usually grab a smoothie after sessions, next door." Gabe thumbed over to a dim bar. "If you…"

Fox had to keep the spark in him down, like, *wait, wait.* "I like smoothies," he said, stupidly. A voice in his head rolled his eyes. *Nice, dumbass.* His eyes to Gabe's, then Gabe's smirky lips, then eyes again.

He watched Gabe head into the elevator, and then stayed on the sidewalk the whole hour. Through the cold drizzle and everything. He couldn't risk Gabe changing his mind and popping out early. *We can't do this again. Look what happens.* Not that he could tell his legs to move, anyhow, with the way his heart rooted him to the sidewalk, like a whole chorus of voices were yelling at him to stay put.

Smoothies that tasted like grass clippings and honey, and they sat at the end of the smoothie bar and met eyes. Talked about their sessions. Fox had a whopper of a latest session with Darius. Gabe laughed. *Oh man, Fox, you had to whip out warring gods and go on a quest?* And Gabe? He'd mostly been storyboarding sessions about Julio and his mom. *Working through some shit,* he said. *I do this thing where I work on shit now. Fuckin' blows.*

"You look good," Gabe said, leaning in. Gold-ringed eyes. And ohgodohgod, Fox could smell his skin. "Happy."

At least Fox was fooling someone. He hid the stomach-sink with another pull of smoothie. Grass stuck to his teeth. "Yeah. Thanks. You, too."

Awkward shuffle out onto the sidewalk. Do they hug? They should hug. After everything, a hug is the least they could do. Gabe looked up at the bar sign then to Fox again and barked one of his nervous laughs. They'd forgotten the Gabe-and-Fox foxtrot. Neither of them heard the music. They stumbled to each other and hugged—warm and too fast, suddenly like they had a hundred elbows knocking together. Gabe squeezed and did that bro pat on Fox's back. Fox wouldn't crumble there on the sidewalk. He didn't do that anymore. He gritted his teeth and looked inside when he felt weak and fumbled around until he felt better on his own. Whiskey down the drain, long ago, not down his gullet. Which sucked. He even cut lemon wedges to put in the metal water jug he carried around.

"Good to see you," Gabe said. Before Fox could mumble something, Gabe was already halfway down the block.

"Yeah," Fox said to the air. And by the time he got home, he actually believed it.

A buzz at the door, after Fox got home and brushed the grass clippings out of his teeth. The intercom, someone at the street.

"Hey, it's me," Gabe said, just a gush. His tinny laugh through the intercom sounded like he was talking out of a can. "Let me in, yeah?"

Fox couldn't cram the unlock button fast enough. And then he held his breath—waiting, waiting—overflowing and his eyes on the door. It'll open. Soon, soon.

ACKNOWLEDGMENTS

I could say thank you, forever, to a number of people for helping me get this book out into the world.

Thanks to my amazing agent, Naomi Davis of BookEnds Literary Agency, for giving me the courage to start fresh and rethink a story that I'd worked on for years and years. Huge thanks to George Sandison at Titan Books for helping me unravel all these threads and bring them together. And for encouraging big, weird swings. Thanks to continuity queen Elora Hartway for spot-on feedback and an incredibly close read of loopy timelines. Thanks, too, to Julia Lloyd for the beautiful cover art and Adrian McLaughlin for not only typesetting the manuscript, but having fun with different typefaces. Shout-outs to Louise Pearce and Tiffani Angus, plus Titan's publicity team: Katharine Carroll, Kabriya Coghlan, Charlotte Kelly, Daisy Saunders, Hannah Scudamore, and Kate Greally.

Thanks to the I-Park Foundation for two fellowships where I wrote in a cabin in the woods. The blue heron that visited the lake there ended up on the cover of this book. And to the Rolling Ridge Retreat Center. The Field of Reeds Center looks suspiciously like that place in North Andover, Massachusetts. Big thanks to Mrs. Florence Taylor for her incredible support during my last year of high school, which has stuck with me years later. When it came time to think of a guide for Fox, she naturally came to mind.

Thanks very much to John Hilton Taylor at the British Museum, who edited the beautiful book Journey Through the Afterlife. His translation of ancient Egyptian spells and funerary texts from the Book of the Dead were huge inspirations for things like chapter titles and the odd spells that pop up throughout the book, and his pronunciation advice on ancient Egyptian words was so helpful.

To the Boston Gay Book Club: I could not have found a more fun and supportive group of guys to talk about books and other things I won't dare mention in print. Thanks for letting me crash the party.

Big thanks for all the support to the really wonderful booksellers I've met over the last few years at events or over emails. Book people are great.

And thanks to you for reading.

ABOUT THE AUTHOR

Nathan Tavares is a writer from Boston, Massachusetts. He grew up in the Portuguese-American community of southeastern Massachusetts and developed a love for fantastical stories at an early age, from superheroes to mythology. He studied English in college and received his MFA in creative writing from Lesley University in Cambridge, Massachusetts. His editorial work celebrates queer culture and historically excluded communities, with pieces appearing in *GQ*, *Out*, and elsewhere.

For more fantastic fiction, author events,
exclusive excerpts, competitions, limited editions and more

VISIT OUR WEBSITE
titanbooks.com

LIKE US ON FACEBOOK
facebook.com/titanbooks

FOLLOW US ON TWITTER AND INSTAGRAM
@TitanBooks

EMAIL US
readerfeedback@titanemail.com